BORDERLINES

**This Large Print Book carries the
Seal of Approval of N.A.V.H.**

BORDERLINES

Archer Mayor

Thorndike Press • Thorndike, Maine

Library of Congress Cataloging in Publication Data:

Mayor, Archer.
   Borderlines. / Archer Mayor.
      p. cm.
   ISBN 1-56054-162-8 (alk. paper : lg. print)
   1. Large type books. I. Title.
[PS3563.A965B7   1991]   91-2310
813'.54—dc20   CIP

Thorndike Press Large Print edition published in 1991
by arrangement with G. P. Putnam's Sons.

Cover design by James B. Murray.

The tree indicium is a trademark of Thorndike Press.

This book is printed on acid-free, high opacity paper. ∞

To Roger, for seeing the stuff
dreams are made of

1

I only half-saw it at first, a slight movement of brown against brown. I was also far away, so to have noticed it at all was sheer luck. I took my foot off the accelerator and let the car slow down on its own. A glance ahead and into the rearview mirror confirmed I was the only one on the interstate.

The deer hesitated at the edge of the bank leading down to the southbound lane, parallel to my own. Its hide was just slightly darker than the frost-killed grass at its feet, its rack intermixing with the grayish-brown bare branches of the small trees behind it. I rolled the window down, letting the cool November air flush out the car's stale, warm interior.

The deer shifted its weight and sniffed suspiciously at the breeze, weighing its own inbred caution against whatever was tempting it to cross both broad lanes and the grassy median in between.

I took the engine out of gear and continued rolling until I ran out of momentum, coming to a stop in the breakdown lane as gently as a leaf striking the ground. The deer barely glanced at me. It took two tentative steps away from its cover and froze again.

It had good reason to be fearful. It was November — hunting season — and the antlers on this buck's head testified to a past ability at staying alive. I moved my own eyes across the distance he had to travel before gaining the trees on my side of the road, wondering, if I were him, whether I'd run the risk.

I decided I wouldn't but he stepped forward, placing his forefeet on the pavement. I looked around slowly, checking for other signs of life. I didn't see a thing, not even a bird. Still, I fought the urge to get out of the car, even to press the horn, and instantly end the debate.

The sun, just inches above the low, rounded, dark purple mountains in the distance, had caught him fully now, revealing the subtleties of his coat, the glistening of his twitching nose. I abandoned any notions of becoming his guardian angel and of scaring him away. He — and all of nature's dominance in this isolated area — was one of the reasons I was up in the sparse northeastern corner of Vermont. Aside from the intrusion of this road and its kin, and a few towns along the way, this was his country, thinly populated, covered with trees, thrust up like a hilly plateau against an omnipotent and often querulous sky. I was the useless outrigger here — far be it for me to tell him what to do.

He moved purposely now, head high, his white-tinged tail flipping back and forth. I could see the tension in his tapered legs, but he kept his poise, as if on parade. He would not give this road the satisfaction of undignified flight.

The rifle shot came as in a church — intrusive, heart-stopping, sacrilegiously loud and startling. The buck froze, its eyes wide with wonder, and then it glanced back at its own hind legs, which were collapsing as if on their own. A second shot rang out as I leapt from the car and began to run toward him. He saw me then, perhaps blamed me as his head fell back and his antlers rattled against the hard, cold surface of the road.

I stopped beside him, breathing hard, the vapor from my lungs encircling my head. The deer was very still, the only movement being the steaming blood slowly spreading from its open mouth. Its eyes were still wide open, still registering my image, I thought.

I looked around. No one was going to appear now. What had happened was flagrantly illegal — discharging a weapon in proximity of an interstate highway. The hunter would wait for me to leave. I wished I had the strength to lift this huge beast onto my car and deliver him to a ranger station, to deprive its killer of the satisfaction of possession and of later tall tales of peerless hunting.

But I couldn't.

I bent over, reached out and touched the warm, smooth hide with my fingertips, reminded suddenly of my own losses — real and imagined. If only I'd given warning when I thought none was necessary.

I stood up again slowly, anger replacing shock. The location of the wounds indicated that the shots had come from the same side of the road as the deer, but farther south. I began to walk in that direction, cutting diagonally across both lanes of the interstate, my eyes glued to the treeline above the road bank, watching for any movement, listening for any sound. I knew, as if I could actually feel them, that another unseen pair of eyes were watching me come.

I was on the southbound lane's divider line when I saw it — a flash of fluorescent orange — accompanied by a hunter's heavy boots crushing the brush underfoot as he moved.

"Stop where you are. I'm a police officer." I began running the rest of the distance to the treeline, straight to where I'd seen that one bright flicker of color.

Just before I entered the woods, I glanced

back to see the two parallel blacktop ribbons, my car, its exhaust pluming smoke in the crisp cold air, and the body of the deer. From this angle, the animal must have presented an almost irresistible target, its muscular outline highlighted against the black of the road and the pale horizon, a temptation only decency and sportsmanship might have stilled, and obviously had not.

I hadn't walked ten feet into the woods before I was utterly enveloped in its dense, dark embrace. I stopped, listening. The hunter had bolted late in my approach, and could only have covered a short distance before I'd reached this spot. I scanned the dark curtain of trees before me, aware of only the absolute stillness, and of the sound of my own heart beating from the exertion of the run.

"I'm a police officer. You've already broken one law; don't add resisting arrest. Come on out."

The vapor from my words hovered briefly about my face and then vanished in the answering silence.

I looked to the forest floor, hoping to see some tracks, but tracking wasn't one of my strengths, at least not in the woods. All I could see was a tangle of twigs, rotting leaves, and frozen brush.

The sudden, blinding combination of a third

rifle shot and the explosion its bullet made in the tree trunk next to me threw me to the ground before I could think, my Korea-bred instincts suddenly as keen as they had been many years earlier.

With my face to the ground, breathing in the damp mustiness of the near-frozen earth, I waited for the ringing in my ears to fade. Behind it, fading also, I could hear a body crashing away through the forest.

It had been a warning from a hunter whose initial purpose had not been sport. That deer in the road had not been shot for a trophy and some bragging, as I'd imagined. It had been meat, a hedge against the winter, a hungry and self-sufficient man's necessity for survival, as he saw it. He had not missed killing me; he had warned me to back off.

I got up slowly and brushed myself off. Ahead of me, some one hundred and fifty feet away, I saw an orange hunting jacket hanging from a tree branch — a single bright beacon in an ever-darkening, cold and silent world. It was another warning; he was a hunter no longer, but a man with a gun, dressed to blend into his chosen environment. He could now stand with impunity next to a tree, invisible beyond fifty feet, and fill his rifle scope with my chest.

I was now in Vermont's so-called Northeast

Kingdom — poor, isolated, thinly populated by people who had chosen to put their independence and wariness of the rest of the world above the hardships of living here. The man watching me had no interest in killing me, but he did want it known that he would if he had to.

I stood absolutely still, watching, listening, aware now that my movements were my only relevant spokesmen. A line had been drawn: I could die defending the rights of a dead deer, or I could retire and leave the field to my unseen opponent and his more ancient, instinctive code of moral right and wrong. It wasn't my kind of debate.

I returned to my car, as depressed as I'd been angry when I'd left it in outrage. It had been a short and violent reminder of the limitations of legal authority. Here, in this high, cold country, the law had less to do with rules, and more with personal honor. Often, they were one and the same, but not always.

I got back behind the wheel, drove around the carcass, and continued north.

2

My trip to the Northeast Kingdom that late fall was an escape. I was heading for a temporary job — a minor embezzlement investigation for Ron Potter, the Essex County State's Attorney — but that was largely a pretense. I was also leaving in Brattleboro an accumulation of tensions, disappointments and heartache with which I'd felt I could no longer deal. In fact, I had telephoned Potter because I'd heard he was searching for a very short term investigator, a need imposed on him because he was the only Vermont State's Attorney not assigned a full-time man.

He'd been tickled pink, for purely selfish reasons, no doubt. I had a feeling his delight and ready acceptance of my offer had less to do with my prowess than to the fact I'd been the first to nibble his hook. A stint as the Essex County SA's investigator was not the stuff of legend in a resume. In fact, not even the SA's job is full-time, and his office is located in St. Johnsbury, which isn't even in the county he serves.

My call to him was also helped by the fact that we knew one another. Potter had been a patrolman in Brattleboro about ten years ago, trying to scratch together enough cash to pay his way through law school. He used to come by my desk for occasional moral support, both as a prospective student and as a fledgling cop. I hoped he was better at serving the people of Essex County than he had been working for me.

For nearly thirty years now, I've been a policeman in Brattleboro, starting as a patrolman and having just wrapped up a six-month assignment as Acting Chief, an event which went a long way in explaining why I was flirting with burnout.

Tony Brandt, the man whose job I'd temporarily held, had been given a half-year suspension so the Town Manager and the Selectmen could save face over a case I'd reopened to prove an innocent man had been falsely jailed. The irony that they'd then asked me to take Brandt's place should have prompted me to change citizenship and head straight for the border.

But I hadn't, any more than I'd scared away the deer. In retrospect, the reasons for this lapse of judgment seemed inexcusably trite. The case, involving a hell-bent homicidal crusader in a ski mask, had attracted national attention, and I, in the public's eye, had emerged the hero of the day. Perhaps I succumbed to the Selectmen's wishes because my own view of myself was considerably less than heroic. The outcome, as I saw it later, had been inevitable from the start — the innocent had been freed, most of the guilty had been punished one way or another — but I had been less the driving force in it all than the conductor, madly trying to maintain order on a runaway train. When the dust had settled, I was the only one left who'd looked good, and I felt unhappy enough with my performance to welcome the flattery of the Selectmen's offer.

Now, a mere lieutenant once more, I found the results of my foray into town government had been a lethal overdose of political soft-shoe, and a painful severing of cherished ties to the street. It had also helped to poison my friendship with Gail Zigman, the only woman I've really cared for since my wife died almost twenty years ago. Not bad for six months' work.

So, through either my own stupidity or the simple workings of fate, I felt I'd taken two shots on the nose, one right after the other. I needed to retire to some cave and lick my wounded pride, and to do that, I had looked back over my personal history to find solace in its highlights and refuge in its memories.

I turned off at the Lyndonville exit, drove through town to connect to Route 144, and headed north toward Gannet — a tiny weather-beaten collection of boxy prefab buildings, tar paper-patched trailers, and, with one garish exception, an occasional, abused remnant of nineteenth-century rural architecture. Gannet was undoubtedly, in the eyes of tourists and outsiders, the epitome of "ugly," but it was also the primary repository of precisely the type of soothing memories I was after.

At the end of every school year, my brother Leo and I would be eagerly packed into the car by my mother — leaving my father to tend to the farm — and we'd drive north to spend the summers with my aunt and uncle. Although we lived in Thetford, only sixty miles to the south, the trip took most of the day, sometimes longer when the roads were out.

This afternoon, the trip had taken less than an hour, which was just as well, since my psychological needs were more pressing. Aunt Liz had died several years ago. She'd been a thin, nervous, somewhat scattered woman, given to much activity to little effect, a characteristic she readily admitted with good humor and grace. My uncle Buster had been her counterbalance, huge, benevolent, slow-moving. He owned and ran a ramshackle garage and service station in Gannet, known more as a halfway house for troubled kids than as a place to get your car fixed. A philosopher of sorts, he'd instilled in me the value of listening not just to what people were saying, but why they were saying it — a knack that was to help me considerably as a cop. Together, Buster and Liz had shown Leo and me an alternate way of life from the more isolated one we knew on our father's farm — one with a volunteer fire department, adjoining back yards, and a soda fountain at the local café.

Route 144 heads off north-northeast, past the struggling Burke Mountain ski resort condominiums, the little village of East Burke, and on into the wilderness toward Island Pond and Canada — a narrow, much-patched, rough ribbon of tarmac, following the connecting valley floors through a tangle of brush-choked forest and meandering streams.

The late afternoon sky was blue and cloudless, the low sun highlighting the bare trees, making them look pale purple brown from a distance. The violent coloration of fall had yielded to this timid replacement, a concession to the anticipated dread of winter. I passed several empty pickup trucks and 4 χ 4s, parked awkwardly on the shoulder, all with gun racks barring their windows. In contrast to the brutal encounter I'd just had, hunting season was a time of quasi-religious importance to most rural Vermonters, when larders were stocked against the barren months ahead, and when young men with their fathers, carrying old 30-30s, entered a crucial rite of passage from childhood, as I had long ago with Buster. It was also a time when well-heeled flatlanders came north to hunt and drop some greatly needed cash in a region of the state that otherwise rarely attracted them.

I stopped the car at the top of the low hill south of town. Below me was Gannet, whose haphazard cluster of houses and buildings contrasted with the almost rectangular grid of its four streets, the only paved one of which was Route 114. Parallel to Route 114 was Atlantic Boulevard to the east, with South Street and North Street connecting the two at the bottom and top of the rectangle. The entire layout was no more than some two hundred yards on its longest side. It was an absurdly regimented layout for such an unruly hodgepodge of buildings and trailers, since not one house was aligned with or looked like another. About three hundred people lived in Gannet, half of them in town and the rest in the surrounding hills.

I put the car back in gear and rolled down the slope, losing my slight aerial perspective and becoming one with the village. Buster's home, an ancient but tidy ramshackle ex-farmhouse, was the first on the left. Originally a squat and clumsy copy of traditional Greek Revival architecture, one of only about five in town, its outer appearance had been transformed by the practical hand of hard economic times — a prevalent regional feature. The roof was a smattering of rusting and multi-hued, brightly painted corrugated metal panels; the walls, intermixed with a few remnants of the original white clapboard, consisted variously of unpainted plywood, asphalt shingles, battened-down tar paper, and more corrugated metal. And yet the whole structure had the appealing look of a neatly designed patch-work quilt. Buster was no slob; he just made do. Subconsciously, like a proud apprentice, I picked out those bits and pieces of the building's exterior that I had nailed into place in years past.

There was a car backing out of the dirt driveway as I pulled up. It stopped, and an attractive young woman with pale brown hair pulled back in a ponytail got out. She stood uncertainly by her open door, but stuck out her hand tentatively as I crossed to meet her.

"You're Joe?"

"That's right."

I smiled and shook her hand. It was strong and muscular, which threw me off a little, given her demeanor and her expression — she had the nervous, shy look of a young girl. I guessed her to be somewhere in her early thirties.

"Hi. I'm Laura. I clean your uncle's house. He's real excited about your coming. Asked me to do an extra special job."

Her hand went a little limp in mine and I realized I'd held it too long.

"Thank you. It's good to be back."

She was wearing tight faded blue jeans, sneakers, and a thick sweater. She wasn't skinny, but she didn't carry any fat, either. I found her enormously appealing, even sensual, in a no-frills, down-home way. It jolted me a little, and made me think of Gail, whom I'd left behind in a rush in Brattleboro, almost without explanation, like a pain too big to bear.

She gave me a small, crumpled smile and looked at the ground. I'd been staring, and now we were both slightly embarrassed.

She put her hands in her pockets. "Well, I better get going."

"Is Buster inside?"

She looked up again, her face clear. "No, he says it drives him nuts to watch me work, makes him feel bad. He's probably at the

Rocky River by now, or maybe at the garage. He's real excited . . . I guess I said that. Do you know which room you're in?"

"Yup."

She smiled again. "That was dumb. Not like it's your first time here, is it?"

"No, although it almost seems like it. I've been away so long."

"Buster told me you're investigating something."

"Yeah. Not here, though. I just thought I'd stay with him while I'm in the area — you know, cheaper than a motel and a whole lot friendlier."

There was a long pause. I suppose neither one of us wanted to start talking about the weather, which was certainly all I could think of at the moment. She broke the silence by turning toward her car, repeating, "Well, I better get going."

I stepped back and shut her door for her. She rolled down the window. "It was nice meeting you."

"My pleasure. Hope I see you around."

She laughed, which made her face suddenly quite beautiful. "Hard not to in this town."

I watched her back out and drive north, up through town, and thought again of Gail. She, too, was younger than I, although in her forties. She was smart and strong and reasonable, both a successful realtor and an effective town selectman. She, like I, enjoyed being independent, and so we lived apart, getting together only when it suited us both, which had been less and less lately. It had been a while since we'd shared a laugh, or much of anything.

I hadn't told Gail I was leaving for Gannet until this morning, thereby highlighting the sorry state of our friendship. I'd decided beforehand what her response would be, and had thereby guaranteed it. She'd greeted the news, and its late delivery, with a chilling-cold anger. It had been a self-fulfilling prophesy, but it had nevertheless come as a shock. I'd orchestrated things so that only her pleas could reverse them. She, predictably, had passed on the opportunity.

I got my duffel bag out of my car and parked it inside the front door of the house. Then I started walking toward town on the left shoulder of the road. The sun had just set, the shadows were darkening, and the evening's chill was now coming up around me like a blanket. The radio had predicted a low in the mid-twenties tonight.

Gannet had no sidewalks, just the road cutting across driveways and the occasional scraggly front yard. A few of the houses, on my left, didn't even face the street. The mobile homes, none of which would ever be mobile again, had a stranded look, as if they'd reluctantly put down roots after being abandoned beside someone else's house.

There was a fence or two, a swing set, a few stray dogs. Properties blended into one another, making it difficult to figure who might lay claim to the odd, rusted weed-strangled car that lay somewhere between two homes — what Gail, with her realtor's acerbic eye, called "Vermont planters."

If there was a nucleus to Gannet, it lay in the large island of land ahead on my right, hemmed in by Gannet's four streets. There, the houses were older but equally dilapidated. They faced the road like circled wagons, with unfenced back yards abutting one another, forming an untamed field of sorts in the middle, pockmarked by seemingly stray gardens, bushes, or leafless shade trees. During summers past, Leo and I had used this inner field, about the size and length of two football fields end to end, as a communal playground, and it was a natural magnet for every kid in the area.

As I came abreast of South Street, I saw the first real sign of life — four children playing with an incredibly mangy dog. They were dashing back and forth in the middle of the dirt road, chasing stones, sending up a thin cloud of dust that glowed in the dying light. I was struck by their identical tattered-quilt suits, reminiscent of what Chinese troops wore in the fifties, when I was being underpaid to fight them in Korea. I couldn't tell if the kids were boys or girls — they all had long hair, tied back at the nape of the neck to keep it out of their faces.

They stopped playing when one of them saw me. I waved, but to no response. They stood stock-still, ignoring the barking dog, staring at me not in wonder or curiosity, but as nervous animals might, transfixed by the sight of a dreaded predator. I was chilled by both implications: that I might be seen as a threat to these youngsters; and that they had been trained to see me, and presumably others like me, as blatant enemies. It made me feel there was a larger presence among us, an invisible authority dictating how people should be perceived.

The ominous spell only lasted a moment. The dog finally bumped one of the kids to gain its attention, and they all returned to their game with the same enthusiasm as before. But the episode startled me, and concerned me, too.

Buster had mentioned these people once on the phone. Oddballs, he'd said, members of a back-to-nature group that had bought most of the buildings on South Street and on the lower half of Atlantic. They didn't use electricity, didn't believe in money, didn't own cars, and, according to Buster, had set up the only legitimate business enterprise the town had ever seen — something called The Kingdom Restaurant. The contradiction about money threw me off at the time, but Buster had merely laughed and said he wasn't going to probe. Some of the people who came to eat there also topped up their cars at Buster's garage.

The garage, on my left, was locked up tight, looking like a rusty beached Liberty ship, far from the sea. What little I knew about cars, I'd learned here, tinkering on an assortment of wrecks. I'd never known if they belonged to Buster, were headed for the dump, or were actually the property of paying customers. Directly opposite — once a demurely rotting erstwhile farmhouse — stood the Kingdom Restaurant, its windows glowing yellow. Several cars were parked out front.

I cut diagonally across the street to where a familiar figure was putting the final shine on the roof of a 1943 Chevrolet fire truck. He was standing on the running board and had his back to me, caught in the circular gleam from the sole streetlight by the road. The truck was parked in front of a two-bay firehouse with GANNET VOLUNTEER FIRE COMPANY carefully painted in red on the wall between the first and second floors.

"Hello, Rennie."

Rennie, a man about my own age, turned with the rag still in his hand. He didn't get down, but just looked at me from where he stood and smiled. "Joe Gunther, you son of a bitch. How the fuck are you?"

I laughed and shook my head. "I've been better. How are you?"

His familiar round, florid face broke into a theatrical scowl. He was a barrel of a man, short, square, and muscular, his body more a monument to hard work and fatty foods than to genetics. The diet had undoubtedly also contributed to his increasingly flushed skin tone, which by now had progressed to the stage where he looked either on the brink of blowing sky-high, or of having a major heart attack.

He stepped down and shook my hand. "Pissed off. I told the others to be here to give the trucks their last wash and wax before winter, and I'm the only one that showed up. I've been here the whole fucking day."

"Can't compete with the deer."

"Deer, shit. Just a bunch of drunks with rifles. What're you doin' up here?" His eyes were shining, and he still hadn't released my hand. I hadn't realized how much I'd missed his company.

"Temporary job for the State's Attorney — moonlighting."

Rennie snorted, dropped my hand, and retrieved a can of car wax from the roof of the cab. "Well, that chicken shit needs all the help he can get. What's the job?"

"Some town clerk dipping into the till. I'm supposed to dig up the proof."

"Murial's dipping? Damn, you'd think she'd live better than she does."

"Not Murial, different town. I just thought I'd stay with Buster while I'm in the area."

He got behind the wheel of the fire truck. "Yeah?" he said nonchalantly, looking completely uninterested. "What town?"

I grinned at him. "Nice try."

He started the engine with a tremendous roar and eased the truck backward into the station. The clearance between vehicle and doorframe was about an inch and a half on all three sides. Another truck — a '55 Chevy — stood at gleaming attention at the mouth of the second door. I crossed over to it as Rennie killed the motor and came around the front.

"Memory row, huh?"

I smiled and patted the red fender. "I remember when Buster first rode this into town."

"Yeah, the only brand-new truck we ever had." He jerked his thumb over his shoulder. "I'm still partial to Engine 1, though, even if it is Army surplus. That son of a bitch has never been a problem."

"And this has?"

Rennie shrugged. "I don't like it as much."

I knew it wasn't the truck — it was the fact that it was Buster's baby. Buster was Chief — seemingly always had been — while Rennie had worked his way up to Assistant Chief through pure attrition. During my first vacations up here, Rennie and I had been "junior firemen," duped by that meaningless title into sweeping, cleaning, washing, polishing, waxing until we'd qualified as Grade-A maids, all seemingly under the stern direction of anyone and everyone in the department eighteen years or older. My willingness to "shovel the shit," as Rennie put it, despite my connection to the Chief, had formed the initial basis of our friendship. That had later blossomed as we'd graduated to manning equipment and fighting fires — albeit only the minor ones — always together, always a team. We'd even exchanged letters throughout the school year, comparing notes on how many ways adults conspire to torture teenagers.

We were young men by the time Buster rolled into town on the new Chevy in 1955

— both veterans. That was the last time I was to spend more than a couple of days in Gannet at one time. My connection to Rennie faded in intensity after I signed on as a policeman in Brattleboro; the correspondence died of neglect and memories began to replace an updated friendship.

It had seemed reasonable to think that Rennie would eventually replace Buster as Chief. Now, I wasn't so sure. Buster was in his eighties somewhere, and it looked like he would outlive us all. I imagined that fact, along with all the other intangibles that had grown between the two of them through the years, had created a kind of low-level but permanent friction.

Rennie, like most of the other people in Gannet, worked in St. Johnsbury. He was a loading dock foreman for a large trucking firm, or at least he was the last time I saw him.

I walked to the back of the station, reflecting on how many hours I'd spent in this building, so many years ago. Attached to the 55's back-step, I discovered two shiny new Scott-Paks, breathing tanks and masks used for entering smoky buildings. I raised my eyebrows and pointed at them. "Pretty fancy. When did you get those?"

Rennie grinned. "Ever try one on?"

"A few times. We used to carry them in our patrol cars in case we had to go in with the firefighters. We dropped it, though. The training was costing a lot and the Fire Chief felt his turf was being invaded."

"Too bad, they're kind of fun. The Order gave 'em to us — good will gesture, I guess."

"The Order?"

"Yeah. The Natural Order. The cult, or whatever you call it. Haven't you heard about them?"

I nodded. "I thought they didn't support this kind of stuff."

"They don't. But their leader is a real politician. He holds all the money, has electricity in his house, drives a car. He's no fool — got the best scam running I ever seen. He gave us those and a couple of new portable pumps; he even tried to buy us beepers for when we get a call, except we don't have a system that would trigger the beepers."

"What's his name?"

"Depends. If you're a member, he's called The Elephant; real name's Edward Sarris. Nice enough for a nut; sure spreads the money around. Christ, when they moved into town, they paid top dollar for all those houses — cash, too."

"Where's the money come from?"

"Damned if I know. The restaurant does

good business, I guess — mail order, mostly; you know, granola head stuff — organic foods. Rumor has it when you join, you got to give all your money to Sarris, but for all I know, they could be printing it in the basement."

I glanced out the door. "Well, I better get going. Haven't seen Buster yet. You coming down to the Rocky River later?"

"Sure. Be along in a bit."

I continued my walk down the street, taking in the sights. The contrasts I saw were familiar and typical of the Northeast Kingdom. Between and beyond the weather-blighted buildings and broken roads of the village, my eye was drawn to the land — wild, undulating, pristine. Its beauty lay in its pocket vistas, rarely extending beyond a mile or two. Farther south, the Green Mountains offered breathtaking views of valley passes and river gorges. Up here, the whole earth was shoved up closer to the sky, its hills and dales more interconnected, less in conflict. Seeing this land, oddly arctic in appearance at this time of year, gave one a comforting, although false sense, that there were perhaps corners of the world where civilization had yet to set foot. I'd always thought it was as much the remoteness as the beauty of the region that made the Kingdom a shrine of sorts to the citizens of Vermont.

I thought back to the man who had shot at me to protect both his freedom and his winter's meat, which made me focus anew on how the once-familiar buildings of this town were being ground down without respite. The Kingdom would live on, but not as it had. The younger generations were already abandoning it, lured by the monied south, and those who had made that money were seeking new places, like the Kingdom, in which to buy real estate.

For the Gannets, tucked away from the main highways, on the outskirts of the commercial centers, things weren't looking too good. I began to wonder if after decades of clinging to this land, Gannet was finally slated to die.

Considering that I'd come back here for some mental and emotional rest and relaxation, this kind of thinking was not the stuff of dreams.

3

The Rocky River Inn was the one glaring exception to the town's generally muted architecture. It took up one entire side of North Street, with one wing at the corner of Route 114, and the other looking straight down Atlantic Boulevard. It was an enormous place, dwarfing any three buildings in town put together. It was also a first-rate Victorian-style dump. It had a sagging rusty metal roof, diseased-looking, paint-peeling walls, and its windows were covered with either torn plastic sheets or dilapidated plywood. Although it had "wrecking ball" written all over it, it had looked that way for as long as I could remember.

It had once been a palace, of course, built in the middle of nowhere in the 1850s by a lunatic logging king named Gannet, who had died one week after moving in. It sported turrets and bay windows, porches and balconies, and more gingerbread than any sane Victorian would have considered tasteful. Now, however, one of the turrets was draped with a moldy green tarp, the balconies had been declared unsafe, and the wraparound first-floor porch groaned under the weight of several cords of stacked firewood. The gingerbread was half gone, and two of the bay windows flickered with the garish light of several neon beer signs.

A combination hotel/bar/café/home, the Inn was owned by a mercurial woman in her fifties named Greta Lynn. She had run the Rocky River for the past twenty-five years or so, inheriting it from her equally eccentric mother, and lived there with a succession of mousy male companions whose names nobody could recall. Greta, Rennie, and I were, as they say "of an age," and had run around with the same crowd when we were younger. In later life, after "Peanuts" had become a popular comic strip, I was convinced that somehow Charles Schulz had met Greta — and had found his inspiration for Lucy Van Pelt.

I climbed its warped, cracked and creaking front steps and entered a huge entry hall. A crumbling carved hardwood staircase rose directly ahead, and two equally large rooms opened on either side. The room to the right had been converted into a café/bar — where I'd slurped sodas of yore — and was segregated by a pair of ornate multi-paned pocket doors. The room to the left had no doors and spilled out into the entry in a seeming attempt to take it over.

I turned left to what everyone called "The Library" to find Buster, for this was his home away from home — a room of paperback-cluttered walls, of tall dirty windows, clanking radiators, and derelict furniture, all overshadowed by a gap-toothed, non-functional, cobweb-choked chandelier. There, at the head of a semicircle of mismatched sofas, armchairs, and ottomans, like some long-dethroned king with his Bowery-bred entourage, Buster held court.

He saw me as I crossed the threshold and raised his beer high. "Goddamn, it's the celebrity. Come here." He struggled to his feet as I approached and placed one gargantuan arm across my shoulders. He was a huge man, fat and bearded, six and a half feet tall, with crooked, yellow teeth and bleary, misty eyes — a man with intimate knowledge of the bottle, yet whom I'd never seen under the influence. Or maybe never seen sober.

I am no grasshopper myself, but standing next to Buster, I felt like a child posing with a hippo.

He waved his beer can at the small group of people sitting around the semicircle of chairs. "You know any of these guys? John. . . ."

The man finished for him. "John Secco."

"Right; not too good with names," Buster muttered. "This is Joey Gunther — sorry, Lieutenant Joe Gunther of the Brattleboro Police Department, my nephew. Remember hearing about that Ski Mask murder case down in Brattleboro? Well, Joey here nailed him."

Several heads nodded, I think out of pure politeness.

He pointed at another man, hesitated, obviously groping for a name, and finally gave up on the general introductions. He pushed me into the chair to his right, settled back down himself with a grunt. He was about to ask me a question when Greta entered the room.

"Thought I heard you in here. How's your mother?" No hugs or kisses from her. There never had been; never would be. Greta Lynn was a square, no-nonsense woman who prided herself on being ready and able to spit any man in the eye — metaphorically speaking. She was short-tempered, opinionated, and brusk and, as far as I knew, had never shown a different side of herself to anyone in all her fifty-six years — except to my mother. To her way of thinking, it would have been sappy and contrived to have made more of a fuss over my arrival.

"She's fine. I dropped by on the way up

here. She asked me to give you her best."

"That's very thoughtful. And your brother?" Here her tone was less solicitous. Leo, who still lived with our mother in the old family farmhouse in Thetford, loved classic cars from the fifties, cheap flashy women, his work — he was a very successful butcher — and our mother, who was older than Buster and whom Leo nursed in his own effective fashion. It was a combination of plusses and minuses in Greta's eyes, and the ambiguity had always made her grumpy. I think she found absolute whites and blacks easier to deal with.

"Leo's fine, too. Making a killing with his new butcher shop."

She made a noncommittal grunt. "Would you like something?"

"Cup of coffee would be nice. Thanks."

"All right." She turned to Buster. "Another one?"

He never got a chance to answer. Suddenly, the front door flew open with a crash and a middle-aged, thick-waisted woman half-fell into the entrance hall. She was disheveled and frightened and was still holding her leather handbag.

"My husband," she gasped as she tried to get up off the floor.

Greta ran to help her, the rest of us looking on.

38

"What happened?" Greta asked.

"It's Bruce. He's gotten into a fight with one of the cult people."

"Where?"

"In one of those houses, down the street." She pointed toward Atlantic Boulevard.

Greta looked over her shoulder at us. "Well, come on, move it." She turned the woman around and charged out the door with her. The crowd, I among them, moved like cattle to follow them.

"You know what's going on?" I asked Buster, as we hurried down the street, struggling into our coats.

"I can guess. She and her husband came up here a couple of days ago trying to find their daughter. Sounds like they got into trouble instead."

"What do you mean, 'Find their daughter'?"

"My guess is she joined the Order and her folks are trying to get her back."

"Has this happened before?"

Buster shrugged. "Off and on. We get parents, clergymen, newspeople. They either come to gawk or raise a little hell. Never amounts to too much."

Rennie, catching sight of us from across North Street, ran over to join us. "What's goin' on?"

Buster chuckled. "I guess that Boston fella

is getting the short end of the stick with the Order."

Rennie looked down Atlantic Boulevard at Greta and the woman. "Oh, Christ, Greta on the warpath." He trotted on ahead to catch up to them.

We were near the bottom of Atlantic when we heard muffled shouting coming from the last house on the east side of the street. Ahead of us, Rennie, Greta, and the woman, who Buster identified as Mrs. Wingate, broke into a run. Mrs. Wingate began calling, "Bruce. Bruce," as she went.

Rennie reached the front door first and pounded on it with his fist, yelling for someone to open up. As Buster and I drew near, I noticed an absolute stillness from the neighboring houses, and felt the odd sensation of dozens of eyes watching me from the dark. I was struck again by the same ominous chill I'd felt earlier upon seeing the four children and the dog in the street.

I stood beside Rennie and tried the doorknob, my adrenaline now pumping at a good clip. Inside, the shouting had been joined by the sound of objects breaking. The knob turned in my hand, but the door was obviously bolted from the inside.

Mrs. Wingate began to cry. "Please, get him out. Somebody's going to be killed."

Rennie glanced at me. "Window?"

I nodded. The two to the left of the door were blocked by a flower box, so Rennie and I ran for the building's south side, looking for another option. The sounds from the inside continued unabated.

As we rounded the corner, a shattering explosion of glass at head level made us veer off, our arms thrown up to protect our faces. As if in slow motion, his jacket fluttering like broken wings, his white shirt glowing in the night as with an energy of its own, a man came sailing backward through a large, ground-floor picture window, accompanied by a million tiny shards of glass, each twinkling fiercely in the light of the full moon.

He landed with a solid thud, flat on his back, his arms spread-eagled, and his expression one of utter astonishment. From his clothing, which included black slacks and penny loafers, I knew he had to be attached somehow to the tweed-and-wool Mrs. Wingate.

His face was bleeding slightly and he looked utterly astonished, but otherwise he appeared more surprised than injured. Above us, standing in what used to be a ground-floor window, loomed a tall bearded man with long black hair, dressed in quilted cotton.

"What's going on here?" Rennie shouted.

"He threw Bruce out of the window," Greta said, emphasizing the obvious.

I stepped over the shattered glass and bent down near the man on the ground. "You okay?"

He looked at me in silence for a couple of seconds. "I think so." I could sense him trying to regain his composure. He was having to dig deep.

"Anything hurt?"

Mrs. Wingate joined me at his side.

"No." Wingate moved a little. "I think I'm okay."

He sounded a little distracted. With his wife's help, I lifted him to his feet.

"I'm a little dizzy," he said as he tried to take a couple of steps.

We sat him down on the grass, away from the broken glass.

"Bruce, what happened?" Mrs. Wingate asked, dabbing at his face with a handkerchief she'd produced from somewhere. His cuts were superficial and had already stopped bleeding. He pushed her hand away.

"That bastard wouldn't let me see Julie. Wouldn't even let me in. I had to use force." He tried for a smile, but his lips were tight and pale. "I guess I lost."

Mrs. Wingate introduced us — her first name was Ellie — and we all shook hands awkwardly. I noticed then he was trembling slightly. I could hear more shouting from inside the house.

"Someone told me you're trying to find your daughter."

"That's right."

The noise inside got louder. I looked over to Ellie. "You okay here for the moment? I think I better get in there."

She nodded. I found the others just inside the front door. Not surprisingly, the noisemakers were Rennie and Greta.

"Goddamn it, Greta, if you'd shut the hell up, we could find out what happened here."

"Any idiot can see that. Bruce came to get his daughter and was beaten up. That's assault and battery."

I interrupted. "Not necessarily, Greta. I'm Joe Gunther." I stuck my hand out to the tall man with the beard, who'd just been watching up to now.

He smiled slightly and took the handshake. "Fox."

I continued: "If Mr. Wingate broke in here uninvited, these people had a perfect right to throw him out, although maybe not through the window. Is that Mr. Fox, or Fox something?"

"Just Fox. Are you a lawyer?" A woman with three small children stood behind him,

43

all dressed identically in their quilted suits. The disheveled room, even with the window permanently open, was quite warm.

I smiled at his question, and at the kids, who looked very small and scared. The oldest couldn't have been more than five. "No, I'm a Brattleboro policeman, up here visiting. Can you tell us what happened?"

"Oh, this is going to be good," Greta muttered.

"We were returning from Evening Gathering when this man approached us, demanding to see his daughter, someone named Julie. I told him I knew of no such person, and would he please leave us alone, but he followed us home. I tried to keep him out when we got here, but he forced his way in, locked the door behind him, and began pushing me around, screaming and yelling. He grabbed that chair and tried to hit me with it. I had to think of the children, so I stopped him. He tripped and went out the window."

"The people in your party are all here now, in this room? No one's missing?"

"That's right."

I nodded toward the woman. "What's your name, ma'am?"

Fox answered for her. "Dandelion."

Greta almost choked. "Dandelion?"

"Give it a rest, Greta." I walked over to

44

the window and called out to Wingate. "Did you break in here uninvited looking for your daughter?"

He froze for a moment, his eyes narrow and angry.

"Did you start the fight?"

He looked up at me furiously. "He wouldn't let me see her, said she wasn't in there and that he didn't even know who I was talking about. I saw her with my own goddamned eyes. We followed her here, for Christ sake. Why do you think I came to this house in the first place? He lied to my face. He's lying right now." I sensed violence surging within him, but for the moment at least the man in the Robert Hall clothes maintained his self-control.

I told Fox, "You can press charges if you want."

"What?" Greta asked, visibly surprised.

Rennie answered for me. "It's the law — Wingate was trespassing."

Greta looked at me. I just nodded.

"We don't wish to press charges," Fox said in a quiet voice.

"You want him to pay damages?"

Again Fox shook his head.

"We may have a kidnapping here," Greta's voice was a notch higher. "I demand that we be allowed to search the building." It was a

45

good line of bluster, but, knowing Greta, I could sense her sails beginning to flap.

"That's way out of line," Rennie said behind her.

She whirled on him. "Since when the hell did you become such a legal hotshot?"

"We don't mind." Fox's calm, resonant voice spread between them like oil on water.

We didn't search so much as amble from room to room, like tourists visiting a museum. And the analogy held, for in many ways, the tour revealed a life style of long ago. There were no lamps or electric lights — the only illumination came from homemade candles; the floors, apart from an occasional small wool or braided rug, were bare; dried foods hung from hooks in the kitchen; the beds upstairs were nothing more than wood frames strung with rope supporting straw-stuffed mattresses. Everything was neat, clean, and frugal to the point of being bare.

At the foot of the stairs, there was a jury-rigged wood stove made from an upended fifty-five-gallon drum. It was supported on bricks and had wire supports running from the wall and ceiling to the stovepipe.

Rennie passed his hand near the hot surface. "This ain't the safest stove I've ever seen. I got no bone to pick with you about how you live, but you better fix this: new stovepipe,

46

new supports, some kind of firewall behind it. We don't really have a fire code around here, but this is dangerous. I'll get you a pamphlet on what you need if you like."

Fox nodded. "Thank you."

He escorted us to the door, his small family mute behind him. Greta suddenly marched up to the woman called Dandelion.

"Do you know where Julie Wingate is? Has she been hidden someplace?"

All four of them looked at Fox. "You may answer."

"No," the woman said.

"Christ." Greta stormed out.

"Would you like to see the basement?" Fox asked politely. I could hear a slight inflection of victory in his tone.

Rennie patted his arm as we filed by, pretty amused by the entire proceeding by now. "I think we're outta here."

The Wingates were standing outside with Greta.

"Better luck next time, Bud," Rennie called over to Wingate.

"My name's not Bud."

The sheer hostility in his voice caught us all off guard. For some reason, it made me think of when the light gets strangely yellow, just before a big storm hits from out of nowhere.

47

Rennie heard the menace in Wingate's voice clearly. "Hey, look, I'm not your problem. If you can't keep your shit together, don't lay it on me."

Greta looked from one to the other. "Never mind, Rennie."

But Bruce Wingate seemed to have found an outlet for his anger and frustration. He was like a stove glowing cherry red.

Rennie stared at him for a moment, typically unwilling to walk away and let the situation cool. "What the hell's the matter with you?"

"You people make me sick." The words slipped out between unmoving lips.

Greta tugged at Rennie's sleeve. "Drop it, Rennie, the man's upset."

"I can see that. What I don't see is why he's pissed at us. Seems to me we put up with enough bullshit from these assholes — them and their fucked-up daughter."

Wingate hit him with his fist hard across the face, making him stagger back. Rennie's mouth was open, his expression stunned. Buster and I instinctively caught him by his arms and held him. But he didn't attempt to react. He just watched as Wingate stalked off, stiff-legged, with his wife in tow.

Buster patted Rennie lightly on the back. "You okay?"

Rennie straightened and shook us off. "Yeah. Fucking dink." He walked away in the other direction, rubbing the side of his face.

The three of us, Greta, Buster, and I, were left standing in the dark street. "Christ almighty," I muttered. "What's been goin' on around here?"

Greta looked at me for a moment, and then left us without saying a word.

As I stood there in the evening chill, I knew one thing: The violence and frustration buried deep inside all of us was working its way to the surface in Gannet, building up slowly, like the sweat of exertion on a hot summer day.

4

Buster and I stood quietly for a while, watching Greta's stumpy figure receding up Atlantic toward the Inn.

He sighed gently, the vapor from his nostrils caught in the light from the moon and the blanket of brilliant icy stars overhead. I sensed in him a resignation of sorts, not just about tonight's behavior, but about the causes behind it. He was one of life's observers, and the social disintegration I sensed in this town must have been a focus of his attention for years. I felt the sadness emanating from him like the heat from dying embers.

Buster shoved his hands deeper into his pockets. "You goin' home?"

I hesitated. "I don't think so, not yet. I thought I might go back to the Inn. I would like to talk to you about all this, though."

He nodded. "I'll walk with you. I'm stiffening up."

I let him hit his stride in silence for a couple of minutes, knowing he hadn't forgotten my request. He wanted to give it some thought.

"You know anything about this group here?" He jerked his thumb over his shoulder.

"Rennie told me they're headed by a guy who calls himself The Elephant. They've spent a lot of money making friends."

"Right. Edward Sarris. Well, Greta and I are still Selectmen, along with Ernie Cutts. About five years ago, this guy Sarris comes to one of our monthly meetings and introduces himself. He says he's moving up here with some friends and that they'll be buying up a bunch of property. He knows people're going to talk 'cause his bunch is a little unusual, but that we're all goin' to be real good neighbors. He's not asking us for anything, you know — it's more like an announcement, just so we don't think he's sneaking around trying to pull a fast one.

"Well, sneaking was hardly a problem. They came in here gangbusters, paying top dollar for about a dozen houses, buying the old Morse farm north of town, building something like a church up in the woods beyond Atlantic, opening that restaurant, spreading money around like snow in January. People were so busy stuffing their pockets, they didn't see half the town had switched hands."

"How many members are in the Order?"

"Oh, I don't know — seventy-five to a hundred. Anyway, problem was, once they were in, the town was split in two; they didn't mix with us and we weren't invited to mix with them. It's against their religion, or whatever they call it. You saw it in that house: They're real structured and keep to themselves. They say they're anti-materialists and that everybody who ain't like them are the bad guys. It's like any other bunch of oddballs, I suppose — you got to hate something or someone to make yourself feel better. Maybe that's what Greta's doing."

I had seen Greta's hatred, and Wingate's, but Fox had seemed downright gracious in the face of our invasion. "Who do they hate?"

"The 'material world,' as they call it: the

pollution, the money-grubbing, the commercialism, electricity and plumbing and cars — us, in other words."

"Does that animosity ever come out? Have they ever threatened anyone?"

He gave a surprised look. "Oh, no, they wouldn't touch us with tongs. Except for Sarris — he's their ambassador in dealing with the outside world."

I shook my head. "So it's a time bomb?"

He chuckled, which came as a relief. "We could be close-minded by now. I don't know. There's more, though, a feel to it that unsettles people. I'm not real bent out of shape myself, mind you. I don't like that we lost half the town, but that was our fault. Other people, though, see 'em as a threat. They dress funny, look weird, keep to themselves. Hell, when you get down to it, I think it's just the hippy thing all over again. They're nature freaks — they fertilize their gardens with their own shit; they don't believe in zippers or in getting married; they call each other by funny names. And then there's the sex. Rumor has it everybody does it with everybody else and Sarris gets the pick of the litter. Doesn't sound too bad to me, but people like Greta ain't too fond of it. She always was a little strait-laced, I thought."

"You told me once the restaurant was the only genuine business the town has."

52

He sighed. "Oh, it is — it's real successful. It has a mail-order part to it, too, that sells 'natural food,' whatever the hell that is. But with the town half-sold off, and the restaurant pulling whatever traffic comes by, Greta's found herself pretty pinched. The whole town has, for that matter." He shook his head and smiled sadly. "Looks like maybe we sold our soul for a few quick bucks."

"How badly off is she?"

"Greta? Who knows? She's gotten pretty wild about them. You want to get your ears burned, just mention the Order. This Wingate couple blowing into town has been like a fuse. She's latched onto them like a mother hen, determined to help them find their daughter. I don't know, though. They seem pretty weird to me, too."

Despite Buster's amiable tone, the picture he was drawing was grim, of desperate people in a face-off, the backs of their heels on the edge of a chasm.

"Has Wingate blown up before?"

Buster frowned. "That was a first; course, he's only been here a couple of days. It wouldn't have happened if that damned fool Rennie hadn't pushed."

I didn't say anything. I wasn't going to fault Rennie. It had seemed to me his irritation at Wingate's tone had been justified, even if he had been a little lacking in sensitivity. Still, that was the Rennie of old — never afraid of being popped if he felt he was right. I'd always loved running in his wake as a kid, glorifying in his bravado. It was the exact trait Buster so disliked in him.

Buster resumed. "Except for tonight, old Bruce strikes me as a pretty tight drum, as buttoned down as his collars. I never seen him so much as smile, I don't think." He shook his head. "I'm not sure I'd be real keen to go home with folks like that."

We had reached the front steps of the Inn.

"You coming inside?" I asked him.

"Nah, I think I'll go home. Laura usually puts something in a Crockpot for dinner. I'll leave it on for you, if you like."

"Hmm, I met her when I came in. Sounds like you're getting decadent in your old age, hiring a housekeeper."

He smiled. "Nice kid. No . . . I helped her out a few years back — alcoholic family, lousy friends. She straightened herself out and thought I had a lot to do with it; said she wanted to return the favor somehow. I got tired of arguing, so she fixes me the odd meal now and then and cleans the house . . . Well, catch you later."

I climbed the steps and looked back at him, heading toward the corner of North and 114.

In the dark, barely visible from the Inn's anemic lighting, he looked like some bear heading back to his cave.

I stepped inside the door and hung up my coat.

Greta was coming out the café's double doors. "I thought you went home."

"I wanted to ask you something."

She looked at me warily. "What about?"

"The Wingates."

She placed her hands on her hips, not the most subservient of gestures. "Is it true you're working for the State's Attorney now?"

I hesitated, suddenly conscious of how I might be perceived here. "I'm on temporary assignment for a specific case. It has nothing to do with Gannet, though."

"Are you going to help the Wingates?"

"I don't know if there's anything legally I can do."

She let out a short bark of a laugh. "Those Order people kidnapped the Wingates' daughter. That's against the law, isn't it?"

"*If* they kidnapped her. Sounds more like she ran away."

There was a burst of laughter from the other room, followed by loud voices competing for attention. Greta scowled. "She's like a zombie — she doesn't know what the hell she's doing. They've got her drugged or something."

She bent forward and thrust her face up at me. "Jesus, Joe, stop tiptoeing around. What do you think this Order is anyway — a summer camp? It's a cult, just like that Jonestown bunch. They're sick. Did you see what happened when I asked the woman about Julie? She looked at Tarzan for permission. These people can't even think for themselves. They're sick and I think they're dangerous."

I opened my mouth but she wasn't finished. "Did you see those kids tonight? They can't read or write, they all act like robots." She held up one hand like a traffic cop. "I know that Fox guy — I've seen him around. He's one of the big shots, one of Sarris's flunkies. If we went back to that house a week from now, I guarantee you'd find him with a different bunch of kids and a different woman. These people move around like rabbits."

I thought about pursuing it, but then I changed my mind, giving in to one of those sudden emotional cave-ins that occur when you're already close to throwing in the towel. It had been a cop's impulse to question Greta instead of going back home with Buster. But Greta was right. I should probably just get out of the way. I should go after my sticky-fingered town clerk for the State's Attorney, avoid further complications in my life, and get the hell back to Brattleboro.

I realized I'd come up to Gannet with false expectations; I'd wanted to find the town unchanged, my friends waiting to greet me. Gannet was a kind of tonic I'd hoped would make me feel better. It had been a silly, self-serving notion.

I turned back to the row of pegs on the wall and retrieved my coat. "I don't know, Greta. Seems to me everyone here's a little too steamed up. If you like, I'll tell the SA to keep an eye on this bunch."

She stepped forward and stopped me from putting on my coat. My vague, evasive tone had made her quite angry by now. "Don't you pat me on the head, Joe Gunther. I don't need you looking down on me."

I watched her eyes, narrow with fury, remembering a similar look on Wingate's face, and Rennie's as he had walked away after being punched. Compared with theirs, Fox's had been cool and superior, displaying an icier, perhaps more threatening anger.

I removed Greta's hand from my coat and put it on, bidding her goodnight, suddenly eager to escape back into the cold. Outside, I shook my head. Anger is no byproduct of self-contentment. I couldn't shake the ominous feeling that Wingate and his wife, Greta and Rennie, and God knew how many other people in this town were all in the process of slipping their mental anchor lines, yielding to the different frustrations that had consumed them over time. I wondered in how many of them this rage might be controllable, and in which ones it indicated a ship drifting toward the rocks.

5

A searing pain in my shoulder blew me awake. "Ow. Damn."

"Wake up — fast." Buster punched me again, hard.

"Cut it out, goddamn it."

"Siren's blowing — we got a fire." He was already out the door and heading for the stairs.

As I stumbled out of bed, groping for my clothes, I could hear the eerie funereal wail of the firehouse siren, rising and falling, a persistent, nagging, penetrating noise that made my hair stand up on end.

Slipping my shoes on unlaced, holding my coat under one arm, I stumbled downstairs to the front door. As I kicked it open, Gannet's siren enveloped me, making the air vibrate.

Buster's pickup was already rolling down

the driveway, the passenger door open. "Come on. Move it."

I half-ran, half-jumped onto the seat next to him. The sudden acceleration slammed the door for me and threw me back against the seat as we squealed down the street.

"There," he shouted, pointing down South Street as we drew abreast. "Looks like that house we were in earlier."

We came to a skidding stop next to the firehouse just as the siren blew its last mournful note. The firehouse doors were already open and I could hear the roaring of both truck engines being fired up. Pickup trucks and cars appeared out of nowhere, parking helter-skelter up and down the road, as half-dressed men ran toward the fire trucks, even as they eased out of their tight berths. Buster and I clambered aboard the 55, next to a young man wearing glasses and a mustache.

"Hi, Chief."

"Hey, Paul. Hand me that helmet." Paul cracked my knee with the stick shift as we pulled into the road. It was a two-man cab, and I was the third man in the middle.

Buster shouted out the window at one of the other firemen, "Call East Haven and East Burke, we're going to need backup on this."

The driver hit the toggles for the red lights and siren, which, considering the size of the town and the short distance we had to travel, seemed a little excessive to me. It also made it hard to hear myself think. I could see Buster's lips moving, but I couldn't tell if he was muttering or shouting.

As Buster had suspected, it was the same house Bruce Wingate had been thrown out of earlier, several of its windows now glowing orange or actually leaking flames. The smoke above the building reflected the hellish pink glimmer. As we pulled up, I saw where someone, presumably Fox, had nailed a piece of plywood over the broken window.

Everyone piled out of both trucks and began grabbing equipment: hats, boots, bunker coats, hose, axes, Halligan tools. Two men each grabbed the two new portable pumps Rennie had showed me earlier and ran for the bank of the Passumpsic River to set up a continuous water supply for the truck pumps.

I had been to fire scenes before, both here as a kid and as an adult in Brattleboro, but what I'd forgotten was the lack of radio equipment in most truly remote, rural fire departments. Instead of the usual crackling of electronic voices and the sight of white-coated officers walking around with portable radios, the people here ran flat out, some with megaphones, shouting out orders like barkers at a carnival.

"Put this on," Buster said as he shoved a

coat and helmet into my arms. "And get some boots — rear compartment."

I did as I was told, jostling with others at the back of the truck, trying to stand on one foot while shoving the other into a heavy, folded-over rubber boot. One of my shoes fell on the ground and was instantly kicked under the truck by someone grabbing for a pair of leather gloves.

I pulled back finally, with boots too big and a coat too tight across the shoulders. I slapped the helmet on and felt it dig into my forehead. At least the gloves fit and I had a working flashlight.

Rennie jogged by, carrying one of the Scott-Paks in his arms. "Joey, come with me." Paul, my erstwhile driver, was holding the other Scott. Only then, hearing Rennie's voice, did I remember that we had done this before, Rennie and I, as a team. For once, here was a memory that was holding true, and I gave in to it happily, the observer no longer.

We half-ran toward the burning house and stopped near the front door. Another crew was laying a one-and-a-half-inch attack line on the ground for use inside the building.

Rennie thrust his Scott-Pak at me and turned his back. "Help me put this damn thing on."

I held it up so he could lace his arms through the shoulder harness and supported it while he tightened the buckles. Paul, both thinner and much younger, was doing the same on his own beside me. But in the flickering red lights from both the trucks and the fire, I saw his face looked wan and fearful. His hands were shaking badly as he fumbled with the straps.

Rennie took his helmet off and was about to slip on the face mask when there was an explosion above us.

"Look out."

We all three ducked and felt a shower of glass and wood splinters pelt our backs. Rennie was the first to straighten up. "Flashover."

Paul, standing still, was shaking his head, his Scott dangling from one shoulder. "No way, man. No fucking way."

Rennie looked at him. "What're you talking about? Scott up, goddamn it."

Paul dumped the air cylinder onto the ground. "Not me, man. The whole fucking place is going. You're going to die in there."

Rennie shook him by the coat. "Paul, come on, don't do this. There're people in there. Once we ventilate the windows, the heat'll escape. That's all that was. Come on."

A firefighter pounded Rennie on the shoulder. "All set, line's charged."

I looked down and saw the hose was now fat with water.

"I'm not going to die for a bunch of granola heads."

Rennie stared at him, his mouth open in astonishment, momentarily bewildered by an attitude as foreign to him as ancient Greek. As prejudiced as he could be under normal circumstances, once that fire coat went on his back, I'd never seen him hesitate to stick his neck out for others. It was a form of unspoken oath with him: To differentiate between victims out of pure prejudice would have been to spit on his own beliefs.

I yielded to impulse, Rennie and I fighting fires again. I began grabbing Paul's equipment. "Give it to me. I'll go in."

Rennie gave me a shit-kicking grin, the years, for just a moment, gone from his face. "Just like old times."

"Up to our knees in shit," I whispered under the noise, and began to load up.

I tightened the air bottle's straps over my shoulders, slipped the face mask over my head, and triggered the positive-pressure lever on the regulator harnessed to my chest.

Scott-Paks are designed to operate in two ways: Demand-pressure allows the air to reach the face mask only with each inhalation of the firefighter. It's the best way to guarantee that the air released from the tank goes into the lungs of the wearer, with no waste. The other way, positive-pressure, allows a little air to leak through the regulator and into the mask at all times so that the pressure inside the mask is slightly greater than the pressure without: It's an extra safety device to keep poisoned air from getting in around the edges of the mask. Considering the size of the fire we were facing, I opted to waste the small amount of extra air generated by the latter method.

Not that the mere flip of a lever took care of all my worries. The face mask is similar to what scuba divers use, with rubber borders and a curved plastic lens. Putting one on made me feel claustrophobic; not only was my peripheral vision blocked off, but the sound of the air rushing into the mask at each breath reminded me that in twenty minutes, at the very most, my bottle would be empty — faster if I breathed harder.

Rennie positioned himself at the front door, nozzle in one hand, an axe in the other. I stood right behind him. My job was to bear most of the weight and clumsiness of the stiff, unyielding hose so that Rennie might move more freely. We both also had flashlights available.

Buster ran up and shouted, "We're ready to ventilate if you're ready to go." He suddenly recognized me behind my face shield. "What the hell are you doing?"

Rennie thrust his head forward, shouting through his mask. "Paul won't go in."

Buster eyed me sternly, "You been trained for Scott use?"

I merely nodded but Rennie's face clouded. "I wouldn't have him in it if he hadn't been."

Buster smiled, gave a thumbs-up, and began shouting orders. I could hear upstairs windows being broken by ladders. This would encourage the flames to course through the house, but it would also draw out the smoke, a fire's primary killer. If Rennie and I could hit the base of that fire during our search and rescue, then the flame problem would be eliminated also. It was a standard best-laid plan that rarely went as hoped.

We crouched to one side of the door as Rennie turned the handle and pushed hard. The door flew open and a bright orange tongue of flame spat out next to us. We waited a second for it to recede, and then entered the building, bent low.

The scene before us, especially as viewed through our plastic lenses, had the unlikely look of a Hollywood inferno. Overhead, the ceiling was totally occluded by a thick, roiling cloud of orange and yellow smoke. About twenty feet ahead, at the foot of the stairs, the wood stove Rennie had criticized earlier lay on its side, caved in and white hot, its contents the heart of an angry, noisy, air-sucking fireball. In its midst lay a darker shadow, and from that shadow, extending out beyond the center of the blaze, was a human arm, charred and twisted.

The heat, especially compared to the twenty-degree temperature outside, was almost instantly unbearable. The flames columned straight up from the destroyed stove with a cyclonic ferocity, flattening against the ceiling and shooting up the stairway like an upside-down waterfall.

Rennie opened the nozzle to a full-fog pattern, putting a curtain of cooling water between us and the fire. The downside to this life-saving maneuver was expected and dramatic; the water instantly turned to steam and knocked out our vision with the abruptness of a plug being pulled on a lamp. Of the split-second sharp picture I'd had upon entering, all that was left was a world of smoke and steam with a blurry heart of orange. We were reduced to crawling forward, dragging the hose along, groping with outstretched hands and relying on our memories of what we had toured a few hours earlier.

Rennie led us straight to the fireball. The sound of water hitting white-hot material was like nonstop thunder, but the effort paid off. We quickly got to the body on the floor —

or what was left of it — and progressed to the foot of the stairs. There, Rennie rolled over and aimed the stream overhead, at the sloping ceiling above the stairs. The splash-back soaked us with soot-stained warm water.

He cut back on the water after the flames went out above us and shouted through his mask: "How many rooms are downstairs? Do you remember?"

The noise of the steam, the fire still crackling upstairs, and the water trickling everywhere blocked off his already-muffled voice. I responded with the one word most frequently uttered by firefighters inside a burning building: "What?"

He repeated his question. I held up three fingers and pointed at the nearest door, just to the left of the stairs, which led to the kitchen. I realized I was panting and made a conscious effort to slow down my breathing.

It probably took us ten minutes to crawl along the walls of those three rooms, arms outstretched, feeling for more bodies. That was faster than it should have been, but we both knew we were doing it for the benefit of the doubt; through it all, our minds were on the bedrooms upstairs, dreading what we suspected lay ahead.

By the time we regrouped near the still-sizzling remnants of the stove, there was no question of where we were headed — upstairs, where both bedrooms faced each other at opposite ends of the landing, with a bathroom in between.

We quickly crawled to the top. Here, too, the ceiling was on fire. Rennie hit it with water, showering us once again. Through the gaps the fire had burned overhead, we could see an ominous glow in the attic. We could also hear the sound of a chain saw being applied to the roof, for the fire to exit and the water to get in from outside.

The flames temporarily contained, we quickly crawled to the left, to where we both remembered the three children slept. Rennie reached for the bedroom doorknob and turned it.

"It's locked."

I crawled to one side to give him room to swing his axe. My knee, already raw and sore from abuse, landed on something sharp and painful. I let out a shout and shined my flashlight at the floor. There was a old-fashioned door key. I picked it up and handed it to Rennie.

"Try this."

He slipped it in, turned it, and twisted the knob again. The door swung back.

There was no fire in the room, not even much smoke. Enough, though — just enough. With our flashlights and the red and white flickering light filtering in through the window from the trucks below, we could make out four human-sized bundles clumped together on one of the three beds. They were huddled under a blanket, the one woman and three children we'd visited before, their arms around one another, seeking protection from an evil that had already sealed their fate.

We peeled back the blanket and felt for signs of life. There were none. The smoke, what little there was, had killed them.

Rennie moved to the window and broke it out with his axe. The sounds of men shouting, the roar of revving engines and of water under pressure filled the room. And on top of it all, a sound I'd missed while concentrating on the search — a dull rumbling, as of a freight train far away; that, from my experience, meant a fire someplace was getting the upper hand.

Rennie banged the outside wall with his axe to attract attention. I heard a voice from below. "Get the hell out of there. The attic's about to go."

Rennie pulled back his mask just enough to shout back. "We've got victims here. Get a ladder."

"They're all being used."

"Well, unuse one, for Christ's sake."

"All right, all right."

Rennie replaced his mask, already coughing. "Let's check out the last bedroom while they're getting the ladder."

"What about the attic?" I shouted back.

He shrugged. "It'll hold. This won't take long."

We backtracked onto the landing. The rumbling was louder, the train getting closer, the threat more imminent.

I pounded him on the back as he crawled across to the other door. "Rennie. Let's get the hell out of here. Something's not right."

He didn't turn around; he just waved his hand back at me and continued. I noticed that the heat seemed suddenly worse. My ears began to sting. I looked around, stabbing at the smoke-stained walls with the feeble yellow shaft of my flashlight. I became suddenly aware of a fearful creaking in the walls. Rennie put his hand on the doorknob and turned it just as I felt the hose in my hand go flat — a firefighter's worst nightmare. We were out of water, and I knew for a fact we were out of luck.

The explosion behind us was like a tidal wave of flaming air, lifting us up off the floor and hurling us through the doorway. The roar of the train was now complete and all-encompassing, surrounding us and making our bodies vibrate with its thirst for oxygen. Through my plastic face shield, all I could see in every direction was a spectrum of swirling red and yellow patterns, curling and lapping like some volcanic river of fire. It was the color of heat, of death in the midst of fire, the last thing a body experiences before it is cremated.

And through the din, as from a small boat on an enraged sea, I heard a bell madly ringing — the alarm on Rennie's Scott-Pak, warning of the few remaining minutes of air still trapped within his cylinder.

I was lying on my back, watching the kaleidoscope ceiling, when I heard that bell. I rolled over, hands out, feeling for Rennie, and landed on the hose. It was still flat, its water gone before the flashover, and the senseless thought occurred to me that I'd make sure the pump operator's life was made miserable if I got out of here alive.

I couldn't tell which end of the hose led to the door, or to the nozzle. The walls were invisible — my flashlight had been torn away. I was aware of my breath coming in short, panicky bursts.

I began to crawl in one direction, feeling the softness of a rug under my knees, my helmeted head bumping against a bed, then a chair. The heat was still terrific, but not as it had been.

I found a wall and stuck to it, moving to my right, one gloved hand gliding along the baseboard, the other outstretched into the room, feeling for Rennie, hearing the bell getting louder and louder. My face broke out in sweat as I heard my own bell join in, an incessant, unyielding, frantic clamor — the sound of a sinking ship with its steam whistle tied open.

I found him sitting with his back against the wall. I shouted at him and shook him.

His head moved, his helmet bumping mine.

I saw his flashlight still gripped in his hand and pried it loose from his clenched fingers. I shone it in his face. His eyes were open — almost vacant — as if he were daydreaming.

"Rennie. Goddamn it." I punched him in the chest, hard.

I saw his face convulse with pain and his mouth open to inhale. At that moment, his bell stopped ringing, its mission over. His eyes widened further as he realized there was no more air and both his hands flew up to the mask to tear it off.

"No, no. Wait." I fumbled at his regulator as I batted his hands away. His body began to heave and twist, trying to fight me off. He rolled away and I rolled with him, banging my head against the wall.

Suddenly, I felt the release ring loosen around the end of his mask's elephant-like air hose. I shoved my head into his chest, up against his regulator, and quickly pulled the hose loose and shoved it up under the rubber rim of my own mask so that we were both breathing what little air I had left. I could hear the urgent hissing rushing through the leak I'd created. I crushed my mask against my face, grinding his air hose into my cheek, trying to stem the loss.

"Come on, come on," I shouted, dragging him beside me, afraid our tenuous connection might be severed, that his hose might tear from his mask, that my air might expire, that no window was on the wall I was feverishly pawing as we stumbled and crawled along the floor.

My hand hit something — a sill.

"Stand up. Stand up. We got a window."

But he stayed there on all fours, a dog beaten down, seemingly unable to expend the one last effort that would save his life.

I reached under and unclipped his harness at the chest and waist, something I should have done earlier but had forgotten, and I dragged the heavy air bottle off his back.

"Come on, goddamn it."

My bell stopped. For a split second I froze, realizing that frantic sound of leaking air had ceased. I closed my mouth, fighting the urge to suck in the poisoned air from around the gap in my mask, and, grabbing as much of Rennie as I could manage, I launched both of us up off the floor and toward what I hoped was a window.

There was a crash, a splintering of glass. I felt cold air on my neck as, locked in an embrace, we both toppled headlong out the second-floor window.

6

We rolled out the window, hit a shed roof, fell off its edge, and landed in some bushes, still locked together like two lobsters in mortal combat. Rennie didn't even get hurt.

But we didn't go back inside. The hot embers from the stove were reignited by the blast, returning the first floor to its hellish first appearance. For the rest of the night, our firefighting consisted of trying to save what we could from the outside, preserving the walls of the coffin for those people within.

It wasn't until dawn, after the last water had flowed and I sank exhausted onto the tailgate of Buster's fire truck, that I realized I hadn't escaped unscathed. It was Laura, there as a member of the women's auxiliary, who discovered that I'd burned my ear, and who set about putting it right.

"Ow. What the hell is that stuff?"

"It's Bag Balm. It doesn't hurt; it's the burn that stings."

I ducked away from her hand. "You're not on the receiving end."

Laura gave me an exasperated look. "Good thing, too; it's all over your hair now. Stay put."

I stayed put, but only because the pain was mitigated by her sitting so close to me. In the cool breeze of early morning, I could smell her cleanliness mixed in with the bitter odor of charred wood. Whether it was the fatigue, my brush with death, or just the fact that Laura stood in such contrast to our surroundings, I found myself swept up by the romantic notion of being tended by a pretty woman in the midst of a virtual battlefield.

She held my chin in her other hand to steady my head. "I can't believe you got off so lightly."

I looked across to the blackened, punctured, sagging building. "I'm not sure I believe it, either." Rennie, in fact, was stuffing his face with doughnuts at a long table the auxiliary had set up in the driveway. That's what had brought Laura over to me in the first place — a sugar-coated, creme-filled monster that had done wonders for my spirit, if not for my arteries.

Laura leaned back and admired her work. "That should keep it from getting infected. It's going to sting like hell if you shower."

"I'll work around it."

She handed me the green tin of Bag Balm. "Here, keep this."

I took the tin and smiled my thanks. Her eyes were on the green side of hazel and looked straight back into mine with refreshing directness. "I'm almost glad I burned my ear."

Her cheeks tinged very slightly, and I regretted having tipped my hand, even when she responded, "So am I."

I shifted my position to lean against the closed rear compartment door, suddenly feeling all the aches and pains of the night's activities. My bunker coat was covered with a thin sheen of ice that crackled and flaked as I moved, but it was tight and warm on the inside, although damp with old sweat, and I didn't want to take it off. I closed my eyes for a moment, trying to sense with my face any warmth from the rising sun.

"What was it like?" Her voice was surprisingly soft.

"In there?"

"Yes."

"Oh, I don't know. . . . Hot, confusing, scary . . . noisy. Very colorful, though."

"They told me you didn't have any air left in that tank."

"Not a whole lot." I opened my eyes. "Good thing I'm not religiously inclined, huh?"

For all the chaos I'd witnessed on the inside, the building was still remarkably intact. Its roof was pretty much history — a good chunk of it had been blown away by the explosion — and all the window tops were charred and smeared black, but the walls remained standing for the most part. Still, my guess was the whole thing was unsalvageable.

I realized my trying to be lighthearted had bordered on being flippant, which was not my intent. "It's funny. I know Rennie and I came close to dying in there, but it all seems kind of far away right now."

"You must be tired."

I smiled. "That I am."

Fire trucks from at least five surrounding towns were parked every which way. The ground was littered with a spaghetti-like maze of hard, frozen hose, glistening in ice-rimmed pools of water that were starting to reflect the sun's washed out daily appearance. Firemen wandered about, collecting equipment, chatting, banging at hose connections with rubber mallets.

And in the midst of all this solemn, dark and brooding quiet, stood the remains of the charcoaled house and five extinguished lives, huddled as we'd found them, wards of the state now — of the arson investigators, the police, and the medical examiner.

What had caused that fire? I wondered, and shuddered suddenly. Mentally replaying what I'd just been through, I recalled the spasm of panic I'd felt when the hose had gone flat, just before the explosion. There'd been no time for reflection at the time. Indeed, it had happened so fast, I'd almost thought it part and parcel with what had followed. But I knew otherwise now, and the realization scared me. My running out of water had had nothing to do with the explosion.

Buster's large profile stepped between me and the source of my reverie. He handed me a cup of coffee. "How're you feeling?"

"Tired."

"I bet." He looked at me steadily, his face solemn. "I'm glad you made it, Butch."

I lifted my cup to him. "Butch," for him, was the ultimate endearment. "Feeling's mutual."

But his expression was steady, almost hard. "How did it happen?"

"Damned if I know. Flashover, I guess; it got incredibly hot just before it blew. I suppose whatever ventilation there was wasn't reaching the landing; maybe the attic had something to do with it. I just don't know. It was pretty confusing." I took a sip of coffee, which burned on the way down. My throat was sore from the smoke.

"Dick said he told Rennie to get the hell out of there when he asked for the ladder."

My mind began to focus on what was going on here. Buster was after something — seeking to lay blame. Any questions I was about to ask concerning the flat hose line were pushed aside. "I heard some shouting," I said vaguely.

"Well, that's what he said. What did Rennie tell you?"

"He said we ought to check out the other bedroom. I agreed with him."

"He didn't tell you Dick warned him the attic was about to go?"

"He may have tried. You know what communication's like with those things on."

There was a long, drawn-out silence between us. Then Buster pushed out his lips and turned away. "I gotta go check on the equipment."

We watched him lumber off.

"Is he mad about something?" Laura asked.

I leaned back again, watching the women's auxiliary, chatting and laughing, serving their hot coffee and doughnuts to all comers. "We were just kind of bumping bellies."

"Over what?"

"Oh, I don't know. Different people have different ways of doing things. I think he feels we shouldn't have gotten so close to getting killed."

She was quiet for a couple of seconds. "And he's trying to blame Rennie."

"He's just upset, trying to find answers when there's no point to it. He'll let it go in a while." I didn't quite believe that — he'd let it go all right, but into a mental filing cabinet with the rest of Rennie's real and imagined transgressions. I didn't want to tell her that. Right now I didn't want to think about it.

Besides, it was history. Buster had always leaned on Rennie, first with high hopes, and then in disappointment. In the early days, I think it was because the older man wanted to mold the younger one in his own image, to shape a son he didn't have. But Rennie had refused to play along, staying independent and wounding Buster's pride. Buster had an admirable track record with most younger people. It was a sad and perhaps fitting irony that the one he'd decided to make his special project had also been the one to consistently stand up to him. Through all these years, they'd stayed locked in harness, linked as much by their differences as by their similarities.

I saw the Wingates approaching, stepping over debris like survivors from a train wreck, carefully wending their way toward us. Wingate had his arm around Ellie's shoulders, which were bowed, as if the arm was heavy enough to grind her into the ground. The last time I'd seen this man, he'd been in almost exactly the same spot, but seething with an anger so intense that he'd vented it on someone who'd been trying to help him. I couldn't help wondering if it all tied together in some way.

He nodded stiffly to me, like we were being introduced at a party and I'd just thrown up all over my shirt front. I was reminded again that I was probably one of the few people in the world to have seen this man in some pretty unbanker-like positions, a point that was probably as important to him as it was immaterial to me.

"Hi there, Bruce."

He frowned slightly at my use of his first name. On the surface, this was not the man of last night; now, his raw passion was a secret only he was supposed to know about. His chilly demeanor further made me wonder how he'd unloaded his excess steam.

"Good morning. I wanted to thank you for your help last night. I'm afraid I was a little overwrought."

"No problem." My response was purely mechanical. I was stunned by his opening concern. The last time this man apparently had seen his daughter alive, she was entering a now almost totally burned building. Even allowing for the fact that we later hadn't found her there, the assumption that she was safe belied common sense. He either had ice in his veins, or he knew something I didn't.

"I don't usually act that way."

"Don't worry about it." I was watching Ellie Wingate, who stood stock-still, her eyes glued to the ground. I had the feeling that if she could have turned herself outside in and disappeared like some black hole, she would have done so on the spot.

"You didn't find our daughter in there, did you?" The question wasn't casual, but it still came too late — like polite but insincere condolences.

"I don't think so."

He suddenly sharpened, thrown off balance. His eyes locked onto mine. "What do you mean?"

"There's one body that's pretty badly burned. I don't know who that is, or even what it is. And one of the victims is a woman. I don't know what your daughter looks like." I could have told him I'd recognized the woman from last night, and the three kids, but something about this man told me not to volunteer much, to make him come to me as much as possible.

He pulled a picture out from inside his coat and handed it to me. It was a face shot of a woman in her late teens, with shoulder-length light brown hair — not particularly attractive. She had the usual expression of a person who's wishing the photographer would drink arsenic. I looked at it for a long time, wondering what lay behind the sulky face. I wondered if the hostility I saw in her eyes was actually there, or whether I was injecting some of my own feelings for her father.

I handed the picture back after Laura had glanced at it over my shoulder, a gesture which caused her hair to brush my cheek lightly. "She's not the unburned victim."

"Thank God," Mrs. Wingate whispered.

Her husband pocketed the photograph. "Can we see the other . . . victim?"

"No. That's all off-limits until the powers that be arrive to investigate."

"When will that be?"

"Several hours, I would guess. They come from far and wide."

He looked concerned. "You make it sound like an army."

"Sometimes is, depending on what you got. Usually it's just the State troopers — there's one here already that I've seen — but in cases like this an arson investigator, the medical examiner; sometimes the State's Attorney and the State Police Bureau of Criminal Investigation get involved if they suspect something."

"Do you think it was arson?"

I looked at him for a couple of seconds. He seemed so removed, as if his mind was being overworked, concentrating on other things.

"I don't know. I guess time will tell."

The State trooper I'd seen stringing a brightly colored plastic ribbon labelled "Police Line — Do Not Cross" around the house came walking up to us. He was thin and carried himself stiffly, as if on parade. This was helped somewhat by his green and gold uniform, which somehow looks more official than most state-trooper getups, especially with the green ribbed commando sweater with the matching elbow and shoulder pads.

He nodded quickly at me and Laura, before addressing the couple before us. "Are you Mr. and Mrs. Wingate?"

"Yes, we are," Wingate answered.

"My name is Corporal Wirt. I'd like to ask you a few questions."

"Of course."

Wirt glanced at us again and gestured down the street, away from the fire trucks.

"Let's step over there."

They all three moved away. "I wonder what that's all about," Laura murmured.

"Cousin Brucie had a fight with one of the unfortunate people in that building."

"He did?" Her eyes were bright with interest. In the midst of all this destruction, the air thick with unanswered questions, only Laura seemed fresh, youthful, and enthusiastic, yet somehow fragile. It was a beguiling combination. Her face had a way of completely altering itself as she shifted from one emotion to another, the way gusts of wind disturb a still body of water.

"He thought his daughter was staying there, so he went in uninvited last night and got himself thrown out the window for his pains. A small group of us trooped down to cart him away. I would imagine Corporal Wirt finds all that of some interest."

"If anything interests him. He walks around like he's got all the answers. Rumor has it he was banished up here because he stepped on some toes. We all call him Corporal Jerk."

"Where's he work out of?"

"Island Pond. He makes no secret about hating this place. I think it's silly they posted him here. The guy the State Police had here before was wonderful — knew everybody's name, used to come by when he was off duty and shoot the breeze. He made the State Police look good, you know? Of course, that was before the Island Pond thing. Wirt was transferred here right after that . . ."

The "Island Pond thing" rang more than one bell for me. Island Pond, a town about twelve miles north of Gannet on 114, was host to a Christian sect called the Northeast Kingdom Community Church. Some years back, over one hundred State troopers and social workers invaded the town, armed with a warrant, and rounded up some two hundred and twenty members of the church, including one hundred and twelve children. The charge was child abuse. It was alleged that adult members beat their children to discipline them. But before anything could be made of the case, a judge declared the raid unconstitutional and ordered everyone returned to their homes. That left a lot of egg on a lot of official faces. To this day, if you wanted to see a Vermont State official start looking for the exit door, all you had to say was "Island Pond."

No doubt, all of that was going through Corporal Wirt's head, too.

Laura tugged at my sleeve and pointed up Atlantic Boulevard at a man walking in our general direction. He was dressed in the quilt uniform of the cult, although the way he walked made it look more like a business suit, and his full beard was trimmed and neat. He carried himself with an air of studied authority and ease.

"Who's that?"

"The Elephant — Edward Sarris. The leader of the Natural Order." Her tone, I was sure, would have jacked his ego up several pegs. Whether influenced by his notoriety or fame, she was clearly impressed. It was the kind of reaction that doubtless stood him in good stead.

As he walked down the street, I noticed for the first time some signs of life from the houses around us. Faces appeared in windows, a few doors opened, a couple of bearded men stepped out on porches to watch. They were all clearly members of the Order. It was only then I remembered not having seen a single Natural Order bystander at the fire — just as I hadn't at the fight between Wingate and Fox. Now, with their leader in evidence, his followers were being drawn out, perhaps as much by curiosity as by allegiance.

He came toward us, his expression neutral, his hand held out in greeting. "Lieutenant Gunther, I'm glad to meet you. I'm Edward Sarris, leader of the Natural Order."

I shook his hand. I noticed that while he spoke, his eyes widened slightly, giving him a slightly startled look. It occurred to me he was probably trying to appear earnest, although his knowledge of my name tilted the scales more toward contrivance. That, however, may well have been my own cynical view. He did cut an impressive figure — tall, slender, with large dark eyes that looked straight at his target. He combined an uncanny mixture of intensity and calm in those eyes, which I imagined had done their fair share of persuading people.

"I wanted to thank you personally for your extraordinary act of valor in trying to save my people. There are many who wouldn't have risked so much for their own children, much less for total strangers. I can understand why you are so widely respected."

It was a perfect little speech, well-modulated, nicely phrased, astoundingly out of place. It wasn't phony or hyped-up, not like a used car dealer's pitch. But it didn't sound like human speech, either; it was too grammatical, as if I'd just been praised by the head of the English Department.

I nodded, momentarily at a loss for words.

"Please extend my thanks and compliments to all your colleagues."

"Is Julie Wingate one of the bodies?" I asked him.

He was unfazed at my abruptness. "No. She left the building just as her father arrived and created that unfortunate altercation last night."

"How do you know that?"

"It is standard practice in our society. This is not the first time parents or other outsiders have attempted to take the law unto themselves."

"Where is she now?"

"Safe." The finality of the word made the speaker's intention clear. He looked around, apparently without purpose, and saw Rennie standing at the coffee and doughnuts table.

"Excuse me," he said, and began to walk off, presumably to dump as much praise over Rennie's head as he had mine.

I raised my arm and motioned him back. "If you're sure Julie Wingate isn't in that building, I think her parents would like to know." I motioned over to where Wirt was just finishing with the Wingates.

Sarris smiled carefully. "Of course — an excellent suggestion. Thank you, Lieutenant." He nodded at Buster, who had appeared from around the side of the truck. "Nice job, Chief. We all appreciate your effort."

"No problem," Buster muttered.

I watched as Sarris strode off, self-confident and almost buoyant. "Not easily depressed, is he?"

Rennie walked up, now cradling three

doughnuts and a cup. His mouth was full. "Man's an asshole."

Buster's brow furrowed at Rennie's approach. "I better check on how the cleanup's going."

He left us and Rennie swallowed before smiling bitterly. "Your uncle thinks I tried to kill you."

"I thought you were trying to commit suicide."

"Guess I fucked up all around, huh?"

Laura, still sitting nearby, laughed. Rennie took a sip of coffee and then looked at me more carefully. "Did he ask you what Dick said to me?"

"About the attic getting ready to blow?"

"Yeah."

"Yup. Told him I didn't hear it. But," I added, "I also told him you decided to search the other room, instead of getting out."

"Over your objections?"

"No, just that you decided and I followed."

He nodded. "Good. I told him I couldn't hear what Dick was saying." He smiled again. "It's driving him crazy."

He laughed then and began to walk away. I stopped him with a question. "What made the hose go flat?"

He rubbed his cheek with the back of his hand. "They told me the portable pump froze.

90

Didn't have any oil in it." He shrugged and filled his mouth with another huge bite, talking at the same time. "By the way, thanks for saving my butt."

"Least I could do for someone who tried to kill me."

He let out a grunt and continued on his way.

Laura was looking at me with increasing concern. "What did happen in there?"

I smiled at her. "It's like Rennie said."

She shook her head in frustration. "You guys . . ." She stood up suddenly and waved. I followed her look and saw a pickup with a young man at the wheel pulled off of South Street. He waved back from the driver's window.

"Gotta go. See you later."

I watched her run to the truck, her hair bouncing. She looked good in jeans, and I felt an unreasonable pang at her leaving. I also felt an odd sensation at her running toward another man, even though, presumably, he was her husband.

"I hear you're a police officer."

I turned around, surprised at the sudden intrusion.

It was Wirt, in full official splendor.

"That's right. Joe Gunther, out of Brattleboro."

We shook hands, although primarily because my hand was flapping in the breeze before Wirt reluctantly grabbed hold of it.

"I was told you and Wilson were the first two in there. What did you see?"

I resisted stating the obvious — like "a fire" — which would have forced him to step outside the Joe Friday imitation.

"One incinerated body at the foot of the stairs, wrapped around the remains of the wood stove, and four more upstairs, apparently dead of smoke inhalation. There were no puddles of flaming gasoline on the floor, but the four people upstairs were behind a locked door, with the key on the outside, on the floor."

He looked up from the notepad he was carrying. "What kind of lock was it?"

I knew what he was after. "Old-fashioned, key operated from either side. It wasn't a dead bolt."

"And there wasn't a key on the other side as well."

"Nope, not in the door."

"But there might have been one in the room?"

"That's possible, but I don't think it's likely. I've never seen a lock like that with more than one key. In fact, usually the one key's been lost years ago and people use a hook and eye to lock the door."

He was scribbling feverishly by now. "Any idea what caused the fire?"

I was beginning to tire of this. Also, I didn't see much to gain by humoring him further. I knew damned well all this would stop dead in his little black book. With the locked-door problem, he was going to have to bring in BCI — the Bureau of Criminal Investigation. None of them would ask him his opinion on the case, and everyone would ask roughly the same questions of me and everyone involved a dozen more times over the coming week. A street cop worth his salt could be an invaluable source and a good friend to cultivate; a disliked ham like Wirt was best suited to directing traffic and nurturing his resentment.

I got up and stretched. The ice that had covered me earlier had melted in the morning sun, leaving me damp and weighted down. I began to peel off the cumbersome and very dirty bunker coat as I answered his last question. My own body odor, finally released, damn near made my eyes water. "Probably the wood stove. Now, if you'll excuse me, I think I'll hit the hay." I hung the coat on the truck's tail light and walked away. " 'Night."

"I have more questions." The tone was supposed to freeze me in my tracks.

"Don't doubt it for a second. I'll be around." I didn't need to turn around to see him glaring. The heat from his eyes on the back of my head was enough.

The truth was, I had some questions of my own. As a rule, accidental fires have a way of explaining themselves, especially where dead bodies are involved. People either die in their beds, oblivious to what killed them, or they're found along the way toward some hoped-for exit. When they appear behind a locked door, with the key on the outside, I have to wonder just how "accidental" the fire might have been.

7

I didn't make a clean getaway. As I walked down South Street toward 114, a red Mercedes pulled in, heading my way. The license plate was marked "QNCY."

I moved out of its way and bent down to the driver's window as it stopped alongside me. "I thought you drove a blue car."

Dr. Beverly Hillstrom, Chief Medical Examiner for the State of Vermont, smiled up at me. "I did. I traded it in. Big mistake. You should stick to the larger Mercedeses; these little ones just aren't the same."

I laughed at that. "I'm lucky to be stuck to a rebuilt Toyota. How are you?"

She patted the back of my hand, which was resting on her door. "In tip-top shape. What on earth are you doing here? You look terrible, by the way." She wrinkled her nose. "And you smell awful."

"Thank you. I'm staying with my uncle. I used to come up here regularly when I was a boy."

"And play fireman?"

"How'd you guess?"

"You should see your face in the mirror. You look like a chimney sweep. And your ear looks medium rare." She gave me an appraising look. "It's hard to imagine Joe Gunther on vacation."

"I'm supposed to be working with the local SA on a small job around here. If you came from Burlington, you made awfully good time."

"The local M.E.'s out of town and I was in Barton anyway. My husband and I are looking for property in the Kingdom. Pure serendipity. Who's the SA — Potter?"

"Very good."

She laughed. "Not really. I was told he'd

meet me here." There was a small pause. "So, what have we got here?"

"I don't know. I figure if I stay around long enough, maybe you'll tell me."

I let her park and opened her door for her. As she swung her legs out, I saw she was wearing a dress and high heels — elegant garb for an elegant woman. "Lord. You'll have a tough time getting around in those."

She stood up and walked to the back of the car. "I used to. I've learned since."

She opened the trunk and pulled out a pair of dirty L.L. Bean boots with bright blue socks stuffed in them. "So, you suspect 'foul play,' as they say?"

I watched as she slipped off her shoes. Beverly Hillstrom was in her mid-fifties, maybe a bit older — tall, blond, and slim — but she looked fifteen years younger. I'd first met her on the case in Brattleboro that had stimulated the local politicos to make a scapegoat of my boss and put me on the hot seat for six months. She'd been the one person who'd supported my reopening what had seemed a closed case and had even supplied forensic evidence she'd been keeping in the deep freeze for years, hopeful that someone with an ornery disregard for protocol might happen along. And that, as Humphrey Bogart would say, was the beginning of a beautiful friendship.

"I don't know what I suspect — nothing specifically. It's got several possible readings as I see it, bit of a surprise package."

"And I'm to unwrap it."

"If you would." I glanced up at the sound of another car pulling up behind us. A man in his late thirties, wearing a bad complexion, thin hair, a pot belly, and an ill-fitting three-piece suit got out and waved to me. "Here's Potter now."

"I should have known you'd be in the middle of this," Potter said to me as he approached. "I thought you were supposed to check into the office before you started trouble." His smile, in direct contrast with the rest of his appearance, was infectiously childlike.

He walked up to Beverly Hillstrom and introduced himself. "I'm Ron Potter, Essex County State's Attorney."

"Beverly Hillstrom, State M.E."

"Oh, yes, I know. It's a real privilege. I was expecting the local M.E."

Hillstrom's tone was noticeably cooler now that Potter had arrived. The warmth she showed me was a sign of friendship, which was something she did not dispense freely. "Pure chance — he was out of the area; I happened to be in it."

Potter nodded and turned to me. "Any ideas about the fire?"

Hillstrom reached back into the trunk and pulled out a camera, a notepad, and a small shoulder bag while I told Potter, "It may just be a guy falling downstairs and knocking over a jury-rigged wood stove."

The three of us began walking toward the building.

"Or it may be something else," Potter added.

"Maybe. There's background for more — a fight last night, some bad blood between townspeople and the bunch that owns the house . . ."

"Ugh," Potter interrupted. "Don't even mention it. I got two calls this morning already from newspeople, wanting to know if it's arson or murder or God knows what. Shades of Island Pond."

"There may be something more. We found four of the bodies behind a locked door, with the key on the outside."

"Were you the one who found them?" Hillstrom asked.

"Me and another guy, just before the whole place blew up. I'm not exactly sure what shape the building's in."

We had just ducked under the police line when Wirt came jogging up. "Where do you think you're going?"

Hillstrom looked at him in amazement, her

chilly Nordic dander up. "I beg your pardon?"

"This is a police line. You can't just ignore it."

The message was appropriate, but the tone was doing him dirt. I tried to smooth things over. "Corporal Wirt, this is Chief Medical Examiner Hillstrom and State's Attorney Potter."

He looked at me with contempt, not accepting the social escape hatch I'd opened for him. "This scene is closed until the arson people look at it."

Hillstrom's back straightened slightly. "Corporal, were your arson people here now, I might concede that point. But they are not and I am. It is my responsibility to examine those bodies, and I am not going to stand around for several hours waiting. Is that acceptable to you?"

Potter chimed in. "As chief law enforcement officer of the county, I'll take full responsibility."

Wirt stared at us for a few moments, his mind obviously crowded with options, some obstinate, some petty, and probably a few quite vulgar. But I guess he decided to pass on them all, or he remembered that his opinions had landed him here to begin with. He muttered, "All right, go ahead," and left us on our own.

We entered through the same door Rennie and I had used before, although you could have told that only from the outside. The inside was unrecognizable — the floor covered with a tangle of glistening, black, charred debris. The walls were stained with smoke and dirty water; the ceiling half-gone, chunks of soggy plaster hanging to shattered pieces of lathing. It brought back memories of the shell-blasted buildings I'd searched as a young soldier over thirty years before, my finger cramping around the trigger, ready to fire at the slightest movement.

Only here, any movement aside our own was out of the question. The smells of damp plaster, wet wood, charcoal, and burned cloth were all of death. The very dripping of water in the walls had a funereal sound to it.

Hillstrom, in the lead, paused to take a couple of pictures. "Which way, Lieutenant?"

Despite our recent friendship, we had never dropped the official titles, perhaps as a token of our mutual respect.

"To the foot of the stairs."

Sunlight was beginning to shaft down the staircase through the open roof above, giving me the sensation of being in a damp cave far below the surface of the earth. Dr. Hillstrom began picking her way slowly and carefully through the tangle, making sure of her footing, conscious not only of her own safety, but of the integrity of the scene as well. All three of us knew that while her goal was to view the bodies in place, other experts would follow with different interests — interests we might obliterate if we just marched through the building, tossing debris aside to make a path. It took us ten minutes to cross some twenty feet.

The foot of the stairs was especially cluttered, since the staircase had acted as a funnel for much of the debris from the floor above. The crystal-clear mental snapshot I had of the night before, of the white-hot stove spewing its column of flame straight up, and the blackened human arm extending from its base, was now smudged and altered, covered with enough clutter to render it almost unrecognizable. Had it not been for the staircase, I might not have even known where to start.

"Here?" Beverly Hillstrom asked, sensing my hesitation.

I scanned the wall for the stovepipe flue and then pointed to the floor. "That's where the stove is, or was. The last I saw, the body was right in the middle of it."

The sunlight was quite bright here. Indeed, looking up the stairs, we could see clouds against a blue sky where once there had been a ceiling. But the shadows were correspondingly harsh, and made looking beyond the surface of the rubble difficult. Hillstrom pulled a flashlight from her shoulder bag and began probing the recesses.

"Here we go."

She crouched suddenly to look more carefully. Both Potter and I instinctively did the same. Caught in the lamplight, its white teeth shining, was a charred human head, its eyes, nose, and lips burned away, its mouth open wide in a silent, agonized scream.

Potter straightened abruptly. "Jesus," he muttered and staggered slightly, shifting a pile behind him.

Dr. Hillstrom looked over her shoulder at him. "Careful, Mr. Potter. Would you like to wait outside? I'm not going to do much at this stage anyhow, and I won't be issuing any findings before autopsy."

"No, no. I'm all right."

She smiled brightly. "Oh, I know that. I just meant this will take a while and won't tell you much. So, if you have other things pressing on your time, you might want to pursue them rather than watch me poking around."

Potter nodded and made a show of checking his watch. "Well, maybe that's a good point. I'll get out of your hair."

"You're not in my hair. You're certainly

welcome to stay."

"No, no. That's okay. I'll see you later."
He began to backtrack slowly toward the door.

Hillstrom didn't say anything until he'd left.
She took photographs and notes, shifting an
occasional piece of wood or plaster and then
replacing it carefully.

"Very diplomatic," I said finally.

She chuckled. "I didn't relish him throwing
up down the back of my neck."

Her investigation was limited by what we
could see without seriously altering the scene,
so we soon made our way slowly and gingerly
up the clogged stairway, occasionally going on
all fours. I noticed her dress was beginning
to suffer.

At one point, she paused to look back and
take a photograph. "So you think he may have
tumbled downstairs, knocked himself out, and
spilled the stove in the process?"

"Maybe. You ruling that out?"

"No. It's very possible — that kind of thing
happens. There was no other source of fire?"

"None that I saw."

"And no smell of petroleum or oil or something similar?"

"Nope." I was impressed she asked. I wondered what was going through her mind, but
I also wasn't about to inquire. Like most investigators, she was assembling pieces in her

head, mentally constructing an incomplete jigsaw puzzle, hopeful that what she had might be enough for her to guess at an overall picture. She didn't need me to bring up questions she'd already asked herself.

As we reached the top of the stairs, she asked, "Right or left?"

"Left."

The bedroom door hung open like the entrance to a dark lair — a black rectangle in contrast to the sun-drenched landing on which we stood.

Hillstrom looked up at the sky. "Amazing. Where were you when this went up?"

"Right over there." I pointed to the opposite door, which had been blown off its hinges.

She shook her head silently and smiled.

We picked our way to the bedroom door. With the sunlight now behind us, the room's shadows receded somewhat. Here there were no great signs of catastrophe; aside from the cloying odor of damp smoke and wet plaster, the scene had an untouched feel about it, a peacefulness enhanced by the shape of seemingly sleeping figures clumped together on the bed. Hillstrom shined her light on them and revealed one small, paste-white face, its dull eyes half open.

She sighed and extinguished the light. I kept

quiet. After just a moment's pause, she adjusted her camera's flash unit and began taking pictures, writing notes, and examining the bodies, being careful not to displace them more than Rennie and I had hours before. I admired her professionalism, tinged as it was by the stray compassionate gesture — tucking a loose strand of hair behind the mother's ear, giving a small head an unconscious pat. It somehow seemed irrelevant that her patients were all dead, since the concern and attention she demonstrated would have been the same had they been living.

She eventually finished and straightened, looking around one last time. "Was the smoke very bad in here when you found them?"

"No. More like a thin fog."

"And the window, presumably, was closed?"

"Yeah."

She nodded, but stayed silent. She had told me once that several years ago, she'd been encouraged to guess at a cause of death prior to autopsy and had been mistaken. Nothing adverse had come of the error; she caught it almost as soon as the body was stretched out in her lab back in Burlington. But she had learned a lesson, and had vowed never to announce her findings from the field again.

I was therefore surprised when she paused

at the foot of the stairs, after we'd spent another fifteen minutes carefully retracing our steps. She stood looking down at the black, flaky skull-like head with its frozen, soot-smeared grin.

"What do you think killed him?"

I followed her gaze. Most of him was under debris, but you could see bits and pieces, if you knew where to look, along with one twisted, charcoaled arm, its fist clenched in midair — the classic "pugilistic stance" of the severely burned victim. I'd taken it earlier as a piece of wood.

"Sounds like a trick question. I'll say the fire."

"Therefore dying of smoke inhalation?"

"I guess."

"Have you seen many people die from falling down a set of stairs?"

"No."

"What are their injuries, usually?"

"I couldn't say — not about stairs — but from similar falls, I'd guess mostly bumps and bruises, broken legs and hips, an occasional neck or two . . . something like that."

"How about being knocked out cold?"

I looked again at the man I'd briefly known as Fox, wondering what he was telling her that he hadn't told me yet. "Not often, I guess."

"How old was he . . . ? Oh, did you even know him?"

"I met him once. He must have been in his late twenties, early thirties."

She pursed her lips. "Well, then you're right, statistically at least. Very few people of this approximate age group die from such a fall. Most of the time, they're nimble enough to take some sort of evasive measures. They might break something in the process, but they rarely die, and they rarely get knocked unconscious."

"Rarely."

She nodded. "True — the exception proves the rule. But there's something else. Are you aware of the AVPU scale of consciousness?"

"AVPU? Sounds like something hatched in the Pentagon."

"It does. It's a mnemonic, actually, with each letter standing for a key word in the descending order of consciousness: a patient is either *A*lert, responsive to *V*erbal stimulus, responsive to *P*ainful stimulus, or totally *U*nconscious." She drew the letters in the air for emphasis.

"Painful stimulus is usually a pinched ear or a knuckle rub on the sternum — some physical way of disturbing this artificially deep sleep, in other words."

I was finally beginning to follow her train

of thought. "Or putting your hand on a hot stove."

She smiled. "Right. You do something like that, and all but a deeply unconscious person will react, usually by pulling away from the stimulus. Again, it's not a guarantee; it's just a statistic."

"But if it's true, this man was out like a light before he hit the stove."

"That's not all. Look at his flesh, high on the chest."

I followed her pointed finger. Fox's skin had split in several places, much as a hot dog's does when it's been cooked too long.

"What color is it?" she asked.

"Sort of beige; a little pink, maybe."

"The classic sign of carbon monoxide poisoning is the cherry-red color of the skin after death. Of course, where the skin is charred, you look for the flesh underneath for the same indicator."

"So he was dead before he hit the stove."

"He *might* have been dead before he hit the stove." She wagged her finger at me. "And don't you tell anyone I told you so."

8

Ron Potter sat on the toilet seat and shook his head. "The BCI and arson teams are here. They helped Dr. Hillstrom get the bodies out. The burned one kept falling apart; I don't know how she does what she does."

I spat into the sink. "It's interesting. If it gets to you, just think of being a proctologist — now there's a curious line of work."

He made a face. "They had to get three different funeral homes to carry the bodies to Burlington. Nobody had enough body bags — we get five people killed simultaneously in this state, and it's considered an official disaster. The guys in New York must have racks in their hearses."

We were upstairs in Buster's house. I'd just spent four hours trying to catch up on last night's lost sleep, with negligible success. Potter had walked in on me fresh from a shower, while I was brushing my teeth, and had been asking me questions.

He watched my technique for a moment. "You think Bruce Wingate killed them?"

I rinsed my mouth out and squeezed by him to cross the hall to my bedroom. He followed me. "I think the fire killed them, at least most of them."

"Come on, Joe."

I began putting on a fresh shirt. "Maybe. I want to see what we get from the scene before I draw any conclusions. We may find out it was an accident, that Fox had a heart condition and died of it on the way downstairs."

"What about the locked door, then?"

"I don't know. Maybe they had an argument and he locked them in. Maybe he locked them in every night. People do strange things, especially this Order bunch, from what I hear."

Potter sat on the windowsill and stared out gloomily. He had not been the brightest cop I'd ever worked with; he lacked the flair it often took to get people to open up. He'd been hard-working and earnest — most of his fellow officers had found him a grind — but it hadn't seemed to do him much good. I'd thought maybe his lackluster style was because being a cop was a means to an end; according to him, he'd always dreamed of becoming the state's Perry Mason, carrying the cop's hard work up to the bench and convincing judge and jury that the bad guys deserved hard time.

I'd never pointed out to him that Mason

was a defense attorney; it was his flat-footed opponents who were prosecutors.

I wondered now, looking at him, whether that kind of misconception should have told me more at the time. Judging from his present lack of enthusiasm, it appeared the idea of his job was more appealing than its reality. It reminded me, albeit cynically, that the State's Attorney was an elective post, as open to politicians as to qualified prosecutors. I made a mental note to keep that distinction in mind before putting all my trust in his hands.

I finished dressing. "Any objection to my tagging along with the arson people?"

He stood up quickly. "Objection? God, no."

"Well, I'm your boy now. I could drop this whole thing and go after your embezzling town clerk."

He waved his hand. "Oh, forget her. Do what you got to do."

Like a model at a fashion show, the burned house had again changed appearances. From the scene of a fight to a five-alarm inferno, it was now playing host to a full police investigation. Instead of fire trucks and hose, State Police and Sheriff's cruisers clustered near its blackened walls. Men in uniform and in plainclothes milled about, measuring, photographing, and collecting evidence. As I approached the front door, one of them came up to greet me. He was about my age, but more hair and more gut, and was dressed in filthy blue overalls with "State Police" stenciled in white letters across his shoulder blades.

"You Gunther?" he asked, sticking out a dirty, ham-sized hand.

I almost winced at the grip. He was also about my height — five foot ten inches — but built like a brick. "Yeah."

"I'm Dick LeMay — State Police arson investigator. Thanks for keeping the scene clean."

I looked for some irony there. Arson sites, aside from their naturally dirty nature, are notoriously abused by others: Firemen, rescuers, cops, medical examiners, homicide teams, and sometimes even insurance adjustors and gawkers trample on the evidence before the arson investigator gets his first glimpse. More often than not, important details that could have told the story of the fire right off are ground into oblivion.

"Unless you're pulling my leg, you ought to thank Corporal Wirt. He roped it off before it was even cool."

"Yeah, well, I don't like him. I also heard you and Hillstrom were real dainty going in for an early look."

We were standing in front of the house, by the front door. Suddenly, there was a crash from inside.

"That's the boss." LeMay grinned, and motioned me to enter ahead of him.

Another man in blue overalls was moving slabs of plaster and lathing away from the middle of the floor. The air was thick with acrid dust. I could see already that a lot had been done to restore the room to its appearance prior to the fire. The space around the wood stove remnants was clear down to the bare floor — or what was left of it — and most of the stairs had been cleared as well. The body was gone.

LeMay made the introductions from the door. "Jonathon, this is Joe Gunther — he's the SA's man we were expecting. This is Detective Sergeant Jonathon Michael; that's Jonathon with an *on* at the end instead of *an* — parents were either hippies or illiterate. He's my supervisor out of St. Albans and he's real sensitive about his name, so get it right in your reports."

"You can spell it any way you want; everyone else does." Michael waved to me from across the mess. "Glad to meet you."

Michael was the Stan Laurel to LeMay's Oliver Hardy, thin and very tall, with a narrow face and steel-rimmed granny glasses that gave him a perpetually surprised look.

"So, what have you found so far?"

LeMay maintained center stage. "Well, the fire started at the stove — burned straight up and out. You can see the V pattern clearly, along with the downburn pattern over here. All that started secondary flareups, especially when the ceiling started to go, but you can tell they were all offshoots."

He guided me around the room, showing me one burned area after another. I nodded — I hoped intelligently — but I couldn't tell one from the other. To me, the whole room looked trashed and burned to a crisp.

We all turned at the sound of someone entering the front door. A small, neat man with carefully combed brown hair and an immaculately trimmed mustache stood there watching us. His hands were buried in the pockets of his tan overcoat, giving him an oddly proprietary look, as if he were appraising the building for possible purchase.

LeMay sounded surprised to see him. "Hullo, Crofter. I thought Appleby was on this."

The small man's face didn't change. "He is. I just wanted to take a look." He shifted his gaze to me. "Who are you?"

"The SA's guy — Joe Gunther." LeMay answered for me.

"What are you doing here?"

There was a momentary pause. The question wasn't harsh, but the inflection was so loaded with suspicion that even LeMay was rendered mute.

Michael cleared his throat. "Hamilton okayed it."

"He did?"

LeMay regained his voice, although he kept it low-key. "Yeah. You can check with him if you like. We're going to be here for a while."

The small man didn't answer, but looked at me carefully once more, turned on his heel and left. The tenseness in the room followed him out like a cloud of after-shave.

I looked to the other two. "Who was that?"

Jonathon Michael answered. "Crofter Smith. He's the senior BCI man under Hamilton at the St. J. barracks. He's a little reserved — good cop, though."

"Even if he does look like a shoe clerk," LeMay added.

Michael gave a short laugh. "Better that than sanitation workers, like us. He's just not real fond of outside investigators; makes him a little aloof."

"I think he's a cold fish."

Michael shrugged. Years back, SA investigators used to be state policemen on rotation. Then the legislature, for whatever reasons, broke up the marriage. It didn't alter the basic system to any great extent, but it did affect the ease that once marked communications between State's Attorneys and the State Police. Many of the latter, and obviously Crofter Smith among them, felt the loss of direct representation in the SA's offices had been a major mistake.

LeMay pawed at the ground for a moment, muttering, "Where was I?" He then grabbed my elbow and steered me over to where the stove had stood. "Okay, so here we have the origin — nice and tidy. But was it dumped? Was coal shoveled out of it onto the floor? Was it doused with an accelerant to make it explode?"

I noticed Michael had found a seat on an evidence can and was watching LeMay's show. I wondered what he was thinking, until I sensed in his expression the simple admiration of a shy man for an exuberant one.

"I know there's not much left of the floor — lucky there's any at all, really, or you and Hillstrom and the SA would have ended up in the basement." He peered up at me from his crouching position. "Bet you never thought of that, did you? First thing we did was shore it up.

"Anyway, look at the alligatoring here. See where the wood has been burned into squares? Well, we had a little debate about that, Jonathon and me. You can get a pretty good idea from the size of those little squares whether the fire was slow and smoldering, or fast and hot. Problem is, if the fire goes for long enough, then everything gets consumed, and you have no way of telling whether it started fast or slow. That's where you get into figuring out the layers of a fire, and sometimes you're helped because something falls on a piece of wood, extinguishes the flame, and preserves the alligatoring up to that point, so it's handy sometimes to have the ceiling fall in."

"Gotcha," I muttered, feeling I had to say something, even if it didn't reveal the depth of my wit.

LeMay jumped on it. "Gotcha, you say. But got what? Here's the evidence. Was it fast or slow to start?"

I stared at where he was pointing, feeling my face flushing slightly. Small for slow, large for fast . . . "Slow."

LeMay slapped his knee. "Damn. Brilliant. You were looking at the wrong piece, by the way — that's fast char — but you're right anyhow."

Michael spoke up from his corner. "He

guessed wrong, too, at first."

LeMay chuckled. "That just puts you in good company."

I straightened, looking for a punch line in all this. "So what happened here? Can you reconstruct how it started?"

Jonathon Michael finally got up and joined us, his voice quiet and measured compared to LeMay's. "We've taken samples for testing at the crime lab — in those clean paint cans there — but we think what happened is that the man you found lying here fell up against the stove and dumped it over; it wasn't very sturdy, and it wouldn't have taken much."

LeMay chimed in. "The fire smoldered for a while, maybe half an hour, building up a lot of smoke; that's what killed the people upstairs. Then, when things got hot enough, whoosh. The whole place went. That's why it was a little confusing telling the fast char from the slow. You have both here."

"So there's no sign of arson?" I asked.

Michael shook his head. "Nothing blatant. There are problems, but nothing that outright says arson."

"What problems?"

"Oh, it's mostly law of averages, like the position of the body. We know he was lying on the stove — a good indicator that he fell on it to make it topple over — but we found him facing up. Usually, they face down."

Again, LeMay pitched in. "See? Unusual, but not really suspicious."

I glanced at the stairs. "What about up there?"

LeMay led the way upstairs, the irrepressible tour guide, pointing to the details. "We didn't find anything up here. The fire spread along the ceiling, just like in a chimney. You can see on the walls how it seeks the highest spot. Then it got to the landing, had nowhere to go, spread out to all four walls, and then began to eat its way through to the attic."

We were now standing between the two bedroom doors, opposite the bathroom, and in full daylight from the hole above. The floor had not been as carefully cleared as the one below. I pushed at a small piece of debris with my toe.

"So there were no signs of any fire being set up here?"

LeMay dropped to his knees, pointing out the details. "You can see char here, just like downstairs, but that's from fall-down, junk from the burning ceiling. See? You can see the outlines of individual pieces of wood and stuff. We took photographs before we moved it, of course, so you can see from those, too."

As he moved, his foot brushed against a small, flaky pile near the mop board at the top of the stairs. Something briefly twinkled and caught my eye. I bent over to look more closely.

"What have you got?" Michael asked, squatting next to me.

"Damn," muttered LeMay, on his hands and knees by my other side. "I better get the camera."

As he clambered downstairs, Michael and I just looked at the object, wondering what to make of it. It was the shiny spent cartridge casing for a 9-mm bullet.

9

By the time I climbed the front steps of the Rocky River Inn that evening, I was seriously wishing I could just go home to Buster's and fall into bed. The day had been spent crawling all over every square inch of that charcoaled house, looking for anything that might explain that one spent cartridge. We had found nothing — no bullet hole, no gun, no other cartridges — nothing to justify wrapping up the day with a celebration at the Inn. Buster, however, had told me in no uncertain terms that this was where I was to be tonight.

My weariness from both lack of success and lack of sleep was helped by the realization that the Rocky River had evidently been designated this evening's official hot spot. Every window blazed with light, and the suppressed tremor of dozens of blended voices seeped out to the street.

I stepped through the front door, and was greeted by a seriously intoxicated Rennie Wilson, shouting at the top of his lungs. "Hey, hey, everybody. Here he is, the hero of the hour, that man among men, that fireman's fireman, the son of a bitch who really truly pulled my fat from the fire: Mr. Joe Guntherrrrr."

A ragged cheer followed his announcement. I gave a feeble wave and found a beer bottle thrust into my hand. Several people, none of whom I knew, slapped me on the back. The air was almost as full of smoke as it had been during the fire, and the noise, now that I was in its midst, was deafening. Greta probably hadn't had a crowd like this in years.

By my rough estimate, there were over a hundred people flowing between the café, the entrance hall, and the Library. At first glance, I didn't recognize anyone aside Rennie, whom I could see lurching off to the bar. That, of course, wasn't surprising — the crowd was mostly made up of younger people, in their twenties and thirties, and many of them were firemen and their relatives from the surrounding towns.

There were a few older faces, I saw finally, some of whom were obviously residents of the establishment, dressed in bathrobes or wearing undershirts; one was only in pajamas. Greta ran less of an inn than a retirement home/hostel for the itinerant; people stayed anywhere from two hours to ten years, and could do so, if they wished, in total isolation. The air was hot and stagnant. I put my coat on the back of a chair near the wall and hoped I'd find it later. Then I made my way slowly toward Buster's den.

Greta found me at the door and tried to push a beer bottle into my hand. It clinked against the one I already had. "Someone beat me to it, huh? Want a refill?"

"It's still full. Thanks." Actually, I no longer drank beer, or anything else, for that matter. Over the years, the appeal had gone out of it.

She kissed me on the cheek, a lifetime first. "You're a good man, Joey, and Rennie's a lucky one. Your drinks are on the house tonight, so enjoy."

I could see the top of Buster's head through the bodies and steered toward it. When he saw me, he punched the arm of the man sitting next to him and motioned him to leave.

"No, stay put," I motioned.

Buster eyed the beer in my hand. "I thought you didn't go in for that stuff anymore."

"I don't. Want it?" I had to shout to make myself heard.

"Hell, yes." He drained the one he was holding and took mine. "Greta's doin' all right, I guess."

"She told me I could drink free all night."

"Shit, Joe. She knows you don't drink. I told her so."

I watched him take a long pull from his bottle. "Hard to believe five people died today."

He gave me a long, philosophical look, a little on the blank side for all the beer inside him. "That's true, Joey, but it just doesn't weigh the same to most people in this town — sad but true."

He seemed content to leave it at that, so I obliged him. Philosophical ruminations obviously were not at the top of his list at the moment.

Watching him made me thirsty, if only for something like tonic water, so I began carving my way back toward the café/bar. As I got to the double glass doors, however, Greta's bullhorn voice cut through the din.

"Quiet down, everybody. Quiet down. I want to listen to the news. Somebody close those doors."

I was the somebody, and the word was passed to pipe down. Greta was on a stool behind the bar, fiddling with the color TV that hung there.

I was considerably less sanguine than she that this crowd would stay still for an entire news program, even with her repeated admonitions. Fortunately — or unfortunately, depending on your viewpoint — we turned out to be the lead story.

"Tragedy struck the small Northeast Kingdom village of Gannet early this morning when a fire broke out in a residence owned by a group calling itself the Natural Order. Five members, including three small children, lost their lives. They were the sole occupants of the building.

"Firemen from five surrounding towns fought several hours to bring the blaze under control, almost losing two of their own in the effort. There is more to this story, however, than a valiant but fruitless attempt to save lives and property, as our own Donna Fields discovered earlier today."

My heart sank as the screen switched to a young, blond, college-aged ingenue standing in front of the Atlantic Boulevard house, mike in hand. Once again, I thought back to the mess I'd left behind in Brattleboro. Much of our troubles during that investigation had stemmed from the overheated media attention, and the predictable political response to it. It suddenly looked like I might be headed for more of the same.

My fears increased as I listened to the report. The fire was dubbed "mysterious," despite Jonathon Michael's statement that while his findings were not final, he'd found nothing suspicious about the cause of the fire. The camera lingered on the gaping hole in the roof as the reporter pondered the significance of the "unexplained explosion" that had almost killed two firemen, followed by some neighboring Fire Chief who said that flashover explosions were a common occurrence in structure fires.

The portable water pump was the next focus of attention, with its now dramatically drained oil reservoir, which one local firefighter I didn't recognize called "real strange" — an assessment with which I couldn't argue. Finally, there was a long shot of several State Police cruisers parked alongside the road and a close-up of the "Police Line — Do Not Cross" ribbon around the house, as the voice-over by young Brenda Starr stressed that a full investigation was "being launched in this case."

Greta, still perched on her stool, hit the off button and picked me out from across the room. "What do you think, Joe?"

To the bottom of my soul, I wanted to be somewhere else. "It's really inappropriate for me to say anything. It's an ongoing case; the best thing is to wait for the final report."

"So there is something suspicious about it." Another voice chimed in.

I held up both my hands. "No, hold it." I walked over to behind the bar, which was elevated slightly above the rest of the floor. "As far as I know, this was an accidental fire, caused by someone falling against a rickety old stove that shouldn't have been lit in the first place."

"The guy was dead before he hit the stove."

I played dumb, although I was amazed the way these things seemed impossible to contain. "That's news to me."

The man speaking was the fireman who had panicked at the front door of the burning house — Paul somebody. "I saw him when they carried him out. He had his arms up like this." He postured in a boxer's pose. "Like he was fighting someone when he bought it."

"That happens in a hot fire; the flames contract the muscles and bring the arms up."

"Well, I heard it from one of the State Police, too."

"And what about that pump? Somebody must have drained it," another voice added.

Greta joined in. "I heard the Wingates were arrested for suspicion. I saw them being driven away."

I banged a glass on the counter like a gavel. "All right, all right. Let me tell you how it works, okay? First of all, nobody outside Hollywood gets arrested for suspicion. The Wingates were taken somewhere for questioning, and they were taken voluntarily. If they hadn't agreed to go, they'd still be here."

"Oh, sure, and if they hadn't agreed to go, they'd look guilty as hell."

"You don't look guilty because you don't cooperate: You look guilty because the facts weigh against you, and it takes a little time to accumulate those facts. Come on, now. I bet a dozen people in this room were questioned by the police today."

A few heads nodded.

"So why take them away?" Greta persisted, an edge to her voice.

I knew they weren't going to like this one. "Probably because they agreed to a lie detector test."

There was a predictable hubbub. The double doors opened and a few more people squeezed into the room. I hoped I could get this over with before word spread too far.

Greta began to warm her jets. "A lie detector test? And you say there's no suspicion?"

"I said you couldn't be arrested for suspicion. Be reasonable, Greta, you saw the fight. The police have to consider the possibility that Wingate returned to the house later."

"I talked to Ellie . . ."

"I'm talking possibilities here," I spoke over her. "Not alibis. The State Police have to look at everything before they can rule anything out. That's logical, isn't it? For all I know, they'll be questioning you as well, especially given your feelings about the Order."

"What are you saying?"

I couldn't believe I'd been that stupid. "I'm just pointing out that cops have to look at everybody at the start —"

But Greta was already craning her neck looking around the room, her face flushed. "Where's Norm? Norm, goddamn it."

"I'm here, I'm here." A small man with a pencil mustache raised his hand in the middle of the crowd. Just looking at him, I pegged him to be one of Greta's boyfriends. They came and went, but they all looked roughly the same. I was impressed she got the name right.

"Wasn't I in bed all last night, after that fight?"

There was an embarrassing pause.

"Answer me."

Norman gave a limp shrug. "I guess so. I was asleep." He looked around sheepishly.

Someone snickered, there was a guffaw across the room, and slowly the entire place was swept with laughter. I took advantage of the gap and headed for the door, half-expecting to feel a spear smack me between the shoulder blades. But either Greta was being drowned out, or she too had beaten a hasty retreat, probably to murder Norm.

I found Buster standing at the door. He stepped aside and let me pass into the entrance hall. "Catching some flak?"

I brushed it off. "Not too bad. People get anxious."

He planted one big paw on my shoulder and steered me toward the counter under the main staircase. "Things are different up here now, Joey. Folks are angry, and the Order is catching the brunt of it. I don't think anyone's glad those people died, but they don't want the blame pinned on Gannet. Look at Greta. She's all tied up in knots 'cause of old-fashioned competition. The Natural Order came in, throwing money around, and we took it. Hell, she and I are Selectmen —

we said they'd be good for the local economy. Now she's going broke 'cause of the Kingdom Restaurant. There's a lot of that anger goin' 'round, blaming them so we don't have to look in the mirror."

He tapped my cheek with his hand. "We can't fight back at the flatlanders, or the economy, or the government, but we can take it out on the Order. They're right here, in our own back yard; we can reach out and squeeze 'em. And unless this shit is straightened out fast, that's just what's going to happen. Somethin's goin' to blow."

He straightened suddenly, either struck with a new idea or reacting to a crick in his back. Then he mussed my hair. "Well, I think I'll get one last one for the road. See you at home." And he lumbered off toward the bar.

It had been a startling little speech, mostly because I'd thought him too drunk to give it, but it left me thinking, and a little worried. The entire state of Vermont was in the same financial straits, but few places were in Gannet's extremely tenuous position. Its gradual decline had been kicked into high gear by the arrival of the Order. And as Buster had pointed out, resentments had been given ample time to become properly misdirected. I wondered now if that resentment was burning hot enough to kill five people and turn their home into a crematorium.

10

I recognized Laura through her car window as she drove by, looking for a parking space. I was standing on the Rocky River's porch, having left behind the noise, the smoke, the heat, and the stench inside. The cool, fresh air felt wonderful. It was warmer than last night, well above freezing for a change — what Buster would call "a warm snap."

I stepped off the porch and met Laura on the sidewalk. "Hi."

She smiled, her face softly lit by the light from the Inn's windows. "Hi, yourself. How's your ear? I thought you'd be in bed by now."

I made an involuntary gesture toward my ear. "It's feeling better. I took a nap earlier. What're you up to?"

"I got bored at home. Are you leaving?" She moved, as if to step aside.

"No, no. I just needed a little air." I nodded back at the Inn.

"You sound like a hunted man."

"Well, maybe hounded a little. People are curious — think I have all the answers."

She laughed. "You're kind of famous around here, 'cause of that Ski Mask case in Brattleboro. Buster's got a scrapbook of everything you've done."

"You're kidding."

"Nope. I know you fought in Korea and got a bunch of medals, and that you went to college at Berkeley for a while . . . He's got your letters stuck in there, too."

"And you've read them."

She was suddenly quiet, obviously embarrassed.

"I don't mind."

Her voice was muted. "You sure?"

"Hell, I wrote 'em to be read."

I had settled on the fender of a parked car. Now she joined me.

"You spend a lot of time with Buster?"

She nodded.

"Why?"

She took her time before answering. I felt she was deciding whether to trust me or not, whether to respond with a social nicety or to reveal something quite personal. "He helped me when I was in trouble."

That was about as much as Buster had told me. Still, her admission was an obvious token of friendship, the sharing of an intimacy.

"I'm a recovering alcoholic. Buster was the only one who figured it out. Or maybe he was just the only one who cared."

I remained silent.

"That was about three years ago."

"How did he and you get together?"

She smiled and shook her head. "Oh, you know how he is at the garage; it's almost like he holds court there sometimes. And a lot of the kids he hires have had problems. I don't guess they're real good mechanics."

I laughed at that. Buster's employees were notorious for putting fluids in the wrong holes, or the wrong-sized tires on cars. She was right — it was less a garage than a halfway house.

"Anyway, I used to pull in there for gas or an oil change or whatever, so we got to know each other over time; he's real easy to talk to. At first, it was just general stuff — who're your folks, what's your job. Turned out he used to know my grandpa pretty well in the old days; I guess they used to go hunting together. But he found out a lot more about me pretty quick; it's not like he asks much, you know? You just end up telling him everything."

She laughed suddenly. "At least I did — real blabbermouth. Anyway, I got busted for DWI once; I don't know how he found out about it. I guess everybody finds out that kind of stuff in a small town like this sooner or later. But they usually don't say anything. He was different. I pulled in there for gas one day, and he asked me to get out and have a Coke with him, and that's how it began."

"Did he get you into AA or something?"

"No, it was just the two of us. We talked a lot; spent a lot of time together. I'd cook for him or I'd hang out at the garage. Somehow he got me out of it — out of depending on the booze."

"Must have had its moments, especially seeing him drink like a fish."

She looked straight at me, her face fresh and open. "That was one of the amazing things about it, though. He got me to focus enough on me that it didn't matter that he drank. He did that for his reasons, and they had nothing to do with me. At least that's how I ended up seeing it. I guess at first that bothered me some. But he's a wonderful man. Not everyone seems to know that."

A small pause grew. I was worried it might present a pretense for ending the conversation.

"So you have family here."

"Oh, sure. I'm a local girl, well, kind of — from East Haven. My husband's family is from here, though."

"Was that who picked you up this morning?"

"Yeah. Tommy." Her tone was not endearing.

"Problems?" It was none of my business, but professional habits are hard to break.

"Well . . . I don't know. He's a nice man. It's just . . . Maybe I'm not cut out for marriage. Buster makes it sound good when he talks about his wife . . . or when he talks about yours, too."

That came as a shock. Ellen, my wife, had been dead almost twenty years, after a long, painful fight with cancer at an unfairly young age. To have this sudden reference to her from someone I barely knew, especially in the context of marital relations, was a little disconcerting.

I guess it showed. Laura quickly put her hand on my arm. "I'm sorry, I shouldn't have said that."

I put my hand on hers. "No, that's all right. I forgot you know all about me. You shouldn't give too much credit to the ramblings of old widowers, you know. No one can compete with the dead, and there's usually no saint quite as holy as a departed mate. It's probably compensation for all the fights you had when she was alive. I don't know . . . the older I get, the more I question the sanity of any marriage."

She smiled wanly. "I can believe that. I might as well live alone. I hardly even get laid anymore."

I burst out laughing at her bluntness. "God, now *that* I don't understand."

She stared up at me then, and I felt my face turn crimson.

"You're blushing."

I laughed again, feeling thoroughly embarrassed now. "I mean, you're very attractive." I felt suddenly hot. I also felt like a total jerk.

She reached up and put her cool palm against my cheek. "It's sweet. Thank you."

She folded her arms across her chest and sighed. "It's my own fault. I could do something about it. We don't have any kids. It's just . . . I don't know. I'm stuck; have been for years."

"What does your husband do?" I asked, happy to change the subject.

"He works nights in St. J. at a lumber company. When he gets home, I'm getting ready to go to work; when I get home, it's his turn to head out. We could probably share a twin bed and never bump into each other."

"I could see where that wouldn't do much for a relationship."

"I guess." She paused. "Do you have a girlfriend?"

I smiled but kept quiet.

"I didn't embarrass you again, did I? I'm sorry."

"No, no, not at all. Yes, I have a girlfriend; I just never thought of her in that light. I'm surprised you didn't already know about her. The scrapbook must get thin at the end."

"What's her name?"

"Gail." It felt awkward saying her name here. With all the recent excitement, I hadn't paused to think about the primary reason I was up here — to ponder just where Gail and I were headed.

"And?"

"She's a realtor in Brattleboro."

"Is she pretty?"

"I think so." I was distracted, suddenly wondering just what it was that had caused things to cool between Gail and me.

"Skinny?"

"Pretty thin, yeah. Why do you ask?"

"I just thought she would be. Skinnier than me, I bet." She slid off the car and opened her coat. I looked at her, again startled by her spontaneity. She was, in fact, remarkably attractive in a close-fitting sweater and the perennial jeans — "full-bodied," as the ads say, but with a flat stomach and nicely rounded hips. I found myself thinking old Tommy must be out of his mind.

"Very nice."

She looked down at herself. "That's it?"

I could feel my cheeks flushing again. "You like doing this to me."

She grinned and swiveled her hips.

I leaned over, took her hands and brought them together, closing her coat. "You know damn well what I think."

Like a burst bubble, her mood darkened. She hugged the coat about her and stared at the ground.

The suddenness threw me off. "I'm sorry. I didn't mean to hurt your feelings."

She shook her head. "You didn't. Just the opposite. You're one of the nicest men I've met." Her voice lifted, regaining an artificial brightness. "So, do you love Gail a lot?"

Her frailty was infectious, and her ability to turn the tables uncanny. I found myself suddenly quite at a loss for words.

She gave me a sidelong glance and a sad smile. "You, too, huh?"

"No. It's different. Well, for one, we're not married. We don't even live together."

"Oh."

A silence grew between us. I looked up at the stars. What a surprising conversation to be having, especially with a woman I'd only known for a day. Not to mention the fact that she was half my age. But I felt I owed her as much honesty as she'd shared with me. "Gail and I are a little like seesaw riders trying to stay level with each other. It only works if we're both at the same emotional height, and at opposite ends of the board."

"I never would have thought of a relationship that way."

I thought about it for a bit. "It's accurate, though. And right now we're off balance."

"Seriously?"

I shrugged. "I don't know. I think that's one of the reasons I'm up here."

"So what're you going to do?"

"Damned if I know. Try to work it out when I get back to Brattleboro."

Another pause. "And what do I do?"

I didn't answer at first, confused by the way she'd phrased the question. "I don't know that I'm the one to ask." I thought for a moment. "Talk to him, maybe change your schedules, look in the mirror and decide what you want from each other. It's very hard. I can only tell you the answers don't get any easier the older you get."

She nodded and slowly straightened up, her hands in her pockets. "Thanks, Joe."

She reached up and kissed me on the cheek. Then she walked down the sidewalk to her car, got in, and drove away with a small wave of her hand. I waved back and watched her taillights.

Maybe it was the empty feeling she'd left behind, or the uncomfortable yearnings she'd aroused in me, but in that moment of Laura's departure, I don't think I'd ever missed Gail more.

11

I paused in front of the burned house, still contained by the thin, sagging yellow Police Line, anemically reflecting the rising sun. This marked the start of the hunt, the point where seemingly random violence yields to the search for an explanation. I wanted to begin that search with the real owner of this house, Edward Sarris, and I wanted to begin it early, before a scheduled morning meeting between Potter and the State Police investigators.

It was a warm morning, or at least warm for November in Vermont. The earth, just twenty-four hours ago crystallized with ice, was now softened and muddy. The tracks of dozens of heavy trucks had lost their definition as if, slowly, they too were melting.

I walked north up Atlantic Boulevard. There still wasn't much activity; sunrise had been but twenty minutes before. I'd been told all the houses at this end belonged to the Order, something I could easily have guessed. For one thing, there were no electrical wires running to any of them. They were all peculiarly blotchy in appearance, as if, after scraping, they'd been repainted with a wash. None of the lawns were mowed. Indeed, seen from a low enough angle, especially from the dirt road, the houses looked like museum-quality prairie homes, originally miles apart, which had been gathered together in one overgrown field for anthropological preservation.

There was something else that struck me, but it took a while to sink in: There were no cars. In fact, there were no trucks, or motorcycles, or even tricycles anywhere to be seen. This entire end of town looked transported from the previous century. The paint, upon closer scrutiny, was indeed whitewash — what Tom Sawyer had applied to his aunt's fence. The clothes lines, the piled split wood, the occasional cross-saw seen leaning against a wall — all harked back to preindustrial times. Aside from a glimpse or two of a woman or child in the ubiquitous cotton Mao suits, all of it could have served well at Williamsburg or Sturbridge Village. Except that all this looked real, including the odd scrap of antique garbage.

I saw a woman hanging laundry by the side of a house partway up the street. "Hi. Excuse me."

She turned and looked at me, her initial smile fading. She didn't answer.

"I'm looking for Edward Sarris's house."

Without a sound, she pointed across the street at the narrow side road where the Wingates had waited for their daughter the night before last, the one that led off into the wooded hills east of town.

"Up that street?"

She nodded, now looking quite grave.

"Thank you very much." I followed her direction, looking back just as the tall grass and the corner of the opposite house were about to hide me from view. She was still looking at me. I waved, still to no effect.

From Atlantic Boulevard the road looked more like a driveway than a road, but once on it, past the houses and across the wooden bridge spanning the Passumpsic, I felt myself suddenly in the country, surrounded by nothing but tall frostbitten grass, underbrush, and a growing number of gray, bare trees.

The road led upward for only a third of a mile, but became increasingly steep, so I soon found myself stripping off my coat and dangling it over my shoulder, despite the dabbled shade the now dense trees were supplying. I wasn't hot, just pleasantly warm, and with the absence of any bugs this late in the year, I discovered I was thoroughly enjoying myself.

The house first appeared as more of a suspicion — something dark and solid amid the dark and distant tree trunks. Its substance grew quickly, however, along with its obvious size. It was built of logs, was no more than a few years old, and was truly gigantic, not quite the Rocky River's three stories, but almost. This sense of size was reinforced by the fact that it was built out from the hillside, its front supported by a small forest of pillars, making it look much like a dock approached at low tide in a small boat.

The road, which turned out to have been a driveway after all, ran past the house, circled around, and ended in a large parking area that had been cut out of the hill to the rear. Several cars and vans were parked there, only one of which — a new Jeep Cherokee — was obviously used with any frequency. The others were all aligned at the back of the lot, and covered with dust and leaves. There were about twelve of them. The license plate of the Jeep spelled "ORDER," a word I'd always found had ominous undertones.

I walked up to what was obviously a hand-made cherry door — quite beautiful in its detailing — and knocked.

Edward Sarris opened up almost instantly. "Hello, Lieutenant. I thought you might be next." He was immaculately attired, as when I'd last seen him, making his cotton garb look like custom-tailored silk. I had hoped to find him at a disadvantage, dripping wet from the shower perhaps, but he either kept ungodly hours, or had already locked into a psychological war plan.

"State Police beat me to it?"

"Yes. Yesterday afternoon."

"Well, I can't promise I'll be the last."

"I'm familiar with the system." His tone reflected the thrill of it all.

I tilted my chin at the building. "This is quite the eagle's nest."

He smiled and ushered me in. "It suits us."

What I entered was one huge room, easily one hundred by fifty feet, and extending two floors up to a web of heavy wooden supports, cross braces, and rafters. The downhill wall, leading out to an equally huge deck, was a mosaic of windows — squares, rectangles, rounds, and half-rounds, which salted the room with multi-fractured light. There was a church-like stillness to it all, enhanced by a view that encompassed the slope I'd climbed, all of Gannet, the hills opposite, and far beyond.

"This is beautiful."

"Thank you. We built it ourselves."

I walked to the middle of the room, which had little furniture, and that mostly benches lining the walls, and looked around. My footsteps echoed majestically on the uncarpeted hardwood floor. "How long did it take you?"

"Not long. We're a very dedicated clan, and we work hard at what we love."

"Well, I tip my hat. You did an amazing job."

He walked by me and threw open a set of French doors to the deck. "Come outside."

I followed him and felt I was stepping aboard an aircraft carrier. The deck was in fact longer than the room, extending a good twenty feet more to the right, and revealing there was more to the building than just one room. It was surrounded by a simple rail, thin enough to be almost invisible from a distance, giving me the impression of being held aloft, above the trees, as on a huge magic carpet. If the intent was to be inspirational, it was a sure-fire success.

"You guys don't fool around with tight quarters."

"Our goal is to be as one with Nature, Lieutenant. Depending on your viewpoint, that is either a practical or a romantic ambition, but in either case, we have tried to capture the poetry of that mission here in our place of worship."

Again, I was struck by his diction and vocabulary. He spoke with precision like a highbrow radio announcer, and had a nice baritone voice to boot. He must have been hell on the pulpit — or whatever he used.

"So this is your church?"

"We choose not to use that term. This is simply our place of worship."

"And what do you worship?"

"Nature."

"It's my understanding that for the average cause to work it has to have not only an appealing goal, but something to unite against as well. What is it you're against?"

He looked at me in silence for a moment before smiling. "Have you always been a Brattleboro policeman?"

"Over thirty years."

"But you went to college."

I smiled back. "Why?"

Now he chuckled, rubbed his chin, and wandered toward the outside rail. I followed him. "Because you display more intelligence than I have come to expect from the local constabulary."

"That's pretty faint praise. There is no local constabulary."

He smiled and waved that away. "I meant the State Police."

"So who are the bad guys in your world?"

He didn't duck it this time, nor did he bother to argue semantics. "The materialists."

"The head of General Motors or the woman buying groceries at the P&C?"

"Both. They both contribute to the erosion of those parts of life that are healthy, benevolent, and in harmony with nature. They are the water that cuts away at the sandy bank of our existence, making our foothold on this planet increasingly precarious."

I leaned against the rail. From the edge of the deck, overlooking a good twenty foot drop, I felt like a bird at the top of the trees. I chose to avoid a philosophical debate, by which, I was quite sure, neither one of us would be satisfied. "Did the materialists burn your building?"

His face clouded. "I don't know. I have no reason to think so yet. Do you?"

"No. What about Bruce Wingate?"

"Bruce Wingate has chosen not to look in the mirror. He blames us for his errors and attacks us for putting his wrongs right."

"But did he kill your people?"

I could see he was wrestling with his composure. I had hit a button with Wingate's name. "I've already answered that."

"I understand Fox was one of your lieutenants."

"We have no such ranking: We are as one."

"You're the leader."

He hesitated. "I am."

"You must need people to help you run things."

He made an impatient expression. "Very well, as you see things, Fox was a lieutenant. An Elder, perhaps, more accurately."

"One of many?"

"Fox was a friend and an advisor. He was among a small group of similarly trusted individuals. We shall all miss him, as we shall miss the people who perished with him." His tone was final.

I switched tack. "What does Julie think about all this?"

"Julie?"

"Cute. Julie Wingate."

I could just hear a small sigh. "I cannot speak for other members of the clan."

"Can I speak to her, then?"

"No."

Now it was my turn to smile. "You want to expand on that a bit?"

"No."

"You'd be good in court."

"I have been good in court."

I laughed at that, and he joined me after a moment's hesitation. There was an appeal to this guy. He used the language well, he had some wit, and although dogmatic, he lacked that self-righteous tone that always made me want to strangle the likes of Tammy and Jimmy Bakker. "I bet. I tell you what. Right now, we've got your man Fox falling head over heels downstairs, knocking over the stove, getting burned to death and killing the rest of the people in the building with the smoke."

"So I gather."

"But I don't swallow that."

He was staring out at the distant mountains, his hands resting on the rail. He nodded. "All right."

"And you don't swallow it either."

"I don't?"

"I'd like to know if I can have your cooperation on this investigation."

"I've always cooperated with the police."

"Why do I think we're beginning to kid around a little here?"

He turned toward me. "Lieutenant Gunther, we are not on the same side. You would like to believe that you are preserving peace and maintaining rationality in a society that occasionally runs amuck. In our view, you are the chief engineer in the belly of an aging, leaking tramp steamer caught in the middle of the storm that will mark your demise. You are not in control, your crew is not in control, and the ship in which you ride is doomed. The sea controls you, the winds control you, and when you die, you will rot, and Nature will repossess your carcass. Nature will out in the end, Lieutenant, regardless of how you might choose to see things. My cooperation with you and minions like you is pragmatic — the price of survival in this society. But do not think for a moment that I will allow you voluntarily to come among us and spread your diseased philosophies. You are the plague to us, the enforcer of the greedy, the corrupt, the polluter, and all those who would take this planet and reduce it to a poisonous wasteland. I will cooperate. I will not embrace."

I smiled and gave him a mock applause.

He turned away in disgust and took several steps — I wondered if he ever wore a cape; the gestures would have gone well with one. He turned back to face me. "I was hoping for better from you."

"From the enforcer of the greedy, the corrupt, and the polluter?"

"You are being flip. Surely that cannot be your intention."

"Look, I don't really care what you and

your little band believe in. You could spend all day worshipping cucumbers and painting yourselves green, for all I care. That's your right. I'm not here to swap philosophies or to measure up to your expectations. I'm here to investigate the deaths of five of your members."

"I said I'd cooperate."

"But only kind of."

"Lieutenant, I do not trust you or anyone else of your ilk. You may believe what you will about us — or me — but I have not reached my conclusions without serious contemplation. You do not impress me with your self-assessed role in all this; you have long been duped into thinking the way you do. You are blind to reality, even as bright as you are, which is a shame."

He began to walk purposefully back toward the house, clearly intending to show me the way out. "However, your societal placement allows you a certain power over me, which I must practically recognize and to which I will occasionally bow. But that's it. Do not expect me to be awed by your office or to view your coming with anything other than dread."

We had reached the front door. He opened it wide to let me pass.

"I guess I'll never get to call you Ted."

He gave me a disappointed teacher's look again. "You may call me anything you please, as long as it isn't libelous."

I shrugged and walked away. I'd liked him better when he was wowing my socks off.

12

The room was stuffy — too small, with too many smokers. It reminded me of Chief Brandt's office in Brattleboro, where he and our SA, James Dunn, dueled regularly with pipe and cigarettes as if the man who passed out last would win the debate. It was a contest I could only rarely witness to the end.

We were at the State Police barracks in St. Johnsbury, and the leader of the band was Lieutenant Mel Hamilton, the local Bureau of Criminal Investigation Chief. Sitting around in his small, bland office, with tiny rectangular windows irritatingly placed six feet up on the wall, were myself, Ron Potter, Dick LeMay, Steve Wirt, and a secretary. In addition, there was Anson "Apple" Appleby, from the Derby barracks upstate, and another plainclothesman whom I guessed was Apple's sidekick. Apple, whom I knew from his earlier career as a Deputy Sheriff in Windham County — where Brattleboro is located — was a twenty-year State Police veteran. He had been called in to head the arson deaths investigation.

Crofter Smith, the chilly BCI investigator LeMay told me was Hamilton's Number One man, was not there. As yet, despite the plethora of questions we all had, the house burning was still being officially listed as "an accident pending the accumulation of further details."

Hamilton was obviously not a smoker, but polite — he didn't ask anyone to crush their butts. "I'm sorry we had to meet here. The conference room is tied up. Does everyone know everyone?"

"Nope." I pointed to the sidekick.

"Sorry. Mike Churchill — Joe Gunther."

We waved feebly at each other.

Hamilton sat on the corner of his metal desk. He was a tall man with a pudgy middle, a pleasant, uninteresting face and, judging from his office decorations, a stickler for keeping things clutter-free, neat, and tidy. To me, that was not necessarily a good sign.

"I've invited the SA and his investigator to sit in so they can get it straight from the horse's mouth." He smiled a tiny smile. "No offense."

The joke landed like a dud. Although he had Waterbury-based bosses who outranked him, as far as we were concerned, Lieutenant Hamilton was the top cop here — the State Police equivalent of Ron Potter. It was he who would be most influential in deciding just how smoothly things traveled between the SA's office and the Bureau of Criminal Investigation. I was becoming worried he might be as guarded and rigid as Potter was skittish and uncertain. If he was, I'd be in a hell of a bind, dangling in between them.

"Dick, what's the arson report?"

LeMay shifted in his seat and cleared his throat, the playful, nonstop manner he'd displayed in the burned house reduced to an official drone. "No better than yesterday — can't prove willful and malicious. What we got so far from the lab shows nothing unusual: no accelerants, no misplaced matches or candles. From what we can tell, nothing of value was removed from the building prior, and nothing was there that looked out of place. There wasn't much in there period, really."

He held out his hand and began counting off his fingers as he went. "There was no sign of violence except the window, which we know about. I didn't get anything unusual out of the firefighters involved — no suspicious smoke or flame color or noises. The spread, evolution, and speed of the fire were natural. The building didn't have any wiring or gas lines or even plumbing, for that matter. The explosion that almost got Joe and his pal was superheated air caught in a natural dead air-space in the attic. Turns out they ventilated the wrong place when they cut through the roof; the attic was partitioned and they entered the space that was fire-free."

He put his hands down. "The building is owned by something called The Elephant Clan, which is a corporation listed under Edward Sarris's name. The insurance was legit for the value of the house, and PILR didn't come up with anything when I ran Sarris, Elephant, The Elephant Clan, the Natural Order, or Jesus Christ through their computer."

Hamilton's face tightened slightly.

"Sorry. Anyway, the whole thing looks clean as a whistle."

"Thank you."

"What's your gut reaction?" I asked.

"I hate it."

Hamilton gave me a baleful look that wasn't neat and tidy. But his tone was utterly neutral. "You hate what?"

LeMay shifted again and flopped his hand over, palm up on his lap. "Lot of things. The bullet, the locked door, the way that body's lying on the stove, among other things. Just doesn't look real. I don't know . . . I'm stuck with a lack of evidence, but I smell a rat."

Hamilton nodded. "Okay. That's good. Appleby?"

The one man who wouldn't call him Apple. Still, I was pleased at the way he'd accepted what LeMay had just said. I began to hope I was selling him short, maybe his mind wasn't as restrained and unimaginative as his exterior had led me to believe.

"We're not getting much help from the Order on this. Churchill talked to Sarris and asked him to get his people to open up. He said he wasn't in a position to do that, gave us some crap about their freedom to interact or something."

Hamilton frowned again and glanced at Churchill, but Apple didn't even pause. These weren't his barracks; he'd be back in Derby before too long. Besides, he was an old-time street cop, less inclined to avoid crude language, and considerably less concerned with impressing his superiors.

"The local who pulled the alarm outside the firehouse said he woke up hearing shouts in the street, looked out his window, and saw people running around the house. Said it didn't look like they were doing much good, and he hadn't heard the siren yet, so he ran off to sound the alarm himself."

"Did he recognize any of the people in the

street?" Hamilton asked.

"Nope. Says they all look the same to him and it was too far away anyway. His house is pretty far off."

"How involved was the house when he stuck his head out the window?"

"He said he saw flames downstairs; he's a little vague about upstairs. Says he might have seen a flickering."

Apple opened a file he'd been holding in his lap. "I got the autopsies back from Hillstrom. The four upstairs died of smoke inhalation. The guy downstairs — Fox — is a different matter." He nodded in LeMay's direction. "Dick's gut is right on the money: Whatever the guy died of, it sure as hell wasn't smoke. Hillstrom says she has no doubts he was dead before he hit the stove. The fire did a pretty good job on him; so did moving him from the house to Burlington, for that matter. His neck was pretty well burned through; lot of bone breakage due to heat —"

"Any guesses what killed him?" Hamilton interrupted.

"She can't say for sure; she's mostly ruling stuff out, like no bullet hole, no depressed fractures, no poison in the system, no bloody knife found nearby, etc. . . . She did find something interesting, though — a feather in the neck."

Hamilton's brow furrowed. "Where in the neck. I thought you said it was burned through?"

Apple closed the file with a small slap. "Well, that's what makes it iffy. I mean, we're talking about a piece of meat that's been cooked right down to charcoal almost. There's a photo in here, but you can't tell squat from it, so I drove over to see it all for myself. What she's got is all burned and microscopic, but she swears it's the remnants of a feather. What she can't swear to is whether it was on the guy when he burned, or in him."

"Like swallowed by him?" LeMay asked.

"Swallowed, inhaled . . . You know as much as I do. Maybe the guy ate raw, unplucked chickens or something. I hear they're pretty strange."

LeMay spoke up. "We found a feather on the landing upstairs."

There was a pause. Nobody apparently could make much of that. The mention of the landing, however, made me think of the four other victims. "Dick, you said the fire smoldered for quite a while before it finally took off, but Rennie and I found the four victims upstairs all huddled together on one bed. Why didn't they open the window if they smelled smoke? Why didn't they shove a blanket under the door?"

I hadn't meant to put Dick LeMay on the spot. He shrugged and looked over to Appleby, who shook his head. "Beats me."

"Maybe they were all huddled on that bed for some other reason. When we first went in, and I saw them under the blanket, I thought it was there to block off the smoke. But I've been thinking — the blanket was around them, not over their heads. They were all crunched up like they were afraid of something."

Apple frowned thoughtfully. "You're saying they were frightened by something before the fire even started, something that may have distracted them from smelling the smoke before it was too late."

"Right," I said. "Like when kids get scared of lightning in the middle of the night, or they hear something creaking outside. They get together; they huddle up. Maybe the woman was playing along, lending them comfort; or maybe she was scared, too."

"Wouldn't the smoke have stunk the place up?" Potter asked, as if pained by the possibility this might all be more than a simple accident.

LeMay answered him. "The stove was a cob job — held together with baling wire, literally. It must have stunk all the time — they were probably used to it; if all of a sudden there

159

was more smoke, and if they were seriously distracted like Joe thinks, they might not have noticed 'til it was too late. Besides, depending on what's burning, the gases can kill you before the smoke is even noticeable."

Hamilton nodded from his perch on the desk — the benevolent moderator. "It's purely speculative, but we should keep it in mind. What about the hose line that went flat? I gather that turned out to be nothing."

His last sentence stunned me. I'd heard with everyone else that the oil had been drained from the portable pump that had supplied water from the river to the tanker, and thereby to Rennie and me, but that hardly sounded like nothing. On the contrary, it had struck me as a coincidence too great to ignore.

Apple nodded. "Apparently Buster Chartier got a little tense at the time, but it turns out it was human error. One of his people forgot to refill the oil pan after he serviced the pump last time."

"Definitely accidental?" Hamilton pushed.

"Anything's possible, but in my book, the guy screwed up. He did the job last month — there was a bill for the oil. Another guy helped him during the initial breakdown and cleaning of the pump, but had to leave because it was getting late and he had to go home for dinner. I found the oil, unopened, and the guy thinks that in the rush — now that he was all alone and late for dinner himself — he just forgot to put the damn stuff in."

I thought back to Buster's odd behavior following the fire. Now it made more sense. He held himself accountable for risking my life because he hadn't checked the pump. His anger at Rennie had been compounded by his own guilt. I now regretted not bringing the subject up at the time.

My mixed feelings were not unique. There was a perceptible sense of disappointment in the room. Had the pump been sabotaged, as most of us had thought, then premeditation and possibly conspiracy became parts of the recipe. That meant a more organized, complicated scheme, which in turn meant more potential rocks lying around for us to look under. Apple's report put an end to all that, and introduced the possibility that the pump wasn't the only thing that merely looked suspicious. Like bloodhounds suffering cabin fever, none of us looked forward to being told the hunt was off.

As if to stem that very possibility, Apple almost cheerfully turned to another sheet in his folder. "I got the report back from the crime lab on the shell casing found in the house. It is 9 mm, like we thought, from an automatic, but they can't say what kind, nor can they say how long ago the bullet was fired. But," here he held up his hand theatrically, "it does have a nice clear, single print on it."

"Belonging to . . .?" I asked.

"Unknown. Hey, you can't have it all."

Hamilton looked a little irritated. "They couldn't match the casing to anything in their files?"

"Nope."

Hamilton checked a sheet of paper lying beside him, presumably an agenda. "What about the identities of the deceased?"

"Ah. There, Sarris is being more helpful, but that's Mike's territory."

We all looked at Mike Churchill, who hadn't said a word so far, no surprise with a partner as voluble as Apple. He cleared his throat. "Yes. We — I mean, I — showed him photographs and he identified everyone including the burned guy. I pushed him a little there, since the guy's such a mess, and at first he seemed to hesitate a little. But then he said definitely there was no doubt the burned guy was Fox. His real name was Ed Sylvester, by the way. Sarris said he'd known him for years; he'd been one of his trusted advisors and one of the original members of the Order. Plus, he said, Fox — or Sylvester — hadn't turned up, and the burned house was where he'd lived. Gave me addresses of next of kin for everybody, too. I'm still working on it, but so far, they're checking out. It'll take a few days for it all to get back to us."

"Did he get those from a file or something?"

"What?" Churchill seemed startled at a question from me.

"The names and addresses."

"Oh. Yes. A filing cabinet."

"He keeps pretty substantial records, I think," Hamilton clarified. "About six months ago, they had an accidental death over there — a small child fell off a bridge into a dry stream bed. Sarris gave us all the information we needed."

"Were you able to look into his files?"

"No. He wasn't that cooperative, but what he gave us checked out." Hamilton smiled ruefully. "I can't deny I would have liked a look, but he made it clear we'd have to get a warrant, and we had no grounds."

"How old a child was it?" I asked, my curiosity piqued.

Hamilton paused a moment, thinking. "He was a little guy — had just learned to walk — fourteen months comes to mind, but I'd have to check the case file."

"And he was walking across a bridge?"

The other man's brow furrowed at my persistence. "He wasn't alone. There was a group of them, supervised by a couple of adults. The

163

children were all holding hands when this one either broke away or was let go and ran to the rail. He was over in a flash. Nothing they could do. As far as we could tell, it was a straightforward accident; tragic, but unavoidable."

Hamilton picked up the agenda before him and referred to it. "I guess that's about it. So our primary thrust right now is to see if Churchill and Appleby can establish a willful and malicious fire."

"What about Julie Wingate?"

Hamilton stared at me for an instant.

"Has anyone talked to her?"

"I'd like to," Apple admitted.

"I asked about her," Churchill added, "but got nowhere with Sarris."

"I didn't either," I told them.

"Nor will any of us," Hamilton said, "unless we prove she did something to warrant getting a court order."

"How did Wingate do on the lie detector?" I asked.

"Inconclusive; and his wife refused to take one."

Ron Potter spoke up again. "Is there any feeling he might have started that fire?"

Apple answered. "Too early to tell, but I agree with Dick. Something stinks here, and I think old Brucie's right in the middle of it."

"I agree," I said. "His reaction following the fire was odd, and he certainly had motive and opportunity. I take it he has no real alibi for his whereabouts that night?"

Apple smiled. "They were in bed together all night — supposedly."

"Did you go with them to take the lie detector test?"

"Yeah, up to Derby. That's what bothers me. I know those machines are supposed to be pretty good, but they can be beat. To me, an inconclusive result might just mean we were asking the wrong questions. I mean, I know in my gut Wingate ain't playing straight."

"Where're they from, by the way?" I asked.

"Natick, Mass. He's a bank manager; she's a legal secretary. Squeaky clean — on the outside."

Hamilton held up his hand at that. "One word of caution. This investigation is just beginning. We have some leads; we have a lot of legwork to do. Let's not jump to conclusions and go after the wrong people. We don't have an arson here — we have an accidental fire. And we don't have a homicide. Right now, it's an unexplained death, quite possibly also accidental. The press is going to have a good time with all this, so let's keep them as bored as possible."

He looked at Potter and me. "I want to thank you two gentlemen for coming today. We will, of course, keep you up to date on everything we find out."

"In other words," Apple laughed, "bye-bye; we have private stuff to talk about."

This time, Hamilton showed his anger. "That's enough."

Potter got to his feet. "No — absolutely. Thank you one and all. We appreciate the invite. I'd like Joe here to be a part of all this, and we'll let you know what he digs up, too."

"So, what do you think?" Potter asked me as we stepped outside the building and headed toward our cars. His voice was falsely jaunty, as if he were whistling past the graveyard.

"Like I said in there, I agree with LeMay and Apple; the whole thing stinks to high heaven." His obvious reluctance to acknowledge the more suspicious aspects of the case made me sound harsher than I intended. "I also wish I could get hold of Julie Wingate and ask her where she was when the house burned down."

"You think she had something to do with it?"

"I don't know. But it's quite a coincidence the house went up in flames only hours after

Wingate broke in fighting mad looking for his daughter."

"Shit. You know goddamn well this whole thing's going to blow up in our faces. The news guys are going to have a ball. I mean, look at this mess: a cult, five deaths, possible arson, a flunked lie detector test."

"Enough to drive you out of politics, huh?" I couldn't resist needling him. This was, after all, his big chance to act out his grand ambitions.

"Enough to get me evicted from politics — damn straight."

"Relax. Island Pond was a big deal because people fucked up. You're just doing your job."

He shook his head and got into his car.

We both drove to his office — the first time I'd been there since my arrival — and he introduced me to his secretary, Florence Ginty. She and I made up his entire staff. For the rest of the day, I set up shop, establishing a filing system to absorb the mountain of paperwork I knew the State Police would soon produce on this case, and getting Flo used to me. Potter stayed in his office most of that time, and then later disappeared "to court," a catchall phrase I've always envied.

Flo left at about six, having thoroughly impressed me with her organizational wizardry. An investigator can either translate police re-

167

ports and files into something usable for his boss' day in court, or he can have others do most of that for him while he hits the street to fill in the blanks. In the best of worlds, he does a little of both. I hate the paperwork, so my particular joy was discovering that Flo was my perfect counterpart. She had no interest in the war stories of how information was gathered; her delight was in seeing it all properly filed, annotated, and thereby transformed into legal data. She would be the perfect bridge between me and Potter, and I promised her that whatever extra help she might need down the road, she would get — guaranteed.

Later, however, sitting in my corner of the office alone, writing lists and timetables of things done and things to do, a feeling of dread began to take over. I sat back and looked out the window onto the street below.

Tony Brandt had asked me back in Brattleboro why I didn't just go on vacation, instead of taking a leave of absence. I'd told him I needed a change of pace, not a vacation. The truth was I hadn't taken a vacation since Ellen had died. I didn't know what to do on a vacation. I didn't hunt, didn't fish, didn't collect butterflies or slides of exotic places. I ate, slept, read, watched TV, worked, and — these past few years — spent time with Gail.

That, of course, was the nub of it. If I had gone on vacation, it naturally would have been with Gail. But that hadn't been an option this time, not with the chill that had descended on that friendship.

I reached out and turned off the desk lamp, allowing the lights from the cars below to filter through the misty window panes and flicker across the ceiling in silence. I was truly between a rock and a hard place. Instead of staying put in Brattleboro and tearing down the elusive, half-seen barriers that had grown in silence between Gail and me, I was now arm wrestling with the ghosts of my childhood memories, while being sucked into a case that threatened the very serenity I'd been seeking.

It made me wonder if there was anything left for me in Brattleboro, beyond the very job which had helped cause my dilemma in the first place, a rather morose perspective, even from my own presently dour point of view. I decided it was time for a short break, before I started checking the ceiling for good places from which to hang a rope.

In the end, I found myself wandering the neighboring streets. The balmy night weather was still holding against all odds. I concentrated on clearing my head, enjoying the same St. Johnsbury sights I'd relished as a kid on the town with a small pocketful of cash. Then, St. J. had been *it* — "The Maple Capital of the World," home of most of the industry in the area, and all of the nightlife. For once, things didn't look too different. It was still an upscale town, with lots on the ball, at least in comparison with the rest of the Northeast Kingdom.

I paused at an odd kind of bric-à-brac store on my way back to the office, and then went inside with no purpose in mind. A pretty girl behind the counter chatted with me as I wandered up and down the empty aisles, picking up objects and replacing them without thought.

I ended up back on the street with a small bag in my hand, containing a twenty-dollar green stone necklace I'd bought for Laura. I'd done the same kind of thing for Gail in the past; purchased gifts on impulse, just things to make her smile. It felt suddenly awkward to have made the same gesture, but for the wrong person.

I stuffed the bag in my coat pocket and returned to Potter's office, determined to stop wracking my brain and to get on with what I was being paid to do. I picked up the phone and dialed the Rocky River Inn.

13

I found the Wingates' room on the second floor of the Rocky River, directly opposite the stairs. Greta stood in the open doorway, waiting for me. That came as no great surprise. When I'd called to arrange a meeting with the Wingates, Greta had answered the Inn's only public phone, and while I hadn't told her I was inviting myself over, I figured she would grill them to find out my purpose.

"You took your time." There was some irritation in her voice, but not what I'd feared, given my hasty retreat from the café during our last encounter.

"Sorry, Greta, I was in St. J."

She reached out and touched my shoulder, an unexpectedly maternal gesture. "Are you all right?"

I looked at her in surprise. For all her cranky ways, I was fond of Greta — we went back a long way together. She was loud-mouthed, unpredictable, thin-skinned, and always convinced she was right; but to my knowledge, she had never told a lie and she never let you wonder where you stood. She was getting old, of course, along with the rest of us, and I seriously doubted she would age with any grace whatsoever, but by now I knew my affection would overcome anything she could throw at me.

"You look tired," she said.

"It's been a long day."

She stood aside to let me enter the room. I was touched by her tentative concern for my psyche, and privately amused by her typical inability to really let it show.

There were only two pieces of furniture on which one could sit — the bed and a single hard-back chair. Ellie Wingate was sitting on the former; Bruce Wingate, naturally, was perched ramrod-stiff in the chair. The room had a single window, rendered milky white by the old, brittle plastic sheet that sagged across it to cut the drafts. A single bulb hung above the peeling white wrought-iron bed. The floors and walls were blotchy with an artistic assortment of earth-colored stains. A crooked, balding velour painting of a toreador was the sole decoration, hanging over the battle-scarred dresser where a mirror should have been. I parked myself against that wall, with my elbow on the dresser top.

Ellie Wingate was staring at the floor, like a penitent in church. The bulb hung behind her, so her face was in shadow. Not so her husband's, across the way. The harsh light endued his face with the graininess of a news photo. "So what do you want?"

I was silent for a moment, wondering how much good this would do me, now that I was here. "I just wanted to talk about a few things."

Greta jumped right in. "Good. We'd like to do that, too."

I raised my eyebrows at her, interested. It didn't bother me if they wanted to get the ball rolling. It might prove more educational.

"What are you doing to locate their daughter?" Greta asked.

"Specifically?"

"Well, yes, specifically. That's why they came up here, after all."

"We aren't doing anything."

Wingate nodded and stood up, as if I'd just cranked his handle one turn too many. "I knew that. I kept telling you."

I wondered for a moment if he was going to march right out of his own room, but he stayed put, immaculate as always in a V-neck sweater and slacks, like a J.C. Penney catalog version of a Brooks Brothers model — barring the Band-Aids on his face.

Greta's voice was firm. "What do you mean, 'nothing'? Don't you think you owe these people an explanation?"

I was, as usual, awe-struck by her grasp of reality. I'd also suddenly decided I needed her out of there. "Wait, stay put," I told the Wingates, and escorted Greta back out into the hallway, speaking in a low voice. "Greta, I will talk to them — I want to talk to them, in fact. But neither I nor anyone else in this investigation owes them anything." I held up my finger to silence her. "It'll be on an even footing, okay? They can ask me questions, too. We'll go back and forth. But I want to do it alone. You've got to butt out."

Her voice was an angry hiss. "What do you mean, 'butt out'? I'm their only friend in this stupid town."

"Exactly. I need some neutrality."

"I won't say a word."

"Because you won't be there."

"Dammit —" She glared at me, but then finally shrugged.

"Okay, Greta?"

"All right."

"Good. Get some sleep. I'll talk to you to-morrow."

I returned to the room and closed the door behind me. Wingate was standing by his wife, trying to coax her to stand also, as if I would then take the subtle hint and dash for the street.

Instead, I crossed the room casually and sat in his chair, placing him awkwardly between us. "Sorry about that. I just thought we might be able to talk more freely without her."

I gestured to the bed. "Please, have a seat."

Reluctantly, as if being asked to sit in a puddle of cold water, he bent his knees and perched next to his wife.

"Do you like Greta?"

They looked at each other, surprised. "She's been very nice," Mrs. Wingate said.

"A little overbearing?"

Wingate's face was set impassively, his voice purposely neutral. I had a sudden image of him refusing bank loan extensions to people right and left. "My wife has already answered that. We appreciate all that Mrs. Lynn has done for us, that everyone has done for us."

"How did things go at the State Police?"

"Fine."

"I gather your wife refused to take the lie detector test."

Ellie Wingate stared at her hands.

"I wouldn't let her."

"Why not?"

"It was inappropriate. No one knows how much she has suffered through all this — for years. That test calls people a liar. It was an insult."

"You took it."

"I wanted to cooperate. I know you have to rule me out — that's part of what you do — but pulling her over the coals wouldn't have accomplished anything."

"We haven't ruled you out, though."

"I passed, didn't I?" His voice quickly bordered on belligerence. His wife reached out and gripped his hand.

"Not really. The test was inconclusive."

It was a tiny gesture — a quick shift of the eyes, right and left — but it struck me as odd, as if something else was struggling with the show of outrage. Right now, Bruce Wingate was very high on my list of suspicious characters, and I was loath to edit out his little mannerisms. Like sunspots, they appeared to me as signs of a body in turmoil.

"Those tests don't mean anything anyhow," he murmured.

"I wouldn't be quite that categorical." I was impressed by both his defensiveness and the fact that neither he nor his wife had asked me a single question about their daughter. Had they been as genuine as Greta thought they were, it seemed to me they'd be brushing aside my questions and grilling me for updates on their daughter's whereabouts.

I stared at him hard, forcing him to look at the floor. I wanted to take advantage of whatever it was that was chewing at him. Conventionally, that would mean giving them both the third degree on their activities on the night of the fire. It occurred to me, however, that in their eyes, the fire was not the monumental event it was to the police. Something else had brought this couple here, far from the decent middle-class values they supposedly espoused back home, something that had torn their moorings and had possibly forced them to desperate extremes. It was that something I wanted to learn more about. "Tell me about your daughter."

"What about her?" Wingate's voice sounded like he was muttering without moving his lips. It wasn't at all like the anger I'd seen explode at Rennie, but it revealed a brooding moodiness totally at odds with the man's appearance, and one which I'd already come to expect. I wondered what he was like to work with — or live with. Presumably, as a banker, he had to present the stereotyped blandness we've come to expect of that profession. What outlet did he have for his other side? How did he blow off that excess steam? I doubted the answer was healthy — or harmless.

"How old is she?"

"Twenty-one."

"What kind of person is she?"

"She's very sweet," her mother almost whispered.

"Ever have any troubles with her?"

"Like what?" Definitely a nerve there.

"Oh, I don't know. Drugs, sex, hanging out with people you didn't approve of —"

"We didn't permit that. We are a hard-working, God-fearing family. Those things never crossed our threshold. Julie was a very . . . obedient girl."

"The threshold works two ways."

"My daughter didn't do those things." Ellie Wingate's voice attempted to match her husband's, an impressive show of dual indignation. I was now quite content to push this line of questioning to whatever limit it might reach.

"Then how did she end up here?"

She pursed her lips. He answered. "She was duped."

"Duped?"

"At college — by her supposed 'friends.' They brainwashed her. She was naive, just a freshman."

"Where?"

"Boston College."

"Was she happy?"

"Of course she was," said Ellie, gaining strength.

"Brainwashing's pretty difficult unless the subject is receptive, at least to a degree."

"You don't know what you're talking about."

I raised my eyebrows. "How did the Order approach her? How did you hear about it?"

"We talked on the phone every week," Ellie Wingate answered. "The three of us. Just a few weeks after she got there, she started to talk about her new friends. It sounded nice at first."

"How long ago was this?"

"When she entered college? Three years ago."

"And there was no mention of the Order?"

"No. Just friends. We thought they were college friends. People she was going to school with."

"How did she describe them?"

Wingate shook his head contemptuously. "You obviously don't have children. They don't describe their friends."

"They do talk about them, don't they — tell you what they're doing? Did they dance, go to the movies, attend religious services, protest in the streets?"

"No, no. They were just friends —" Ellie's voice trailed off.

"They talked. Bull sessions — typical college stuff."

"What about?"

"I was hardly there, was I?"

179

"You talked every week. She mentioned these new friends. What was the context?"

Wingate rolled his eyes. "I don't see that it matters a good goddamn what the context was." From the quick accusative glance Ellie gave him, I gathered cursing was considered among the social diseases. I, on the other hand, found his increasing brittleness encouraging.

"I think she mentioned these new friends and you told her to dump them — sight unseen. So she stopped talking about them, and then stopped talking to you altogether. When did you last communicate with your daughter?"

It was a long shot. As Wingate had said, I didn't have children of my own. On the other hand, I had dealt with more troubled kids than he ever would, and I knew that the bridges from children to their parents were among the first to be burned.

There was an embarrassed silence before Ellie Wingate murmured, "Two and a half years ago."

Her husband gave her an angry glance.

Six months after she entered college. "How was that? A phone call?"

"A letter."

"And what did it say?"

"A bunch of crap," Wingate burst out. "She

180

was babbling about finding a higher plane and needing to cut her ties with her past. It was utter nonsense."

"And it took you this long to find her?"

They both looked at the floor and didn't answer immediately. When Ellie finally did, it was in a whisper. "We didn't look at first; we tried to honor her wish to be treated as an adult. Later we tried to locate her on our own, but we both work, and . . . there were some other troubles. We finally joined FTC, and Mr. Gorman introduced us to a private detective. He found out last week that she was here, in Gannet."

I interrupted. "What's FTC and Mr. Gorman?"

Wingate sighed, the impatient executive dealing with a dull-witted subordinate. "FTC stands for Freedom to Choose and Paul Gorman runs it. It's a Boston counseling group for parents of children who have been brainwashed by cults. He's like a deprogrammer and counselor combined — he's had a lot of experience in these matters."

I made a mental note of both names. The sudden introduction of a deprogrammer was significant, I thought, especially given their less-than-pristine reputation.

"Did you tell the State Police about Gorman?"

Wingate's tone was indulgent. "They didn't ask."

I certainly would, but a little later. Right now, I wanted to get them back to the present. "And you saw your daughter for the first time two nights ago?"

Mrs. Wingate was becoming almost conversational. "Yes. Mrs. Lynn has been letting us sit in her café so we can watch the street. We hoped we'd see her that way. We asked around at first, but those people wouldn't talk to us. Then the night before last, Bruce saw a large group of them headed into the woods. We figured there must be a meeting — they have a kind of church up there in the woods — so we waited by that small bridge near the street. That's how we found Julie. She just walked out in front of us."

She shook her head. "She wouldn't talk to us, wouldn't even look at us. It was as if we weren't even there. All I can think is that they must have brainwashed her. It was as if she didn't recognize us. Then her friends all grouped around and crowded us out. It was so frustrating . . . after all this time." She shook her head again. "She looks terrible. We followed her to that house, but the others wouldn't let us enter. Finally, Bruce decided to go in anyway."

Wingate's face tightened.

"But Julie was gone?"

"She must have gone out the back," he answered.

I thought of Fox's self-confidence when he'd offered to let us search the cellar. I was pretty sure now I'd been outmaneuvered on that one. I also imagined Wingate being confronted by that same arrogant confidence, being denied access to the house, and to the daughter he'd been hunting for years. It wasn't hard to see how any father might have exploded. What hung in my mind, though, was his punching Rennie. Despite forcing his way into the house, and being forcibly ejected, Wingate's punch had showed his rage to be still hot, and still uncontained. It made me wonder what he might do to quench that anger, and what he had done in the past when similarly denied.

Wingate was by now struggling for self-control. "This is nonsense. We've been all over this with your colleagues."

I stood up, walked to the window and sat on the sill, changing tack somewhat. "Look, Mr. Wingate, I'm trying to find out how the Natural Order ticks, not just what happened two nights ago. Sarris says he won't talk for his members, and they won't talk at all, probably because he's got them under his thumb. So that leaves you two. I've got to understand how their system works, at least that part of it you've witnessed."

This wasn't strictly true. I was enlisting their alliance less for what they knew than for how they expressed their knowledge, or their prejudice.

"Paul Gorman calls it love-bombing —"

"I'll talk to Gorman later. What I need to know now is what you saw, not what you learned from him."

Wingate slapped his knees in exasperation. "What's the point of all this? Who cares how it happened? It happened, that's all — they stole our only child, they turned her into a freak. I want my daughter back. Is that so unreasonable?"

Maybe not, I thought, but the means might have been. I remembered Fox's blackened skull gritting its teeth at me, and the pale-faced children, huddled together on the bed.

"Did Julie have many friends as a kid?"

"Of course," he answered just as she shook her head.

In the embarrassed silence that followed, I asked, "Since you both work, did you have someone stay with her after school?"

"No. I began working after —"

Wingate stood up, not angrily, but determined. "I've had enough of this. Unless we're under arrest, we don't have to submit ourselves to these questions. I'd like you to leave."

"Tell me about Gorman. How did you find him?"

He tugged at her arm, in an attempt to make her stand. "Enough. You go after the people responsible for Julie's abduction. We're not the guilty party here. And if you're tiptoeing around them because you're afraid you'll get sued, let me warn you — I'll end up doing the suing and you'll never know what hit you." He looked down at his wife. "Goddamn it, Ellie, stand up," he said, dragging her to her feet.

It occurred to me that both Wingate's sudden bluster and his manhandling his wife were reactions to his inability to control me; she had become my surrogate. Despite her obvious discomfort, I was quite satisfied with the way things were going.

I stayed put, my voice calm and my posture relaxed. "Mr. Wingate, if we were to do our job the way you'd like, you'd be the one in jail right now, not Sarris or any member of his organization. You seem to forget that we are not investigating your daughter's dropping out of college, but the deaths of five people in a fire in which you are a primary suspect."

"Oh, come on." His mouth fell open in indignation, but his eyes slid back and forth again nervously.

"You started the fight with Fox."

"He threw me out the fucking window."

"Bruce." Ellie Wingate stared at her husband.

"And you screwed up the lie detector test." For a moment, he seemed disoriented by his own excessive language. "You, you people —"

"And you own a 9-mm, semi-automatic pistol." Wingate's expression froze.

I couldn't suppress a smile. I'd hit a home run to center field. I felt that if I'd leaned forward and sneezed just then, I could have dropped them like bowling pins — pure Hollywood.

"What?" he finally said in a strangled voice.

"You're a law-abiding man. I'm sure Massachusetts has a file on it somewhere."

Neither one of them moved.

"Where is that gun right now?"

"I . . . I don't know. I lost it." He was staring at the floor, as if mesmerized by one of the mysterious stains there.

"When?"

"I don't remember."

"How do you know you lost it?"

"I looked for it. I couldn't find it."

"At home?"

"Of course at home."

"Why were you looking for it?"

He hesitated. "I was going to practice with it."

"When?"

"A few months ago . . . a year ago." He scratched his head nervously. "No . . . wait, several years ago."

I found the confusion interesting. "When did you buy the gun?"

"What's the point of this?" he said, making a halfhearted attempt to assert himself.

"The file will indicate when you bought it, Bruce."

"It . . . it's been years. I don't remember the dates. It's got nothing to do with all this." I noticed his forehead was shiny with sweat.

I let that sentence hang in the air for a while. "So, tell me about Gorman."

Ellie Wingate was looking bewildered, staring at her husband. I half-expected him to invite me out again, but he just set his jaw. "What about him?"

"How did you meet?"

"An ad in the paper."

"And you called him up?"

"No. He flew in the window." He tried for a sarcastic smile with minimal results.

"Then what?"

"We offered him lemonade."

"Steady, Bruce."

He glared at me, suddenly hot again. It reminded me of fishing — a little tension, a little slack in the line — the fish alternately fighting and yielding.

"Do you meet one on one?"

"We meet in a group. I told the State Police all this."

"We repeat ourselves. It helps cover our tracks, keeps us from missing things, like the gun. How many were in your group?"

"I don't know; maybe ten."

"All couples?"

"No; some."

"What was Gorman's role?"

"He was the discussion leader."

"All the time, or did he have associates who ran the meeting, too?"

"No. It was always him."

"What did he charge?"

There was a hesitation. "Two-fifty."

"Two hundred and fifty bucks a session? How long were the sessions?"

Wingate's tone became a little defensive — the banker being called out for spending too much. "Two hours, sometimes more. He didn't run it by the clock, and we could call him any time, day or night. And he helped in other ways . . . He's no con artist;

we got our money's worth."

"What other ways did he help you?"

"He put us in touch with the private detective who found Julie."

"What was the detective's name?"

"John Stanley."

"Out of Boston?"

Wingate nodded, his resistance reduced to a sullen expression.

"Did he find Julie?"

"He found out which group she'd joined, and traced her here."

"You definitely saw her?"

He glared at me a moment before finally nodding.

"When?"

"We already told you."

"What about the second time?"

He froze at the implication. "I only saw her that once."

Well, it had been worth a try. "What else does Gorman offer?"

"He gives us support, emotional support . . ." His voice trailed off.

"Have you been in touch with him lately?"

"Why?"

That struck me as an odd response. "To bring him up to date. Seems like you'd want to tell him you located Julie, ask him what to do next."

"No."

"When was the last time you spoke with him?"

"By phone or in person?"

Another strange answer. I could sense the interview winding down, but I still wanted to reel in everything I could — the trash fish along with the catch. "Your last contact with him."

"I called him when we spotted Julie, the night of the fight."

"And not since?"

"No."

"Not after the fire?"

He hesitated. "There was no point. Julie wasn't in the house."

I was puzzled that he was so sure of that fact, even before his visit to the fire scene. "The State Police will be checking the Inn's phone logs."

He smiled — bad sign. "Be my guest."

Ah, I thought, pay phone. "We'll also be talking with Gorman."

"That seems to be what you do best."

I'd finally lost the edge here. I stood up. "We do what we have to do, Mr. Wingate. And we usually end up with the right people in jail."

I crossed the room, opened the door, and left on that note. Not a bad night's work, I thought.

14

When I returned from the Rocky River, I found Buster in the kitchen, in his bathrobe, cleaning up the dishes before heading off to bed. For half an hour, I sat with him, nursing a coffee I knew would keep me up half the night, trying to get a feel for what was left of the town that had done so much for me as a kid.

I was in better spirits than I had been earlier. My interrogation of the Wingates had made me keen for the task ahead. What I'd gotten from them hadn't broken the case, or even changed things dramatically, but it had been progress — something valuable to be used later, like bricks for a future house.

Now I was sitting in the near dark of the living room, seeing only by the dim hall light upstairs, which filtered down the staircase around the corner. Buster had left it on for me after he'd gone to bed, some two hours ago. I could hear him snoring in his room above.

I'd been very touched when Laura had told

me Buster kept a scrapbook about me. It had been tangible evidence of the affection I'd always sensed was there. The feeling was mutual, in fact, which explained why I didn't find it odd. Buster had been for me, even long before my own father died, the man to whom I naturally looked for emotional support.

My father had been a farmer. My first and last memories of him are of an earth-soiled man, slightly stooped from his labors, working his land. I used to stare at him at the table when we shared breakfasts and dinners, not only because he struck an impressive figure, which he did with his huge, gnarled brown-stained hands, but because those were the only times I ever got to see him up close. The rest of the time he was out there — in the fields, in the barn, among the animals — working. He worked consistently, constantly, mostly by himself, and mostly without a word. Every year, there were times he hired extra hands to gather the crop. Then, suddenly, briefly, the farm resounded with laughter and coarse voices, the kitchen was crowded with men and noise at mealtime. Leo and I tore around, watching, listening, helping our mother, reveling in it the way other children revel in Christmas carols in late December. And then the silence would resettle around the house.

It wasn't oppressive, because there was

nothing to fear in it. It was just my father's way. He was older — over forty when he married my mother — supporting his family in the classic mold, through the Depression, through the war, through the bad years and the good. He did so with the same metronomic doggedness as a cave drip building a stalagmite. He never yelled at us, never lost his patience as he taught us our chores, never showed anything but quiet pleasure at our company. Rarely, I caught him glancing at Leo or me and smiling privately. But that was it — that smile was the extent of his emotional volubility.

My mother picked up the slack, caring for our emotional needs, encouraging us, nurturing us. Realizing that we needed a father who was also a friend, and realizing my own father's limitations in that department, she had merely substituted him with Buster during our summers in Gannet.

It was a perfect example of her inborn genius at mothering. Father was our father — the point was never denied nor denigrated. Indeed, we sensed she worshipped him, albeit from afar and without demonstration. But Buster was fun, and while as a year-round influence he probably would have ruined us, as a summertime dad, he was as necessary for us as the occasional candy-bar binge is for a ten year old.

If my father had his fields to till and make flourish, Buster paid just as close attention to the human spirit. Nowdays, he was given to drinking too much and giving marginally coherent lectures on the human condition, but back then he was a hands-on soul massager, as eager as a young school teacher to expose his charges to the ins and outs of life. He did so using his garage, the surrounding hills and streams, and his wife Liz's tolerance at having their house and kitchen perpetually invaded by boisterous, ravenous kids.

Under his guiding eye, we fished and hiked and worked on cars, painted and repaired houses, and worked as willing slaves at the fire department. We were taught the value of everyone's private dignity.

Only when I was much older did I realize the price Buster had paid for his generous excess. Like a rich man desperate to make an impression, he had exchanged his wealth for friendship. By the time Liz died and most of the town's younger citizens had either grown up or moved to greener pastures, Buster had found little left in his reserves with which to bolster his own spirit. He'd begun to drink more, to reminisce, and to hold court among people who, barring a few exceptions like Laura, didn't give much of a damn what he had left to offer.

In that, he'd become much like the land around him. Listening to him talk earlier, as I sat sipping my coffee and watching him do the dishes, I had my concerns for the Northeast Kingdom confirmed as he elaborated on what he'd said during the celebration at the Rocky River.

When I was younger, the Kingdom had been much as the name implies — a magical other world, removed from the mainstream and endowed with a specialness in the minds of those who knew of it. Its topography, both rugged and cursive, could reject and embrace, kill and nurture. It was a place where land and weather ruled, where the beauty came less from the majestic mountain views found farther south, and more from the perpetual surprises that lurked behind the low, ever-present hills. Even at its harshest, the Kingdom was seductive, as when its omnipotent sky darkened with boiling blue-black clouds, low slung and pregnant with threat.

Its people, like those of Gannet, clung to this mercurial terrain mostly out of choice. It was not a place to come to work, for jobs were few and far between, and demanding on the body when found. It was not a vacation retreat, since it offered no glitzy ski slopes or lake-side spas. Even during deer season, outside hunters were forced to work for their kill, finding shelter in uninsulated hunting cabins or weather-worn motels with no TVs.

Native Northeasterners preferred it that way. They were independent, self-supporting, proud, and generally uninterested in what was happening outside their boundaries. Ignoring the police and social agencies, they turned to themselves or their neighbors for help and justice, and scorned whatever innovations the rest of the state touted as invaluable.

But, obviously, the fabric of the Kingdom had begun to strain and yield. The Gretas, Rennies, and Busters, with the modern world pressing its demands, were no longer envied for their conservative self-sufficiency, but rather seen as quaint and out of touch, even gullible. The marketplace began to put a price on all they'd taken for granted, and in many cases transformed an unimportant poverty into grinding penury. It went a long way in explaining Greta's anxiety about keeping the Inn, and her xenophobic view of the Order and its practices. It also helped to explain a new bitterness I sensed lurking beneath Rennie's time-worn friendly exterior, working like an infection from the inside out. That, of course, was purely an impression on my part; I hadn't had a real chance to sit down and talk with him. But he seemed tired, his laughter was harsher and more brittle, and his eyes, once clear and determined, tended to look away. He struck me as a man running scared.

I was sitting in Buster's exhausted armchair in the living room, my mind clotted with thoughts of Gannet, before and now, with fire and death. I felt an overwhelming need to share what was bottled up inside me, despite the late hour.

The idea of calling Gail was instinctive, more natural to me than any concern about the present strain between us. This is not to belittle the latter — it was real and painful and not to be taken for granted, but its basis was in a friendship temporarily gone awry. I knew in my heart that in a time of need, even now, neither one of us would be unavailable to the other. I'd used the image of two seesaw riders to describe us to Laura. In my mind, it had gone without saying that a seesaw without two people, no matter how out of balance, was a choice with no options.

The only phone in the house was located in the hallway, as the crank phones had been of old. Buster had never seen the need for privacy on the phone, especially since he rarely used one in the first place.

I dialed in the gloom, the number known by heart.

The answering voice was sleepy.

"Hi. It's me."

"Hi."

There was a pause. I tried to gauge her mood from that one word — just a sound, really — and got nowhere.

"Sorry to be calling so late."

"It's okay."

Again, the brevity left me hanging. There was no hostility in the voice, but no encouragement either. She was letting me stick my neck out.

"How are you doing?"

This time, a stunned silence preceded any words, and I rued the banality of my question. Her delayed response had the predictability of the pain following a slap. "How the hell do you think I'm doing? I'm angry. I feel like you walked out on me without ever telling me why. I thought grown-ups talked through their problems — you just ran away."

"I told you I wanted time to think."

"That's bullshit, Joe. What good is thinking in isolation? This problem belongs to both of us. I'm not interested in what you come up with on your own. Christ, we're friends; you'd think this would be the time to work together."

Her precision undermined any defensive maneuvers I might have attempted. She had hit on the exact subconscious motivation behind my dialing her number in the first place.

"Maybe that's what I'm trying to do now."

Her frustration boiled over. "On the phone? I hate the goddamn phone. It's a business tool, Joe, something you use to fire people you can't look in the eye."

"I don't want to fire you." Only after I'd said it did I realize how idiotic it had sounded. The realization prompted a more accurate rejoinder. "But I'm not sure I want to look you in the eye, either."

She sat on that for several long seconds. This was not an impulsive, highly charged individual. Gail had walked a long, experience-paved road, from the free-love, drug-stimulated sixties to a middle age of thoughtfulness and reflection. Her answer echoed that, and made me glad I had phoned. "That's fair, but only if you're coming back so we can talk properly."

I was surprised by the implication. "Of course I'm coming back. I won't deny I ran for cover, but I didn't run away. Your anger scared the hell out of me. It was like standing too close to a hot stove."

Again, the reflective pause. "I didn't mean to put you down."

It was a classic Gail line, a little bit of psycho-talk, of I'm-okay-you're-okay. It was an extraordinary and endearing trait, her ability to nail down unstable emotions so they wouldn't run amuck and cause undue injury. She, unlike anyone else I knew, understood when it was time to put down the weapons and make peace — long before I ever did.

"You felt I was that angry?" she asked.

"Weren't you?"

"I think it was more frustration. I felt totally cut off from you. The last time you left my house, I felt like a hooker who'd been underpaid."

"Good Lord, Gail."

"Hey. You weren't even there. You were God knows where, at the office, feeling sorry for yourself, waiting for Tony Brandt to get back so you could retrieve your freedom, or whatever the hell it was. When you said you were going up north, it was like hearing the other shoe drop. It was the predictability that made me mad — you had totally cut me off."

"I'm sorry."

"I don't want to hear that. I'm sorry, too, but is that going to get us anywhere?"

"I hope so. It's a start."

The thoughtful pause. "You're right. I'm sorry."

"You're sorry I'm sorry, or you're sorry you're sorry? Or are you sorry you said we shouldn't be sorry?"

She laughed, and I realized I'd been clenching the phone. I relaxed my grip.

"God, life is such a bitch."

She was right there, and by making the choices we had, we hadn't made it any easier. We'd taken an ideal situation, one as potentially transient as a burst of laughter, and had tried to freeze it in place. She was single, as was I; she had a career, just like me; we both liked knowing the other was there, available sexually and morally, but not dependent. How long, in a world crammed with other people and events, could such a static emotional state exist?

"So what do we do about it?" she continued.

"I'd like to do something — have I done any permanent damage here?"

She sighed, and I could hear the pillow rustling against the headset. She was right again: Times like these are not good on the phone. I longed to be next to her. "No, and nor have I, at least I hope I haven't."

I picked that up quickly. "I made the call, and you didn't hang up."

She laughed again gently. "All right. That proves something, but I don't want this to happen again. I can live with the fact that things might change and we might choose separate paths, but not this way, okay?"

"Sounds good to me."

But she wasn't going to let me off that lightly. "I thought it might, but I mean it, Joe. You're good at talking to people in trouble, or giving them the third degree. You're even pretty good at snowing the Selectmen, but you're not that great talking to me. I think you hope all our little problems will just die natural deaths of their own."

Despite the urge to do so, I couldn't deny it.

"You know that's not the way it happens, right?"

The hint of maternal superiority suddenly irritated me. "I may not be the only guilty party here."

There was a long, dead silence, followed by, "Ouch."

This time I chuckled. "This may work, after all."

"You are a bastard and I hate the phone and I wish you here."

"I love you, Gail."

"I love you, too, Joe, but it can't stop there."

I had to give her high marks for persistence. "I know. I'll try to do a better job. The Chief coming back is bound to help — at least my professional life will be back to normal."

"How's your professional life doing now? From what I heard on the news, it sounds like you stepped into it again."

"Did my name come up?"

"I could arrange for it to."

"Oh, please, spare me that. What did they report?"

She told me what she'd heard, which didn't vary much from what I'd seen on Greta's TV. I told her the details and the cast of characters. I also told her of the changes that had come to Gannet, and of the damage they had wrought. She listened and asked questions and heard the sadness in my voice and became again, as she had been for years, my best friend.

She reminded me before we hung up that we had work to do, that things were going to change between us, for the better if we paid attention, and that she was looking forward to that.

So was I, although as I replaced the phone on its cradle, I thought of Laura, opening her coat to show me her curves. It made me doubly glad Gail and I had talked, before I'd been tempted to try something that was preordained to fail. But then, that had probably been my driving stimulus — that in the midst of a complicated case, in a town whose memories were becoming at best bittersweet, I needed to connect with a person whose motives were clear and clean, and whose alliance was unquestioned.

Laura had said of Gail, "Skinnier than me, I bet." Skinnier, more complicated, more intellectually demanding, more emotionally precise, but only a small part of me wondered why I'd reached out to Gail, when getting her back meant so much more work.

15

Early the next morning, none of us had any doubts a crime had been committed. Bruce Wingate was found stabbed to death.

A breathless, half-frozen teenage boy had been dispatched by Rennie on a bicycle to fetch me. Buster's only comment had been, "Better grab a coat. Cold's back."

There was frost on the grass; the surrounding bare trees looked old and withered in their icy, silver sheaths. The "warm snap" had ended like the slam of a door, leaving the air brittle and raw, almost painful to breathe too deeply. In the low spots — the ditches, the dips in the road, the hollows between the hills — ground fog lay as if clinging to dry ice.

The three of us piled into Buster's pickup,

placing the boy's bike into the back. Dulac's ravine, where Wingate's body had been found, was a mile north of town, bordering a road off of 114. Dulac had been a farmer in the region years ago, and the road had once led to his house. Both he and the house were long gone, but the road remained, a major attraction to those who had to opt for backseats over bedrooms for their moments of intimacy.

Rennie's pickup — green, battered, and flamboyantly splotched with dark red Rust-Oleum spots — was listing like a sinking rowboat at the edge of the road. We parked behind it and got out. A good twenty feet below us, at the bottom of a treacherously steep and ice-slicked slope, wreathed in a smokelike mist, stood Rennie Wilson and a man in fluorescent orange carrying a rifle. Between them, barely visible, lay Bruce Wingate, looking like the fallen ghost of a bird, dropped from the air in midflight, with one wing still outstretched.

The ravine was dry, walled in on the opposite side by a gentler, much taller, heavily wooded slope that curved away above us.

To my right, a footpath angled down from the road to the mist-wreathed bottom, a time-worn pedestrian trail used by anyone who wanted to climb the hill on the other side. The boy who had driven back with us was already running off toward it to join Rennie and to ogle the body.

"Buster. What's his name?"

"Jimmy."

I shouted after him. "Jimmy! Hold it. I don't want any more footprints around there. Stay up on the road."

The shout caused both Rennie and his companion to look up at us. I waved them toward the path. "He's dead, right?"

Rennie answered. "As a doornail."

"Then come on up. I want to keep that scene as clear of people as possible."

I walked down the road a bit and met them at the top of the path. Rennie introduced us. "This is Joe Gunther, with the State's Attorney's office; Joe, this is Mitch Pearl. He found the body."

We shook hands. Pearl was about thirty-eight years old, with brown hair and eyes, a clean-shaven square face, and a respectable beer gut. He wore a worried look on his face.

"When did you find him?" I asked.

"About a half hour ago. I was following a set of deer tracks along the bottom of the ravine. I drove back to town and told Mr. Wilson here."

"Anyone else know yet?"

"I called Wirt, so I guess he'll be here soon."

"Okay. Let's try to keep this under our hats until the State Police show up. It'd be better if we could keep the road blocked off, as well as both slopes. So far, only you two have been to the bottom, is that right?"

Both Rennie and Pearl nodded.

"What's the ground like down there?"

Pearl answered. "Crusty, but pretty soft still from the last few days. That's why I went down there; I figured I'd find some tracks."

"Crust isn't enough to hold you," Rennie added. "By the end of the day, it should be like concrete."

"All right. All the more reason to keep people away. Where do you live, Mitch?"

"Connecticut."

"You staying nearby?"

"Lyndonville — the LynBurke Motel."

"Can you stick around to give a statement to the police?"

"Sure."

"Okay. Who's got some paper — something to write on?" The words and gestures were all automatic. Despite the location, and my being far from my home turf, I was still a cop, and this was something, unfortunately, I knew all too well how to do.

Buster pulled a couple of large receipts out of his pocket and handed them over. "Back sides are blank."

"Thanks. I'm going down to have a look. Just keep everyone away and let me know when the troops arrive."

Everyone nodded. I started down the path, tendrils of mist shrouding my feet and legs. The more I immersed myself between the two banks and into the fog, the more I felt like I was being sucked into the earth, surrounded by smoke without odor. The effect was heightened by my concentration on the path, muddy and slick with the passage of several pairs of feet already. In a few hours, unless the cold really set in, we were going to have to set up ropes to save people from skidding straight down to the bottom.

I stopped at the foot of the path and looked around. Above me, I could hear muffled voices, the occasional scrape of a boot on gravel; but here, in the ravine, I felt as if I was underwater. I was as aware of my breathing as if I were wearing a scuba tank.

I took Buster's receipts and my pen out of my pocket and began to sketch what I found: the number of footprints and their directions, beer cans, food wrappers, an occasional condom, assorted other trash. Slowly I walked, taking inventory, aware all the time of Wingate's body gaining definition the closer I got to it.

Finally, we were together, the only sharp-edged objects in the middle of a cloud. I looked up and saw the hazy outlines of people looking down at me. It made me think of the gladiators in the center of a locked arena. I turned my attention back to Wingate, trying to concentrate.

He'd been stabbed many times by the look of it. His upper back and neck were covered with slash and puncture wounds. One ear was severed, lying two feet off to the side. He was wearing khaki pants, sneakers, and a pale windbreaker — not enough for the present cold temperature, but enough for earlier last night, when we'd last talked.

I studied the ground. There was a lot of blood, particularly from the left side of his neck. I bent over, trying not to move my feet and thus add to the confusion of tracks. There was a gaping laceration just to the left of the trachea: a bull's-eye to the carotid. He would have died within a minute of receiving that wound alone.

I looked over my shoulder and examined the grassy slope behind me, the one leading up to the road. There were no gouges, no scrapes, no prints, no bent vegetation. No body had rolled down it on the way to the bottom.

I slowly began to separate the footprints: Wingate's sneakers, my own shoes, Rennie's and Mitch's lug soles, which I'd made a point of mentally cataloging at the top of the path. There were others, what looked like one more pair of small smooth-soled sneakers and a third set of lug soles. Besides ourselves, at least three other people had shared this spot with Wingate. But that was far from certain; there'd been a lot of activity, much of it from Rennie.

"Hey, Rennie, how long were you down here?" I didn't bother looking up to distinguish one shape from the others.

"Not long. Just enough to check it out. Why?"

"Looks like you tap-danced all over the place." It was said at half volume, more to myself than to him, but I shouldn't have said it at all.

"Fuck you, Joe."

"Sorry, out of line."

"I didn't know if the son of a bitch was dead or not."

"I know, I know." The entire exchange had been pointless, reflecting more my own frustration than any anger toward Rennie. It irked the hell out of me that I'd been speaking to Wingate just hours before, too dull to sense something in the offing. The fact that I wasn't clairvoyant never seemed an adequate explanation at times like these. This, I kept thinking, had been preventable somehow.

"Joey."

"Yeah, Buster."

"Wirt's here."

Great, I thought. The Hun himself. "Okay. Tell him I'm coming up; I'll meet him at the top." I quickly added a few last notes to my diagram and backtracked as carefully as I could.

Wirt was not happy at my involvement, and demonstrated the fact at his officious best. "What were you doing down there?"

I handed him the map I'd drawn. "Nailing down the scene before anyone else messed it up. It's damn near unreadable as it is."

He took the map without looking at it. "You shouldn't have been down there," he snapped. "You're the SA's man, not BCI."

I walked over to his patrol car and opened the door. "Can I use your radio?"

"Absolutely not." He scowled angrily.

"Look around, Corporal, and think about what you're doing here. Your problems aren't my fault, but I can sure as hell make my problems yours." I swung into the car and unhooked the mike, telling the dispatcher to get hold of Hamilton for me. I knew my anger at Wirt was irrational. Wingate's death made my elation following last night's interview seem conceited and smug. I'd dropped the ball in midplay, and I was taking it out now on Wirt.

"You know what we've got here?" I asked Hamilton when he got on the radio.

"Affirmative."

"But not the identity."

"Correct."

"It's the man from Natick."

There was a moment's silence. People love to listen in on police frequencies in Vermont. Part of that is due to the large number of volunteer firefighters in the state, most of whom listen to scanners the way elevator operators listen to Muzak; the other part is because in areas like the Kingdom, everybody knows, or once knew, everybody else; scanners have become the electronic version of the old party line, and a primary reason why cops try to be as oblique as possible in their communications.

"Ten-four. What do you advise?"

"Keep the scene locked up until the crime lab arrives instead of letting your boys have first crack."

"Why should I do that?"

"Lots of foot prints. Any more people and you'll lose them. Also, there's nothing here that's going to change over the next couple of hours."

There was a pause. My request was neither unreasonable nor unprecedented, but Hamilton still had to suppress a cop's natural urge to jump in and start digging. "All right. Give me Wirt."

Wirt was already there, of course, seething down my neck. I handed him the mike and slipped out of the car.

I walked over to Buster. "Can I borrow your truck?"

"Sure."

"For what it's worth, I just cleared with the State Police lieutenant in charge of all this that no one, not even cops, are supposed to go down that path or get near that scene before the lab guys show up."

"So I can drop Wirt if he tries?"

"You can have fun thinking about it." I walked over to the truck and noticed the bike was missing from the back. "Where's Jimmy?"

Buster shrugged. "Beats me."

"Damn. I think we can assume the cat's out of the bag." I'd known from the very start that we'd never keep this a secret, but I had hoped I could at least interview the man's widow within scant minutes of his discovery without being beaten to the punch. Now I doubted I'd be able to do even that.

I drove directly to the Rocky River Inn. For once, the place was completely empty. It looked like an abandoned warehouse, the dirty, plastic-filtered light seeping through onto unswept floors and strewn-about furniture, highlighting the grime on the walls and the cobwebs on the light fixtures.

I walked up the stairs to the second floor,

two at a time, finding, as before, the Wingates' door open. Ellie Wingate was sitting on the bed, half-dressed in her slip, with Greta beside her.

Greta looked up at me scornfully. "Oh, the great Brattleboro detective — come to save the day."

I nodded at Ellie, who seemed to be listening to distant whispers. "She knows?"

"I wasn't going to let the police tell her."

I crouched down in front of her, putting my face in her line of sight. "I'm sorry, Mrs. Wingate. I'll need your help to find out who did this."

"You've been no help so far," Greta muttered.

I looked over at her. "Greta, either be quiet or leave." The depth of her anger mixed with my own. I fought back the impulse to air my own frustration and tried instead to concentrate on the drawn-out process of picking up the pieces.

Greta gave me a withering look, but didn't say anything more. I got the impression, though, that some bridge had been burned in her mind, that I would never be "Joey" to her again.

"Mrs. Wingate, when did you see your husband last?"

Her eyes were startlingly blank. She blinked once in a great while, but otherwise didn't move. Her mind was filled with so many other, more insistent voices, that mine must have had the impact of a mosquito hitting a window.

"Ellie." I reached out and touched her cheek.

Her eyes shifted onto mine, but without appreciable recognition. Her brow furrowed just a hint. "Last night," she said in a whisper.

"When last night?"

The furrow deepened. "Bedtime."

"You both went to bed at the same time?"

Two blinks in a row. The eyes seemed to focus a little. "Yes." The voice was stronger, but somehow less real.

"He didn't wake you when he got up?"

"No. I'd taken a Valium."

"How many?"

Her body English all seemed very odd to me, a cross between being entranced and rehearsed, as if two behavior patterns were tugging at her simultaneously.

"What did you do after I left last night?"

"We went to bed."

"You didn't talk to anyone? Didn't see anyone?"

She shook her head.

"You saw me," Greta said. She sounded hurt.

Ellie Wingate nodded but didn't look at her. "Oh, yes."

"What did you talk about?"

She shrugged. Greta answered. "I gave them a letter and they told me how you'd treated them . . . I should have known."

I turned back to the stricken woman, trying to make my voice sound as bland as before. "What was in the letter, Ellie?"

She didn't answer. I straightened and glanced around the room. The bed was still unmade, there were a couple of suitcases in the corner, some odds and ends on the bureau top and the bedside table, some clothes hanging over the chair — basically the same as I remembered last night.

I glanced at the trash basket near the bed. On the top was a crumpled, balled-up envelope. I squatted down and poked at it with my pen and the back of my fingernail, trying to spread it open wide enough to read. I made out "Bruce Wingate" handwritten across the front in script. My high hopes fell a little when I saw the envelope was empty.

I tapped it with the pen. "Is this what Greta gave you last night, Ellie?"

She glanced over distractedly and became very still.

"Where's the letter that was inside?"

"I don't know." She went back to studying her hands.

"What did it say?"

"I don't remember."

I thought a different approach might shake more out of her. "When did you tear your stockings?"

She raised her head disconcertedly. "What?"

I repeated the question. "Yesterday," she said, frowning.

"The envelope was on top, Ellie. It was put in the trash after you threw out the stockings last night, after you took them off. Isn't this the same envelope Greta handed you?"

She closed up again. "I don't remember."

Greta had been fidgeting in silence, either in deference to me, which I seriously doubted, or because even she was beginning to realize that not everything was as it seemed. Prolonged silences, however, were not her strong suit. "Enough, Joe. She's in shock."

I struggled with a surge of anger. Ellie Wingate's husband was now lying dead with his face in the dirt and yet she still seemed as unwilling to help me now as they'd both been earlier. Her reaction was baffling.

"How did you get the letter, Greta?"

"It was in their cubbyhole downstairs. I don't know how it got there."

"Any idea when?"

She shrugged. "Could have been anytime — from midafternoon on."

I rose and crossed to the bathroom. Over the sink were several prescription bottles. I tore off a piece of toilet paper to keep my fingerprints from contaminating the one labelled Diazepam and then opened it, pouring the contents into my palm. There were twenty tablets. I read the label again carefully.

Ellie said she took a Valium before bed. Prescription medicine labels sometimes border on Sanskrit, but this one I could figure out. The date of issue was about a month ago; the contents listed twenty tablets. None were missing.

16

I had called Mel Hamilton from the pay phone downstairs and was sitting on the top step of the staircase when he found me fifteen minutes later. The Wingates' door was still open, but Greta had moved Ellie to her own apartment at the end of the hall, albeit with a predictable amount of grumbling. Even she, however, could see that events had progressed beyond her ability to control them.

Hamilton was slightly winded when he reached the top. "You've been busy."

I raised my eyebrows, surprised at his acerbic tone of voice. "Oh?"

"You've contaminated a crime scene, overrun the attending State trooper, and now you've presumably ransacked the dead man's apartment and interviewed his widow. I'm surprised you bothered to call me."

His face was as bland as ever, but he was truly irritated. He was also correct. While a Vermont cop is a cop anywhere in the state, regardless of jurisdiction, I had been acting more by instinct than with good manners. The worst part was, I hadn't given it a second thought until now.

"I did contact you about cordoning off the crime scene." It sounded lame as I said it.

"True, but you didn't tell me you'd treated my trooper like a doormat or that you'd wandered straight into the middle of the crime scene."

We looked at each other for a moment. I was at a loss for words. Antagonizing the local State Police head of the BCI had not been my intent. He was a man who could make things very difficult for me down the line, when time came for his people and the State's Attorney's office to coordinate the building of a case.

But a slow half smile crossed his face. "Thanks for the crime scene sketch, by the way, and for locking the area up. It was a good call."

That was a relief, and deserved a reciprocal peace offering. "I'm sorry about Wirt."

"Well, he can be a pain in the ass, but he knows his job. So, what did you call me for?"

I explained about the envelope, the Diazepam bottle, and the fact that Ellie was under Greta's care down the hall, ripe for further questioning.

Hamilton nodded and turned on his heel. "I brought along a couple of people I want you to meet before we do any more interviewing."

He led the way down to the lobby. There, admiring his surroundings as if he were at the Metropolitan Museum of Art, stood a tall, slender man with glasses, straight blond hair, and the angular grace of a giraffe. He gave us a demonic, ear-to-ear grin and stuck a thin, bony hand out to me. "Joe Gunther, right? I hear you're the one who planted the 'hurry-up-and-wait' order in the lieutenant's ear here."

Hamilton allowed a tight smile, more reminiscent of the man I'd seen yesterday at the barracks. It made me think suddenly that his stiff demeanor was a conscious attempt to create precision and order in the midst of those people who relied on their guts for guidance. "This is Detective Sergeant Lester Spinney. He's under my command in the St. Johnsbury BCI; he's also one of the four members of our new Major Crimes Squad."

"Hello," I said, and shook his hand, wondering if his opening line made him for me or against me.

Spinney laughed. "Come on, you're faking it. You don't really know what MCS is, do you?"

He had me there. "I'm a little behind on reading the mail I get from you guys."

He smiled and looked at Hamilton. "And you wonder why I'm such a great detective. We're supposed to be the A-Team — Don Johnsons driving Fords."

"Supposed to be?" I asked.

He smiled apologetically. "Well, that's the way it would be in the movies."

Hamilton sighed. Spinney, all fresh-faced and boyish, didn't look like he'd been away from home that many years. It was difficult imagining him as the elite of anything outside an intramural basketball league.

"How long you been with the State Police?"

"Twelve years."

I was impressed.

"Gotcha, right? Everyone always thinks

they screwed up the paperwork."

"It did occur to me."

He shoved his long, thin hands deep into his pockets. The gesture seemed to calm him. His voice was abruptly quieter, his sentences more measured. Still, an almost juvenile enthusiasm remained in his eyes. "No, I've been at this awhile. Being made a member of MCS has been the high point of my career."

"You still haven't told me what it is."

He laughed and shook his head. "Right, right. Sorry. They also call us the Homicide Unit. Any time there's a crime like this, they call the four of us in to support the local barracks BCI team. That way, we get a lot of experience and become the homicide experts within BCI."

"Sounds reasonable. How long has MCS been around?"

"About six months."

I glanced over at Hamilton. "MCS is not in control; they are purely support. The local barracks Bureau of Criminal Investigation crew still supplies the case officer and heads the investigation; MCS does what the case officer tells them to do. Of course, their advice is appreciated."

I'd always been a little slow to follow the ins and outs of the State Police command structure — it seemed so much larger than the number of people within it. "I thought you said he was from your barracks."

"He is, but he's still in a support mode as a Major Crimes Squad member. Crofter Smith, one of our regular BCI, will be the case officer on this one." He looked at Spinney. "Where is Smith, by the way?"

My spirits sagged at the mention of the name. I knew nothing about the man, and I had obviously misjudged Hamilton at first glance, but the impression Smith had made when we'd "met" inside the burned building had been less than overwhelming. I did recall, though, that Jonathon Michael had rated him a good cop. I tried to hang some hope on that thought.

"He's outside — the local decor was getting to him, classic as it is. We have different tastes."

I decided to ask the question foremost in my mind before Smith crossed the threshold. "Where do I stand in all this? I don't want to be hung out between you and Potter on this thing. I'd like to know how you people see me."

"As an asset." Spinney answered immediately, which came as a partial relief.

Hamilton was slower and more diplomatic, and a whole lot more uncomfortable. "We're talking apples and oranges. It's not up to me to place you anywhere in our structure. Technically, you're an independent with whom we share what we find. Plus," he added more sternly, "you've been a bit of a loose cannon so far."

"Come on, Lieutenant, put him in with me under Smith. God knows he'd be a good buffer between us."

Hamilton looked like he was being forced to eat something distasteful. "This is inappropriate; it's not the way it works."

"If I'm a freelance, so to speak, couldn't I just keep Spinney here company, as his sort-of guest?"

Hamilton shook his head. "That's between you two and Smith. On paper, it's an unstructured relationship. You guys do what you want; just make it work and don't step on people's toes anymore."

He wandered toward the front door, as if for some fresher, less impulsive air, although I knew it was to fetch Smith.

"So, you and Smith need a buffer?"

Spinney shrugged as an answer and changed the subject. "I'm a big fan of yours."

"Yeah?"

"Yeah. I followed that Ski Mask case you handled down in Brattleboro — very 'damn-the-rules-full-speed-ahead.' . . . Balls."

I followed his look. Crofter Smith had entered the building and was coming toward us

224

with the studied expression of the serious official.

"What's his problem?" I muttered.

"I used to be, but from what I've been hearing about you, I think it's going to be both of us now."

Smith stopped in front of us and nodded his head curtly at Spinney. "Les."

Spinney aped the gesture with a small smile. "Croft." I had taken an instant and instinctive liking to Spinney, but it occurred to me that if you ever ended up on his bad side, as Smith obviously had, Spinney's quirky humor could be used to peck you to death. It evoked in me a tiny quiver of sympathy for Smith that I hoped I could nourish.

Smith stared at him for a couple of seconds, his expression blank, before turning to me. "So you're Potter's man." His voice had the same monochromatic quality I'd noticed earlier.

"Among other things."

"I'm Crofter Smith. I've been put in charge of this investigation." He didn't offer his hand. "Is this yours?" He handed me the sketch I'd made of the scene.

"Yup."

"What do you think we have over there?" His monotone reminded me of a bad 1950s science-fiction movie.

"Don't know. That's why I suggested the lab go in there first; there're a lot of footprints."

"There's also a lot of time being wasted."

"Maybe."

"Hamilton didn't argue the point." It struck me as I said it that shoving his boss down his throat was not the way to get on Smith's best side. It was possible I had nothing to lose, but I didn't know that yet and instantly regretted the comment.

Smith gave me a baleful look. "I'm not Hamilton."

"I know, dumb thing to say."

He paused, I think a little startled by the apology, and then turned to glance at the closed front door for no apparent reason. He spoke to me with his back turned. "So tell me about him."

I glanced at Spinney, who rolled his eyes and smiled before I catered to Smith's request. I gave him everything I knew, from Wingate's defenestration to his admission last night of owning a supposedly stolen 9 mm. I was in the middle of replaying my interview with Ellie Wingate a few minutes ago when his portable radio squawked that the Vermont State Police Crime Lab had arrived at the ravine.

Smith acknowledged the message and marched for the door. He turned back when he noticed that neither Spinney nor I had moved. "You coming?" he asked his colleague.

Spinney shrugged. "Not much I can do until they're finished. If it's all right with you two, I'd like to follow up with Mrs. Wingate."

"Suit yourself," and Smith was gone.

We both stood silently for a moment, looking at where he'd been standing. "Well, he didn't say we couldn't team up," Spinney murmured.

I smiled. "Glad to have you. What's he like to work with?"

Spinney made a face. "What you see is what we got."

"Is he any good? I was told he's Hamilton's senior man."

"He is that." Spinney waved his hand, as if to shoo away a fly. "Oh, hell, he deserves it, too. He works hard, gets results — he's good at what he does. I just think he has no personality."

I gave a shrug and turned toward the staircase. "Want to meet the widow?"

We were halfway up the stairs when the front door opened below us. We both looked down to see a tall, tanned, immaculately dressed man in loafers, tan slacks, a herringbone sports coat, sweater, and tie. If Bruce Wingate's wardrobe had once struck me as

J.C. Penney striving for bigger times, this guy was an advertisement for *Gentleman's Quarterly*.

He turned a vaguely George Hamilton-type face toward us, obviously startled. "Who are you?"

Before either one of us could answer, I saw Ellie Wingate swing into view at the top of the stairs, with Greta hard on her heels. "Paul, thank God you're here."

"Paul" double-stepped up the stairs. Spinney and I moved aside to let him float on by. His after-shave lingered in the air behind him, causing Spinney to cock an eyebrow and tilt his head slightly to one side, like an emaciated owl spying a vole from afar.

At the top of the stairs, Spinney introduced us both to the stranger. "We're with the police."

The other man shook our hands. "Paul Gorman, a friend of the family. Have you found out anything yet?"

"We're just beginning."

"Of course, and no doubt you want to speak with Ellie. Give us a couple of minutes, will you?"

Without waiting for an answer, he returned to the women and swooped them up. We watched them wend their way down the hall to Greta's apartment.

Spinney gave a theatrical gaze toward the blotchy ceiling. "Ohhh-kay — and who was that cast of characters?"

"The square one with the red face was Greta Lynn, who owns this dump; the lady in distress is Mrs. Wingate; and Gorman heads up Freedom to Choose, or FTC, some sort of Boston-based deprogramming organization for parents with children 'abducted' by cults."

"I thought FTC was the Federal Trade Commission."

I glanced down the hall. Greta had been left standing outside her door. She saw me looking and turned her back, obviously embarrassed at having been so obviously excluded from Gorman and Ellie's little get-together.

"Interesting," I muttered.

Spinney followed my look. "Not in the mood to share, I guess. So tell me," he added, leaning his bony hip against the newel post. "What's going on here? You think Edward Sarris has anything to do with Wingate's death?"

"Him or anyone else. If this were the movies, he'd be the bad guy for sure."

"Wingate burns five of Sarris's people to death, so Sarris knocks off Wingate?"

Spinney had obviously been briefed on the case earlier. "Right."

"But you don't like that."

I ran my fingers through my hair and scratched my neck. "It could be that simple. I'd like some details, though."

Greta's door opened and Gorman's inappropriately smiling face appeared. "Please, come in."

"Sounds like a dentist," Spinney muttered.

But to me, it sounded worse, like a man who had taken control. I very much doubted that the interview we were about to conduct would get us very far; Gorman would see to that. The question was, why?

He led us — including Greta, who seemed more like a guest in her own home — down a short, dark, somewhat sour-smelling corridor to another door.

We entered a large living room, the corner windows of which looked down onto Route 114 and North Street. The surprise was that it was bright, cheery, immaculately clean, smelled like roses, and was furnished not with antiques, but with an assortment of beautifully maintained, well-coordinated pieces. It was embracing, gently feminine, and very homey — an unthinkable jewel buried in the middle of a gigantic rotting hulk of a building.

"My God, Greta, this is amazing."

She didn't answer, indeed, she looked quite angry that her secret had gotten out.

230

Gorman settled comfortably onto a sofa next to a strained Ellie Wingate and waved us to the various seats around the room. "Now, how may Mrs. Wingate help you?" he asked, with all the charm of a yacht salesman.

I looked at Spinney. He sat back in an arm-chair and stuck his long legs out, an easy smile on his face. "Just a few questions, nothing remarkable."

Ellie Wingate sat as before, her hands in her lap, her eyes focused on the ground, but her back was ramrod-stiff — not the curved, caved-in posture I'd come to expect from most people with her recent grief. This was a woman far more nervous than bereaved.

"Fire away, Sergeant." Gorman leaned forward and put his elbows on his knees, his hands gathered loosely before him, his body language shifting to a let's-shoot-the-shit-with-the-boys kind of guy.

"Why are you here?"

Gorman let a second pass before smiling. "Ellie called me. Told me what had happened."

"When did you call him, Mrs. Wingate?"

Gorman answered for her. "This morning. A little over an hour ago. Actually, she had Greta here do it for her." He looked like the cat that ate the canary.

"Where were you?"

"In Hanover, New Hampshire."

"And you knew to call him there?" Spinney looked to Ellie again.

She looked up, but Gorman answered for her once more. "I have a car phone. All my calls get forwarded to wherever I am."

Ah, I thought, aren't we clever. I glanced at my watch. If the call had been a little over a hour ago, that would have meant that immediately upon hearing of her husband's death, Ellie had dispatched Greta to the phone. It struck me as an unusual reaction, especially in someone as hard hit as Ellie Wingate obviously was. What was she trying to cover up?

"And you dropped everything to come tearing up here."

"Of course. Wouldn't you have done the same thing?"

Spinney shifted in his seat. "Mrs. Wingate, how are you feeling?"

"She's upset — pretty natural reaction, isn't it?"

"Mrs. Wingate?"

She looked up, her lips tight.

"Feel like talking?"

She nodded.

"I know you already talked to Joe here. But I just want to hear it for myself."

"That's fine," she whispered.

"Okay. So you two went to bed last night, and when you woke up, your husband was gone. Is that right?"

"Yes."

"What did you do then?"

"Then?"

"Yes, after you realized he was gone."

"I started to get dressed. Then Mrs. Lynn came and told me Bruce was . . . had been . . . killed."

"Where did you think he'd gone?"

"I don't know."

"Were you concerned?"

"No, well . . . I mean . . . I don't remember."

"Did you think he'd gotten up early to go for a walk?"

"What does it matter, Sergeant? She was barely awake."

"Mrs. Wingate, what did you think?"

"I was sleepy."

"Was your husband in the habit of going out early, before you got up?"

"You were the one who said that."

Spinney, as always, ignored Gorman. "Was he?"

"No."

"So it was odd, his not being there?"

Gorman sat forward on the edge of his seat, his voice harder than before. "I'm not sure

I like this. You're implying Ellie knows something she's not admitting."

"Am I?"

"I think so. And as her friend, I think I ought to tell her not to speak any further with you."

"Is that right, Mrs. Wingate? You want to stop talking with us?"

She looked from us to Gorman and back.

"We're trying to find the man who killed your husband. Anything you could tell us might help."

"I would like to help, but I took a Valium last night. I was asleep."

I cleared my throat and Spinney glanced over to me, cocking an eyebrow. "Ellie," I said, "I looked at your prescription bottle. It was filled a month ago. All twenty pills are still in the bottle."

Ellie's eyes shot up and flitted nervously between Spinney and me. "I . . . I was asleep."

"This has nothing to do with finding out who killed this poor woman's husband. If you suspect her of something, then come out and say it. Otherwise, I'm going to ask you to leave."

I heard a car drive up outside and a door slam. A few moments later there was a knock at the door. Spinney rose and left the room.

"Ellie, do you have something you want to tell me?"

"No."

"I think you do. I think you know who wrote that note last night. I think your husband may have gone off to meet someone. Was that note from Julie? Or from someone claiming to know where she was?"

Her hands were a tight ball in her lap, the knuckles white. "No."

I heard Spinney talking with someone in the hall, then steps going back down toward the stairs.

"That's enough. What are you implying?"

Spinney spoke from the hall door. "We're implying that Mrs. Wingate knows more than she's telling us. She lied about the Valium and we think she's lying about the identity of whoever wrote that note."

Gorman stood up and grabbed Ellie's elbow, just as her husband had earlier. The repetition of the gesture deepened my already keen interest in her — she was taking on the look of a talisman of sorts, the keeper of the secrets. Did she know if Wingate started that fire? Did he kill Fox beforehand? Did she know who killed her husband?

Gorman's voice pulled me back to the present. "We're leaving. Bruce is lying dead out there, and you're in here badgering his widow.

If you're so hung up on getting who killed him, talk to Sarris. That's your man, or one of his goons. Bruce Wingate challenged his authority, and now Bruce is dead. It doesn't take Sherlock Holmes to figure that one out."

I rose as Mrs. Wingate did. "Are you leaving, Ellie, or do you want to talk with us further?"

Spinney stood in the doorway, filling it. Ellie looked around the room.

"Please get out of the way, Sergeant."

"Ellie?" I asked again.

"I want to go," she whispered.

Spinney stood aside. "Where're you headed?"

"Home," she said vaguely.

"You're not going to try to find Julie, after all this?" I asked.

"That's my job now," Gorman answered. "I'll be staying at the White Horse Motel in St. Johnsbury until this mess is cleared up." He steered her past Spinney into the hallway.

Spinney reached out and touched his arm as he passed. "I know Mrs. Wingate is eager to get home and put this behind her, but like it or not, we're going to have to ask her more questions over the next couple of days."

"So?"

Spinney leaned forward just a hair — a hint of aggressive body language. "Mr. Gorman, you know and I know that there are some problems with all this, some unanswered questions. It would be a lot easier if she stuck around here for a while. Cooperation from you will play in your favor."

Gorman started to answer, but then paused a moment. "All right. I'll put Mrs. Wingate up at my motel for a couple of days. But no more, you understand? She needs to get back to a familiar environment —a routine."

Spinney smiled. "Thank you, appreciate it."

Leaving Greta behind, we followed them downstairs and watched as Gorman piled Ellie into his car. "We'll send along her things after the crime lab's through with them."

Gorman flipped a hand at me. "Whatever." He walked around to the driver's side of the car, got in, and drove off toward 114. As they left, I saw Ellie's white face looking back at us, drawn and strained — stressed, I thought, as much by her knowledge as by her grief.

Spinney looked at me. "Holding out on the sleeping pills, hey?"

"Not on purpose. I was about to tell Smith when he took off."

"No sweat; it went okay. We got other problems, though."

"What?"

"You know a guy named Rennie Wilson?"

"Sure." The introduction of Rennie's name

237

in this context startled me. I looked at Spinney's serious face and felt the plug being pulled from some small but sensitive vial in my chest. "Why?"

"They just found his lighter at the scene, under the body."

17

"I don't want to talk to these butt-heads."

Rennie sat on the tailgate of his pickup, his feet dangling, his arms crossed over his chest, his torso rocking slightly back and forth like a tightly wound-up toy.

"So they told me."

"Fucking assholes."

Spinney stood nearby. Slowly, without much movement, he got all the troopers and most everyone else away from the truck.

"Shit. I was the one that got all these bozos up here in the first place. Some murderer."

From where I stood, I could see into the ravine. Bruce Wingate's body was being placed into a black body bag, his hands enveloped in clear plastic sacks. The almost mystical feeling of this morning — of the lonely corpse wreathed in foggy tendrils — had been replaced with one of mechanical industry. Crime lab technicians, troopers, and plain-clothesmen were slowly combing the outlying reaches of the scene, using tape measures, cameras, and assorted esoterica. The ground was littered with evidence cans, tool boxes, and odd pieces of equipment. Wingate, in his bag, looked uncomfortably out of place, as if he'd fallen unnoticed out the back of some ambulance.

Rennie followed my gaze. "What the fuck kind of airhead do they think I am? I'm going to kill a guy, ditch his body in that hole, and then call everyone except the fucking National Guard? Get real. I'd have to be some kind of dick-head, you know?"

Procedure is that the body stays as found while the search team goes through its routine. Only then does the medical examiner come in, do an examination, and finally roll the body over to check the other side. That's when they found the lighter, lying on the ground. I noticed the medical examiner was a man this time, presumably Hillstrom's local rep. He was a heavyset bald man with black-rimmed glasses who seemed to have difficulty moving around.

I looked at Rennie. I'd known him a long time, had seen him fly off the handle many times, although never violently. Still, he was impulsive, bull-headed, and right now, incredibly angry. God knows I didn't want him to be guilty of Wingate's murder, but in all honesty I couldn't rule him out. "It's not unheard of for the guilty party to scream the loudest, just to divert attention."

"Well, what about the lighter? Shit. If I was that smart, why would I've left the fucking lighter behind? Besides, I haven't seen that damn thing in months."

"The lighter might have fallen out of your pocket by accident."

"I told you I lost it months ago."

I didn't reply.

He looked around at the now distant state cops. "Assholes."

"You told them you'd only talk to me. So talk."

"I didn't do it."

"Okay. So how 'bout I ask some dumb questions, just for the record?"

"Do I have a choice?"

I was starting to feel he was protesting too much for his own good. "You're not under arrest, Rennie. You can leave right now, if you want. In fact, maybe you ought to just stay quiet and get a lawyer."

"You're shittin' me."

"If I were in your position, that's what I'd do."

He gave me a devious sidelong glance. "What is this, reverse psychology?"

"I'm just saying we can talk if you want to — you're under no obligation."

"I didn't do it, Joe."

"So you want to talk?"

He shrugged, considerably calmer. "Got nothin' to hide."

"Where were you last night?"

He laughed bitterly. "Oh, I love that. I was carving up that asshole, you know?"

"I told you you wouldn't like the questions."

"All right, all right. I got off work; I went home and cleaned up a little; I went into Lyndonville to have a few drinks; drove around a little; and went to bed. End of story."

"Where did you have the few drinks?"

"Some bar."

The vagueness sent a small but palpable chill through me. An innocent man in a tight squeeze would know the value of accuracy. "Which bar?"

"Shit, I don't know — The Maple Door. It's on Route 5, down from the Miss Lyndonville Diner."

"Anyone see you there?"

He looked at me, his face flushed with anger. "No. I went alone into the place; nobody was there. I poured myself a drink, left the money on the counter, and then I left."

"I meant anyone who might know you."

He muttered something. "No. I never been there before."

"Talk to the bartender?"

"No, except to order."

"What did you drink?"

"Shit, I don't know — beer."

"What time?"

"Who knows?"

"What time you get home?"

"Late. Nadine was asleep."

"You wake her up?"

"No. I slept in the spare room. I do that when I come in late."

None of this was what I wanted to hear. Rennie had always been belligerent in front of authority, so his blowing steam didn't bother me. But I sensed he wasn't being straight, and that troubled me a lot. It made his bluster less childish and more like a cover-up.

"How'd you lose the lighter?"

He paused, obviously weighing his response. "I don't remember."

I was beginning to hate this; the scales were tipping farther and farther against him. It was difficult keeping the skepticism out of my voice. "And you don't have the slightest idea when you lost it?"

242

He shrugged. "No, maybe six months ago. I don't know."

I let a few seconds pass. I scratched my forehead. Perhaps I was overreacting; I had hoped to find him absolutely innocent. Now I was having some serious doubts.

His voice, sounding tired, broke through my thoughts. "Am I really in deep shit here?"

I looked at his face — florid, worn, made older than his years through hard times and hard liquor. "As far as they're concerned," I nodded toward the troopers and Spinney, "you're their Number One prospect. And I got to tell you, your story doesn't help you much."

I half-wanted him to blow a cork then, but he didn't. He just said quietly, "No, guess not."

"Did you see Bruce Wingate after you two had that fight — the night he was pushed out the window?"

"No. I went home."

"Not even walking around later?"

"No."

"You didn't see him and his wife the next morning after the fire?"

"Yeah, I guess I saw them then. That was it, though, and I didn't talk to them. I didn't even go near them."

"When do you get off work?"

"Six-thirty. I worked late."

"Alone?"

"Yeah. I had some paperwork to shove around."

"Night shift wasn't there?"

"Sure they were there. I was working in back."

"So you got home about seven?"

"Yeah."

"Nadine home?"

"Yeah. She doesn't get out much," he said matter-of-factly. I knew she was in a wheelchair, which obviously restricted her somewhat.

I rubbed my eyes with my fingers. "Jesus, Rennie, you're not helping yourself much here."

He flared a little at that. "Not my fault I wasn't giving some judge a blowjob all night. How did I know I'd need an alibi?"

"All right, anything else to add?"

"Nope."

"Well, you want to talk more, I'll be around."

I walked over to Spinney; Smith was standing next to him. "He says he quit work at six-thirty, went home, went drinking at The Maple Door, drove around a bit, and then hit the sack, all without seeing anyone or being seen by anyone he knew."

"What about the lighter?" Smith asked. I was struck by the fact that Smith must have acquiesced to Rennie's demand to talk to me only. He didn't seem any friendlier — his body language still told me I was as welcome as a head cold — but I decided I'd take it as a good sign.

"Says he lost it six months ago, but doesn't know where."

"When but not where? That's a little odd."

"I know."

Smith's furrow deepened. "Well, it's too early to do anything about him yet. Let's wait until the lab results are in. I'll have people check the bar and his workplace. We better get a search warrant for his house."

"What grounds?" I asked.

"Footprints," Spinney piped up. "Unless he flew in for the kill."

"What about the shoes he has on?"

Smith gave me a peeved look. "I already checked. They don't match." He looked at his watch. "I'll get the warrant. If I'm lucky, I should be back in an hour or two."

We all three looked up as Rennie drove by, his rear tires spitting gravel. He ignored us, staring straight ahead.

"He had a fight with Wingate a few nights ago."

The other two turned to stare at me. I described everything that happened on the night Wingate was thrown out Fox's window.

Spinney shook his head. "But Rennie didn't come back at Wingate after he was punched? He just walked away?"

"Yup."

"I don't know Rennie, but that seems a little out of character."

I couldn't answer that. I wasn't sure I knew anything about Rennie's character anymore.

"I wonder why he was killed way out here?" Smith mused, looking around.

I shrugged. "Quiet place for a meeting if you don't want witnesses."

"Or for a murder," Spinney added.

Smith checked his watch. "I'll post a discreet watch on his house to see if he tries to remove anything before we can get in there with a warrant. I'll also have the lab guys go over Wingate's room to see what we can find there."

He walked off toward the large green van that housed the crime lab and its crew of four.

"What're your plans?" Spinney asked me.

I looked to the bottom of the ravine. "I think I'll poke around here for a bit, maybe talk to the M.E. I'd like to look at the footprints again, just to get them straight in my mind — that is, assuming there's anything left to see. How 'bout you?"

"I want to check out Wingate's room. Why don't I meet you at the Rocky River in about an hour and a half?"

I nodded and headed down the steep trail leading to the bottom of the ravine, using a rope someone had anchored to the top to help keep my footing. As I'd suspected would happen with all this traffic, the trail had become treacherously slippery.

Below me, the medical examiner was directing two troopers to place the loaded body bag onto a stretcher. He glanced up and studied my slow progress. "Are you Joe Gunther?"

"That's right."

"I'm Dr. Hoard, the local M.E. Dr. Hillstrom told me to keep an eye out for you."

I got to the bottom finally and walked over to him. "That was nice of her."

"She said to tell you what you wanted to know, not that I have much at this stage." Despite the cool air, I noticed his forehead was beaded with sweat. He took off his glasses and wiped them with a handkerchief.

"So what do you have?"

"He was killed by a good half-dozen blows of a knife, a big one by the looks of it. Probably a kitchen knife." He bent down and undid the zipper to the bag. It was a little startling to see Wingate reappear, pale and dirty, his deadly, almost yellow cast emphasized by his black shroud.

Hoard rolled him over slightly and pulled down his jacket and shirt to reveal the base of the neck. "See how some of the wounds gap and others look narrow?"

I squatted down and looked. There was little blood — it had mostly drained away — and the cuts looked like they could have been made in a pale, bloodless chicken carcass. "Yeah."

"That's because of what we call Langer's lines. The skin is a fabric of intermingled dermal collagen and elastic fibers that tend to run lengthwise along a body and form a pattern called the lines of cleavage. If a knife cuts across Langer's lines, the wound gaps, because the underlying fabric tension is pulling at a ninety-degree angle to the incision. If, on the other hand, the cut is parallel to Langer's lines — and the lines of cleavage — the wound is narrow."

"Does that tell you anything?"

"If the stab wound is straight in and out, and if it runs parallel to Langer's lines, you can often tell the blade's width and thickness. Here," he pointed to a single gash. "See? It's wide, but the back of the blade isn't thick like a hunting knife's would be." He let Wingate roll back. "Of course, that's pure speculation. He's going straight to Burlington now, where Dr. Hillstrom can do a more detailed analysis."

"When do you think he died?"

He smiled. "Last night sometime."

I looked at him.

"Sorry, I wish I were joking. Actually, it's about all I can tell you. He wasn't fresh when he was found. Lividity had set, which generally happens eight to twelve hours after death. Of course, that's not a law. Rigor mortis is still ongoing — his hips and legs and part of his torso are still flaccid. But that's all sensitive to cold, which delays the process; at room temperature, it's usually complete at twelve hours, so we're still in that ballpark."

He squatted down again and placed his hand on Wingate's forehead. "The other indicator is that his cornea has just begun to cloud over, something that again usually happens in twelve to twenty-four hours following death if the lids were closed, which they were here."

He moved his thumb and lifted back the right eyelid to show me. "Incidentally, it may not be of great importance, but he's missing the hard contact lens from his left eye. See how the cornea's just slightly cloudy?"

I glanced over his shoulder, but without great interest. That kind of detail was more fascinating to him than to me right now, especially since it didn't tell us much. "Anything else?"

Hoard nodded, stood up and took his glasses off again to wipe them. I wondered if some sweat had fallen onto them or if that was just his particular nervous habit. "He was found clutching his testicles with one hand."

I remembered from this morning that one arm was pinned under his body. "You think he was kicked?"

"It's just speculation, but it would be an excellent way to render him defenseless, and it's consistent with his wounds. Also, it increases the odds that anyone could have killed him, even an adolescent."

18

Spinney languidly cracked a knuckle. We were sitting on the steps of the Rocky River Inn, waiting for Crofter Smith to arrive with the warrant. We shared a view of the low, tired houses opposite and the ratty, brown grass field behind them. There were two withered trees out front, their limbs bare, skinny, and gray, already in despair before winter's first snowfall. The watery sun still hadn't made much of a dent on the cold.

"What did you make of the envelope in the trash?"

"Interesting. Wish we could match the handwriting."

"Think it might be Julie's?"

He looked at me sharply. "Yeah, it's possible."

"The M.E. said a woman might have killed Wingate."

Spinney mulled that over for a moment. "Of course, the letter didn't have to come from anyone they knew. It could've been from anyone: one of her friends, Sarris, an informer of some kind. Who knows? In any case, Ellie's not cooperating. She won't show us anything with handwriting on it, and we don't have enough for a warrant. So we're stuck."

"They haven't tested it for prints yet, have they?"

"No, they'll do that back in Waterbury — better control. Why?"

"I was wondering if you could ask them to save a bit near the glue strip. If whoever sealed it used their tongue, there might still be some saliva on the paper that isn't polluted by the glue — you know, some overlap. Maybe they could get a blood type."

Spinney pushed out his lower lip and nodded. "Excellent. You don't mind if I tell them it was my idea?"

"Go for it. They dig up anything else?"

"Nothing obvious. They gotta cook up their chemical stews and see what comes up, but I doubt they'll find much, except for the envelope. You know the Wingates are — or were — up to their asses in this. I mean, we're not talking innocent mugging here." He laughed and shook his head. "You know, standing there in their bedroom, watching the lab crew at work, I was half-tempted to interview the walls, just to see what I'd get."

I glanced over at him. My liking for Spinney grew the more I got to know him. Somehow, over years of service in what could be a pretty grueling business, he'd managed to keep a poetic flicker alive in the back of his brain, something that allowed him to stay out of the ruts, to keep his mind open to any suggestion. I gave the State Police high marks for putting him on a special platform from which he could work freely; most other outfits would have labeled him a flake and buried him in the typing pool.

We were still sitting there in comfortable silence when I saw Buster, presumably coming from the garage. I rose to greet him and introduced him to Spinney.

Buster looked worried. "Rumor has it Rennie's tied into this somehow."

Spinney nodded, mostly to himself. "Ah,

the reliable beat of the jungle drums."

"Maybe," I answered. "We did find something."

"What?"

I looked at Spinney but he merely shrugged. Smith would have had a fit — cops are not supposed to volunteer their findings. "Did Rennie mention losing a lighter within the last ten months or so?"

"Is that what you found?"

I nodded.

Buster shook his head. "Not that I remember. You talk to Nadine yet?"

"No; we're about to — we're waiting for a warrant now."

"Nadine's a friend. Would you mind if I came along? She might like some comfort with you people tearing the place apart."

I ignored the bitter tone in his voice and cast an inquiring look at Spinney. "She's in a wheelchair; might be nice if he could hold her hand."

Spinney nodded down the road. "We can ask the boss himself."

Smith was approaching in his car. As he drew abreast of us, he rolled down his window and waved the warrant at us like a flag.

"Think he's surrendering?" Spinney asked hopefully, as he rose to climb down the steps.

I forwarded Buster's request to Smith.

Smith looked at Buster with those expressionless brown eyes. "Just have him stay out of the way."

I was surprised. I'd fully expected Smith to reject the idea out of hand. I was having a hard time pinning the man down, and beginning to think that Spinney's constant putdowns were throwing me off. I didn't like Smith much, any more than I had Wirt. But Wirt was a malcontent, while I suspected Smith, despite his instinctive prejudice against me, had a pretty good analytical mind. In fact, I wondered if his dislike of me wasn't restricted to the office I held, and that it was utterly impersonal.

We drove in separate cars out to Rennie's place, north of town, past the cutoff leading to Dulac's ravine. It was a nondescript, two-story house, patched together like Buster's, but lacking the neatness. Everything about it looked worn, in need of repair or paint. The rusted metal roof had countless black daubs of tar across its surface, the marks of a losing battle against leaks; part of the foundation had rotted away, making the house list slightly, as if it were about to slip back into the earth that had supported it too many years. Aiding this desolate, familiar picture was a yard littered with a wide variety of rusting metal hulks — truck frames, gaping auto bodies, the remains of a tractor, what looked like a harrow — intermingled with old tires, washing machines, bales of rotted wire, and piles of mysterious debris. The only area clear of clutter was a long ramp that ran straight out from the front door to where a vehicle could be parked. There was, however, no vehicle beside ours and three state cruisers.

The four of us assembled with four troopers at the foot of the ramp. "Anyone seen Wilson?" Smith asked.

One of the troopers nodded. "I saw him getting out of his pickup in Lyndonville and heading for a bar about a half hour ago."

"He never came by here," another added.

"Okay. Let's go."

Spinney, standing next to me, muttered, "Charge!" as we all followed Smith up the ramp to the front door like ducklings behind their mother.

The door was opened by a heavyset woman in a wheelchair. Her voice was as high and soft as a young girl's. "Yes?"

Smith brandished his warrant. "I am Detective Sergeant Crofter Smith of the Vermont State Police. I have a warrant allowing me to search this house for any shoes whose tread may match those we've collected at the scene of a recent crime."

Christ, I thought.

Buster stepped out from the mob in front of the woman. "Hi, Nadine. The police found Rennie's lighter at the scene of a murder. They gotta check it out."

"A murder?" She spoke the word as if it were foreign. The look in her eyes reminded me of a small child's when confronted with its worst imaginable fear. I was glad Buster had come along.

He stepped around her and pulled the chair away from the door, so the others could enter. Her hands lay motionless in her lap. Smith lay the warrant on top of them and directed his men to spread throughout the building.

Buster moved Nadine across the living room to a large window overlooking the yard, and positioned her so she could see out. It was a gentle, thoughtful gesture, designed to help her turn her back to the chaos overtaking her house. I thought it all the more considerate when I noticed the house was as neat and tidy inside as it was tumultuous outside. Like a tidy, conscientious model prisoner, she'd maintained control over that part of her world she could reach — until now.

That, however, brought to mind a further point. I remembered that even before Nadine's accident, their house had reflected this odd contrast. In other couples, I would have taken it as a sign of conflict, as a difference of styles so sharp that it could only split the marriage. But not with Nadine and Rennie; with them it had been a badge of successful compromise, reflecting a decades'-old ability to walk a central line. The apparent disparity had been a curious symbol of enduring affection, as when, I suddenly recalled, he always took off his boots as soon as he entered the house through the kitchen door.

Buster sat facing her on a small table underneath the window, one of his hands around hers. I half-perched on the sill.

"You remember Joey, don't you?" Buster asked her.

She gave me a wisp of a smile and nodded. "Buster, I don't understand."

"It may not be anything, Nadine. Some guy from out of town was killed, and Rennie's lighter was found with him."

I finished what Buster didn't know. "We talked to Rennie, and he said he hasn't seen that lighter for six months. Do you remember what happened to it?"

"No . . . Who was murdered?" Her voice was so soft, it was hard to hear, especially with the clomping of feet in the rooms around us.

"Nobody you know," said Buster. "The father of one of the kids in the Order."

"Bruce Wingate," I said, watching her face

for a reaction. There was none.

"Did Rennie know him?" she asked.

Buster squeezed her hand. "No — barely."

He was trying to shield her with a tenderness exceeding his usual soft touch with people in distress. I wondered what it was I didn't know about their friendship. I hadn't known Nadine when we were all growing up; she was from another town, and I'd only met her briefly during the few times I'd visited over the past thirty years or so. I'd heard about her accident — falling down a flight of stairs or something. It had happened almost ten years ago.

I decided to let him take care of the sensitivities while I asked the questions, although his look showed me he wished I'd turn to dust on the spot. "A few nights ago, Rennie helped us rescue a guy who got in a fight with some people from the Natural Order."

"Yes. I remember."

"Well, that was Bruce Wingate. He'd followed his daughter to one of the Order houses, and was determined to go in and get her. Later he picked a fight with Rennie and ended up punching him. Did Rennie tell you any of that?"

She dropped her eyes, as if admitting to a crime herself. "Yes — he was pretty angry."

"What did he say or do?"

"He slammed a few doors and talked about it a bit, but you have to understand Rennie." She reached out and touched my arm. "He wasn't angry at . . . What did you say his name was?"

"Bruce Wingate."

"He was angry about more than just that. The slap was only a trigger, sort of. He's had fights before; they don't mean as much as you'd think. They're just a way for him to blow off steam."

"What else was he mad at?"

She shook her head sadly. "Oh, everything in a way: the flatlanders, the economy, how the town's falling apart. If anything, he was more frustrated with Greta than with Mr. Wingate. He kept saying she's gotten obsessed about the Order, that she's letting it ruin her life, and that she's bringing everybody down with her."

"He took her problem that personally?"

"They're old, old friends."

Buster shifted his weight. I could tell he was becoming angry with me. "You don't have to answer these questions, Nadine. You've got nothing to do with all this."

She looked over her shoulder at the sound of a loud bang. A trooper across the room had dropped a picture off the shelf he was checking.

Buster stood up. "Hey, do you mind? This ain't your house."

The trooper looked genuinely embarrassed. "I'm sorry. It slipped." He carefully replaced it on the shelf — a small framed photograph of a grinning young man in mountain-climbing gear, with a coil of rope slung over his shoulder.

I brought it back over to her. "It's fine — no breakage."

"Thank you." Nadine placed it on a small table next to her. "That's my favorite picture of my brother —" She pulled at Buster's hand. "Sit down, Buster. I don't mind all this. Maybe I can help Rennie."

I smiled at her. "Thanks. When did you see Rennie last night?"

She looked down at her lap and shook her head. "I never did. I think I heard him very late, but I don't know. Wednesday nights he always plays cards with Pete Chaney."

I wondered why Rennie hadn't told me that earlier. It was a custom-made alibi, for at least part of the evening. "Where does he play?"

"Pete lives in East Burke. He runs a small market there, out of the front of his house. They play at his place. They've been doing it for years."

"And that's where he was?"

"I think so."

"He didn't come to bed when he got home?"

"Well, we don't . . . I mean, when he comes in late, he usually sleeps in the spare room. He doesn't like to wake me."

"And that's what he did last night? Slept in the spare room?"

"I think so. I didn't see him this morning, either. I usually don't. He gets up early . . . Always been an early riser, even before this." She tapped the arm of the wheelchair.

"How about after work? He said he left work around six-thirty and got home about seven to change. Did you see him then?"

Again, she looked elsewhere and sighed. "No. I wish I had. I'm not being very helpful, am I?"

"Were you in the house?"

"Oh, yes. I was in the bedroom. At seven, I would have been watching television and knitting, like always, but it makes a lot of noise."

"The television?"

"The knitting machine," Buster growled. The "you jerk" went unheard, if not unnoticed.

"You didn't have dinner together?" I asked.

"Oh, no. But that's not unusual — Rennie eats out a lot." She shook her head suddenly. "This is coming out all wrong, Joe. It makes it sound like we never see each other, or care

261

for each other. We do, but differently from other people. That was true even before this blasted thing." She thumped the chair's arm. "People are always looking at it, thinking they know everything."

I wondered how many times that was true of other couples whose lives centered around a wheelchair.

"Joe."

I looked up. Spinney was standing near a back hallway. He motioned to me.

"Sorry, Nadine. I'll be right back."

"Don't hurry," Buster muttered.

"What's up?" I asked Spinney in the hallway.

"Follow me." He led the way down the hallway through the kitchen, to a small mudroom beyond. A narrow, cluttered, stale-smelling bedroom lay off to one side by the back door. It was as incongruous with the rest of the house's interior as spilled garbage on a clean floor, and obviously Rennie's home away from home. The room's location made it clear why Nadine hadn't heard Rennie come home, if he had come home. Smith and several troopers were also in the room.

"Take a look at these." Spinney bent down and picked up a pair of work boots, already encased in a plastic bag.

"A match?"

Smith opened an envelope he'd pulled from his coat pocket. Inside were a handful of Polaroid pictures, all of footprints found at the scene. They were not "official" — those were taken by the crime lab with larger, fancier cameras and would yield sharper results — but they served an immediate purpose. Smith selected one and showed it to me.

I compared it to the tread I could see through the plastic. They fit, right down to a stone caught between two of the lugs that showed up as a dent in the photo. Furthermore, I could make out circular stains on the boots that looked a lot like dried blood.

I let out a heavy sigh. "Where'd you find them?"

Spinney pointed to the top shelf of the one closet in the room. "Buried in back, under this." He held up a shirt. "It's 'plain view' inculpatory evidence, along with a pair of pants, too." He spread them both out on the bed, the shirt above the pants, like flat paper-doll clothes. There was a single red-brown spot bridging where the shirt would have met the pants, and several more splotches descending the right leg. The pattern was consistent with Dr. Hoard's hypothesis that the killer kneed Wingate in the groin to double him over, and then knifed him from overhead.

"Your friend's in deep shit," Smith muttered.

"I realize that." As usual, his voice had been utterly without intonation, which technically made his comment a mere statement of fact. But the utter lack of sympathy angered me, especially when I knew he was right. Not wanting to count myself as one of the people roping Rennie in tighter and tighter, I chose to dislike Smith all the more for his relentless, lifeless enthusiasm.

"I'm afraid that's not all." Spinney led me back into the kitchen and showed me a large carving knife, lying on the counter.

I bent over — not touching it — and looked carefully. There was some clotted material caught between the blade and the wooden handle.

"Look at the tip."

About an eighth of an inch had been broken off — recently, by the gleam of the metal. I was grateful Smith wasn't at my side to gloat about that, too. To him, these were rewards, sought-after pieces of the puzzle. To me, they spelled heartbreak and doom, the tearing of a fabric I'd cherished most of my life.

They also hit a rebellious chord deep inside. The more I found out about Rennie, the more I realized how much he'd changed since our time together. Time had obviously ground him down considerably, making him drink to excess, become moody and pessimistic, neglectful of his wife. But that was hardly unique to him — even Buster was a shadow of his former self, albeit still a benevolent one. What I couldn't believe was that the same person who had risked his life a few days ago entering a burning building in an attempt to save others would stab a man six times with a kitchen knife because of a punch in the face. Unless there was something more I didn't know about his relationship with Wingate.

I played dumb and shrugged at the broken tip. "So?"

"Smith called Burlington just now to see if Hillstrom had gotten far enough into the autopsy yet to make a possible connection. She found a blade tip — same size — stuck in the spine. The lab'll have to prove it, but it sounds right." His voice was solicitous, like a doctor's with bad news.

Smith came out of the small bedroom carrying several plastic bags. "All right, pack up the knife. I think we're out of here. What did you get out of the wife?"

"She didn't see him or hear him all night. She did say, though, that every Wednesday night, for the last several years, he's gone to play cards with a guy named Pete Chaney in

265

East Burke; he runs a small grocery out of his house."

"Good, good." Smith wrote the name down in his notebook. He checked his watch. "We better get out of here. Hamilton wants a pow-wow with everybody in an hour."

"Him too?" Spinney jerked his thumb at me. It was the first time the subject of my tagging along had actually come up for discussion. So far, I'd just managed to lay low and avoid the matter. For once, I'd wished Spinney had put a cork in it.

Smith looked at us both with obvious distaste, almost as if by bringing the subject up, we'd ruined the delicate shelter under which he'd allowed us to operate. Now he could no longer pretend I wasn't what I was. "The State's Attorney's office will get a full report."

Buster was still holding Nadine's hand when we returned to the living room. "It looks like they're about to wrap up here. I'm sorry for the intrusion, Nadine."

She shook her head. "That's all right, Joe. I know it's your job. Did you . . . find anything?"

"Odds and ends. We won't know anything until we can look at them closer, and even then, they may not mean anything. There's a lot of this that goes on in an investigation like this. Most of it doesn't mean a thing."

She nodded. "Thank you."

"You will give us a call if you see Rennie again, though, won't you? He and I ought to talk. I'm staying at Buster's."

"Of course."

I gave her shoulder a squeeze and straightened. "By the way, does Rennie ever go without a belt?"

"Not wear a belt?"

"Yeah."

"Oh, no. He always wears one." She gave that ghost of a smile again. "With his tummy, he has to."

I smiled back, but for other reasons.

19

I leaned back in my chair and put my feet up on the table. I was in Potter's office, having completed another couple of hours of paperwork with the meticulously accurate Flo Ginty. She was gone now, I was alone, and the office was dark, except from the single lamp on my desk, just the way I liked it.

I pulled the phone onto my lap and dialed Beverly Hillstrom's number, reading it off a scrap of paper I had tacked to the wall in front of me.

"I was wondering when I'd hear from you," she said after we'd exchanged greetings. "I take it you'd like a rundown on Bruce Wingate."

"If it's not too inconvenient."

"Not at all. It was a transverse laceration of the carotid — from that alone, he would have been dead within a minute. But he also had a good gash in the aorta, a severed spinal cord, and a variety of other less spectacular injuries."

"And he'd been kicked in the scrotum, like Hoard thought?"

"Oh, yes, and not tenderly, either. The testicles were quite engorged."

"Lending weight to the theory that he was stabbed after being doubled over."

"That's correct."

I mulled that over for a couple of seconds and then changed subjects. "So tell me about feathers."

I heard her chuckle at the other end of the phone line. "I thought that would attract your attention."

I could hear soft classical music in the background. "Was the feather you found ingested, inhaled, or just placed there?"

There was a long pause. "I honestly can't

say. The neck was burned entirely through, and the feather was just below that point of total incineration — near the top of the trachea, but also bridging the esophagus."

"Could it have been carried to the spot by a bullet?"

She thought a bit. "Possibly. If so, it's the only sign of a bullet we've got. The soft tissue was too damaged for me to find any of the usual traces. Why would a feather be involved?"

"The killer might have held a pillow over the gun. We found another feather at the top of the stairs. Also, their clothing is insulated with goose down — a bullet could have carried a feather from there into the body." I looked at a small pad on my desk where I'd scribbled some notes. "By the way, did you hear whether the crime lab made a match between your knife tip and their knife?"

"Yes, they did. I hung up on them just before you called."

"And I suppose the dimensions they gave you of the knife fit the wounds."

"Yes."

I chewed on that for a while. I wasn't surprised, but it was hard to accept.

"That's not good news?" She asked tentatively.

"Well, it is what it is. It puts a friend of mine into pretty hot water."

"I'm sorry to hear that. There was one last thing about Bruce Wingate that I thought you might like to know — he'd brushed his teeth just before he died."

"How long before?" Like the feather, it was one of those tiny tidbits that were either uselessly distracting, or on which an entire case could hinge.

"A half hour at the most. I discovered it because he had a small smudge of something white at the corner of his mouth, which I had analyzed."

"That's interesting," I muttered.

"I thought you might like that."

"Well, it means one of two things: Either Wingate brushed his teeth before he went to bed every night, which means he died about a half hour after that, or he brushed them especially because he was meeting someone he wanted to favorably impress."

"Someone he thought he might stand close to, or even kiss," Hillstrom added.

I was silent for a moment. That opened up possibilities I hadn't considered. "You're very good at this."

She chuckled.

We talked about Wingate and Fox a bit more, going over known material, looking for possible new avenues, and then finally gave it up.

I turned off the light after I hung up and just sat there in the dark, turning it over again and again in my mind.

Bruce Wingate fights with Fox, loses, and takes it out on Rennie. Then what? Fox and the entire household die in a presumably accidental fire, only Fox is dead before smoke gets in his lungs, the woman and kids are on the other side of a locked door, a spent 9-mm cartridge is found at the top of the stairs, and Bruce Wingate admits later to having owned a gun of the same caliber.

Then, the next day, Wingate takes an inconclusive lie detector test and won't let his wife take one at all.

Conclusion? The Wingates are up to their chins in this. Only Wingate is now dead. Who could have set up a meeting with Bruce Wingate and killed him? And why were there so many footprints found at the scene? If Rennie did kill Wingate, who were the other two people? And what motivation did Rennie have to do in Wingate? I had a difficult time believing it was because of a punch in the mouth.

I shook my head, remembering Smith's satisfaction at finding the boots, the clothes, and the knife. I also recalled the sour feeling in my gut when I'd heard him tell the troops to pick up Rennie for Wingate's murder. Just as well I didn't get an invite to their little powwow — might have raised more questions than they wanted to hear.

I knew Spinney wasn't entirely happy with what they had against Rennie, and for all I knew, maybe Smith wasn't either. He didn't like me. I was Potter's man and an outsider to boot. But his going by the book with Rennie didn't mean he was ignoring other possibilities. You grab at what you can in this game, nailing down what loose ends you've got before going after new ones. Smith was a cold piece of work, it was true, but it was a piece that seemed to work well, without cutting corners.

So who else wanted Wingate dead? Sarris? If Wingate did torch the building, revenge might certainly be due. Of course, Sarris would probably have someone else do it, which then brought up the possibility of any one of dozens of men. Or women, for that matter, as Hoard had pointed out. Certainly the fact that there were as many as three people present when Wingate was killed argued in favor of Sarris and his group.

Then there was the mysterious Julie Wingate, the reason Bruce and Ellie had come up in the first place. Was their relationship so far gone that she'd murder her own father? She could have mailed the note to her father, arranging a rendezvous, and then killed him when he showed up. Could Ellie and Julie have been in cahoots? Ellie's sleeping pill story was almost certainly a lie. Bruce Wingate was no charmer; maybe this was an elaborate scheme for the two women to finally get rid of him, the ultimate in mother-daughter bonding. But if so, why leave the envelope in the wastepaper basket?

I laughed at myself in the dark. Jesus. Besides, none of those theories explained why all the evidence pointed at Rennie. Good old Rennie, with your ass in a crack. What have you been up to?

I thought back for the umpteenth time to our teenage years. You never do know what your friends will become. Charles Manson no doubt once played tag and pigged out on Hershey's kisses. But I had always thought Rennie and a dozen other people I'd known would grow up pretty much as they had. They'd move around a little, they'd grow fat and bald, but they wouldn't offer too many surprises. And that's the way it had turned out — except, apparently, for Rennie.

I heard footsteps on the landing outside, followed by a knock on the door.

"It's open."

The light from the landing backlit Spinney's gangly silhouette. I leaned forward and lit my desk lamp. We both squinted at each other.

"You get a lot done this way?"

"Secret of my success. Have a seat."

He crossed the room and took the chair by my desk. He was carrying a folder, which he placed delicately on his bony knees. "Thought you'd like to know what we've dug up."

I raised my eyebrows at him. "Does Smith know you're here?"

He allowed a half smile. "He said you'd get a report." He opened the folder. "I'll skip the stuff you already know. The fire is still legally an accident, nobody saw a thing, and nothin's goin' nowhere fast. But," he raised a finger for emphasis, "we are chipping away at it. Remember the 9-mm casing, which *could* have come from anywhere, despite Wingate's having owned the same kind of gun?"

"Sure."

"Well, the print we lifted from it belongs to Bruce Wingate. It 'puts him at the scene,' as they say, for the first time."

"It puts his print at the scene."

He gave me that loopy, wide grin. "Right. We kicked that around, too, especially since he says he lost the thing."

"Which he may or may not have." I remembered what I'd been kicking around in my head just minutes earlier. "If he didn't, then he might have been there and fired it. But if he did lose it, then anything's possible."

"Like the daughter."

I shrugged. "Sure, the daughter — or the wife. What do we know? Maybe Ellie tried to kill Julie and frame Wingate, or kill Wingate and frame Julie, or killed Fox on purpose or by mistake, or tried to kill herself and missed."

Spinney was laughing. "All right, all right. Apple dug up a lot more on Edward Sarris. Want to hear it?"

"Sure."

Spinney blinked a couple of times to focus on his notes. "He's pretty bland, really. Used to be a college professor, wrote a book about some of his back-to-nature ideas, dropped out and formed the roots of this outfit in Chapel Hill, North Carolina. Did pretty well, and then came up here because things were getting too crowded and tense down south."

"How so?"

"He was a real pain in the butt to the town government, constantly ragging them about what they were doing. He'd show up at council meetings and raise hell. It was legal but it caused problems. They started going after him for code violations of one kind or another, and he'd stall 'em with lawyers. But that was about it — no big deal. They think he finally left more because of his success than because of any hassles with the town."

"Where's he get his money?"

"They give it to him. That's part of the deal. When you join up, you hand over every dime you own, along with all your material possessions. He keeps the cash and sells the rest. Then he's got the restaurant, which has almost no overhead since all the workers are volunteers, and he's got a mail-order business for all the natural foods they grow for nothing. He gets into a jam every once in a while — relatives of Order members try to sue because of the money angle, one state agency or another sticks its nose into labor relations, or the vital statistics law, which he just ignores, or health and sanitation. Things like that. None of it ever sticks — he runs a tight ship, he's got good legal advice, and he knows what he can get away with. As far as anyone can tell, he's smart and weird, but he ain't crooked."

"What about the kid that died? Hamilton said some kid fell off a bridge a while back."

Spinney shrugged. "I looked at the file: pretty cut and dry. They said it was an accident, we investigated, and we agreed. The kid took a nose dive off the bridge. We gave a more careful look than we might have otherwise, because of the people involved, but that kind of thing happens. The bridge railing was a joke — designed for adults. The little guy just squirted underneath, according to the witnesses."

"So there was a bunch of them there."

"Oh, yeah — it was an outing. Twelve kids and two adults. The kid apparently broke ranks and ran to the edge of the bridge."

"How old was he? Hamilton thought fourteen months."

Spinney closed his eyes for a moment, concentrating. "Yeah, that was it, just a toddler. It was a real shame. Apparently he was mentally retarded. That might have been why he made a run for it — never understood the danger he was in, plus at that age, what does anyone know?"

He pulled a drawing from the file on his lap and handed it to me. It was a scaled sketch of the crime scene with Wingate's outline and six sets of footprints in different colors spread out around him like multi-hued flower petals.

"Pretty."

"Crofter's handiwork — he loves stuff like this." Spinney had another copy for himself. "Still, it helps, considering the crowd that was there before us. There is one caveat that Crofter wanted us all to understand, though. This is all pre-crime lab. They haven't reported back on their version of what happened, so we don't have details like the estimated weight of the individuals involved, the shoe sizes and manufacturers, or even who went where first or last or whatever."

"Okay." I studied the diagram. "So, let's see. Two sets belong to Rennie Wilson — blue and red. The blue set was made this morning just before I got there, and after he'd been called to the scene by Mitch Pearl, the hunter. The red set was made earlier, and matches the blood-stained boots you boys found in his house."

"Yeah. Red for blood, get it?"

I looked up at him and deadpanned, "Got it. The green ones belong to Pearl, and the black ones to Wingate himself — black as in dead, I suppose. So that leaves the yellow and the white, the two that are unaccounted for. The yellow appear to shadow Rennie's red tracks, and the white come from an entirely different direction." I paused. "Rennie and the white tracks seem to have a couple of odd connections . . ." I pointed at clusters at opposing distances from the body. "Maybe both of them stood around for a while, shifting their weight, as if waiting. Rennie's seem the busiest, and are concentrated near the head of the victim, while whites are the least busy, just coming in, turning around, and leaving."

Spinney looked up at me. "Christ, you're good at this."

"Practice."

"I guess so." Spinney shook his head and returned to the diagram. "Crofter thought the other mysterious tracks — the yellow — were a bit unusual. They're smaller than the others and smooth, as if they were made by bare feet or moccasins."

"So that might point at someone in the Order, since they all wear homemade shoes, or it may be a setup." I sat back and laid the sketch in my lap. "Have you confronted Rennie with all this yet?"

Spinney gave me a long, enigmatic look. "Well, that's proved to be a little difficult. We can't find him. We went by the bar that trooper told us about. He'd been there, knockin' 'em back pretty steady, but he'd staggered out about a half hour before we got there. Now he's vanished."

I looked out the window at the traffic below, imagining Rennie out there somewhere. What the hell was he doing? If he had killed Wingate, and then played dumb at the crime scene with me, then why had he stashed his bloody clothes where we could find them? It was a logical question that played in his favor. "You follow up on his story about last night?"

"He checks out at the job. We found one guy who says he saw him walking out to the parking lot and getting into his car at around six-thirty; the guy added that Wilson often stays late, wrapping things up. The Maple Door was a washout, though. The bartender

I talked to was there all last night, knows Wilson slightly from seeing him around, and says he definitely never showed his face. The only waitress confirmed that, and she said she knew him pretty well; he's got a reputation as a boozer and a ladies' man."

"And you talked to Chaney."

"Chaney and a bunch of other people — nothin'." He handed me a xerox copy from his file. "Here's a photo of Julie Wingate. We'll be getting a sharper version later, but Smith figured the sooner the better."

"Any luck finding her?" I eyed the picture, a slightly grainy but faithful copy of the snapshot Bruce Wingate had showed me the morning following the fire.

"The Order's not cooperating, and until we get something legal against her, we can't force 'em to open up. It's almost too bad Rennie and you did such a thorough search of that house — now you're their best witness that she wasn't there hours before the fire. We're doing what we can, though. We've instituted two twelve-hour uniformed shifts, two cruisers each. With the rest of us making rounds, maybe we'll luck out and bump into her — or Rennie, for that matter."

"Do you have anything new on Paul Gorman?"

"No, we're just starting on him."

"I have my doubts about his mobile phone routine this morning. I mean, what was he doing, sleeping in his car? When I spoke to Wingate and his wife last night, he said he hadn't called Gorman since two nights ago — Monday — right after they'd spotted their daughter. I told him we would be checking the Inn's phone records, and he suddenly looked very pleased with himself. It struck me that he'd probably called Gorman more recently and that he'd used a public phone to do it — not the ultimate innocent gesture. If that pulls your chain, you might want to subpoena a few public phone records." I slid a stapled sheaf of papers over to him. "That's my report on the entire conversation."

Spinney nodded and wrote himself a note, muttering, "Great, thanks." He looked up suddenly. "By the way, Gorman's been making friends."

I hesitated a moment and then rubbed my forehead. "Greta?"

"The one and only. She's asked him to address a small crowd tonight and tell them of the evil that lurks among them." He said the last in a tremulous voice, reminiscent of Boris Karloff.

"Where?"

"The Rocky River. We thought it might be a little confrontational to send one of our own to listen in, but you're a good ol' boy . . ."

I exchanged a sour expression for his ear-to-ear grin and heaved myself to an upright position. "And here I was thinking it was nice of you to have dropped in."

20

My entrance had the subtlety of a wasp up the nose. Aside from the bar, the Rocky River's entire ground floor was lined with rows of seats: armchairs, sofas, straightbacks, metal folding chairs taken from the fire department — enough to seat the thirty or so people who were staring at me as if I was the only drunk at a temperance meeting.

"Lieutenant Gunther. Welcome." Paul Gorman stood with his back to the closed double doors of the darkened café/bar. Beside and slightly behind him, looking a whole lot less thrilled to see me, sat Greta.

"What do you want, Joe?" she asked warily. I sensed the same antagonism that had risen between us this morning. But there was also something else, a defensiveness perhaps at my

282

having found her with Gorman, as if her innate, almost buried common sense agreed with my own skepticism of the man and his motives.

"Heard there was a meeting."

"You weren't invited."

"Whoa, whoa." Gorman raised his arms, his professional smile glued in place. "Lots of people here weren't specifically invited; we just got the word out. I certainly have no objection to Lieutenant Gunther being here. Have a seat."

I found a seat near the door. Looking around, I noticed the crowd was relatively young — couples and individuals in their twenties and thirties. There were also several reporters with cameras, whose roles in all this were not going to make things any easier for the police.

I also saw Laura there, which surprised me; I hadn't thought she'd be interested in Gorman's rap. She glanced over and gave me an embarrassed smile. In my mind's eye, I'd endowed her with more sense than to be part of this crowd. It made me realize how little I knew her, and how I'd presumed we shared some basic assumptions.

"I was telling everyone a little about cults in general, Lieutenant Gunther — may I call you Joe?"

"Joe's okay." I saw several of the reporters stare at me before feverishly scribbling in their notebooks. So much for maintaining a low-profile.

"I was explaining how cultists, no matter how different they may appear on the surface, usually operate similarly in their recruitment and indoctrination. They focus on people that are essentially unhappy or uncertain in the first place, and then exploit these characteristics to win the recruits over. Have you ever dealt with a cult before, Joe?"

He was a slick son of a gun, I had to give him that. While Greta would have preferred to throw me out a closed window, Gorman was trying to embarrass me to death.

I chose my words carefully, sounding like a press release. "Not specifically. I have dealt with individuals with some of that in their background."

"No doubt you found them disoriented, often depressed, at odds with how to cope with their lives?"

"That fits almost everyone I know."

There were a few snickers. Gorman smiled more broadly. "Good point, and it applies just as aptly to cult recruiters. But where the police mostly deal with aggressive types, cult recruiters go after the passive ones. They don't want people who think they can conquer the world;

they want people they can mold." He held up a finger for emphasis. "The irony is that in some cults, the goal is to *create* conquerors — but only as soldiers, never as leaders."

He was addressing the crowd by now, no longer just me, and the cadence in his voice betrayed the practiced rhythm of an actor saying his lines for the hundredth time.

I looked at the faces in the crowd as he talked about Sarris's megalomania, his preying on those weaker than himself, and a bevy of other Psychology 101 catchphrases. The reporters were mostly bored; some of the crowd looked interested, and several more — Laura not among them, I chose to think — seemed positively entranced. Greta was the easiest of these to spot, since she was facing me. She smiled when his sentences encouraged it, nodded just perceptively when he hit a standard chord note, frowned when he spoke of the duplicity of those who'd subvert others to support their own egos.

It was an interesting phenomenon, since none of these local people were related to anyone in the Order. For me, the message became darker the more I listened to it. Gorman was stoking intolerance, not sympathy for the downtrodden, and yet he was using the same fuel, the same words he would have used on the parents of lost children.

And it was working. As he progressed, drawing more and more comparisons to the "cult" at hand, his explanations became less professorial and more impassioned; he let up on the *theys* and increased the *yous* as he built up the threat of the cults to the people living near them. The number of captivated faces around me grew.

The paranoia that Greta had been displaying since the moment I'd seen her three days ago was legitimized as fear in the face of real danger. As Gorman spoke, the Order gradually metamorphosed into a human toxic waste dump, planted in disguise among welcoming, friendly people, but designed and destined to leach out beyond its boundaries, infecting and polluting the minds and hearts of those who so innocently gave it harbor. It was a feat of elocution that set my hair on end.

Greta stood after Gorman had finished talking. There was no applause. There was no shuffling, no coughing, no whispering to be heard. These people were caught up, believing that what they valued was at stake, and that salvation from their nemesis was at hand.

"Most of you know me," she said. "I've been in this town all my life. I've served most of you food and drink, or at least drink, and I've even cleaned up after a few of you. I'm not the easiest person in the world to get along with — some people call me bitchy, and maybe they're right. On the other hand, nobody in this town can call me a pushover, and they can't say that I ever stood around and let something happen I thought was crap.

"Well, this cult is crap. It came in here all smiles and sweet talk, buying its way into the town, dumping gifts on the fire department and the school and whatever, just like Paul Gorman was saying. But then their true colors showed, and now look what's happened — a fire, a murder, an innocent man being railroaded by the cops for killing a guy he barely knew —"

I found myself standing before I knew what I was doing. "Greta, that's nonsense. Nobody's being railroaded."

"You saying Rennie's not a suspect?" She met my eyes with open hostility.

I regretted my hastiness. Speaking up wasn't a mistake, but I should have done it when Gorman held the floor. Now, it was just Joe and Greta circling the tree again, snapping at each other's tail. "He is, you are, the Order is, and everyone else is, for that matter. It's like a jigsaw puzzle."

"Cut the bullshit, Joe. You guys have a manhunt out for Rennie right now, and as soon as you find him, you're going to say, 'case closed.'"

I tried to ignore Greta's mounting fury. "Sure we're looking for Rennie. It was his lighter under the body, now he's vanished. We're working with what we've got. Rennie and I are childhood friends — I'm not about to railroad him. But I sure as hell want to talk to him."

"You guys were searching his house. Nadine says you found something." Greta was like a runaway train, determined on a collision.

"Yes, we did. Some of it makes him look bad and some of it doesn't." I winced internally when I said that; the reporters were scribbling again, words I hoped Crofter Smith would never see. I tried to tone it down. "We're looking under every rock in this town. For a time, everybody thought that the fire department water pump had been sabotaged. Rennie and I were at the other end of that deal. Was it sabotage? No. Some poor bastard screwed up and left out the oil. We found that out because we asked questions instead of jumping to conclusions."

"I haven't seen any of the cult's houses being searched."

"Nor will you, Greta, unless we find a search is legally justified. We're not a bunch of Nazis kicking down doors and rousting people just because they look different. How many of you have even spoken to a member of this group?"

"They don't want us to talk to them," someone answered.

Greta walked over to me and grabbed my arm, her face clouded with frustration and rage. "This is my place, Joe, and my home, too. I want you to leave." She opened the door, letting in a blast of cold air. "Get the hell out," she growled, and gave me a shove.

I stood out front for a few minutes, salving my ego and ruing my big mouth. One of the standards in police work is the ability to listen carefully and keep quiet.

But, like Greta, I was becoming frustrated, as much by my friends as by the case. I was not detached and objective as I should have been, nor was I in control of the investigation, as I normally was in Brattleboro. This was a State Police investigation, and it involved personal friends whom I hated to see removed from their pedestals. I sympathized with Greta's desire to reach out and strangle the cause of this disruption — only I still didn't know who or what it was.

The door opened and shut behind me. I turned to see one of the reporters adjusting his coat, a young man, probably in his twenties, with slicked-back dark hair and an overly friendly expression. Behind him, standing hesitantly with her hand on the doorknob, was Laura.

"Lieutenant Gunther?"

"Yes."

"Of the Brattleboro Police Department?"

"I'm on temporary assignment with the Essex County State's Attorney's office."

"But you are the Brattleboro Gunther?"

"I live there, yes."

"You were the policeman who was involved in the Ski Mask investigation about six months ago?"

"Yes."

He stuck out his hand. "I'm Tim Chapman, of the *Caledonian Record* in St. J. Were you brought up here to help with this case?"

"No. And that's all I'm going to say. You can ask Lieutenant Hamilton of the State Police for any other information. He's the official spokesman."

"Right. But what did you think of what Gorman said?"

"No comment."

He looked at me with a slightly startled expression. "I didn't mean for a quote, just for background."

"No comment."

"I won't mention your name."

"You won't mention I was at that meeting and spoke?"

"Well, I'll have to do that; that was news, after all."

"Right. No comment." I felt like an idiot, having to sound like a robot, which made me feel more foolish than I had been before.

He shook his head, looking disappointed. "People have a right to know."

"I know they do. They also have a right to keep their mouths shut."

"So you won't give me anything?"

I admired his grasp of the obvious. "No."

He stared at me a moment and went back into the Inn, brushing by Laura at the door.

She waited a moment after the door had shut. "Hi." Her expression was wary.

"Hi yourself."

"I thought you were pretty good in there."

"Not good enough."

"Paul Gorman's pretty slick."

"I'm glad you think so. I got the feeling half the people in there were ready to carry him out on their shoulders."

She made a rueful face. "Maybe they were. The fact they showed up for the meeting in the first place shows how uncomfortable they are with all this."

"Are you uncomfortable?"

She smiled. "Me? A little — I'm mostly curious. And I have too much time on my hands. Dangerous thing for a woman, they say."

I ignored the one-liner. "But you must have thoughts about this."

"Sure I do. I think people have a right to do what they want if they don't hurt other people. But I don't know if that's what's happening here."

"What about Greta?"

She made a face. "I think Greta's full of it. She runs a lousy business, and now she's losing money. It's her own fault. If they'd opened a McDonald's, she would have been in the same fix."

I found myself laughing at the image of Greta bringing in Gorman to rid Gannet of the Golden Arches. I felt my earlier ill humor slipping away.

Looking at Laura, smiling, I was suddenly grateful that she'd been there to lift my spirits. "You had dinner yet?"

"No, I was about to head home and put something on. You interested?"

Something in her tone prompted me to be cautious. "No, let me treat you. Your choice."

She hesitated, "Well, there's . . ." She stopped and gave me a mischievous look. "How about the Kingdom Restaurant?"

My astonishment showed.

"Is that all right?" She looked suddenly doubtful.

"It's fine. I'm just surprised. I would have thought you'd never set foot in the place."

She grinned. "I haven't."

21

The Kingdom Restaurant was, to the average tourist eye, quite charming. The interior contained lots of wood — beams, rafters, exposed floors — and plenty of greenery, plants hung from almost every available overhead spot. There was a fire crackling in a large hearth, surrounded by a semicircle of comfortable-looking rocking chairs. The lighting was muted, mostly supplied by candles, including one at each of the gingham-covered tables — a city dweller's dream come true.

Not that there were too many tourists there. The timing was lousy for them, or for anyone else outside a twenty-mile radius: It was too cold but with no compensating snow; it was fall but the colorful leaves were gone. Of New England's many unofficial seasons, "T'Aint Season," this pause-before-the-snow-flies, was a general bust, except, of course, for the hunters. There were three of them in "Day-Glo" dress parked at a table near the front window.

Laura was obviously impressed. "Wow."

"See? You might even like their filet of materialist flambé."

"Not funny. There sure are a lot of them here."

That was true. A dozen or so men, women and children in quilted pseudo-army garb were sprinkled behind the bar counter, around the kitchen door, and about the fire. Apparently, the Kingdom Restaurant doubled as a hangout for its owners.

One of the women approached us, smiling pleasantly, and led us to a booth off to the side. Walking in her wake, I noticed an odd but not wholly unpleasant scent wafting behind her, some complex mixture of things herbal and animal, including a subtle dollop of old-fashioned body odor. Laura followed me so closely, she stepped on my heels.

The waitress indicated a small slate on the table, with elegant chalk writing on it, propped against the wall. "That is your menu. Our meals are made from our own products, grown or raised on our own land, and prepared daily. I'll give you a few minutes to get settled; would you like anything non-alcoholic from the bar in the meantime? We have a wide variety of fruit juices, natural sodas, and sparkling and nonsparkling waters."

I looked at Laura, who was slowly peeling off her down windbreaker like a reluctant warrior shedding his armor in the face of the enemy. "Want anything?"

She looked from the waitress to me. "Coke?"

"I'm sorry, we don't carry Coke, but we do have something like it."

"Okay," she said doubtfully, and slid into the booth.

"I'll have one, too," I said as I took off my coat and hung it on the hook by the booth. The waitress went off to fulfill our order.

"So far so good. They haven't asked us to step into a huge stew pot yet."

She gave me an exasperated look. "All right, I'm a little nervous."

I reached out and patted her hand. "I'm glad you suggested this. It occurred to me I was criticizing the people at Gorman's meeting for not getting to know the Order, when I was guilty of the same thing."

She looked around. "It is a nice looking place." She was wearing a very pretty, close-fitting, V-necked blouse. Her throat was bare and her smooth, pale skin ran uninterrupted to the edges of her collar, to where the first button rested like a medal on her chest. It was startling to realize that this was the first relaxed, social moment I'd had since I arrived in Gannet.

The waitress returned with a couple of glasses and two cans of Robert Corr's Cola. I quickly glanced at the menu and ordered the least pure thing I could find, chili, with a side order of ketchup. Laura settled for lemon chicken.

After the waitress left again, Laura looked at her drink suspiciously.

"It's a national brand. I've seen it around."

She sipped gingerly.

"So?"

"Not bad."

I decided to ply her for a little more information about the Order. "What was it like when they first came to town?" I indicated the people around us with my eyes.

"Kind of exciting, in a way. Sarris made a point of being friendly. They paid top dollar for the buildings and the farm. People were saying it might be a good thing, give the town a shot in the arm, but that was all wishful thinking. I remember Greta saying she'd benefit from the business this restaurant pulled in. Overflow, she called it. Can you imagine that? She must've been dreaming. No one in their right mind would come to this town to eat at the Rocky River, especially the flatlanders."

I already knew that the backbone of the Kingdom Restaurant was its mail-order business. With that as an extra source of income, Greta's financial outlook looked doubly doomed. "Did anyone try to roll out the welcome mat for the Order?"

She shook her head. "People talk about it now, but no one really went out of their way. I don't think it would have worked anyway. Sarris brought his group up here to get away from the locals. The Northeast Kingdom isn't exactly famous for its hospitality, and I think that suited him."

"Where do they grow their food?"

"North of town. There's a dirt road called McCallister's Road. It leads to an old farm —"

"Which used to be called McCallister's Farm. I remember."

She laughed. "Right. It was abandoned when they bought it, but they've done a lot with it. It's in full production now, or so everyone says."

"Who's 'everyone'?"

"Oh, other farmers around. Early on, the Order asked surrounding farmers how to work the land. They wanted to know how Vermont farming differed from down south. They paid well, so people were happy to help. But there's been less contact lately, now that they know what they're doing. In fact, they have several advantages over the local farmers."

"How so?"

"Well, they don't use any middlemen, the mortgage is paid on the farm, they don't use any power machinery, and the farm hands work for free — and there're a lot of them, too."

"Any resentment from the locals?"

"Some, I guess. It's not really the same market — these people avoid the mainstream — but still, some of them feel the cult's setting a bad example. Same as with the townspeople; at first, they were well paid, then the money handouts stopped."

She took a swallow of her drink. During the pause in conversation, I thought I could hear sounds from the seashore, mixed with rain. I looked around, trying to locate the source, and found it leaking from a loudspeaker high in one corner — "natural" Muzak.

"How do you know so much about this?"

"My father and father-in-law are farmers," she said shortly.

I watched her swirling the ice cubes around in her glass, her eyes on the tiny whirlpool. Her tone had revealed as much as her brevity on the subject. Their life was not to be hers. Apparently, however, that's where her determination had run out; she knew what she didn't want but had no alternatives.

Our waitress returned bearing our meals,

her smile still in place. I focused on her more carefully as she placed the dishes before us. "That was fast."

"Well, we're not too busy, and a lot of the ingredients are prepared ahead of time."

"You work in the restaurant full-time, or do you do other things?"

She looked at me closely then, her smile fading just around the edges. "We all work at everything: It's a sharing community where all are equal."

"So you all get to know each other pretty well, I guess."

She looked at me as if I'd suddenly lapsed into Arabic.

"You ever meet Julie Wingate?"

She looked over her shoulder nervously. A man at the bar, watching us, came over to our table. The waitress faded away as he drew up. "Can I help you?" The tone of voice was neutral, but I found the sequence unsettling.

"No, not really."

"I got the impression you were asking your waitress questions she couldn't answer."

"I don't know if she could or not; she didn't."

"That could be because she knows who you are, Mr. Gunther."

"Ah, very flattering."

"I'm glad you think so. Well, if there's

nothing I can do, I'll let you enjoy your meal."

"You know, we're trying to protect you as much as anyone else; we don't want to see any more of you hurt or killed."

He smiled. "What you want is irrelevant to us." He turned his back and returned to the bar.

There was a prolonged silence after he left. "Maybe this was a bad idea," Laura finally said.

I poured ketchup into the chili, crumbled some crackers over the top, and stirred it all together. It tasted pretty bland — Tabasco might have helped. "Hell with 'em — food's good."

She looked doubtful, but cut off a piece of chicken and ate.

"Good?"

She stared at my bowl. I was adding salt and pepper. "Mine's fine. What are you doing?"

"Spicing it up a bit."

She had the kindness to keep quiet. I didn't really mind; my eating habits were legendary in some circles and I'd already survived a lifetime of harassment. More important, it had taken Laura's mind off her sudden discomfort at being here.

"So," I said after a few spoonfuls, "have you decided what to do about you and Tommy?"

She chewed a while longer before answering. Then she put down her fork. "I don't think I have your courage."

"Courage?" I was disturbed by her choice of words. Her view of me, I'd come to realize, needed a good dose of reality, something a person like Gail would be an expert at administering.

"You can live alone; you can come up here and do this job, with people you don't know; you can handle yourself in tough situations and not have it faze you. I don't think I could be that way."

"That probably makes me callous, not courageous."

She reached out and grabbed my hand. It was a perfectly natural gesture, but the sentimentality of it made me uncomfortable: It spoke too well of her need to make me the solution to her problems. "I don't think so. It's not callous to be strong enough to not care what other people think."

I shook my head. "You're making me sound too good to be true."

"You are good."

It was a painful signpost of her inexperience — or my skepticism. I turned my hand so that I held hers in mine. "What I am is a crusty old cop. Some of what you're talking about comes from my just not giving a damn anymore. And the rest is flat out wrong. I care about what people think; I have concerns about coming across well and not looking like a fool. Everyone does. I want you to like me, for instance, but that's just a normal thing for men and women to do — for anyone to do."

Her face softened. "I do like you. I think I liked you before we even met, just from what I heard from Buster. And now that we have met, I know I was right."

I was angry at myself. Subconsciously, I'd been playing her up, encouraging her. I'd been enjoying the attention, using it to soothe my frazzled ego.

"Laura, you don't really know me. I live alone for good reasons. I'm narrow-minded in a lot of ways and I'm selfish as hell — can't share worth a damn. Don't look to me for examples of how to run your life; look to yourself and find out what it is you want out of life. Like you said, you've got no kids, nothing really to tie you down. If leaving Tommy is what's best, then do it, but if you think the two of you still have a chance, then maybe it's worth fixing up."

"I don't know if I'd be good at that," she muttered, staring at her plate.

"Come on. You said you lacked courage. That's baloney — you beat your alcoholism, didn't you?"

"For the moment."

"Did Tommy help at all?"

"Not much. Tommy doesn't do anything much." Her face became hard. "I'd try to make it work if he was interested. Hell, I'd make it work if anyone was interested." With that, like quicksilver, she was looking softly into my eyes.

I felt like a tugboat pushing an ocean liner away from the rocks. "If Tommy's not the man for you, Laura, then find someone who is. But don't tie yourself into knots for the first nice guy who comes along. That'll bite you in the nose in the long run."

"Do you like me?"

I was getting a little frustrated with this. "Of course I like you, but I'm set in my ways. You're stuck on me because you're unhappy with Tommy."

I'd been harsher than I'd intended. Indeed, even as I spoke them, I half-regretted my own words. To a guy my age, the palpable yearning of an attractive younger woman was a seductive proposition, as pleasing to my vanity as it was foolish and misguided to my inner moral compass. In any case, I had pricked whatever bubble had been swelling between us. She took her hand back and began finishing her meal.

I took her cue and attacked my chili again,

but the taste had gone out of it somehow. After a couple of mouthfuls, I put down my spoon and quit. As I looked up, I saw Edward Sarris staring at me from across the room.

Moments later, he walked up to the table. "Enjoying your meal?"

Laura froze in midbite.

Sarris smiled. "Please, continue."

She did, though obviously with limited enthusiasm. I gestured to the seat beside me. "Join us?"

"No, thank you." He leaned against the table opposite us instead, his hands in his pants pockets, his ankles crossed — the perfect picture of leisure. "So, business or pleasure?"

"The meal was a pleasure, the fact that we had it here was, I admit, a concession to curiosity."

"Nicely put. So, what do you think?" He pulled out a hand and gestured around the room. "It's pretty similar to the way The Common Sense Restaurant is set up in Island Pond, but, as they say, imitation is the highest form of flattery."

"I think it's materialistic as hell. How do you justify it, given your philosophy?"

"Of which you know next to nothing, I might add."

"Okay, but isn't there some truth to that?"

"Perhaps. What you fail to recognize is that

we deal with principle mixed with pragmatism. We intend to outlive you to the end of this demented world, and to do that we must live on the fringes of your world, not utterly apart from it."

"I hear you collect all valuables from entering members and that you have insurance on all your buildings. How's that fit in?"

"I doubt you are truly curious how that 'fits,' as you put it. Suffice it to say it's perfectly legal and that you needn't waste your time trying to prove I'm a despot leading a bunch of deranged half-wits to poverty."

"I have heard that."

"I don't doubt it. You've probably also heard about sacrifices in the night."

"What about Julie Wingate? Have you seen her around?"

"No, I'm afraid not." His manner was consistently relaxed on the outside, ice-cold on the inside. I had to give him high marks for composure. So far, he had avoided all the easy clichés — no temper tantrums, no outright refusals, no bald-faced lies that I could immediately expose, although I knew in my bones his last comment was pure baloney.

"I hear you're not cooperating in locating her."

His eyebrows shot up. "Really?"

"You claim you can't force your followers

to help us out, and they won't move a muscle without your okay." I glanced at the man behind the counter. "Or one of your lieutenants."

"The first half of that is true; not the second."

"That's not what we just witnessed. We asked our waitress a simple question, and she immediately was replaced by that man over there."

He followed my pointed finger. "She didn't know the answer to your question, I suppose."

"I asked her if she knew Julie. Surely she knew the answer to that."

He smiled. "It would seem so. I have no explanation."

It was a wonderful answer, a total roadblock disguised as beguiling truthfulness. It occurred to me that until we had some concrete evidence that the Order was involved in all this, Sarris would be happy to play verbal footsie 'til the cows came home. As he'd said earlier, he was quite good at it.

I glanced at Laura. "You finished?"

She nodded.

Sarris looked disappointed. "No dessert?"

"Not this time." I put a twenty on the table, more than enough to cover the bill and tip.

He reached for the money. "Let me get you your change."

"No, keep it." I rose and helped Laura into her coat.

Sarris unhooked mine and handed it to me. "After this is all over, Lieutenant Gunther, I'd like it if you could come back informally. We're antagonists now, to be sure, but I have enjoyed our conversations."

"Seems like all I do is ask questions and all you say is, 'No comment.' "

"Surely, you've glimpsed better than that."

"I haven't glimpsed much of anything."

Laura preceded me through the door. We stopped on the walkway outside and adjusted our coats against the chill, which, compared to the warmth of the restaurant, had a pleasant bite to it.

"You two guys sure have strange conversations. I can't figure out if you like each other or not."

"I don't like him but he has a certain style."

She shivered slightly, getting used to the cold. "He gives me the creeps. Thanks for dinner, though. It was nice."

"Let me walk you back to your car."

"Okay."

I stuck out my arm in a Cary Grant gesture. She didn't know to loop her arm through mine, and instead patted my elbow awkwardly — different movies.

Suddenly, I heard a soft crack beside me,

along the dark wall of the restaurant. I turned my head in time to see Rennie Wilson standing in the shadow.

"Rennie. We've been looking all over for you."

He turned in an instant and vanished around the edge of the building.

"Rennie. Hang on, goddamn it. We gotta talk."

I bolted after him but had to contend with a small picket fence that blocked the alley. By the time I cleared it, his crashing footsteps were at the far end of the building.

The narrow alleyway that ran alongside the restaurant was pitch-black and choked with high weeds and brush. I ran with my hands in front of my face like a blind man, praying I wouldn't lose an eye or be knocked senseless by something hanging low from overhead.

I was driven as much by desperation as by adrenaline. Christ only knew what risks Rennie was running by not coming in, but one of them for sure was a small army of policemen, armed and convinced he was a violent killer.

I broke through the end of the alley into the overgrown rectangular field behind the Order residences. The grass was chest-high and there wasn't much more light here than in the alley. The sky was overcast and there were no streetlights aside from the one blocked by the dark hulk of the firehouse.

I stopped dead in my tracks and listened. A dog barked far away; a car door slammed. Somewhere I heard muted laughter. In the houses to the north, lights shone through the windows. I watched them, hoping to catch some movement between them and me.

My eyes scanned slowly, trying not to skip from light to light, trying to see more than was humanly possible. About midway from left to right I saw a short shadow, too broad for a sapling, too narrow for a shed, about a hundred feet away. I moved slightly to one side, sliding a distant-lit window along so it would backlight the shape. It was a man, standing stock-still.

I crouched and began moving toward him, hoping to hell I wouldn't step on anything that would give me away. I got about three yards before my left shin struck something thin, horizontal, and resistant — a wire. As my momentum pushed me forward, I tried to lift my foot over, got my shoe caught, and began to fall. I made a giant step with my right leg, hit the same low-strung piece of wire, and fell headlong into someone's abandoned fenced garden.

I scrambled up as quickly as I could, but I knew I'd lost my one chance. The shadow was gone, leaving only the faint sound of a distant body moving swiftly through the grass.

Again, as when I'd seen Bruce Wingate lying dead at the bottom of that ravine, I felt as if I'd let something slip through my hands, something that was to cost me dearly.

22

I called Hamilton after losing Rennie, and he'd rallied the troops. For most of the night, we drove, walked, and talked our way across what seemed like the entire county, all for nought. It was Rennie's backyard, and he obviously knew it well enough to stay out of our way. On the other hand, it gave me plenty of time to think.

Despite the case against him, I still couldn't shake the feeling that Rennie was running for reasons other than Wingate's murder. There were too many inconsistencies; too many leaps of logic, like the assumption that a punch in the face merited a lethal revenge.

Also, there were the other actors in the play — Sarris, Ellie, Gorman, Julie among them — none of whom glowed with innocence.

Rennie's actually running only made him the most blatant of these, but the others were just as shy of the limelight.

All night long, I mulled this over, leafing through flashcards in my mind, trying to piece together some reasonable sequence of events. After hours of this, the only common denominator was the opening line to each and every scenario — Julie's migration from home to college and to the Order had set the whole game into motion.

The more I looked at it, the more I saw the missing Wingate as the catalyst for most of the police's problems. We'd been spending virtually all our efforts trying to locate Rennie and prove him guilty, largely because he custom-fit the role. The evidence was against him, his actions were self-incriminating, and warrants with his name on them were easy to secure: He was a natural.

Just what Julie was not.

With her, warrants were unobtainable, evidence was nonexistent, and no one had even set eyes on her. And yet there she was, like a stage-front actor with no lines to deliver.

All that, after less than two hours' restless sleep, had brought me down out of the Northeast Kingdom and into Massachusetts — to Natick, specifically — to find out all I could about the elusive Julie Wingate.

I parked just shy of the town's central square of updated turn-of-the-century red brick buildings. It was still dark, although dawn's first gray blush was just beginning to touch the sky. I stretched, rubbed my eyes, and crossed the street to a small restaurant. Inside, I sat at the counter and ordered coffee and a sugar-covered cinnamon roll. Natick, from the little I knew, had been transformed over the years from a small rural town to one of Boston's "bedroom communities," meaning, I had always supposed, that its population decreased during the workday. It was built low and spread out, with lots of quiet residential streets lined with middle-aged trees, occupying an economic middle ground among Boston's wide variety of satellites. A good town, as they say, in which to raise a family, benefitting from a nearby metropolis and an inordinate number of nearby malls, and yet enjoying the slower pace of suburban life.

On the surface, Bruce the banker and Ellie the secretary fit in here like peas in a pod — white, middle-class, hard working. Looking through the restaurant window at the early, Boston-bound commuter traffic, I wondered what had made Julie so desperate to escape.

As I ate, I flipped through the pages of a borrowed phone book. Bruce Wingate was listed as living at 4 Maple Avenue. I got directions from the woman behind the counter.

Maple Avenue was a short dead-end street, very pretty and quiet, lined with small, World War One-vintage homes located on tiny plots. Bare trees stood guard by the sidewalk and pinned down the neatly mowed, frost-covered lawns. An occasional tricycle and swing set attested to warmer weather scenes of children enjoying life on a street with no through traffic. Number 4, with its narrow front, high-peaked roof, and dark wood trim, seemed right at home.

The Wingates' residence, however, was not my primary interest. I wanted to talk to someone, anyone really, who might tell me of its inhabitants. I parked in the middle of the block, where I could see most of the street, and waited for some activity. The first sign of life appeared as a concession to the day's gathering light — the bulb above Number 7's porch was switched off.

I got out of the car and climbed the steps to the porch. Whoever had hit the switch had also seen me coming. The door opened a crack, too narrow to let me see who was standing there.

"Yes?" It was a woman's voice, sharp and thin.

I pulled out my badge and showed it to the

crack. "Sorry to disturb you so early in the morning. My name is Joe Gunther. I'm a policeman working with the Vermont State's Attorney's office, and I was wondering if I could ask you a couple of questions."

"Vermont?" The woman stayed hidden behind the door. "I've never been to Vermont."

I gave my best genial smile, feeling like an idiot with no one to look at. "No, ma'am, this isn't about you. I wanted to find out a few things about the Wingates."

"Who?"

"The Wingates — they live right across the street."

"Oh. I don't know them. I've only lived here a few months. What did they do?"

"Nothing. I just need some background."

"They kill someone?"

"Not that I know of." It wasn't strictly a lie, although I had my suspicions about Bruce Wingate.

"Rob a bank?"

"No. I wonder if you could tell me who on this block might know them."

"Try Number 6 — she's pretty nosy. Name's Grissom. They in the drug business?"

"Thank you for your time." I left Number 7 and crossed the street to Number 6. The door opened wide to my ring of the doorbell, revealing a pleasant-faced elderly woman wearing a full-length fluffy robe. She gave me a smile as I ran through my cumbersome introduction.

"Vermont — you're a long way from home."

"Yes, ma'am."

"What questions could you possibly have that I might answer?"

"I'd like to know about the Wingates, what they were like as neighbors; things like that. Did you know them?"

"Oh, yes. I've been living here for quite a while." She eyed me carefully for a couple of more seconds, and then opened the door wide. "Would you like to come in? I was just fixing myself some tea."

I thought of the gallons of coffee I'd been swilling half the night and suppressed any thought of caffeine poisoning. "Sounds wonderful. Thanks."

I followed her through to the back of the house, a combination of dark wood, flowered upholstery, and ancient, sturdy carpeting. The air smelled of warm wool and medicine. I could hear a parakeet upstairs.

The kitchen was catching the first sun of the day, giving the room a bright, embracing warmth. The woman, who confirmed she was Mrs. Grissom, gestured me to an alcove with a permanently mounted breakfast table lined on either side with a wall bench. It made me think of riding in a train.

"So, you're interested in the Wingates," she stated. She was moving about between the stove and the sink, accumulating the paraphernalia necessary for her tea tray.

"Yes."

"Why?" It wasn't said with any hostility; it was merely direct, which seemed to be Mrs. Grissom's general approach to everything.

"We're investigating a crime, and the Wingates might have some involvement with it. I just need some background, something to help me understand what makes them tick."

She was pouring hot water into the teapot with her back to me. "It must be a pretty serious matter for you to come all this way just for that."

"It is."

She finished pouring and brought the tray over to the table. "You look tired."

I smiled at that. "A little. I've been up all night."

"Would you like a doughnut? I make them myself."

"Thank you. That sounds great."

She crossed over to a cabinet and brought back a Tupperware container filled with dark brown doughnuts. I bit into one and immediately eyed the rest; best doughnut I'd ever tasted, even without a creamy middle.

"Eat all you want." She sat opposite me and began to fill our cups. "Are you going to tell me what's going on, or is this to be a one-way conversation?"

I recognized I was not dealing with some prehistoric busybody, as her neighbor had implied. Whatever Mrs. Grissom had done in her heyday, she hadn't kowtowed to other people. "Bruce Wingate's been murdered."

She didn't pause in her activities, but she stayed silent for a moment. She pushed my cup over to me and looked me in the eye, her face serious. "I'm sorry to hear that. How's Ellie?"

"Hard to tell. She's bottled it up. She also has a guy running interference for her, so it's hard to get close."

"What guy?" The way she pronounced the second word, I could tell she wasn't fond of casual English.

"He's some kind of anti-cult counselor — organizes peer support groups for parents of children who have joined cults. He probably has other irons in the fire, but that's the gist of it."

She nodded. "I'm not surprised. So Julie is mixed in with this?"

"They drove up to Vermont to find her."

"I thought that's what it was. They gave

317

me their keys so I could water the plants and feed the cat."

I was a little disappointed by that. The implication was that Mrs. Grissom and the Wingates were old friends, which made her an unlikely source for objective information.

"Silly mess. All three of them should have run away to separate parts of the country."

I raised my eyebrows questioningly in mid-sip of tea.

"Theirs was the most unnatural-feeling family group I've ever seen."

"Really?"

"I never heard any music from over there, or any laughter, not even any shouting. They never held a party, never had friends over, little Julie never played in the yard with a playmate. Any time I saw them together, they were mostly silent. Who killed Bruce?"

"We don't know. Were you good friends with them?"

"No," she answered immediately. "Nor do I think they had any. I think that was Bruce's doing more than Ellie's. My impression was that he dominated the family."

"How?"

"Oh, you know, seeing them coming and going, it was always, 'Don't get Daddy mad,' 'Daddy wants this done,' 'I've got to get Daddy's dinner ready.' Daddy obviously pulled all the strings. It was more than that, though."

"Oh?" My mouth was half full of doughnut.

Mrs. Grissom looked out the window. "Well, what I've described isn't much different from many homes — my own father was a bit of a disciplinarian. I don't know how to put it, really, except to say that Bruce controlled them. He was with that child all the time, especially when she was a youngster. The only times I saw her in the yard was in his company."

"You mean playing?"

She tilted her head from side to side in a vague gesture. "Playing . . . Some would call it that. I would stand at that window years ago," she indicated the window over the sink, "and watch them together, throwing a ball back and forth or shooting marbles in the driveway. He would constantly instruct her, his face serious, as if what they were doing had long-range, almost grim consequences. Neither one of them laughed or smiled. They would just go through the movements — throwing a ball back and forth, back and forth — without any feeling whatsoever. It was almost as if Bruce had read somewhere that he was supposed to do these things with his daughter and, being a man of sound character, he would therefore do them. There was an utter lack of spontaneity."

"Did you ever suspect there was anything unnatural going on?"

Her eyes opened wide. "You mean child abuse?"

"It happens."

"Yes." She paused a moment, reflecting. "I would have no reason to say that. I certainly sensed that Bruce was the unchallenged authority of that family, which I think is abusive, but in the sense you mean it? I'd have to say I don't know — I wouldn't rule it out."

I figured I'd better stop with the doughnuts and leaned back against the wall, cradling my teacup. I was suddenly struck by a notion. "Do you have anything with Julie's handwriting on it?"

Her brow furrowed in concentration. "No, I don't think so . . ." She looked up abruptly, her eyes bright. "Wait a minute; yes, I do."

She rose and crossed to a bulletin board littered with calendars, notes, photographs, and postcards. "They went on a trip to the Berkshires several years ago and she sent me this." She unpinned one of the postcards and brought it back to me.

On the back was scrawled a brief note describing the weather and the fact she was writing this in a hurry. It was signed, "Julie."

"May I keep this? I can get it back to you later."

"It doesn't matter. I have no sentimental attachment to it."

I slipped it into my pocket wondering if its author had also addressed the envelope that Bruce Wingate had received the night of his death. "You seem to be talking about long ago all the time, when Julie was a little girl. What about recently?"

"I can't say. Once Julie began going to high school, Ellie got a job. Every morning, I'd see them head off in the car — Bruce driving, of course — and that would be that. I assumed he dropped the two women off on his way to work, and picked them up later."

"But school got out before five. What did Julie do in the meantime?"

"I don't know. They always came back together."

"And on the weekends?"

"I never saw much of them. Julie never seemed to have any friends over, or go out on dates, though, if that's what you mean."

"You said you 'thought that was it' when I mentioned they'd gone up to Vermont. Did you know Julie had run away?"

"Yes — Ellie had told me — oh, more than a year ago. She seemed almost embarrassed by the fact, as if Julie's action had brought shame to them all."

Mrs. Grissom leaned back and gave me a long look. "You know, I can't say I was surprised when you told me Bruce was dead. It may sound cruel to say, but I always thought it would take his death to allow the other two any kind of freedom, especially Julie. Knowing that family was like seeing a life raft foundering because it carried one person too many."

Growing up in Thetford, there had been two centers to my life. One was at home, where I was lucky enough to benefit from great comfort and support, and the other was at high school, where my emotional state bounced around as routinely as a basketball in full play. I proceeded to Julie's high school.

The parking lot was full. Mrs. Grissom had told me how to get there, but from then on, I was on my own. I walked to where I thought I might put the administrative offices if I were an architect. I found a chemistry lab instead, filled with surprised, white-coated students and one teacher, who gave me directions.

Once at the principal's office, with much talk and much display of my essentially worthless credentials, I was ushered into a small, bare office to meet a nervous, chain-smoking rail of a woman. After listening to my request to talk with Julie's guidance counselor, she tapped her pencil on the metal-topped desk for a few moments of reflection, then finally gave me the name I needed and further directions to the teachers' lounge.

There, I was met at the door by a fat, balding, pink-cheeked man with an old-fashioned pencil mustache that looked absurdly at sea on his enormous face.

"Mr. Gunther?"

"Yes." We shook hands. His was damp and flaccid.

"Miss Stevens called me on the intercom. You want to ask me about Julie Wingate?"

"That's right." The lounge was a tired, threadbare room, smelling of stale cigarettes and burned coffee. The furniture had been colorful and modern twenty years back; now it was stained and exhausted.

Harvey Mullen led me to a couple of fabric-covered tubular chairs by the window. "Would you like some coffee?"

What I wanted most now was a bathroom. I declined his offer and we both sat, facing each other as if we were at some encounter group. Mullen began rubbing the palm of one hand with the thumb of the other. His eyes blinked, I noticed, with the precision of a clock — once every two seconds.

"I gather you were Julie's advisor."

He nodded a few times too many. "Right."

"What kind of girl was she?"

"Oh, average."

"How do you mean?"

"Well, you know, there was nothing special about her."

"Did she have a lot of friends?"

"I don't know."

Right, I thought Mullen was as obtuse as Mrs. Grissom had been perceptive; too bad their roles in Julie Wingate's life hadn't been reversed. I started over. "What kind of advice do you give students here?"

"All kinds. If they have problems with their grades, I see about tutoring; if it's drugs, I see about counseling. I help them with their college choices, assuming they're interested. I try to find their strengths, so the school can help them out in the best way."

"Julie went to college?"

"B.C." I took that to be Boston College.

"Did she have good grades?"

"So-so."

"What was her strength — was she particularly good at any one subject?"

He pushed out his lower lip for a moment. "No, not really."

"What was she like to talk to? What did you discuss together?"

He gave me another big smile. "Nothing,

oh . . . headaches."

This was starting to get to me. "I'm investigating a murder, Mr. Mullen, which well might involve Julie. Could you be a little more generous with your answers?"

Now he looked hurt. "I'm trying to help. She just never said anything to me. Every time we sat down together, I'd do all the talking and she'd just sit there. The only time she said anything was about headaches."

"What about them?"

"She got them a lot, and she complained to me that the nurse wasn't giving her aspirin anymore, said she was taking too many."

"What did you do?"

"Told the nurse to lighten up. It was just aspirin, after all."

"And that was it? The two of you never spoke about anything else?"

"Not really."

"What about when you discussed college choices?"

"We didn't discuss. She said her father wanted her to go to B.C. and that's where she was going. That was almost the longest talk we ever had."

Mr. Mullen finally did admit that Julie spent more time in art class, under the supervision of Mr. Petrovic, than she did anywhere else in school. Art class became my next stop.

Mr. Petrovic was everything Mr. Mullen was not — tall, slim, thoughtful, concerned, and very aware Julie Wingate was not average in any way.

"She spent every afternoon here, after school let out. She was supposed to be waiting in the library — that's where her father picked her up every day after school — but I let her hang out here. She loved to draw, she was good at it, and she never got in my way. Had she been a little less uptight, it would have been a joy to have her here. I could've felt I was nurturing the creative process, you know? An art teacher's dream. Most of the kids I get here can't paint their fingernails."

"So she kept to herself?"

We were in a large room, mostly empty of furniture aside from dozens of easels and a few pedestals with odd lumps of clay on them. One entire wall was made up of glass windows, and with just the two of us here, it was a little like sitting in a secular church; it reminded me a bit of Sarris's lair.

"She kept to herself, all right, like a volcano with a loose lid."

The image startled me mostly because it fit my image of Bruce Wingate to a T. "Did you ever meet her parents?"

He rolled his eyes. "Oh, yeah. The kid had my sympathies."

His expressions and outlook reminded me a lot of the young jaded cynics who'd grown up in the sixties, the ones who hadn't trusted people over thirty and still didn't, despite being ten years beyond that themselves.

"What were they like?"

His expression turned bitter. "Martinets, both of them, although he was the bandleader. She just sort of tagged along. It was the damnedest parent conference I ever had. You know, some of them just want to know how their kid is doing, others are worried because the little genius isn't painting like Picasso — or maybe he is painting like Picasso and they hate it — but most of them are looking to the teacher for some input. Not this duo. The old bastard basically told me what the kid should be doing and let me know that if she wasn't, it was because I was a shitty teacher. He told me he taught her himself how to paint — and how to read and write, and tell time, and do math, and everything else. I got the feeling he sat on her like a mother hen, telling her how to do everything but pick her nose. It was incredible. I tried to encourage them to let her go a little, let her try some things on her own. He damn near bit my head off."

His eyes were blazing by now. Mullen, who

presumably had received the same treatment from Wingate, hadn't given a damn. Petrovic had probably cared too much. I wondered how many times he'd taken Julie aside and encouraged her to fly on her own — while her parents were holding on for dear life.

"You said Julie was like a volcano with a loose lid. Did she ever explode?"

Petrovic's eyebrows shot up. "You bet. We had to call the ambulance once."

"Why?"

"She flipped out. She took the place apart, smashing equipment, kicking the furniture over. She stuck a palette knife in her arm. It was scary. I was in the room with her, doing something in the far corner; she'd been painting for a couple of hours, wrestling with something. She talked to herself when she got mad, although never loud enough for me to hear what about. Anyhow, this time, all of a sudden, she hit the roof. I didn't even get near her 'til after it was over, you know, to see what I could do for the arm — she'd have taken my head off."

"Did she do this other times?"

"I heard she did. I only saw it that one time."

"What kind of paintings did she do?"

"Mood stuff, at least that's what I call it. Some of her work would be normal, everyday landscapes, portraits, whatever. But then, every once in a while, she'd turn out something dark and pessimistic, like something out of a concentration camp, you know? Introspective and ugly. Powerful, though."

"You keep any of it?"

"I wanted to, but she kept track of it; destroyed it all. She only brought the bland stuff home."

"Did you ever talk to her about all this?"

He hesitated before answering, and I wondered again how much he wasn't telling me. There was an edginess to the man, an element of caution in his eyes. My instinct wasn't to imagine the worst, however, for I'd seen the same expression in other teachers, especially the good ones. Their concern for their charges often overran pure education, spilling over into the personal and becoming possessive. Their frustration with poor parenting often made surrogate parents of them, with all the worries, despair, and occasional pride that entailed.

His voice was hard. "I tried, but she wasn't very receptive. I think her parents had her on too short a leash. Being open with people, or herself, had pretty much been bred out of her."

Before leaving Natick, I stopped by the Police department. The Chief was a man whose Italian name was so complicated, I never did catch it. He was short, wiry, and nervous, with a quick smile and an efficient manner.

He led me into his office, a spacious, well-lit affair with comfortable furniture and good lighting. I grimaced at the thought of the office I'd occupied during the six-month leave of Brattleboro's Chief, directly over the ancient basement boiler that shook the pencils in the cup on my desk.

"So you have no warrant? This is purely courtesy?"

"That's right."

He thought about my request for all of three seconds and then turned to his computer. "Bruce Wingate, right?"

"Right."

He tapped away for a while, paused, tapped some more. I visualized other computers across the state waking up to his knocks on their door, blinking a few times, and then pawing through their own files.

Finally, he leaned back in his chair, his eyes on the screen. "Registered as owning a Smith & Wesson 9 mm, purchased about eight years ago, and a Colt .38, purchased two months ago."

I stared at him for a second, my mind suddenly crowded with voices. "No reports of anything stolen or lost?"

"Nope."

I thought about that for a moment. Wingate had told me he'd noticed the 9 mm was missing when he'd wanted to do some target practice two months ago. He'd then changed that to three years ago. It had struck me an odd mixup to make. Now I understood — the .38 had been bought two months ago, a fact he hadn't wanted to reveal.

I scratched my head. Also, he hadn't said the 9 mm was missing; he'd said he'd *lost* it. "Do you have any record of his reporting the loss or theft of anything else of value?"

The Chief leaned forward and tapped a few keys. "Not directly, but his insurance company let us know, just in case they surfaced — looks like someone broke into his car once a few years back; took the radio, a camera, a coat." He paused and scrolled the screen. "His wife reported a lost ring last year; according to this, it came off her finger in the cold and fell in the snow. We never got any of it back."

What did that tell me? That he either lied about losing the 9 mm — in which case, why did he buy a .38 to replace it? — or he feared that by reporting the loss, he'd get someone in trouble. Someone he was always protecting.

23

I found Mel Hamilton in his office, talking on the phone. From what I could hear, he was still running the manhunt for Rennie, collecting additional troops from every barracks he could.

He hung up and looked at me. His bloodshot eyes were resting on dark, tired pouches. "What's up?"

I handed him my report on the Natick trip. "No luck on Rennie, I guess."

He just shook his head.

I then gave him the postcard Julie Wingate had written to Mrs. Grissom and explained where I'd gotten it. "It's a few years old, so the handwriting may have changed a bit, but it might match the writing on that envelope Wingate received the night he died. I want to dig into Julie Wingate a little bit — background material. We may not have paid enough attention to her. Who have you been using for your background information on the Order? Was that a single source?"

He rubbed his temples with his fingertips.

"No, but I know what you're after — the human interest angle. What the hell's her name? A Dartmouth prof, bit of a nut, according to Appleby . . . Kaufman, Ruth Kaufman."

"What department?"

"Religious Studies or Religion . . . Something like that. She has a degree in anthropology, too, but I don't know how that plays in."

I wrote down her name. "How about a consultant shrink, someone you use for criminal profiling?"

"Barb Barrett, out of Burlington. Good lady. Maybe a little uptight 'til you get to know her. The front desk'll have their numbers."

I thanked him, picked up the numbers, drove to Potter's office, and asked Flo if she could set up a teleconference between Burlington and Hanover, New Hampshire. Two hours later, the earliest convenient time to all parties, I had a phone in my hand and a blank note pad before me.

We introduced ourselves. It turned out the two professors didn't know each other. Kaufman had a surprisingly low voice and a nice laugh; Barrett was more precise — professionally neutral, giving credence to Hamilton's description. I explained what had led me to call them up, that I was faced with a town confronted with several violent deaths and torn by the presence of a cultlike organization. That the possibility existed that at least one member was involved. I then gave details of the Natural Order and of the situation in Gannet.

I laid out my opening question so that both of them might address it from their different vantage points. "What does an outfit like the Natural Order do to encourage a kid to join?"

Barrett spoke first. "I'm not going to answer that until I know more about the Order."

"No problem; that's why Dr. Kaufman's here."

"Ruth, please. Unless I'm grading your papers, call me Ruth."

I noticed Barrett did not extend the same invitation. "I gather you've studied this . . . is it a cult, by the way?"

"I have studied it, and no, I wouldn't call it that, although technically, you could call the Catholic church a cult, or the Republican party, for that matter."

I laughed. Barrett did not. I started regretting I hadn't done this in person.

Kaufman resumed. "But the word has negative connotations, involving rituals, psychological abuse, and a generally unappealing attitude."

"Like Jonestown," I interrupted.

"Right. I've studied The Natural Order for about three years now, and it's a far tamer beast. It still carries a lot of cult baggage, but I've found it to be more benign somehow. Edward Sarris, the leader, is a fairly typical megalomaniac — a man with a mission — and he has surrounded himself with a hierarchy in which only he holds the absolute power. But there is a mitigating element to it all that softens the hard angles."

"Like what?" I asked.

"The environmental aspect, for one. Unlike many of these organizations, which proselytize themselves as alternatives to the establishment, the Order throws in the added backdrop of saving the world. Their enemies are polluters and consumers, rather than religious blasphemers. It's an interesting, off-beat and curiously pragmatic choice. It gives Sarris's group added appeal."

"Okay, but what about the down side? I mean, this isn't Greenpeace."

"Oh no, far from it. That's the beauty of this group. It's either hopelessly cynical or bizarrely idealistic; I suspect a little of both. I do think Sarris's environmental concerns are quite genuine — he was once a fully tenured professor with an activist background — but I also think he found a way to practice them that makes him the master of a virtual harem. His contention is that humans do not mate for life; that they are designed, emotionally and biologically, to mate at random, as much for sex as for replication. So Sarris breaks up any shows of strong affection, especially between male/female couples. He often takes a temporary fill-in role himself with the woman. As a male, he must have to pinch himself at night, wondering if this is a dream come true."

She chuckled a little at that. "The treatment of the children bolsters this. They are brought up by the group as a whole, rather than by their natural parents. That way, they are more easily influenced by the group ideology and are removed from the adult male/female bonding process. The children are continuously shuttled around from couple to couple for lodging. And, of course, the couples themselves are in constant flux. The idea is to reduce adult relationships to the purely sexual or communal, as in working together for the common good."

"What about the other men? Where do they fit in?"

"It's like a pyramid, with Sarris at the top, holding power over them all — males and females. Below him are what you might call Elders or lieutenants, people who have stuck with him a long time and have accumulated a certain amount of power, some of it official, some not. Below them, you get a kind of new guys-old guys hazing relationship, where people who have been inside awhile hold sway over the newcomers. Now the males higher in the hierarchy exercise control over the lesser males by taking their women and by assigning menial tasks; the women, who are essentially without official status in this setting, achieve status by sleeping with powerful males, and supplanting one another in the process. It's an incredibly complex society, almost entirely directed by interpersonal relationships rather than, say, competence, rank, or age, barring Sarris and a few of his inner circle. It's kind of like saying that only the blond can lead in a world of redheads. 'Course, I'm trespassing here."

"How about it, Dr. Barrett? Any arguments?"

There was a small pause. "I think it's always misleading to superimpose our own values onto a personality like Mr. Sarris's. People in his position — that is, leaders who live among their followers on a day-to-day basis — usually can't afford our cynicism. It would trip them up sooner or later. What we see as opportunism might well be a form of spiritual expression."

Kaufman laughed, which made me wince,

but Barrett joined her. "I know, it's a little hard to swallow, and it may not be true in this case. You disagree, Dr. Kaufman?"

"No, no . . . Well, maybe a bit. I think a good part of him is just plain horny and self-serving."

"Okay," I said once the laughter died down. "That takes care of Sarris. Now what about the people he recruits?"

"That covers a lot of territory," Barrett hesitated.

"Well, try it in general terms first, and then I'll get very specific, down to one person, in fact."

"Okay . . ." There was a moment's silence as she collected her thoughts. "The kind of people we're talking about, the ones that stick it out in a cult, or whatever you want to call this group, tend to seek an authoritarian environment, be it military service, or a state hospital, or a cult. The irony is that they're often looking for exactly what they've run away from at home."

I perked up at that. "From authoritarian parents, you mean."

"Stern, overprotective, or downright abusive parents. In any case, the kids you're talking about — although they aren't all kids — often come from stifling homes, homes in which the parents exercise absolute control over their children. These kids, as a result, yearn for independence, but are incapable of making decisions on their own. So they run from home and head for a life on the streets, or to outfits like The Order, places where they can just *be,* without having to be responsible, and where they can focus on an authority figure — orderly, street cop, drill sergeant, cult leader, whatever — who is not their parent. Indeed, cult recruiters often comb the streets for just these types."

"And the college campuses."

"Yes, there, too, but for slightly different types. The college recruits share many of the same characteristics as the people I mentioned, but they're less apparent — the mental illness aspects have often been hidden by other, more socially acceptable sobriquets, like 'high-strung,' 'moody' . . ."

"Or 'uptight,' " I said, remembering Petrovic's word for Julie.

"Precisely. The higher educated, wealthier elements of our society are sometimes far more deluded and dishonest about these things than the street people."

"Okay, I have a specific person in mind, a single child — a girl. She's in her early twenties, is now in the Order, and her parents have come looking for her. From what I could interpret from people who knew her in high school and before, it sounds like life at home was suffocating: She didn't have friends; her father was constantly hovering over her, and she had chronic headaches and explosive temper tantrums, times when she would just flip out. Her art teacher said she was extremely moody, sometimes painting normal scenes, sometimes turning out what he called concentration-camp art, which she then apparently destroyed.

"She even stabbed herself once. In fact, that was interesting. The art teacher witnessed that — and called the ambulance — and he seemed to imply that the self-stabbing calmed her down. Can you make anything of that?"

"Not legally."

"This is off the record; just the three of us."

There was a heavy sigh at the other end. "I almost hate to say anything. On the face of it, without knowing this girl or anything more about her, I'd guess you might be dealing with a borderline personality. That's a very strong 'might,' by the way. I have no way of knowing for sure. I'm merely going by the vague signposts you described."

"What's a borderline personality?"

"A pretty unpleasant type, actually. It's a little unclear whether they develop or are born with their personality disorder, but their primary driving force is rage."

"Sounds charming," Kaufman said softly.

"Hardly. Your mention of the violent temper tantrums would fit here, as would the headaches and the suffocating, isolated home life. They are often hyperactive, difficult to manage and impulsive, and when their fuse is lit, they blow sky-high."

"Doesn't sound like someone like that would last three days in a cult." I also had never heard any mention of hyperactivity in Julie; in fact, my reading had been that she was unusually repressed and quiet.

"On the contrary; a cult might be just the place. Borderlines are not happy with their condition. Their lives are often solely directed at finding a solution. But without proper guidance, they're likely to seek help from strong disciplinarians. You remember when the solution to a 'problem child' was to send it off to the French Foreign Legion or the Marines? The old 'They'll straighten you out' school? Often the borderline himself will try to apply the same sort of medicine. They have the sense that since they can't control their own rage, they ought to find an environment that will do it for them."

"So how do they function?" Kaufman asked, by now thoroughly caught up in the conversation. "Request regular beatings?

Sounds like they're in search of accommodating sadists."

"Quite the contrary. They internalize their rage. Usually the people around them haven't the slightest idea that they are half-consumed with anger. Remember, having chosen their surroundings, they try to conform; they follow the rules and regulations precisely and often stand out as exemplary citizens. The cost of all this is on the inside. They hate themselves — growing up, they've often been told repeatedly that they're bad, even 'evil' — and so once in place in their chosen society, they often turn their rage on themselves, sometimes even cutting themselves again and again as self-punishment. Your mention of the self-inflicted wound thus becomes relevant. But I would like to stress again, Lieutenant, that this is all hypothetical. We may be talking of someone who's hysterical, schizophrenic, clinically depressed, or any number of other things."

I was listening, but I didn't want to get sidetracked. "Are borderlines suicidal?"

"No, well, they can end up that way, but generally pain is the goal, not death. Often, they regularly slice themselves, usually in places that can't be seen; they become quite adept at it. I've had borderline patients who were literally covered with scars, but not where it showed when they were fully dressed. Incidentally, since the subject of sex has been mentioned, these people often also engage in painful sex."

"Can this desire for pain be turned around? Can they harm others?"

"Anyone can. Little old ladies have been known to summon homicidal instincts at just the wrong moment. Obviously, someone who whittles on her arm or leg every night is going to have a violent personality. Do borderlines kill? No more than other people."

After I hung up the phone, I pulled Julie Wingate's picture from my pocket and studied it.

That bland, sullen face merely looked back at me, unanswering.

24

I'd spent the day far from the center of action in this case, and yet I felt now that new possibilities had been introduced like a truckload of bricks at a building site; they weren't part of any clearly defined structure yet, but they had all the makings of a firm foundation.

Now Wingate's death was the possible accumulation of years of pent-up anger. If Wingate had killed Fox and the others, and if Fox and Julie had been lovers, Julie's motivation for revenge was iron-clad.

Wingate had told me his 9 mm had gone missing just about the time Julie left for college. Had that been a coverup, or had Julie stolen her father's gun? Wingate's recent purchase of the .38 certainly bolstered that theory.

But if Julie had the 9 mm, and killed her father in the ravine, why had she used a knife? And why had a 9-mm shell, with Wingate's print, turned up in the fire-gutted house? And who were the other people in that ravine?

I turned away from my desk and stared out the window. Edward Sarris controlled the lives of almost half the population of Gannet. Was he behind all this? Did he use Julie to lure her father to a meeting, and then take over from there? That might explain Julie's vanishing act; she might be under lock and key somewhere. Or she might be dead.

And what did Rennie have to do with any of it? And if he had been deliberately framed, then by whom? And why?

I rubbed my eyes with my palms. The problem was, that even with the additional facts I'd dug up on the Wingate family, we still didn't have enough information to draw any conclusions. The truckload of bricks I'd visualized earlier were still jumbled in a useless pile.

We needed more to go on — to find the missing pieces that might act as a blueprint. I knew for a fact that Rennie was in the middle of all this for some reason I didn't understand.

It suddenly occurred to me there was at least one man from whom I might get some answers.

Pete Chaney's place wasn't hard to find. His store was advertised with a big sign — PETE'S MARKET — right on Route 114 in East Burke. The place had the shopworn look of a local hangout, its outside walls papered with posters of local events, new and ancient, its entrance cluttered with several sleeping dogs, the parking area half-filled with patched-up pickup trucks. The market part was actually the front of a residence, an aggravated hallway extending the breadth of the building, each wall jammed with sagging shelves of boxed and canned goods. Opposite the creaking front door, there was an ice-cream freezer with a counter behind it supporting the cash register, a large coffee maker, and a wide assortment of plastic-wrapped, inedible-looking doughnuts. There were several men in stained work clothes standing around the coffee machine chatting and drinking coffee, making passage to the rest of the place a challenge. Considering the instant but brief attention my entrance made, I mentally pitied any good-looking shy woman who might blunder in here unprepared.

Behind the counter was a small, round man with an enormous nose and a single eyebrow, who greeted me with a friendly wave of a beefy hand. "Hi there, what can I do you for?"

"You Pete Chaney?"

One of the other men let out a whoop. "Watch it, Pete — you're in trouble now."

The others laughed as Chaney nodded, his smile fading.

"I'm with the State Attorney's office. I was wondering if we could have a chat."

More hoots followed that. "Better call your lawyer, Pete — chats from those guys last from five to ten years."

Chaney made a face. "Sit on it, you clowns." He gestured to me to follow. "We can talk back here."

He led me behind the counter to a door which opened to the rest of the house. We stepped into an evil-smelling, ill-lit den of sorts with a TV in one corner, a half-smashed coffee table listing in the middle of the room, and an assortment of stained, disemboweled stuffed furniture shoved up against the walls.

There might have been a rug, or even a floor underfoot, but it was invisible under the layers of old newspapers, magazines, paper plates, discarded clothing, and various mysterious piles, the identification of which was impossible in the gloom.

"Have a seat." Chaney sank back into a sofa that damn near swallowed him whole.

I settled more gingerly on the edge of an armchair. I didn't want to call for a winch later to help me to my feet. "You've spoken with the State Police a couple of times already."

"Yeah."

"Well, this is a followup."

He looked at me quizzically, but with very watchful eyes. "You guys don't talk to each other?"

"Your problem is we talk too well to each other." I'd decided on the way here that bluffing was about the only trick left in my bag.

"I'm going to ask you roughly the same questions you've been asked before, but you're going to give me totally different answers. Okay?"

His tongue quickly passed across his lips. "Why would I do that?"

"Because you've been lying so far."

Chaney's face darkened. Otherwise, he didn't move.

"One more thing: You have the right to remain silent, because anything you say might be used against you in a court of law."

His mouth fell open. "Am I under arrest?"

I put my thumb and forefinger about an inch apart. "You're that close. You want to talk?"

"Sure, I got nothing to hide."

"Was Rennie here last Wednesday?"

"No."

"Where was he?"

"How would I know?"

"Why did you claim he was here?"

"He's a friend. I thought it might help."

"Pete, you're on a slippery bank, heading toward deep shit. Covering for Rennie is stupid. He's wanted on a murder charge now, which makes you a possible accessory. Covering yourself will just cause a delay that I'll make sure you pay for."

"I didn't actually say he was here *last* Wednesday."

"You said he was here Wednesdays. How about that? Is that true?"

He turned his head and scratched an ear, crossed his arms, shuffled his feet.

"Was he ever here on a Wednesday night?"

"No."

"So where was he?"

"Around. It depended . . . sometimes on

348

the weather, you know."

I stood up, grateful I could do it with a certain controlled violence, instead of having to ask for a rope out of the seat. "Okay, you want to talk weather? Fine. Let's close this place down and spend the next few days talking about it somewhere less comfortable."

He looked up at me, his hands spread out and his eyes pleading. "What do you want? I'm talking; I'm telling you what I know."

"You're giving me grunts and groans, playing twenty questions. I don't have the patience for that. You start talking now, or I'll hand you more legal problems than you've ever dreamed of."

"He got his rocks off every Wednesday night, all right? He was fucking around on his wife and he got me to cover his ass in case anyone asked."

"Who was he seeing?"

"Hell, I don't know. Different people."

"Give me some names."

"They don't got names — not normal ones."

The effect of his words was like being hit with cold water. "Rennie was fooling around with women from the Order?"

"Yeah."

A crucial — and for me, a feared — connection had just been made. Was this enough motive for Rennie to stab Bruce Wingate at the bottom of that ravine? I sat back down. "Did anyone else know about his affairs? Anyone in the Order?"

"Sarris knew."

"Sarris?"

"Sure, he set it up. Rennie made a deal with him."

"What kind of deal?"

"I don't know exactly. Rennie wouldn't tell me. He said he had something on The Elephant, something that could shut him down. Rennie told me he was set for life; any of those cunts he wanted he could have."

"Did you ever meet the women?"

Chaney did his shuffle routine again instead of answering.

I tried a friendlier, more companionable tone. "Rennie and I grew up together, Pete. He's one of my oldest friends. Now right now, the state cops are crawling all over the place looking to nail him for that stabbing the other day. You think he did it?"

"Murder a guy? No way."

"I don't think he did, either," I said with false conviction. "But we're a minority, and unless I can find out who did, they're going to nail him, and maybe you with him."

"That's bullshit." But he didn't say it with much assurance.

"You think so?" I stood up, my voice suddenly harsh. "Then let's stop right now. You can deal with the State Police yourself."

He wearily motioned me to sit. "Yeah, he brought one of 'em here."

"Why here?"

"Maybe I told him I didn't want to cover his tail when he was gettin' all the action. So he brought the first one over, like a peace offering."

"Who was she?"

His voice went up a note. "How do I know? I sure wasn't goin' to mess with her."

I was becoming impatient. "What the hell's that mean? You were the one who asked for her."

He glared at me sulkily. "She was a real nut — into S&M. She liked to be hit, had scars all over her, like she'd been in an accident. They did it and I watched for a while, but I finally threw 'em out. Told Rennie to keep 'em all to himself."

"So there were others?"

"Hell, yes. He dumped that one later, but he was hooked. I told him I wasn't interested anymore." Chaney looked half-embarrassed by the admission.

There was a lull in the conversation as Pete Chaney studied his dirty knuckles. I felt weighed down inside. Part of my early enthusiasm in this case, I suddenly realized, stemmed from my desire to establish Rennie's innocence. Subconsciously perhaps, I'd seen myself as the prodigal returning, showing my affection for the town of Gannet by freeing one of its prominent citizens from scandal.

Reluctantly, I pulled the xerox copy of Julie Wingate's picture from my pocket and showed it to Chaney. "That the woman?"

He peered at it in the gloomy light. "Yeah, I think so. She looks a little fatter here. There wasn't much to her when I saw her." He shook his head.

"Did you ever see her again?"

"Not her or anyone else. Rennie took me at my word and never brought any of 'em around again."

"How long ago was all this?"

"I don't know — a while."

"A month? A year?"

"Half a year."

"Are you sure he dumped her?"

"That's what he said. He had his pick. No need to get hung up on one of 'em."

"And how did this little cover work, the Wednesday night thing?"

"Usually he took them to the firehouse in Gannet. That way, if someone called him here, I could say he was taking a shit and would call right back, or something like that, and

352

then I'd call him at the firehouse and let him know."

"That happen often?"

"Not too much — sometimes."

"And he always went to the firehouse? What about if they had a fire all of a sudden?"

"Didn't matter. He had a deal set up in the attic. A mattress on the floor, pillows, stuff like that. If the siren went off, he'd just stay put. Never happened anyway."

I made a face. "I know that attic — must have been hotter than hell in the summer."

"He said it was sexy. Anyway, he had a fan set up in the back window, where you couldn't see it from the street. Before he figured out about the attic, he used to go out in the woods — he had a spot."

"Where?"

"Off the end of Lemon Road. There's a kind of rock point that sticks out of the mountainside. You gotta go through the woods a few hundred feet to reach it — it's like a picnic rock. Nobody knows about it."

"You do."

"It used to be a hangout of mine. I told him about it when he was lookin' for a place to get laid. At the beginning I took my phone off the hook and claimed it was out of order, or I took a message and then said I forgot to give it to him. It didn't happen 'cept once in a blue moon. He didn't really even need the attic deal and me calling him up. I just think it made him feel smart, that he had all the angles covered . . . Asshole."

I stood up, feeling like hell. It was almost as if the Rennie I knew had died — a long time ago. How could he have done that to Nadine? I was struck by a sense of bewildered loss. "You've helped yourself a lot with this, Pete. The police or I or somebody will come back and get it all down for the record later."

He didn't look too pleased at the prospect.

I paused as I headed for the door. "What about your end? What did you get out of it?"

He was still sitting there, like a fat egg on a pillow, his hands in his lap. He seemed as bereft as I was. He shook his head. "I didn't get shit out of it — none of it was worth it. We used to play cards together — way back. He was a good guy. But all this stuff ruined everything. I hardly knew him anymore."

25

It gave me little satisfaction to have finally solved the riddle of Rennie's involvement with Bruce Wingate — that there'd been something more than a brief flare-up between the two of them. Had Rennie's affair with Julie continued without Pete Chaney's knowledge? Maybe Rennie had taken care of Wingate as a favor to Julie. And what did Rennie have on Sarris that Sarris would kowtow to him in the first place? Maybe Rennie was innocent of Wingate's murder and Sarris set him up — killing two birds with one stone, as it were. Much as I'd been disillusioned by Rennie's behavior, I still hoped the latter scenario might be closer to the truth.

I was walking into State Police barracks to file the report on my chat with Chaney when Mel Hamilton met me in the lobby. "I just called your office — your secretary said you were headed this way. You might like to come along."

"What's up?" I handed the report to the receptionist.

"They found Rennie Wilson's truck west of Hartwellville on Lemon Road. They think whoever was in the truck headed off into the bush. I'm having Fish and Game send a tracker to meet them."

The trip was fast and lugubrious. Hamilton took a patrol car so he could use his blue lights and siren as necessary. He also had to use his headlights, although it was still midafternoon. The air was misty, greasing the road and reducing visibility, and the clouds hung so low that the hilltops vanished from view. The light was gray and dull, and sudden patches of ground mist lingered menacingly in odd places, as if dropped by accident from the bruised and glowering sky. It suited my mood and helped color my expectations of what we might find in the vicinity of Rennie's truck. During the trip, I filled Hamilton in on what I'd discovered at Pete Chaney's.

Lemon Road doesn't really lead anywhere. It branches off Radar Road out of Hartwellville, starts out paved, turns to dirt, and then just peters out on the heavily wooded slope of East Haven Mountain. It's not very long, has only a house or two at its start, and leaves the impression of some half-forgotten municipal project whose planners ran out of both ambition and funds. Rennie's truck was parked at the end, its right wheels in a shallow ditch and its body half-covered with broken branches and dead leaves, a camouflage job either half-completed or half-cleared away.

Spinney's unmarked sedan and a patrol car were parked in a line on the opposite side of the road. We pulled in behind them to lessen the number of extraneous tire marks in the dirt. A trooper I didn't know was standing nervously near the pickup, his right hand picking at the yellow stripe that ran down the outside seam of his dark green uniform pants; Spinney was stretched out on the hood of his car, his back against the windshield. He snapped a salute from that position as Hamilton and I got out of our car. I could tell from Hamilton's expression he wasn't pleased with the informality.

Obviously, even Spinney got the message. He slid off the car and gave a boyish smile to both of us. "Car hood was keeping me warm."

Hamilton smiled back and placed his hand on the car, warm vapor escaping from his mouth as he spoke. "I hadn't thought of that. Fish and Game ought to be here pretty soon; you come up with anything new?"

"Not here. We looked in the truck without disturbing anything, but there's nothing unusual. You can see where the grass has been flattened leading into the woods. I didn't want to risk messing things up."

Hamilton nodded. "No, no. I think that's right. How long do you think the truck's been here?"

"Hard to tell. Engine was cold; there was frost on the windshield. A blind guess would be last night sometime, but that's mostly because I figure Joe saw him last around 2300 hours and he must have driven here soon after."

The lieutenant nodded again and shivered slightly. "Cold," he muttered, and wandered over to the truck, greeting the trooper as he passed.

"You get any sleep?" I said.

"Some — still feel like shit, though. You figure this mess out yet?"

"No, but it prompted me to talk to Pete Chaney again." I gave Spinney the abbreviated version.

Hamilton came back as I finished. "Makes you wonder how many other people are involved in this case."

I laughed at that, but without any humor. I was just grateful that both of them had restrained from saying, "I told you so." My conversation with Chaney put Rennie right in the middle of this case: He wasn't the framed local bystander anymore, even in my own mind.

While there still wasn't proof he'd killed Bruce Wingate, it wasn't so farfetched to assume Rennie might've had a serious personal grudge.

My bitter ruminations were interrupted by a muffled, grinding, metallic sound from down the road.

"That must be Fish and Game."

A somewhat battered Ford 150 four-wheel drive lumbered up the road and stopped behind my car. The Fish and Game emblem — what hadn't been scratched off by too many encounters with brush and low branches — was emblazoned on the door. A man in a dark green uniform with black epaulettes and breast-pocket flaps piped in scarlet stepped out onto the road. He was somewhere in his forties, tall, very lean and muscular, and wore a .357 Magnum on his belt. Looking at him, I felt like Elmer Fudd next to a young Burt Lancaster. He nodded to us, looking around briefly, seemingly cataloging the scene in his mind. Then, still not having said a word, he walked silently and gracefully up to us and shook hands, barely murmuring his greeting. His deep-set blue eyes, contrasting with a tan face and dark brown hair, were startlingly sharp. If I hadn't seen him drive up, I would have thought him capable of just appearing from the woods, much like the deer that were pictured on both his shoulder patches.

Hamilton made the introductions. "This is Lieutenant John Bishop. He's been with Fish and Game for over twenty years and is probably one of the best trackers they have."

Bishop shook his head slightly, downplaying the compliment. "What've you got?"

Hamilton waved at Rennie's truck. "Owner of that's wanted for questioning in a murder. He disappeared yesterday. Wiley here," he nodded at the trooper, "found the truck about an hour ago."

Bishop nodded and walked a few steps toward the truck, his head bent, watching the ground. He stopped a few feet from it and crouched, looking underneath. "Any of you walk around here?"

Wiley spoke up first. "I went to the driver's door, then around to the other side, just to see if anyone was maybe in the ditch. But that was it."

"You walk around the front or the back?"

"Front."

"Anyone else?"

"I did about the same thing," Spinney admitted. "I also looked inside, using the driver's door."

Bishop placed his hand on the truck's hood and then stepped away, coming back toward us. "Well, it was parked here last night." He looked at both Wiley and Spinney. "Could I see the bottoms of your shoes?"

Both men turned and lifted their feet up for Bishop to see. He nodded after a few seconds of study. "Thanks, I just want to rule them out — don't want to mix them up with other prints."

He walked out to the middle of the road and crouched again, scanning the surface with those careful eyes. He got up, moved a bit, crouched. He did that several more times before nodding to himself. The nodding was something I learned he did a lot, the gesture of a man who spends much time alone in serious conversation with himself.

He crossed over to his truck and retrieved a camera, a large knife that he attached to his belt, and a tape recorder, into which he muttered several notes. He glanced over at us, clustered together, looking back at him. "Saves on time and paper. I type it up at the office."

He pointed to the road. "You had two vehicles here last night. One of them parked over there, and then turned around later and left in no big hurry."

He returned to Rennie's truck, this time from the rear, and got down on one knee near the exhaust pipe. He muttered something to himself I didn't catch and strode quickly to the driver's door again, this time opening it and looking in.

He slammed the door and faced us. "Well, that explains why the branches and leaves were taken off the front — the engine was running, and whoever did it didn't want too much heat to build up and cause a fire."

I scratched the back of my neck. "Why run the truck half-covered with leaves and junk?"

"The lights are on, or they were until the gas ran out and the battery died, and they're aimed right to where the tracks lead off into the woods. I guess he was lighting the way, or maybe just showing which way to go. That's not a good sign, by the way."

Hamilton said it. "Why not?"

Spinney answered. " 'Cause it means he meant to come back and turn off the engine and never did."

I'd understood instantly, too, and it opened a void deep within me. Over the last several days, I'd had to relinquish much of what I'd held dear of my memories of Rennie and of Gannet. What had been planned as a spiritual homecoming was fast becoming a wake.

Bishop gave a small smile and ducked his head slightly. "Right you are."

He followed the erstwhile path of the headlights to the edge of the woods, where the road petered out. "More bad news. Three sets of prints head off here; only two come back, both leading to where the other vehicle was parked."

We walked toward him as a group, but he stopped us. "Tell you what. I'd like your company — all except Wiley — but I'd like you to follow my tracks and not these." He pointed at the ground where, to be honest, I hadn't seen much from the start. "Wiley, I'd like you to stay here to watch the truck and to act as liaison between us and your car radio. That okay, Lieutenant?"

Hamilton nodded. I noticed Wiley seemed relieved as he tramped back to his unit — and its heater. Hamilton, Spinney, and I tucked ourselves into Bishop's wake as he led the way into the woods.

Now in his element, and in obvious control, Bishop became as talkative as he'd been quiet earlier. Bending over at the waist, frequently dropping to one knee, switching suddenly from one bearing to another and back again, he chatted freely about what he was seeing, his eyes rarely leaving the ground. I was tempted to think of him as a hunting dog on the scent, but somehow the image didn't stick. The gun, the quiet, unemotional voice, and the sheer litheness of his movements lent him a more lethal air. There was an element of limitless determination to him — a rare thing in a human being, and a potentially dangerous one.

"The owner of the truck went first — alone. The other two followed later, and not too well at that; not too used to walking in the woods. Look at this — you can see where one of them tripped. And over there, the other one did it; looks like a woman or a small, light man, maybe a teenager. The lights must have been left on for them, although they wouldn't have been much good for more than a few feet. That part still doesn't make much sense to me."

I was staring at where he was pointing. All I saw were minute disturbances in the leaves, a slightly rolled twig, a tiny smudge in the dirt. "How can you tell the other two followed later?"

Bishop pointed to a spot on the ground. "Heel marks are the easiest to spot. All the weight comes down on them, at least when you're on flat ground or going down hill. And you see where there's like a tiny skid mark from the top of the heel mark to the bottom? That indicates the direction they're taking . . . It's a little hard on this partly frozen ground. Okay, there's another one, but it's on top of the first, so obviously it came along behind."

"I can see that, but the time thing —"

Bishop straightened and pointed behind us, back toward the road. "See how we've been walking? All in a line? That's normal in the woods, especially stuff that's pretty thick like here. Now the first guy came pretty much like we did — straight ahead, and along that row of small, white birch trees there. The other two wandered some. They went to the other side of those trees, and over there they got into a bit of tangle, so they backed out and went the other way. All that indicates, by the way, that they were in tight formation, the little guy following the larger one. Here they crossed the first guy's tracks, but they didn't keep on 'em; they wobbled off instead slightly to the left. They wouldn't do that if all three had been in Indian file. I also think the first guy knew the area like the back of his hand, while the second two obviously didn't, but that might be stretching things a little."

We came to a depression, a wet-bottomed swale that might have once been a small creek or a runoff during the rainy season. Bishop held up his hand and went ahead, going up and down the edge of this area. He stopped suddenly, far off to the left, and straightened, looking ahead and behind. Then he took his knife out and slashed a foot-long blaze on a small tree beside him.

"What the hell's he doing?" Spinney muttered next to me.

Bishop, now bent almost in half, had begun walking slowly in circles around the tree he'd marked, reaching out in an ever-widening spiral. Around and around he went, slowly and purposefully.

Spinney pointed to the damp depression ahead. "Even I can see the tracks through that, coming and going, even on the rocks where they left muddy footprints."

Hamilton smiled. "Don't worry. We've worked a lot with this guy. He's so good it's creepy."

Bishop had stopped his circles. He seemed to be backtracking on a parallel course, about twenty feet away from ours, frequently marking trunks as he went. Through the forest of bare trees, we could see him heading back toward the road, his green uniform barely distinguishable from his cold and gloomy surroundings. I looked up at the dark, swollen clouds, seemingly just beyond the reach of the uppermost branches. I didn't like the additional clammy feeling that was beginning to creep inside me, like a confirmation of my fears.

Finally, he came back to us, returning to the edge of the swale. "Found a fourth guy."

We all looked at one another, but stayed

silent. If he'd had more to add, we knew, he would have.

We followed him across some stepping stones, slightly above the tracks Spinney had pointed out. On the far side, where the trees clustered together again, he stopped and let out a grunt of surprise.

We followed his look. Tied to a tree, about chest-high, was one of those mini-mag lights. Its reflector top had been entirely removed, so that its halogen bulb stood exposed at the top, making it look like a miniature lighthouse. The bulb was not burning.

"I'll be damned," he said, looking back the way we'd come. "That explains the truck lights." He twisted and pointed ahead. "If I'm right, we'll either find more of these, or something like it, until we get to the place they intended on meeting."

We could no longer see the end of the road from here; the trees had accumulated enough to totally block the view, but we could have seen the glow from a pair of car lights at night. "He was guiding the way," I muttered.

Bishop grinned. "Right — back and forth. That's why the top's off this light, so you can see it from both directions. The first guy must have told the second two to bring a flashlight, and to pick their way from light to light."

"Why not just escort them from the road?

367

Or just meet at the road and have done with it?" Hamilton asked, half to himself.

"He's a wanted man," I answered. "This rig allows him to see if there's more than his guests coming."

"And it lets him fade away into the night while the other two're picking their way back," Spinney added.

"It didn't work, though," Hamilton said. "There's the fourth guy."

There was a moment's silence. Bishop filled it quietly. "I think that's because the fourth guy was trailing the first one, not the other two. He didn't need this," he pointed at the light in the tree, "because he could see the first guy's flashlight as he set this whole thing up. Also, he's a natural: From what I can find of his tracks, he's spent a lot of time in the woods; knows just where to walk. He barely left a single sign behind, even in that muddy area — he rigged a rope with a grappling hook on one end from one tree to another and went hand over hand there."

Bishop headed off at a faster clip, surer now of what he was trailing. He still made occasional side trips, but obviously for confirmation only. In fifteen minutes, we stepped out of the woods onto a large, moss-covered rock outcropping, stuck like a giant's foothold onto the side of the mountain slope. To our left, the slope continued up; to our right, it angled past and below the rock ledge, creating a twenty-foot drop straight down to a tangle of thick brush and small trees. The entire hike had taken us almost an hour, although we had probably covered no more than four hundred feet.

The view extended due west for almost a mile, its dramatic effect gloomily heightened by the low, threatening cloud cover.

Bishop had stepped ahead, not far from the edge, and now dropped to one knee. "You better stay where you are for a bit here, while I look around."

Hamilton picked up on his cautious tone. "What'd you find?"

"Blood."

Again, he began moving in ever-widening circles around the spot he'd marked with a red handkerchief. I noticed he had several more of other colors sticking out of his two back pockets.

He stopped right at the edge of the cliff and looked over for a while. "If you want, why don't you stand over here and keep an eye on me. I'm going to cut around to the bottom and see what I can find."

The three of us did as he asked, as he moved left toward the mountain, gained the slope, and then cut around to the area below us. He went very slowly, muttering into his tape recorder, once or twice taking a picture, while we scanned the bushes and undergrowth for any movement. None of us had missed the possibility that if two people had come and gone, and another was fatally lacking the blood Bishop had found, then the fourth, whose return to the road still hadn't been documented, might still be out here, watching.

Bishop finally stopped directly below us, where the brush was particularly thick. Had it not been for his movements, we might have lost sight of him entirely. We saw his face look up at us.

"Lieutenant, I think you better get down here. You, too, Lieutenant Gunther."

During our slow-motion trek through the woods, we had filled him in on our suspicions about Rennie, along with the fact that he and I had almost grown up together. There was little doubt in my mind now that Bishop wanted me as well as Hamilton because I knew best what Rennie looked like. I was no tracker, but I had seen the torn moss at the cliff's edge, and had recognized from the broken shrubs and twigs sticking from the rock face that something heavy had brushed against it on the way down.

It was Rennie, of course, at least most of him. His body had been sliced from belly to mid-chest, giving him a crude similarity to a gutted deer.

He was lying on his side, facing me, his head pointing downhill, his eyes half open and dry. There was brush and dirt in his mouth and left ear, and I noticed a tiny insect crawling across his pupil. Even during the war, where I'd seen more dead people than I'll ever see again, I didn't remember anyone appearing quite so lifeless. Rennie looked tossed away, like some ancient discredited rag doll that had been thrown from a passing car.

Bishop was watching my face. "Wilson?"

"Yup." I squatted down, my forearms on my thighs. Because of his position, the blood had pooled to his head, giving him a florid color, much as he'd had when he'd gotten angry in the past.

I'd been preparing for this, certainly since I'd heard his truck had been found and maybe, subconsciously, even before. But this was a death in fact. I realized, watching this dead body, that I'd been mourning his loss long before that knife had ripped him open. Still, now that it was real, I missed him, and what he represented to me, terribly.

"You okay?" Hamilton asked.

I nodded. Dead people have such a different look to them, even if they've been tidied up. I could see where the concept of the soul had won acceptance over the centuries; it really did look as though something had fled this man, something that had once given him more than what lay before me now. Now, he was something busted up and filled with dirt; then, he'd been an active, cantankerous, opinionated, obscene and very honest friend. That man was gone — and maybe had been gone for years.

I stood back up. "Yeah, I'm okay. What do you think happened?"

"The tracks of the two that came together never show any speed. They stumbled around a lot, not being used to the dark and the woods, but they came in slow and left slow. Remember their tire marks? They drove away slow, too. I'd guess they had their meeting with your friend here, and then left him alive, picking their way back to the car following those lights. It wasn't 'til after they'd gone that the fourth guy came out of hiding."

Bishop pointed to the rock shelf above us, from where Spinney was still watching us. "They didn't have much of a fight up there. It looks pretty much like the fourth guy just came up and let him have it with enough force to pitch him right over the edge."

"From the front or the back?"

"I didn't want to move him or mess around much, but I don't see any blood on his back.

'Course, he may have a big hole on his right side — the M.E.'ll have to tell you that."

"What else?" Hamilton asked.

"The killer came down here, probably to check his work. His tracks lead off back toward the road, but lower down the mountain than the way we came. While there's light left, I'd kinda like to find out where he headed. I'm betting we'll find tire tracks further back on the road than where the other two cars were."

Hamilton gestured in that direction. "Be my guest."

We returned to the ledge and Hamilton told Spinney what Bishop had found. We radioed Wiley and told him to activate support troops, the Crime Lab, and the local medical examiner. The three of us then returned the way we'd come. I figured if everyone got here in an hour, which would be pretty surprising, they'd only have an hour or two left of daylight in which to work.

Some unhappy troopers were going to wind up pulling all-night guard duty in the cold, in the dark, and in the middle of nowhere. As for Rennie, he was beyond caring. The gloom and the frost would settle on him and lay claim to a body whose soul, I now believed, had been ailing for a long, long time.

26

It had been dark for over two hours before Hamilton and I finally left Lemon Road ourselves and headed back to St. Johnsbury. He wasn't a man prone to chattiness, but I could tell by his grim demeanor that Hamilton was distinctly unhappy. The hope of nabbing Rennie and putting this entire case to bed had just turned into smoke, and the latest crime promised to whip the press into a frenzy. Indeed, it was partially in an effort to control what information might reach the media that he'd called a mandatory, all-hands meeting at State Police barracks.

But before we even pulled off Route 5, I knew the lid had already blown sky-high. The entire front of the barracks was bathed in television lights, and a crowd of people was standing around the parking lot, forming a gauntlet I would have paid money to avoid.

Hamilton gently nosed the car into a space, moving through the crowd like a farmer among chickens. As soon as we'd slammed our doors, the lights swung over to blind us.

"Lieutenant, apparently you and the deceased were old friends. How are you taking his death?"

"What about the cult, Lieutenant? This murder was reported as having ritual overtones."

"No comment."

"Are you close to solving this? Or are you still all in the dark?"

"Is anyone under arrest yet?"

"How is the cult involved?"

We finally made it to the door and stepped into the front foyer. A trooper was standing guard, keeping people out. "Everyone else here?" Hamilton asked.

"Yes, sir — conference room."

We walked down the hallway to the conference room. The smoke, the noise, and the smell of too many bodies stopped me dead at the door; Hamilton plowed ahead to the front of the room. The place was packed; every chair around the long table was full, others had been brought in from every corner of the building, people were lining the walls. The shades were drawn across the windows — the nervous lights and shadows outside played across them like gigantic moths wanting in.

I parked myself next to the door with my back against the wall. From that distance, Mel

Hamilton was wreathed in a mist of tobacco smoke. Beside him sat a uniformed State policeman with more bangles and baubles than I'd seen since the service, obviously a bigwig from Waterbury. I noticed Ron Potter nearby, too, which gave me a jolt. While I'd been dropping by the office to help Flo Ginty keep things running and write reports, I hadn't actually seen him over the last forty-eight hours. It made me wonder whether he'd been busy, or trying to avoid all this.

Hamilton surveyed the room, checked his watch, and banged on the table with a glass. "Quiet down everybody. Sorry I was late — let's get this started."

What had been a roar shrank to a general muttering and finally subsided altogether.

"Thank you. Before we start, I'd like to welcome Major Imus, head of the Criminal Division. He came down here from Waterbury on very short notice and would like to say a few words. Major Imus?"

The man I'd thought of as a human Christmas tree stood and smiled. Being head of the Criminal Division put him about third or fourth from the top of the State Police hierarchy, the kind of guy the lower ranks saw either at ceremonies, or after the shit had truly hit the fan.

"Gentlemen, you have a great deal of work

to do here and I don't want to get in your way. This has become as heated a situation as some of you will see in your careers, and it's liable to get worse. I am not here to breathe down your necks or to supersede your present chain of command. You have all been doing an excellent job so far, and I am only here to let you know that we are aware of your efforts. Please understand you have our full support. Whatever you need, we will attempt to supply. Keep up the good work and thank you. You make us proud."

He sat back down. Had the audience been larger still, or had it been comprised of fresh Academy graduates, I would have expected applause. Here, everyone just watched him.

Hamilton cleared his throat. "Thank you, Major. You probably all know by now that Rennie Wilson was found dead this afternoon. Crofter Smith will give you what we have so far."

Smith rose from the crowd and opened a file before him. When he'd appeared at the Lemon Road scene at the head of the troops, he'd looked a little piqued, half visible in the gloom. Now, under the fluorescent tubes, I doubted I'd ever seen a man look so exhausted. He had bags under his eyes I could see from across the room. As case officer on the Wingate murder, his compulsively rigid personality probably hadn't allowed him to catch more than two hours sleep at a time, and then only when he was sure no one was around to catch him napping.

"This is going to be a little unusual. Because of the time factor, I haven't been able to condense all our findings into a single report. So, I've asked several of the people directly involved in the investigation of Rennie Wilson's death to give verbal reports tonight, with the understanding that tomorrow, you will all be issued written versions after some of us have had some sleep. I'd like to start with Fish and Game Lieutenant John Bishop."

Bishop stood up slowly and began to speak in a gentle, measured tone, as if he were addressing a group of keenly attentive children. He described the process he'd used to discover Rennie's body, and what the tracks had told him. He had indeed traced the killer's footprints back to the road. Apparently, the vehicle had arrived after Rennie, but before the other two, and had been parked farther down the road, out of sight, disguised with leaves and branches, just as Rennie's had been.

Bishop stuck to a recitation of the facts, but I was struck by a pattern — as if the killer, having followed Rennie to Lemon Road, had followed his every move thereafter, from hiding the car to creeping through the woods to awaiting the arrival of Rennie's mysterious guests at the rock outcropping. It struck me that the killer had bided his time, waiting not just for the proper moment, which must have presented itself again and again in the isolated woods, but more out of curiosity.

One by one, Smith called on his witnesses, including the local M.E. — Dr. Hoard — who confirmed what Bishop had told me, adding that the weapon had probably been a large hunting knife, and who reported that an autopsy was being performed as we spoke. Various members of the Crime Lab, here on their way back to Waterbury, gave preliminary reports on their findings and on the samples they had collected for analysis. Of immediate interest was the fact that while the killer's footprints did not match any of those found at Bruce Wingate's murder scene, the smaller of the visiting twosome did conform to the small ones found at the ravine — the ones that had been colored yellow on the sketch of that scene.

It was an impressive display of police procedure, and no doubt of use to those who had not been at the scene, but it still boiled down to very little. Rennie had been murdered by a person unknown. That much, including relevant details, could have been said in five minutes or less.

Hamilton, too, had obviously reached the same conclusion. He checked his watch, thanked Smith for his effort, and launched into his own spiel. "In the interest of time, I'm going to summarize some aspects of this investigation. The primary purpose tonight is to brainstorm on what we've got and where we're headed — the written reports will supply any detailed background information we might skip over here. Agreed?"

There were general murmurs of relieved assent.

"Okay. Item One: the fire — the beginning of all this. Appleby and his crew have been hard at work, but still haven't found much to add. The members of the Order are still playing dumb, Sarris refuses to actively cooperate, and the investigation, in and of itself, isn't going anywhere, to the discredit of nobody, I might add. That will remain a particularly tough nut to crack until or unless we can use some sort of legal pry bar to open it up, but until such warrants or whatever appear, we'll have to work around the edges. We do have additional information on Freedom to Choose, Inc. — Gorman's company — but nothing that particularly connects to this case."

Apple raised his hand. "Just a couple of quick ones for clarification. Bruce Wingate did buy a Smith & Wesson 9-mm semi-automatic with a nine bullet clip capacity about ten years ago. This morning, Joe Gunther drove down to Natick and found out in addition that Wingate bought another gun — a .38 — just two months ago. Also, we interviewed John Stanley, a private investigator from Boston, and he confirmed the Wingates' story about tracking their daughter to Gannet. He'd been hired to do that about two months ago."

"Thank you." Hamilton opened a file and pulled out a single sheet of paper. "Item Two: the Wingate homicide. Some more Crime Lab stuff has come in. The lighter found under the body was indeed Rennie Wilson's. It was a Zippo-type and while there were no prints on the outside, the inner casing — exposed only while refilling the lighter — had a perfect of Wilson's left thumb.

"They can't match every wound on the body to the kitchen knife found at Wilson's home, so the possibility exists that another knife was also used. However, it has now been proven scientifically that the metal fragment recovered by Dr. Hillstrom was indeed the broken tip of the Wilson knife. There were no prints on that knife, by the way.

"Item Three: the clothing found at Rennie Wilson's home. The stains were blood, and that blood is compatible with Bruce Wingate's. Unless we do a DNA test, we can't swear it's the same stuff, but we're assuming it is for the moment. In addition, there was some dirt found on the cuff of the pants, which also matches the dirt at the scene."

He distributed a sheaf of papers down each side of the table. "Pass these around — they're the details that led them to their various conclusions.

"The footprints around the scene have still not been linked to any particular people aside from Wilson, but we have discovered that these," he swung around to the map of the scene and pointed at the yellow footprints, "are definitely moccasin tracks, completely compatible with what all Order members seem to wear, and with those found at both the Wingate and the Wilson scenes. This does not mean, of course, that any member of the Order was at either place. The easiest thing in the world would be to try framing those people by wearing moccasins. It is too early to draw any hard conclusions right now, of course, but the lab is paying careful attention to see if the 'yellow' prints and the small ones we found off Lemon Road are one and the same.

"In addition," he waved a stapled sheaf of papers at us, "a more in-depth analysis has been made of the sequential order in which the prints were made at the Wingate scene.

All the lab findings will be combined after this meeting into a single volume for reference."

He put down the papers and leaned forward a little for emphasis. "The thing about the moccasins brings up something a little out of context. Those people out there," he pointed at the windows, "are dying to pin this whole mess on the Natural Order. Now in the long run, they may get what they want, but I want that to happen only if and when everybody involved in this process is absolutely positive that's the case. Once the Order — or whoever — has been indicted, then the press can have a field day. But until then, I want them kept in the dark. Nobody is to talk with them — is that understood?"

"Tell Gunther that." It had been a muttered aside, but from the voice, I was pretty sure it was Wirt, whom I hadn't even noticed, buried against the far back wall.

Hamilton stiffened. It was the first time I'd seen him really pissed. "Just a goddamn minute. This is just what I was talking about. You people can bitch and moan all you want about whatever you please, from your salaries to your hours to the way your wives treat you at night, but I will not tolerate any backstabbing. If you have a legitimate complaint about one of your fellow officers, you can bring it to the proper authorities. If you don't, if you just happen not to like the guy, you stick it in your ear and you live with it. Joe Gunther is attached to the SA's office. He is not a member of the State Police. If it's all right with his boss, he can goddamn well serenade the press if he wants. It's none of our business.

"But, for your information, that is not what happened," Hamilton went on. He bent down and pulled a newspaper out of his briefcase on the floor. He held it up. It was a copy of the *Caledonian Record*. The headline ran, "Brattleboro Cop Joins Investigation."

My head began to ache.

"Lieutenant Gunther sat in on a meeting being run by Gorman and Greta Lynn last night. That action was entirely appropriate. Unfortunately, he was recognized by one reporter as a Brattleboro policeman and the press tried to make hay out of his being here. If you read the article, you'll find he didn't give them a thing.

"Furthermore, I'd like to state for the record that while I had my doubts initially about having the SA's man closely linked to this investigation, those doubts are long gone. Lieutenant Gunther has been an asset to us, adding to the case and proving himself a constructive and integral part of the process."

He dropped the paper and leaned forward

again, his fingertips on the tabletop. "Watch out for this kind of thing, people. The press see us as the bad guys, and they'll generally do anything to get us to open up, including making us fight among ourselves. We can't afford that. So ignore 'em and just do your jobs."

He straightened and resumed his usual passive mien. "All right, enough of that. Let's look at all this as a linked chain of events — any and all of you dive in if you have something to add. Early Tuesday morning, we have a fire in which five people die, one of whom had a fight with Bruce Wingate on Monday night. Four of those people are found dead of smoke inhalation behind a door locked on the outside, and the fifth — Ed Sylvester, aka Fox — is found lying on his back on the over-turned wood stove downstairs. He was dead before he landed there and we suspect, but cannot prove, foul play.

"On Wednesday night, Bruce Wingate apparently received a letter instructing him to meet with someone at Dulac's ravine. We've been able to compare the handwriting on the envelope to a sample of Julie Wingate's that Lieutenant Gunther procured, and it appears to be a match, which only establishes that she addressed the envelope. At the ravine, Bruce Wingate was murdered, with all the evidence pointing at Rennie Wilson, with whom Wingate had had an altercation on Monday night following an argument concerning Wingate's daughter. We also now know — thanks to Lieutenant Gunther — that Rennie once had a sexual relationship with that same daughter.

"Thursday night, last night, it looks like Rennie Wilson arranged a meeting with two people off the end of Lemon Road, one of whom had probably also been at the fatal get together with Wingate. That meeting took place, but somebody else followed Wilson, watched the meeting, waited for the other two to leave, and then murdered Wilson."

Hamilton stepped away from the table and began to pace back and forth in front of the blackboard. "One scenario has it that Wingate killed Sylvester — or Fox — lit the fire and killed the others indirectly. Two nights later, someone, perhaps his daughter, contacted him and killed him at the ravine, framing Rennie Wilson to avert attention from herself or the Order. There are several problems with that, however. A) It is unclear whether Wingate was in possession of the gun we think was fired at the top of the stairs. B) The assumption that Julie Wingate might have killed her father is complicated by the presence of several other people at the meeting at which her father died. C) The growing evidence seems to be reinforcing, rather than weakening the premise that Rennie Wilson did indeed kill Bruce Wingate."

He stopped pacing. "So, we switch around the cast of characters, see if we can get a better fit. Our own people reinterviewed Nadine Wilson today to ask her of her husband's whereabouts on the night of the fire. She knows he was there later; in fact, he responded from home to fight the fire, but she's vague about his actions or location earlier. Vague enough, in fact, to suggest that he could have been in the Order house and shot Sylvester, perhaps with Julie Wingate as his accomplice. This possibility is given credibility if we assume that Julie and Rennie were still lovers. If so, they both killed Sylvester — Fox — because Fox kept Julie on a short leash, perhaps against her will. Later, they killed her father out of revenge, as well as to get him off Julie's back."

He leaned forward on the table and smiled. "None of that, of course, helps us to understand why — or by whom — Rennie was killed. It seems, according to Lieutenant Bishop, that, if Julie was involved, she and some man went to meet with Rennie, had a chat, and then left peacefully. We're saying Julie, obviously, because both sets of moccasin prints were apparently made by the same person; in point of fact, we have no proof Julie was anywhere near any of these scenes of violence."

"So maybe it was a small man, or a fat child, or maybe Ellie and/or Greta," Spinney muttered, audibly enough so the whole room heard.

I gave Hamilton high marks. He actually chuckled. "Or an envoy of Sarris's, for that matter. Lieutenant Gunther found out Wilson had been blackmailing him for a steady supply of Order women."

"Doesn't that place Sarris pretty high on the list?" Apple asked. "He had good reason to want both Wingate and Wilson dead."

"Why would he frame Wilson just to kill him later?"

Apple shrugged. "Just because it sounds off-base doesn't mean it is. Is there at least enough on the blackmail angle to get some sort of warrant and force Sarris to talk?"

Hamilton looked at Potter and raised his eyebrows.

Potter shrugged. "It's pretty thin. Chaney doesn't even know it was blackmail — just that Rennie 'had something on Sarris,' to quote Joe's report. And we can't go after Julie now any more than we could before. As the lieutenant said, we still can't place her at any of the crimes."

"Lieutenant Hamilton," I asked, "did you get a report back on the saliva on that envelope we found in the Wingates' room? Maybe that'll help us."

Hamilton nodded and started pawing through the pile of papers before him. He finally located a sheet and held it up. "Here it is."

"Does it say what the blood type is?"

He scanned the report. "B, but we don't know Julie's."

"We could get it, though."

Potter pulled at his chin a couple of times. "It seems to me a whole lot of people are refusing to talk in this case. If we held an inquest, we might get them to talk."

"Yeah," Apple said. "We could get the whole goddamn bunch of 'em in front of a judge and sweat 'em individually." Apple was smiling at the thought. Of all of us, he'd had the most frustrating time, knocking fruitlessly on doors, getting nowhere with people who might as well have lost their tongues. He looked like Potter had just made him a gift.

"It is true, Lieutenant," Smith chimed in, "that we might make better time using an inquest."

An inquest, as legally described in Vermont, is almost unique to that state. It is a secret criminal proceeding in which almost anybody and his uncle can be subpoenaed to appear before a judge to answer questions from the State's Attorney. The person so summoned cannot bring his or her lawyer into the courtroom, although they can leave the room and consult with their lawyer outside if and when they like, but if they do not answer or cooperate with the process, the judge can order them jailed for contempt. In the short run, inquests give frustrated cops a moment of joy — as Apple had just demonstrated. In the long run, however, they can become legal nightmares, later triggering cumbersome discovery motions by the defense — if the case ever goes to trial — and even raising questions of constitutionality.

I spoke up from the back of the room, aware, once again, that I was differing with Smith. "I disagree. If we set up an inquest now, I think we'll end up taking it on the chin."

"Why?"

"First, it'll take a week or so to set up, which is a long time with the vultures circling around outside." I jerked my thumb at the window. "Second, once we do set it up, the press'll be standing around outside grilling everyone who goes in or out of that courtroom. An inquest is a rumor mill almost by design."

"If we get what we want, who cares about

the press?" Apple countered. "We're stuck with 'em anyhow."

"I don't think we'll get anything. Apple, you've been scratching at these people for days. What makes you think they won't stay clammed up in front of a judge?"

"He'll throw them in jail, that's why."

"That'll play right into their hands. Sarris can then say his people are being persecuted, that they didn't say or do anything. I'm afraid an inquest now could stop us dead in our tracks. We've done a lot in a few days. Why risk screwing it all up with a potential circus?"

I noticed heads were turning from me to Potter, as if they were watching a tennis game. I looked at Smith to check for any vicarious enjoyment, but as usual, his face betrayed nothing.

Hamilton put an end to it. "The subject's been broached; if there's time at the end of this, maybe we can go back to it. I'm sure Mr. Potter has some feelings on it he hasn't expressed, and I'm not sure, if I were him, that this would be the place I'd choose to air them. There's still a lot we can do on what we've got at the moment, and as Lieutenant Gunther pointed out, even with an inquest, we'd still have a week before anything happened. Thomas, what did you get on those phone records — I don't seem to have anything here."

Sergeant Thomas straightened in his seat. "I just got them, sorry. I was down in Hanover checking on Paul Gorman's alibi." He, too, pulled out a sheet of paper and looked it over.

"According to Bruce Wingate, he last called Gorman on Monday night, after his altercation with Fox. That must have been at 17:57 — the call was placed from the phone at the Rocky River Inn to the FTC headquarters in Hanover."

"Not to Gorman's mobile phone?" Hamilton asked.

"No. Later another call pops up from a pay phone in East Burke."

"Where?" Spinney asked.

"The Mobil station. The call went to a Hanover number belonging to one of FTC's employees, a Heather Spinelli. I spoke with Mrs. Spinelli and she denies getting a call and claims Gorman spent the entire night at her house in the guest room."

"What time was that?" I asked.

"Four-forty, early Tuesday morning."

"The fire was called in at five, more or less, and the arson team figured it might have been smoldering for up to half an hour before then."

"There was one other call from that phone,

at 17:18 the same day."

"What had the Wingates been up to just prior to that?" I asked on a hunch.

Smith answered. "We'd given them the lie detector test."

Thomas interrupted. "And the call was placed to the White Horse Motel."

"All right," Apple muttered with satisfaction. I liked that bit of news myself. If it was accurate, it might mean Gorman was in the area before Wingate died, and didn't just show up afterwards, as he'd claimed. That would link Gorman tightly to the Wingates, making him either an accessory to whatever illegalities Bruce Wingate had committed, or at least the repository of some information we badly wanted. Most ominously, it opened the possibility that one of the mysterious footprints surrounding Wingate's body had belonged to Paul Gorman.

"It may not mean a thing," Hamilton cautioned. "We don't know Wingate made the call, and we don't know who was at the other end."

"It sure puts Gorman on our hit parade," Spinney smiled.

"Yes, but let's be careful here. Don't screw this up. We can't get a court order here — it's all too vague. Lester, why don't you go down to the White Horse tomorrow and nose around a little? See if you can't get us enough for a warrant. Crofter, arrange with your team to watch Sarris's house and put a tail on him. If we can get anything on him, it might be the first crack in the dam."

"What about the call from the Rocky River, the one Ellie Wingate asked Greta to make to Gorman right after she heard of her husband's death? That was supposed to have been made to his mobile phone."

Thomas made a face. "I couldn't get it. The phone company lost the records."

"What do you mean?"

"It happens," Spinney said. "It's got something to do with retrieving the records from the computers. Apparently, it messes things up and sometimes they just lose the stuff."

"All right. We may have enough anyhow. It's been a long day for everybody. Tomorrow morning, all reports will be available here, including autopsy and Crime Lab updates. Is there anything else? You want to kick around the inquest idea some more?"

Potter spoke up. "Unless anybody has a new angle, I think I've got enough to go on. I'll let you know tomorrow."

Apple chuckled. "So button your lip, boys."

Hamilton frowned his maternal frown. "Major Imus? Any last words?"

Imus couldn't resist. He stood up. "I'm

very impressed by what I've seen tonight. As you no doubt know, I don't show up at meetings like this very often, and I was worried that my doing so would make you feel we were doubting your abilities. That's what I told the Commissioner. The Governor, however, is very concerned about all this, and the Commissioner felt there was no choice but that I should come. I can now return to Waterbury and lay their fears at rest. It is obvious to me —"

It was also obvious to me what else the man had to say. I slipped around the edge of the door and wandered down the hall.

I found a small, dark office with a desk, a chair, a phone, and nothing else. Leaving the light off, I settled in the chair, put my feet up on the table and leaned back, mulling over what had just been discussed.

The inquest angle still rankled, although there was little I could do about that now. I also had to sympathize with the urgency to do something, even if it wasn't particularly well thought out. The frustration of having to constantly fall back onto hypothetical possibilities instead of progressing with accumulated facts was beginning to tell.

Not with me, though. I didn't see things that way. I remembered going to the seacoast as a child once, and playing in the soft dunes.

I'd discovered that when I dug small tunnels into the dry sand, the sides didn't hold. For each scoop of sand my hand removed, an equivalent amount slid in from around the edges. I placed a small, black stone almost five feet up the dune, and by just digging in one small spot at the base, I caused the stone to trickle slowly all the way down, until it finally fell into my hand.

Investigations are like that. We dig and scoop, piling up evidence, but we also draw things in from the outside, things that before had appeared either out of reach or even superfluous — like Paul Gorman.

Only now, I'd come to realize, Paul Gorman was far from superfluous, and he was quickly coming within reach.

27

When I got home that night, I found another car parked in Buster's driveway, something small, blue, and covered with frost. It wasn't until I got out that I realized it was Laura's old Toyota. I stopped by the driver's door to look. The car was empty.

The house looked pretty lifeless, too. It was already almost midnight. The porch light had been left on, and I could see the hall light was on upstairs, but that was it.

I entered quietly. I could hear Buster snoring in his bedroom. I could also smell the remnants of a meal, something more substantial than Buster's usual Crockpot glue. I walked back to the kitchen and switched on the light. From the dishes in the drying rack by the sink, I could tell two people had enjoyed a dinner together. I smiled at the mental picture of them, comforting each other's special loneliness.

I returned to the front of the house and poked my head into the dim living room, lit only from the small flames in the open wood stove. Laura was asleep on the sofa, covered with a blanket. Her face looked very serious, her eyes shut tighter than they should have been; it reminded me of a child wishing the evils of its world away.

I sat on the sofa next to her and watched her for a while, all bundled up, her cheek half-covered by her dark hair. I brushed it aside and she turned her head and looked at me.

"Hi," I said.

She reached out and laid her hand on my chest. The gesture swept the blanket back and revealed she was wearing a light blue shirt with several of the top buttons undone. She saw me taking that fact in and smiled.

"You and Buster have a nice dinner?" I was suddenly feeling uncomfortably warm, aware that I'd both dreaded and wondered about this situation possibly arising. Now that it had, I was as torn as ever over my role in it.

"Yup."

She languidly rubbed a warm hand against my shirt, her eyes still half-closed in sleep. She looked very seductive, especially by the light of the fire. I swallowed hard, hoping she wouldn't notice. The cliché has it that at times like this, the air becomes electric. Suddenly, I didn't find that hard to believe.

"I wanted to see you. Buster said I could stay." Her voice was as soft as water held in the palm. "I fell asleep thinking of you."

She slid her hand down my arm to my hand, which was resting on the cushion next to her. She lifted it and placed it on her breast, closing her own hand on top of it. Her eyes closed and she sighed contentedly.

The heat of her under my hand was mesmerizing. I could feel her heart, the slight movement of her skin under the shirt fabric, even the rush of blood through her veins. I made the most minute gesture — a barely perceptible flexing of my fingers. She took in a deep breath and I felt her nipple grow against me. Her eyes were closed, her whole body as sensitive as sunburned skin.

Gently, carefully, but no longer reluctantly, I removed my hand.

Her eyes opened in surprise, her mouth forming a question. She looked at me, studying my face. Her eyes moistened with tears and her mouth quivered. "Why not? What's wrong?"

"I'm a guy in a scrapbook; it's got little to do with the real me."

Her expression darkened. "That's right, you've already got a job, people who need you, even a girlfriend."

I bit off the knee-jerk objection and kept silent for a moment, struggling to put honesty over diplomacy. "I told you I was selfish."

She seemed to close in on herself for a while then, her eyes averted and half-closed. I stayed where I was, waiting to take her cue. I hated this, for all sorts of reasons. The fact that it was the right thing to do only made it more bitter.

She finally sighed and passed a hand across her face. When she looked at me again, the raw emotion was gone, if not the fragility. "If you were really selfish, you would have made love to me first."

I smiled at that. "Now you're making me feel stupid and selfish."

She smiled back and again placed her hand on my chest. "You're not either of those." Her hand slid off and she pursed her lips. "What am I supposed to do?"

The question was so soft, I wasn't sure I was supposed to respond. Not that I had the answer, in any case.

I leaned over and kissed her briefly. "Thank you, Laura."

"For what?"

"Thinking of me as you do."

Her smile returned. "That's not hard . . . Joe?"

"What's up?"

"I'm not saying I'd ever do this, but would it be okay if maybe I called someday, maybe if things get tough? Or write a letter or something?"

I squeezed her hand. "I'm not going anywhere, at least not for a while."

"I know, but I think I need a little time alone at first."

"Want me to stay out of the way?"

She pursed her lips, her eyes brimming. "I do and I don't, you know? But it might be easier."

"I understand." I stood up. "You going to be okay for now?"

She nodded, just barely. "I'll be fine. I just want to lie here for a bit."

I bent down and touched her cheek. "Good night, Laura."

As I was getting ready for bed, I found the necklace I'd bought in St. Johnsbury a few nights ago in my jacket pocket — shiny green stones intended for her. I placed them in the dresser's top drawer. Maybe she'd find them while she was cleaning, or Buster would, and wonder whose they were, or maybe they would remain there forever, like a gesture never completed.

Never before had a woman made me such a gift, or been so gracious when it was turned down. I was too sentimental to think she'd fail now. It half made me wish, now that I was safely too late, that I'd accepted her offer.

28

I missed breakfast the next morning. Spinney called me as I was dressing, his voice sharp with excitement, to tell me to meet him at the White Horse Motel in St. J. — "toot sweet." I was to stop by the barracks on the way and pick up a tape recorder and the foot-print photos from the Bruce Wingate scene.

He came out to my car as I pulled into the White Horse parking lot. "Got the photos?"

I handed him a large envelope and the small tape recorder. "What do you have?"

He flashed that huge, toothy grin and waggled his eyebrows. "Follow me and learn something about superb police procedure."

I got out and trailed after him up the exterior metal stairs to the second-floor balcony that ran the entire length of the building.

"I already spoke to the manager," Spinney said over his shoulder. "Gorman checked in about five in the afternoon on Tuesday, a full thirty-six hours before he claimed he did. So we got him in a bald-faced lie."

"He could say he got the days confused."

"Yeah, well, he can say what he wants. I still think we got his balls nailed to the wall. What was he up to in town that he doesn't want us to know about?"

He stopped at an open door, outside of which stood a room-cleaning cart, filled with tiny bars of soap, sheets, towels, and cleaning supplies. I could hear a vacuum cleaner whirring inside.

We entered the room and found a small, plump, middle-aged woman pushing the cleaner around in a haphazard fashion. She turned off the machine when she saw us. "Boy, that was fast."

Spinney grinned and patted her shoulder, in an overly friendly manner. Next to her, he looked like an oversized scarecrow — all bones and straw-colored hair. He placed the tape recorder on a side table and turned it on and recited the day's date and the time. "We are here with Joe Gunther, who works with the State's Attorney's office of Essex County, Vermont. I'm Detective Sergeant Lester Spinney of the Vermont State Police, and you are who, ma'am?"

She gave an indulgent half smile. "Angie Cowley."

"And you work as a cleaning lady?"

"Yeah."

"Where?"

"Right where I'm standing — at the White Horse Motel."

"In St. Johnsbury, Vermont, is that correct?"

"Right, in Vermont."

"Tell Lieutenant Gunther what you told me."

She looked at both of us as if we'd lost our minds. "I found a pair of dirty shoes in Room 212, day before yesterday."

"Room 212," Spinney informed the tape machine, "is registered to Paul Gorman. Miss Cowley, what made you notice the shoes?"

She stared at him for a second, perplexed. "I clean rooms."

"So it was the dirt?"

"Yeah, there was dirt all around the shoes on the carpet."

"So what did you do?"

"Like I told you. The boss doesn't like us to touch any of the guests' things, but this was different, I mean, I had to clean, right? So I took the shoes and turned them over, so the dirt wouldn't fall off no more. Then I vacuumed. That's it."

"What did the bottoms of the shoes look like?"

"Bumpy. You know, with those super-deep treads."

"Lug soles?"

"Yeah, I guess."

Spinney rummaged through the envelope, pulled out a series of photographs and spread them on the unmade bed beside him. "Okay. Look at these carefully. They're all shots of footprints. Do you see one that looks like the shoes you described finding in Room 212?"

She shook her head but bent over to study the pictures. "Kind of hard to tell. It's not like these are real shoes. I mean, look at this one — you can hardly tell anything at all. It's not even in color."

Spinney impatiently emptied the envelope

across the sheets, scattering glossy prints everywhere, He rummaged through the pile, finally pulling one out from the rest. "Here, same shoe print, better shot." He replaced the one she'd criticized.

She picked up another one. "This one."

"You sure?"

"You asked, I told you. What'd you think?"

"It's something we have to say, all right? You are sure this photo matches the prints of the shoes in Room 212."

She suddenly looked cautious. "Am I going to get in trouble?"

"No. You're just telling us what you saw, that's all."

Her words came out reluctantly. "Well, I hope you're not puttin' me on." She waved the picture in her hand. "Like I said, this looks like the shoes I saw — there's the same squiggle-like pattern in the middle."

Spinney took the picture from her. "Great." He read the identification number off the back of the photo for the record and turned off the tape recorder. "We're set."

We left Angie Cowley shaking her head. Again, I tagged after Spinney as he half-ran down the length of the balcony toward the stairs. "Now we'll see what kind of clout the State has. You missed it, but last night, after telling us what super dudes we all were, Imus said he'd arranged to have a judge on permanent stand-by to consider any warrants we might request. We are priority business over everything."

"You gonna tell Hamilton?" I asked as I slid into his car next to him.

"I'll do it from the courthouse." He started the engine.

It took only about four minutes to drive to the courthouse. The weather from the day before was still holding — damp, cold, and gloomy, with a cloud cover so low you could touch it. Spinney came up the Atlantic Avenue hill, right by the front of Potter's office, and cut left onto South Main. The courthouse was on the immediate left.

"Shit, reporters."

There were three people — two men and a woman — loitering outside. One was sitting on a cement bench planted under a small bare tree, the other two balanced on the iron railing on either side of the roofed entryway. Call us paranoid, but I thought he was right. Who else in their right minds would sit around outside a courthouse, early in the morning and in weather so cold you could see your breath? Even the rummies knew better.

Spinney parked across the street. "You better stay here. They see your face, we'll never get rid of them; worse than driving around with Batman."

It was irritating but I could see his point. At least he left the engine running so I wouldn't freeze to death at the height of my fame. I looked out the side window at the courthouse, a one-hundred-year-old red brick pile with a slate roof. It had two floors of tall, skinny windows, capped with what looked like wooden eyebrows painted green. The building looked perpetually surprised at what was going on inside.

As it turned out, Spinney could have taken the car keys. He was back in fifteen minutes, looking pleased with himself. "Damn. That's got to be a record. Son of a bitch was right there, just as advertised. He even stood around while I filled out the form."

We returned to the motel and found Hamilton already waiting, standing next to a fat, nervous man with thin black hair and glasses so thick they looked like they'd been cut from the bottoms of Coke bottles.

Spinney held up the warrant. "Efficient, huh?"

Hamilton smiled and motioned to the motel manager to lead the way.

"Do we know if he's home?" I asked.

"Thought we'd surprise him," Hamilton answered. He seemed in a remarkably good mood, understandable considering the heat he'd probably been feeling, and which he'd spared passing on to us.

But Gorman wasn't in. We pounded on the door several times, and then stepped aside to let the manager use his passkey. From the door, the place not only looked empty, but unused. Aside from a suitcase, a few items on the night table, and some clothes laying about, it looked ready to rent — bed made, towels unused.

Hamilton stopped us from going beyond the threshold. "What's your name again?" he asked the manager.

"Petrone, Arthur." I caught a hint of military obsequiousness lurking in the man's past.

"Mr. Petrone, this warrant allows us to search for a pair of shoes whose soles match those pictured in this photograph. We are not here to ransack the room, nor are we allowed to take from it anything not mentioned in the warrant, unless we know it to be directly linked to the criminal investigation now under way. Do you understand all that?"

"Sure . . . I think."

"Good. I want you to stand right here and watch us. Later, if they ask you in court, you can tell them exactly what we did here, okay? So try to remember."

Petrone nodded silently. Despite the cold air entering through the door, I could see he was sweating. "What did this guy do?"

"Maybe nothing, that's why we're here."

Hamilton looked at us and nodded. We both made a beeline for the alcove with the sink at the far end of the room. To its left was the bathroom, with a toilet and tub; to the right was a doorless closet. We both fell to our knees like kids at the Christmas tree.

"I think we got it, Lieutenant."

Hamilton approached, tugging Petrone behind him, and looked over our heads. On the floor, still lying bottoms up the way Angie Cowley had placed them, were a pair of low-cut walking shoes. Hamilton handed the photo to Spinney, who held it next to the shoes.

"What do you think, Mr. Petrone? Is it a match?"

Petrone, beginning to enjoy the newfound authority, nodded gravely. "I believe it is."

Hamilton pulled a brown paper evidence bag from his pocket and gave it to Spinney. Spinney snapped it open and gingerly placed one shoe inside, careful not to lose any dirt. As he began doing the same with the other shoe, I stopped him.

"What?"

"I thought I saw something, something shiny."

I took the shoe from him and held it closer, angling it in the light from over the sink.

"There it is. I'll be damned."

"What?" Spinney asked again, this time with some insistence.

I moved the shoe so he could see. Hamilton stuck his head in from the side for a better view. Even Petrone balanced on one foot and tried to see without intruding. It made me think of a bunch of frustrated miners finally catching a glimpse of a tiny speck of gold.

Which wasn't far from the truth, for what had caught my eye was a small sliver of glass wedged in between two lugs and held there by dried mud. It was broken and scarred, but still recognizable. It also went a long way in explaining why Gorman had appeared so nervous when Spinney and I had first met him, the night after Wingate's death.

It was a contact lens.

29

Gorman, however, wasn't available. Upon leaving the motel, Hamilton got in touch with the surveillance crew that had been put on him and discovered Gorman had returned to Hanover, New Hampshire, the night before.

410

Spinney was all set to get a court order and hunt the man down. Hamilton, as usual, took the dispassionate, reasonable view. Gorman had left his belongings in this motel room and was slated to appear with Greta at a televised news conference at the Rocky River in a few hours. Why not just wait for him to come to us? Spinney continued to growl until it was pointed out that by being in Hanover, Gorman was out of state, and the paperwork to extradite him would take days.

That left Spinney frustrated, but without recourse. Not so Hamilton, who decided that since Gorman was temporarily out of reach, he would head off to the Waterbury lab and have the contact lens scientifically matched to the one that had remained in Wingate's eye — just to be sure.

That had left Spinney at barracks, with me to watch him pace.

I went over to the projection screen at the head of the room, released the catch, and eased it back into its cannister near the ceiling. The diagram of the murder scene was still displayed on the blackboard behind — with all its multi-colored footprints. "What color are Gorman's prints supposed to be?"

"White."

I studied the diagram, using a pencil as a pointer. "White — the one guy who was standing off by himself."

"And for a long time," Spinney added. He was now sitting down, with his elbows propped on the table, staring at the board intently.

"Right. Hamilton said last night the lab had come up with some new information about all this, something about chronological sequencing?"

Spinney looked over the paper debris littering the table and came up with a thick binder. He leafed through it a bit, scanning the indexes. "Yeah, here it is. What do you want to know?"

"Any sense of who went where first."

Spinney read quickly, flipping through several pages. "Well, let's see. We got Mitch Pearl and Rennie's tracks on top of all the others."

I scanned the board. "Okay, that's when they found the body. What else?"

"Of the earlier prints, it looks like white is on top . . . Well, he didn't hit all the other prints. He is on top of black and red — he missed yellow."

I translated, using Crofter's color key. "Gorman's white, so he came after black, which is Wingate. So Gorman either entered the picture while Wingate was still alive, hitting some of Wingate's prints but not all,

412

or he came in after Wingate was already dead."

"Which means he could have killed him."

"Maybe. What else?"

"White — Gorman — is also on top of several reds."

"Red. Crofter called him the busiest —"

"And Gorman the least busy — in and out."

"Right, so he is; one line in, one line out, pretty clean if you're going to hack someone with a knife a half-dozen times."

"Perhaps."

"Red is stomping all over the place, particularly near where Wingate's head finally wound up."

I stepped away from the board and faced Spinney. "I kick you in the balls; what happens?"

"I shoot you and sing soprano the rest of my life."

"Which won't be long. You double over, clutching yourself with one hand, and I finish you off with the knife. You fall at my feet. Ergo, my footprints end up all around where your head ends up, right?"

"Possibly. Maybe you kick me in the balls and I fall down like a sack of potatoes and the little lady finishes me off."

"Oh?"

"Yeah." He pointed at the binder. "Let's assume the yellow tracks belong to Julie for the moment, a likely choice since she addressed the envelope to her father and none of our other suspects fit those small, light moccasin prints. Now, this report says both she and red step all over each other. No way to tell who went first."

I nodded my acknowledgment. "But Gorman's definitely on top of red?"

"Yeah."

"So if yellow — Julie — and red are intermixed, we might assume Gorman appeared after Julie, too."

Spinney shook his head and dropped the book in front of him. "Maybe. This is like reading tea leaves. Just because one set of prints is on top of another set doesn't mean they came later than a few seconds. If you have ten guys walking in a line, did the last guy follow the first nine by two hours, or was he holding a short rope attached to the ninth guy's belt? You can't tell."

"Okay, I'll grant you that. But nowhere does it say Gorman's prints appear under anyone's, right?"

"Right."

"And since yellow's and red's prints are mixed together, it's reasonable to assume they were together at the time."

"Two against one? Yellow and red against Wingate, with Gorman entering the scene after?"

"It works, doesn't it?"

Spinney rubbed the sides of his nose with his forefingers. "Yeah, but so does three against one."

"Does it?" I used the pointer again. "Here's Wingate standing around, shifting his weight, staggering finally, and then falling. Here's yellow, also standing around, back and forth, in front of Wingate. And the same's true for red. But Gorman . . ." I tapped at the two neat parallel rows of white marks, "goes straight in, pauses — maybe squats down or something — and then leaves."

"In a hurry."

"What?"

Spinney pointed at the book. "In a hurry. The lab says he left running, leaving only toe marks, no heels."

"It fits," I said, tossing the pencil onto the table. I felt disappointed in some ways: Gorman, obviously, was not our killer.

"So who's red, and *is* Julie yellow?"

The first question had a numbing regularity to it; it seemed we had fit everyone except Buster into those red footprints. I ducked answering. "And what was Gorman doing there in the first place?"

Spinney leaned way back in the chair and locked his hands behind his neck. "You know, Joe, red could still be Rennie."

I shook my head and sat down.

"Concede the point. It is possible."

"I'd be happier conceding it if he hadn't gotten killed."

"That's because you're linking all three events together — the fire and the two murders. What if they're not connected?"

That struck me as unlikely. "Remember when we visited Rennie's place, and got the boots and clothes and knife? Well, I asked Nadine, just as we were leaving, whether Rennie ever went without a belt. Remember what she said?"

He looked at me closely. "That he always wore a belt."

"So what was blood doing on the waistband of the pants we found? If he always wore a belt, the blood would be on the belt."

Spinney rolled his eyes.

"Wait, I know it's not evidence, at least nothing that would stand up in court, but to me it shows something fundamentally wrong with Rennie being the killer."

Spinney decided to skirt the issue. "Those red prints were definitely made by his boots, and he definitely had ties to both Wingate and Julie. It wouldn't be the first time lovers attempted murder."

"They were hardly lovers, from what I hear. Chaney said Rennie dumped her."

"Come on, we don't know that. For all we know, they were still nuts about each other. Plus, Wingate took a swing at Rennie; some people have killed for a parking space."

I remembered something else. "Rennie said he lost his lighter about six months ago, just a short time after Chaney said Rennie dumped Julie Wingate. Maybe that's why he clammed up on us. I thought at the time it was odd that he knew when he'd lost the lighter, but not where or how. If he suspected Julie stole it, or that she picked it up after one of their trysts, then he also suspected her of planting it under Wingate's body."

"Which might explain what Julie's footprints were doing off Lemon Road. Rennie called the meeting to find out if she'd framed him."

I got up to look out one of the windows. "So who killed Rennie?" That, almost more than anything, was what was sticking in my craw. "If Rennie was framed, why kill him off? Especially when he was the most obvious suspect?"

"How about asking, 'who didn't kill Rennie'?"

"All right."

"Not Julie, because her tracks come and go, leaving Rennie alive."

I nodded, content for the moment that my assumptions about Julie's actions were reasonable.

"Not Gorman."

"Why not?"

"All right, probably not Gorman. Because he would have used his one pair of hiking shoes, just as he had the night Wingate died, shoes which obviously haven't been used since. Also, as a city boy, he'd have crashed around the woods like the twosome who met with Rennie. He's no woodsman. The guy who iced Rennie walked around like a cat."

"So, by the same logic, Gorman couldn't have been part of the duo who met Rennie at the rock."

"Right. Plus, it wouldn't make sense. From what we've established, it looks like Julie was there, so what would Gorman be doing with her meeting Rennie?"

"All that's based on the hypothesis that Gorman knows nothing about moving in the woods — which we don't know for a fact — and that he only has the one pair of boots that he would naturally wear to that kind of meeting. Beverly Hillstrom has a pair of boots permanently stored in the trunk of her car."

Spinney looked sourly at the tabletop. "All

right, so it might have been Gorman."

"Among others," I added, looking out the window. "Like Sarris, or one of his people, or someone we haven't even thought of."

"It gets easier all the time," Spinney sighed. "Well, at least let's start with Gorman."

30

"Jesus, we should have booked ahead."

Cars and pickups lined both sides of 114, and several television trucks filled North Street, across from the Rocky River. We made the corner down Atlantic Boulevard and were damn near back out of town before Spinney said, "Fuck it," and parked in someone's yard.

It had begun to snow as we made our way back up the street, returning to the Inn on foot. "What the hell's going on? I thought this was supposed to be a small interview," Spinney said, looking at the trucks.

"It's a big story; everybody's had enough time to send in the hotshots. My guess is that Gorman's been working the phone like a regular P.T. Barnum."

"The only crew missing is MTV."

As we rounded the corner into North Street, we found a throng of people milling about the menagerie of electronic equipment. I saw Buster standing by the side of the road, looking like the bear rousted from his cave.

"What d'ya think?"

He shook his head. "Damnedest thing. They come all the way up here from cities where they get thirty killings in a week, just to jabber about how the country's going to the dogs. Beats the hell out of me."

"Anything happen yet?"

"Hell, no. The fancy boys with the hairdos are talking to each other, the local guys are taking pictures of the fancy boys, and the rest of 'em are taking pictures of each other just to prove they were here. Now I know for sure why we end up with the politicians we get." He stumped off into the falling snow, presumably to sit in contemplation amid the isolated splendor of his filling station.

Spinney and I climbed the steps to the front door, stepping over a nest of tangled wires and cables leading to trucks with dish antennas on top. Inside, on the left, the Library glowed with an eerie blue-white light. People jammed the entranceway, balanced on top of radiators, and challenged the strength of the staircase, all craning to see over or through the forest of lights, reflector umbrellas, cameras, and sound equipment that had been crowded into Buster's favorite evening den.

We muscled our way through to the double doors, where we found a man with a headset around his neck, guarding the entrance.

"Greta Lynn and Paul Gorman in there?" Spinney asked in his best G-man tone.

The man looked at us like we'd just wandered out of the woods. "Yeah, they're the show."

"We need to talk to them — now."

"We're about to tape."

Spinney pulled out his badge. "Now."

The man caught his breath for a moment, apparently fighting down a hysterical reaction. "Wait here."

He returned a minute later with a flabby-looking man with blow-dried hair, a gold chain around his neck, and tinted aviator glasses, a look I thought had faded years ago. "What's going on?" he asked with thinly veiled hostility.

Spinney smiled — barely — and introduced us, complete with lofty titles. "We're conducting a criminal investigation. We need to talk to Mrs. Lynn and Mr. Gorman."

"Is this going to take long?"

"I don't know."

"You know, we'll be out of here in an hour.

Maybe you could wait. I'll give you a ringside seat."

"No."

The man, presumably a producer or director, pursed his lips. "Since what we're both doing ties in with your case, why don't you let us film your talk with them, and then we'll do the interview right after? Kind of like "Sixty Minutes," you know?"

Spinney just looked at him.

"You may be missing the boat here. People open up when a camera's rolling — we might be able to help you get more out of them. It'll make you look good. Your boss'll be happy and your family can see you on TV."

That explained the tinted glasses and neck hardware, I thought. The network put this guy out to pasture years ago, at least I hoped so.

Again Spinney said, "No."

Finally, the producer caved in. "Kill the lights. We'll hold for a while."

The other man checked his watch. "We can't hold forever."

"I'm aware of that fact, Charlie. If it takes too long, we'll fold our tents; this is hardly a summit conference."

I was grateful Greta wasn't within earshot. They might have been suddenly covering a live homicide.

Several reporters had caught wind something was up and began to cluster around the doorway.

"Aren't you Joe Gunther?" one of them asked.

"Oh, for Christ sake," Spinney muttered and grabbed my arm. "Don't let anyone past," he told headset-Charlie as we plowed into the electronic jungle littering the Library.

Greta and Gorman were on the other side, sitting in director's chairs, having their noses dusted. Spinney stepped up in front of Gorman. "Show's over. We need to talk."

Greta looked around at the dying lights. "What the hell's going on?"

"Actually, Greta," I said, "unless Sergeant Spinney objects, I'd like you to hear this." The makeup man was standing awkwardly to one side. I waved him away.

Spinney shrugged. "Fine with me." He reached forward and took Gorman's arm. "Come on, let's go find a quiet corner."

Gorman shook the hand off. "Am I under arrest?"

"You might be, depending on what you've got to say."

Several technicians and hangers-on discreetly gathered within earshot, straining to hear.

"On what charge?"

Spinney looked around. "You know and we know what the charges might be, Mr. Gorman. If you want to have this conversation in front of the network crews, that's fine with me."

Greta crossed her arms. "Fine, let's do it."

Gorman hesitated. "No, I think maybe a little privacy is called for."

Greta stared at him, her mouth half open.

He quickly covered himself. "I'm sure what they've got to say is totally ridiculous. But there's no point feeding it directly into the pipeline." He stood up. "Where to?"

Spinney shot me a questioning look. I turned to Greta. "The stairs are blocked. Is there some place on the ground floor we can go? The kitchen, maybe?"

Reluctantly, her face mirroring her suspicions, she got up and began to lead the way. I noticed she kept looking back at Gorman as if he had suddenly sprouted horns. Deceit was not something she handled with grace, especially from those for whom she'd let down the drawbridge.

The side door to the kitchen was off a short hallway around the corner from the Library's entrance; our wade through the crowd was short and without comment, at least from any of us.

Once in the kitchen, Spinney locked the

door behind us. Gorman strolled into the middle of the room, seemingly interested in the pots and pans hanging from hooks overhead, the numerous large, deep metal sinks, and the long wooden work tables, their surfaces scarred and eroded by years of slicing and hacking. Glancing around, I wondered if the place would survive even a cursory glance from the Health Department. The accumulated grime of thousands of greasy meals was parked in every nook and cranny, and the walls looked painted with a thin, dark sheen of old, rancid oil.

Gorman turned theatrically on one heel to face us, a great show of forced indifference, belied by his watchful eyes. His hands remained in his pockets. "So, what's this all about?"

"You checked in at the White Horse Motel thirty-six hours before you said you did," I said.

He stared at us with mock surprise. "Checked into the motel?"

Greta laughed. "You got to be kidding. Is that what this is about?"

Spinney took over. "I have to inform you you don't have to talk to us, and that if you have a lawyer, you might want to call him."

Gorman waved it away. "Such melodrama."

"It's your choice. You told us you arrived

on Thursday morning after receiving a call from Ellie Wingate about an hour earlier. That was a lie — we've got the motel records to prove it."

Gorman held up his hands. "A lie? That's a little strong. I may have gotten my timing confused; there's been a lot going on."

"You checked into the White Horse on Tuesday afternoon, two days earlier, after receiving a phone call before dawn the same day at the house of Heather Spinelli, in Hanover."

Gorman smiled. "I told you I'd been in Hanover."

"Do you deny checking into the White Horse on Tuesday afternoon?"

I liked Spinney's style. Some cops get a routine over the years, a favorite approach that works in most situations. But Spinney switched around — tough with some people, endearing with others, solicitous if necessary. With Gorman, he was like a chess player, relentlessly knocking down his opponent's defenses, pushing him into a corner.

"Sergeant, if you say you've got records proving I was at the motel on a certain day, they must be accurate. I travel a great deal."

"Do you remember the phone call? You also got one about fifteen minutes after you checked in. Bruce Wingate told you about the lie detector test, the one he wouldn't let Ellie take. That ring a bell?"

Nice move. We had no idea what they'd talked about, but we did know that a call went out to Gorman following every jam Wingate had found himself in. I noticed that Greta had become silent.

"I remember some phone calls, but I don't recall exactly what was said."

"Where were you Wednesday night? You told us earlier you were in Hanover."

There was a ghost of a pause, and then Gorman's face relaxed into an indulgent smile. "I *was* in Hanover, Sergeant. It's only an hour away. I had interrupted business in Hanover, so I was doing a little shuttling."

Greta stepped forward, grasping at this reasonable explanation. She addressed me instead of Spinney. "If you guys had any balls, you'd go after the Order, instead of coming after innocent people like us. You just don't like the idea we may be right, that the answer to all this has been staring you in the face all along. Why do you think so many people are listening to us? Why do you think the news people are here?"

"We're not finished, Greta," I told her.

She rolled her eyes and walked over to lean against one of the work tables.

Spinney continued. "We searched your

room early this morning, Gorman, and we had the dirt on your shoes analyzed. It matches the dirt where Wingate was killed. In fact, there's some blood mixed in with it."

Gorman looked shocked. "You searched my room?"

"With a warrant."

Gorman was fighting for composure. Greta stood rooted in place, her face pale. I made a move toward her, but she stiffened and put her hands up, her eyes glued to Gorman. She reminded me of a cornered animal, boxed in by some fierce and merciless stalker.

Gorman was trying to recover. "You found dirt on a pair of hiking shoes. Are you telling me that Bruce was lying in some sort of specialized mud, only found in that ditch and nowhere else? Come on, Detective. You're fishing."

"Bruce Wingate wore contacts — you know that?"

Gorman looked puzzled. "I may have. I don't remember."

"When we found him, he was missing one of his lenses."

Gorman's voice was slow and cautious. "So?"

"We found the missing lens stuck to the bottom of your shoe, held there by the mud."

There was a sudden sound and Greta

jumped on Gorman, landing a punch on him that knocked him clean off his feet.

"You son of a bitch. You used me." She was about to kick him when Spinney pulled her off balance. She shook herself free, ran for the door, unlocked it and vanished.

"Greta."

The door slammed and I could hear her running down the hallway. I started to follow, but I could see it was useless — the crowd had absorbed her like the sea. I hesitated and then closed the door. I'd talk to her later.

Gorman was sitting in the middle of the floor, rubbing his head. She'd caught him near the temple and had probably done more damage to her hand than to him.

Spinney chose to ignore the entire incident and continued in the same quiet, chilly tone. "In a lot of murder cases, Mr. Gorman, we don't actually find a guy with a gun in his hand, standing over the body. We have to put the case together, sometimes with circumstantial evidence, sometimes with physical evidence. With you, we've got both. Judges, prosecutors, and especially juries really like that; it's something they can get their teeth into."

Gorman looked totally bewildered. Not only had he been assaulted by his erstwhile ally, with no visible concern from either Spinney or me, but the former was still addressing him as if he was a confessed axe-murderer. "I didn't kill Bruce," he said, struggling to his feet again.

"You were there."

"But I didn't kill him."

"Are you denying you were there?"

"You know I was there. You just said it, but I didn't kill him."

"I'm glad to hear it."

"Don't you believe me?" Gorman's tone began to border on the hysterical.

Spinney shook his head in wonder.

"I saw who did it."

Spinney and I looked at each other. I felt as if the small stone had finally made it from the top of the dune to the palm of my hand. It was a sense of victory that quickly proved premature.

"Who was it?"

"I don't know, it was dark. He stood back, letting Julie Wingate do the talking, until . . . You know, until he killed him."

So Julie was there, I thought, relieved at last to have that piece locked into place.

"You couldn't see him at all?" Spinney's voice was slightly incredulous.

"I just knew somebody was there. Bruce was holding a flashlight, and I could sometimes see the guy's legs — his pants legs were too short. He was standing maybe ten feet behind her, maybe a little more. I knew Bruce could see him; he referred to him, not by name, but just that he was there because she didn't trust her own father. He was saying a lot of nonsense. Anyway, it happened all of a sudden. I don't know who did what first — whether the guy rushed in or Bruce did something — he had a gun on him — but all of a sudden they were at it, or the guy was at it. Bruce never had a chance. The guy kicked him in the nuts and then started stabbing him with this huge knife."

Gorman suddenly sat on a stool near one of the work tables. He was staring at the floor, his hands intertwined in his lap. "It was horrible. Julie screamed and the guy hit her — without breaking stride. He was like a butcher, like the Devil himself. Bruce just dissolved into the ground. I'm not sure he even knew what hit him."

"And you never saw the guy's face?"

"All I could see were outlines — he was tall and thin. Bruce had dropped his flashlight. That's partly what made it worse; it was all so vague, almost like it wasn't happening at all, like a dream. And then it stopped. The guy picked up the flashlight — I got real scared then — but he didn't look around. He stuck something under the body, as if to pin it down, like it might blow away or whatever, and then he did something really odd. He pointed the flashlight at his feet and looked at them carefully, twisting them in the light, and then he rubbed one of them against Bruce's neck, smearing it with blood. It was disgusting, like Bruce was a dead animal or something. Then he took the gun from Bruce's pocket and left with Julie."

The mention of the lighter and the boot being smeared snapped another piece into place in my mind. It also eased that fierce and tiny pain I'd been carrying since the morning Bruce's body was discovered: Whatever else he might have done, whatever changes his character might have undergone, Rennie had not ended his life as a killer. That meant a great deal to me.

Spinney hadn't paused in his questions. "What was Julie Wingate doing through all this?"

"Crying and babbling — it didn't make any sense to me. She just sounded hysterical, like she had no idea what was happening. After they left, I waited until I thought they were long gone, then I turned on my flashlight and went to him. He looked horrible. I was just standing there feeling sick, not knowing what to do, when another light went on and caught me. I heard Julie scream a little again, so I know it was them. I guess they'd been waiting on the road above. So I took off as fast as I could."

"They didn't follow?"

"They might have tried, I don't know. I wasn't listening for them, and I sure as hell wasn't going to wait around. I'd parked my car way up the road and I just took off."

There was a slight pause while Spinney and I absorbed all this. Major questions remained unanswered: What had motivated Wingate's assailant to kill him? Since we now knew the killer wasn't Rennie, then who was he? Sarris, perhaps, hell bent on eliminating both Wingate and Rennie with one blow?

"Why were you there in the first place?" Spinney asked.

Gorman was sitting slumped on his stool, absentmindedly rubbing the side of his head. "Bruce called me. He called me several times — after the fire, after the lie detector test. He was falling apart. He'd gotten a note from Julie late Wednesday night asking him for a get-together later that night. We talked about it some; I said I'd come along to back him up, but we decided I should stay out of sight."

"Why come along at all? Weren't you running the risk of scaring her off?"

"Bruce was scared. I found out at that meeting that Julie had tried to kill him once already, just before the fire —" Gorman hesitated, obviously aware he'd opened a potential can of worms. He spoke rapidly to reseal the lid. "I know nothing about the fire, by the way. When Bruce called me that morning, all he said was that there had been one, that he'd gone back to the house after the fight with Fox, had argued with Julie, who'd reappeared, and that 'things hadn't worked out' — those were his words. He made it sound like the fire was just an accident."

"Did he tell you if Julie got away before the fire?" I asked, remembering Wingate's minimal interest in the victims the following morning.

"Not in so many words. I asked him something like, 'Is Julie okay?' and he said she was fine. I guess he lied about part of it to keep me involved. He knew I'd have nothing to do with violence."

Spinney ignored the self-righteous undertone. "You said you found out that night that Julie had tried to kill her father. What did she say exactly?"

Gorman looked pained, ruing his own indiscretion. "I don't remember exactly; it was something like, 'I'm sorry I didn't kill you.' "

"To which he said?"

" 'You don't know what you're saying.' "

"Was there any mention of how she tried

to kill him? A gun or a knife?"

"No."

"Or whether anyone else died as a result?"

"No, they both knew what they were talking about. They didn't go into detail for my benefit."

I spoke up. "If they didn't go into detail, how did you know she tried to kill her father before the fire — that's what you said. The fire could have been the method she tried."

Gorman was looking increasingly uncomfortable. "I'm trying to remember all this, okay? It was pretty wild. I think that's just something I assumed. As far as I know, they never saw each other after the fire, except for the night he died, so it must have been before. And I think the fire was accidental, because they both blamed each other for that."

Spinney mulled that over and returned to his original line of questioning. "So you say Wingate was scared, and that's why you agreed to be his backup?" His voice was totally neutral.

"He *was* scared — he even brought a gun. But all he told me was that he thought they were crazy and that he wouldn't know what to do if a bunch of them showed up at once."

"So you were supposed to be the cavalry? I find that hard to believe."

He hesitated.

"You're facing felony charges already, Gorman. Don't start dicking around now."

"All right, all right. Bruce was hoping he could talk her into coming back home — most parents do. But he also thought that if she wouldn't come, maybe the two of us could grab her. I'd told him that, if you can get a kid like that in a neutral place, sometimes you can turn them around, make them see the cult for what it is and give it up."

"So you were hoping to kidnap her?"

He didn't like the phrasing. "As a last resort. I didn't know she was homicidal. He lied to me."

"What was the meeting like, before the attack?"

Gorman looked bitter. "I was hiding up the hill a bit. It was dark, the sky had been covered by clouds, couldn't see your hand in front of your face. Bruce was at the bottom with a flashlight. Julie appeared out of nowhere — it was creepy. They talked. He accused her of causing the fire, and said if she came with him, no one would ever know about it."

"Did she admit setting it?"

"Not directly, but she talked about it. She said he was as much to blame as she was, that if he'd just left her alone, none of it would have happened. She made it sound like an accident, but one they'd both caused. It didn't make much sense to me."

"Go on."

"It was pretty obvious she hadn't called the meeting to talk about going home. She wanted him to leave her alone or she'd 'turn him in' — those were her words; I don't know what she meant. Anyway, he said she couldn't do that without implicating herself. She answered she didn't care because he'd ruined her life anyhow and now it was her turn, that her merely speaking out would screw up his job and his cherished reputation forever. She was incredibly angry. I mean, I'd never seen such hatred. She loathed the guy. I was thinking I'd tell him later that he was well rid of her and that he should dump the whole thing."

Spinney scratched his head in puzzlement. "Why didn't you report any of this? You weren't guilty of anything. In fact, you made yourself an accessory by keeping quiet — you must have known that."

Gorman looked at us with wide eyes. "You weren't there. This guy just took him apart. I mean, this wasn't some sort of fight where a gun goes off or something. This guy butchered him — like a madman. I was scared to death. They had that light right on me. I looked up into it — they saw my face."

"So why not get in your car and drive off into the sunset?" Spinney asked.

"I thought about it. But I had to talk to Ellie first, to tell her what had happened."

"Did you?"

"Not right away. I went to the Inn, but that old bat was around. I could see her through the windows."

"Greta?"

"Yeah. I don't know what she was doing, but she was up and about in the middle of the night. I was stuck then, because I didn't want to go back to the motel, in case they'd found out where I was staying, and I couldn't leave Ellie high and dry. So I drove around all night. I figured the motel would be safe after dawn, so then I waited in my room for Ellie to call me. I knew she would as soon as she heard about Bruce."

"Why didn't you just call her on your car phone?"

"It doesn't work up here, no cellular relay stations. Besides, I knew they didn't have a phone in their room. If I'd called, Greta would have answered and might have wondered later about the coincidence of Bruce dying and my telephoning the same night. I wasn't even supposed to be near here, much less at the scene of a crime."

"So why didn't you leave then?" Spinney persisted.

"I was going to, but then I saw what was

happening. Julie and whoever it was were trying to frame Rennie Wilson. That's when I realized I was probably okay. They'd seen who I was, but they weren't going to do anything about it because it would have blown their frameup."

"Come on, they could have rigged it some way. You could have had a fatal accident," I said.

"Running away wasn't going to guarantee my safety. I'm a public guy, easy to find. I figured maybe the best defense was a good offense, especially after I met Greta. If I made a big enough stink, with lots of publicity, it would not only give me some protection, but the extra heat would keep you guys on your toes, and the sooner you caught Julie and her father's killer, the sooner I could stop looking over my shoulder."

Spinney's voice was like acid. "Well, I don't know about you looking over your shoulder, but I'll guarantee you some protection." He slapped a pair of handcuffs onto Gorman's wrists and steered him out into the hallway, reading him his full rights.

31

Spinney and I were standing in the parking lot of the correctional facility on Route 5, just a little south of the State Police barracks, having hand-delivered Gorman there. The jail was high on a hill looking east, and we were both idly facing that direction without actually registering the view, which the falling snow had reduced to a blur in any case.

"So he was tall and thin." Spinney's voice was reflective.

"Yeah. He must have put Rennie's clothes on over his own — to keep himself warm and to expose the clothes to any blood. And he must have kept the pants up with suspenders. That's why that one spot of blood showed up where a belt would have been." I felt particularly vindicated with that last detail.

"So who do we know who's tall and thin?"

I looked at him. "Sarris."

Sarris, as usual, didn't seem surprised to see us. His only greeting was a single world-weary, "Ah."

"We'd like to speak with you, if we might," Spinney said.

Sarris shrugged and led the way through the big hall with its dozens of sparkling windows. At the far wall, he opened a small door I'd never noticed and ushered us in.

We stepped into a brightly lit room, very woodsy and warm, which looked like something torn out of an Aspen real estate brochure — bright ponchos on natural wood walls, beige wool upholstered armchairs and a sofa, a thick hand-woven rug in front of the fireplace, a huge slab of polished maple as a coffee table. There were watercolors hanging about, a couple of wooden duck decoys on the mantle, odd pieces of quaint metal farming tools propped about as decorations. The air was filled with soft classical music.

"Is this the cutting edge of anti-materialism?" I asked.

"Please, no polemics. Have a seat." He gestured to the various seats.

"Electricity too?"

He settled into an armchair opposite us and crossed his legs. He looked only at me. "What do you want?"

I glanced at Spinney, who merely nodded. I was to kick off. "A few more questions."

"I've already answered your questions." He was definitely more peevish than before, his polished, urbane patina worn down by current events — a good sign, I hoped.

"More have come up."

"I'm afraid that's your problem."

"Not really. You're in very hot water."

"It can't be too hot, or you would have arrested me for something."

"There are seven dead bodies out there, all of which have ties to you and the Natural Order. I wouldn't be too optimistic, if I were you, or so cocky."

"I have broken no laws."

"We have evidence that suggests otherwise," Spinney murmured gently.

"You know one of the things that threw me off?" I asked, to stop him from asking us to produce Spinney's "evidence." "It was why you were being so coy. If Julie killed her father, why didn't you just hand her over? You said your opposition was philosophical, but it's been forcing us to chip away and chip away, looking for a way to crack your whole organization wide open. She couldn't have meant that much to you. Besides, you've cooperated in the past. You helped the State Police when that child went over the bridge, and you supplied the identifications to the five people who died in the fire."

Sarris sighed. "I apologize for making you tax your brains unnecessarily. I'm not sure

I understand why you choose to continue doing so here and now."

Spinney spoke up again. "We want you to understand your position. Picture yourself on top of a mountain, with all of us climbing up in order to nail your hide. Each time we establish another fact, we take another step in your direction, and you've got nowhere to go — you're stuck where you are."

Somewhere, in the back of my brain, a bell was beginning to sound.

"I've committed no crime," Sarris repeated.

I was lost in my thoughts, digging furiously through a mental index file, trying to match two separate pieces of information.

Spinney kept going. "That's not true. Julie, for instance. Now there's one hot potato. As soon as we get our hands on her, your world is going to fall apart. But even if you've buried her in some ditch, and we never get to lay a legal hand on you, you're still out of business. Because what we can't do to you, the bad publicity will."

He hunched forward in his chair, warming to his task. "This is no Island Pond. We're the good guys this time. Have you been reading the papers?"

Spinney looked at him impassively. "Not good. Questions are being floated about your being the next Jim Jones. In fact, there was an editorial this morning that suggested we ought to close you down right now to protect the people under your thumb. In fact, your only chance of survival is if you start cooperating with us."

I stood up, the adrenaline pumping, a previously negligible tidbit of information suddenly large in the front of my mind. That I was about to pull the rug out from under Spinney was of little consequence at that moment, and I was convinced that in the long run, Spinney would agree with me. I made a lame attempt to end the interview with the upper hand by fixing Sarris with a stern eye and saying, "Think about it — if you meet us halfway, you might be able to salvage something."

Spinney looked at me, his mouth half open in stunned surprise. He struggled quickly to his feet so as not to look completely left out.

I led the way to the door. "We'll show ourselves out."

Spinney waited until we'd both gotten into the car. "What the hell was that all about? I hadn't even started with him. He must think we're out of our minds." For the first time since we'd met, Spinney was truly upset.

"You can sweat him later, and you can pat yourself on the back now."

"Why?" His voice was incredulous.

"Your flowery images do you justice." I

turned on the wipers to brush the snow off the windshield. "The hypothesis so far is that the guy who killed Wingate wouldn't have killed Rennie because he'd framed Rennie for Wingate's murder in the first place."

"So?"

"What do we know about Rennie's killer?"

Spinney pursed his lips, still mentally switching gears. "He's a woodsman, or at least an outdoorsman, good at tracking, good at keeping quiet."

"And athletic — probably slim and fit."

"Okay."

"I think I've seen him before."

With no cars parked out front, Nadine's house looked abandoned. Spinney and I walked up the long ramp to the front door and pressed the buzzer. The snow had stopped as abruptly as it had begun, leaving the entire countryside blanketed in a thick, white, sound-absorbing shroud.

We waited a long time before the door opened. Nadine looked up at us from her wheelchair and gave us the ghost of a smile. "Hi, Joe."

"Sorry to bother you, Nadine. Are we interrupting anything?"

"Just television."

"We can come back." That was diplomatic;

I had no intention of leaving.

She retreated a little from the threshold. "No, please. Come in."

We entered the house, closing the door behind us. I was again startled at how good the air smelled in here, especially in contrast to the Beirut-like front yard.

"This is Lester Spinney. He was here earlier."

Spinney bent over and shook her hand. "I apologize for not introducing myself then. We tend to lose our manners sometimes. I'm sorry about your husband."

She nodded and let her eyes drop to her lap. We were still standing at the door — the high, tinny sound of a television came from somewhere down the hall.

"We were wondering if we could ask you some questions," I said.

"Of course." She still didn't move or look up. Her voice was just above a whisper.

"How about over here?" I gestured to a living-room gathering of armchairs and a sofa near the large window I'd sat at before.

She raised her head then, embarrassed. "Of course, I'm sorry. Turn on some lights." She wheeled over to one of the lamps and switched it on. I did the same with another, shoving back the gloom of the overcast day outside. Spinney and I settled on the sofa, facing her.

"How're you holding up?" I asked.

"All right, I guess. I daydream a lot. It's hard being interested in anything. Buster's a help."

"He's been coming over a lot?"

"Oh, yes." She smiled that smile again. "I've had to throw him out a couple of times."

"He's very fond of you — I know that." I was aware of Spinney staring at me, wondering why I had made a total fool out of him in front of Sarris so that we could both come chat with Nadine about my uncle.

Nadine got a soft look in her eyes. "Buster's like a surrogate father. My own father was aloof and judgmental — he's dead now. But when he was alive, Buster would come over to drink and play cards. On the surface, that made him Dad's friend, but I always had the feeling that Dad wasn't the reason Buster came over at all. I think he did it for us, to see how we were doing."

"He had reason to be concerned?"

It was an open question, possibly innocent, but we all knew what I meant, and Nadine didn't duck the darker connotation, even while a faint smile played on her lips, an homage to lost innocence. "Looking back, I think he did. Earle and I didn't know it, though; life was what was handed out to you. Dad yelled a lot, sometimes he'd give me the back of his hand. Earle usually caught worse. I never understood what fueled Dad's rages, but he never let up. Buster knew what was going on — he became our guardian angel."

She chuckled briefly. "Buster's no saint, of course. He talks too much and drinks too much, and I would guess he's a terrible businessman, at least that's what Rennie always said. But he was a godsend to us."

"How did Buster and Rennie get along?" I had to go slowly here, despite Spinney's growing restlessness. What I wanted from Nadine had to come naturally; I didn't want her to later blame herself for what her information would help me to do.

"It's funny you should ask . . . I think Buster looked at Rennie like a son who'd never measured up. That always made me sad, because they were the two men I loved most. They both had very good qualities that I could see, but which they couldn't see in each other. Still, there must have been something good between them, or they wouldn't have spent so much time together. Maybe their problems had to do with competition."

"What about Earle?" I asked, finally getting to where I wanted to be. "How did he get along with Buster and Rennie?"

"He and Buster got along — to a point. I think he appreciated that when Buster was here, Dad left him alone. But after Buster left, and Dad would start bad-mouthing him — just like he did everybody — Earle would go along, like a backup singer. Somehow the bad-mouthing kind of stuck, like some oil that won't wash off."

"And Rennie?"

There was a pause at that. Nadine had her head bent, apparently looking at her hands. Only after a few moments did I notice her shoulders gently shaking as she wept.

"I'm sorry, Nadine. Maybe we should go." I still didn't mean it. By now, the stimulus that had put me in front of her was strong enough that I was prepared to be ruthless in its pursuit.

She raised her head then and reached out to touch my knee, possibly sensing my dilemma. "It's your job, Joey. It can't be any worse than what I've just been through."

I took hold of her fingers and gave them a squeeze, looking into her tear-stained face. Her gesture allowed me to be more sincere with my regret. "I wish I could be more like Buster and help you, instead of adding to your troubles."

She shook her head and smiled weakly. "One Buster is enough."

I was impressed and touched by her strength. When we'd first met, when suspicion on Rennie verged on conviction, she'd struck me almost as a lost child, caught in her chair, swept aside by events. She'd spoken in a whisper, struggled morally to stand by her man, and had backed up his Wednesday night alibi. But during the course of this conversation, I'd totally changed my view of her. What I had thought was a fear of the unknown had now proven to be a firm grasp on reality: Her husband was dead, she was on her own, and she had the ability and the emotional wherewithal to deal with that.

She took a deep breath. "What did Earle think of Rennie? He hated him. It was an irrational kind of thing, the kind of thing my father would do."

"Why the hatred?"

She looked like someone trying to move a huge weight out of the way. She gave that sad smile and tapped the arm of her chair. "This had a lot to do with it — and those Wednesday nights."

I was stunned. "You knew what Rennie was up to?"

She pursed her lips but her voice was steady. "I had my suspicions. It made me unhappy, but I didn't blame him.

"We hadn't had much of a physical relationship since this." She touched the chair. "And he was a very physical man. I knew he'd replace what we had with someone else, and I appreciated that he tried to spare my feelings."

I crossed the room to the picture of Earle I'd noticed days earlier, the one of him with a looped bandolier of climbing ropes. "And Earle found out about Rennie's infidelity?"

She shook her head in frustration. "Nobody understood what Rennie and I had. They all thought he was a crude, short-tempered womanizer, and that I was a fool for putting up with him. Earle used to go on and on about him, telling me I deserved everything I got for hanging on. The funny thing was, I agreed with him. I did deserve Rennie, just as he deserved me. What people chose to see as major problems were nothing to us — little glitches, as we saw it. We loved each other. He didn't change after the accident; people's view of me did. Just because I was in this chair, people thought he was supposed to become a whole different person. Well, he didn't and I loved him for that. The fact that life's disappointments wore him down a bit, and that we no longer had in bed what we once had was our business, and we'd come to terms with it. I love Buster but he looks at me as a cripple. Rennie never did that, and to me that was worth putting up with a lot."

It was an eloquent and suitable note to end

on, but I had one question remaining. I noticed Spinney was now sitting on the edge of his chair, watching us carefully. "What did you mean when you said your wheelchair had a lot to do with Earle hating Rennie?"

Nadine took a deep breath and then lifted her eyes to meet mine. "Rennie pushed me down the stairs. It was an accident. He was drunk, didn't know what he was doing. But Earle never forgave him."

"I never heard Rennie pushed you," I said. "Word had it you just fell."

"Small town, Joe, you keep things like that to yourself. Even Earle did, which always surprised me. I didn't think he had it in him."

I stood up abruptly, trying to keep my voice neutral. "Maybe he had his reasons."

Nadine had said we couldn't miss it, a single rectangular building, alone among the trees, the only house within a ten-square-mile area, at the end of a rutted, dead-end track in the woods.

I stopped the car about a hundred yards away, watching for signs of life.

"No smoke from the chimney," Spinney said.

It was a one-story rectangle with one of the narrow walls facing us. We could see a door, with a small window on either side.

"He could have a bead on us right now." Spinney scanned the trees all around. They were packed so close together that even without their leaves, they cut what feeble daylight there was in half.

He took his shotgun from the backseat of the car.

"Think we ought to call in the troops?"

He chambered a shell and looked at the house again. "We don't even know he's in there. I did tell 'em where we were headed."

We got out at the same time and stood silently for a while on either side of the car, listening. The trees and ground were heavy with undisturbed snow, including around the front door of the house. It was so cold the snow creaked underfoot when we finally began to walk forward. The cold steel of my service revolver caused my bare hand to ache slightly.

We kept about fifteen feet apart until we reached the wall. Then, ducking under the windows, we reconvened on either side of the door. Spinney shifted his shotgun and pointed at the door frame. There was a slight gap — the door was slightly open.

I reached out and pushed inward. The door swung back without a sound.

"Earle? This is the police. We want to talk to you."

Nothing. We strained to hear anything beyond the occasional groaning of a tree and the isolated scurrying of an invisible woods animal.

Spinney cautiously poked his head around the corner, his features etched in nervous strain. Then, slowly, gaining confidence from what he saw, or didn't see, he nodded to me and made his move, gliding around the edge of the door and to the left, as I did the same to the right.

We both ended up in a kitchen, crouched against the wall, our guns pointed at an empty room with an open doorway opposite. The place was as cold as the outside. On the floor before us lay a short jumble of climbing rope, an Army-type web belt with various pouches, and an empty scabbard. Next to it was an enormous bowie knife. The knife lay slightly to one side, as if thrown there, its otherwise gleaming blade tarnished with smears of dried blood.

We crossed the kitchen to the other door and looked in. The curtains were drawn across the windows, but enough light filtered through to reveal a small, messy living room with an assortment of cast-off furniture and a short, dark hallway beyond. Now well inside the tiny house, we were cut off from even the rare sounds of the frigid forest. Spinney and I looked nervously at each other. As before, we split to either side and crossed the room to the cavelike opening of the narrow hall.

Keeping our bodies out of sight, we craned our necks to see what lay ahead. The darkness was virtually total, a corridor leading to an absolute black void.

I shut my eyes briefly and then reopened them. What lay ahead was not entirely blacked out; there was something there. I could sense from Spinney's sudden stiffening that he'd seen the same thing. In the midst of the gloom, barely visible, there was a single tiny red point of light — the tip of a burning cigarette.

"Earle, this is the police. Come on out with your hands up."

Nothing, not a sound nor a movement.

Spinney began to back toward the front of the building. "This stinks. I'm calling for backup. I'll bring back a flashlight, too. Wait here."

I nodded my approval. Not to have asked for backup earlier had been a judgment call, one on which we'd both agreed. Now, there was no alternative. Christ only knew what Earle had waiting for us in that bedroom.

I stared long and hard at the small point of light. "Come on, Earle, give it up. This is stupid."

Again, no sound and no movement. And no brains, I thought suddenly. I grabbed a pillow off the couch beside me and tossed it like a Frisbee into the bedroom, directly at the cigarette. I missed, but not by much, and still the tiny red glow didn't move a hair.

"Shit — we've been had." I still didn't dare enter the bedroom; he might be standing in the corner, waiting for one of us to do just that, but I was also afraid for Spinney. If the cigarette had been a lure, it might have been rigged precisely to split us up.

I ran back to the kitchen and looked out the window toward Spinney's car. I was just in time to see him being handcuffed to the doorframe by a thinner, dirtier version of the man in Nadine's photograph. As I watched, the man began returning to the house.

He was about one hundred yards away, a distance he would take cautiously since he didn't know whether I was still standing by the bedroom door, or waiting to blow him away. I didn't want to kill him, but I thought about putting him in my sights and telling him to drop the rifle he was carrying. But Spinney was directly in my line of fire. If I had to shoot, my bullet could pass right through Earle and hit Spinney. I retreated toward the bedroom, scooping the rope off the kitchen floor as I went.

I quickly pulled back the blanket Earle had rigged across the open window, flooding the place with light. Taped to the iron bed's headboard, facing the door, was a barely smoldering cigarette. Without pausing to admire the man's style, I quickly tied one end of the rope around the leg of a side table and passed the rest of it out the window. Then, poking my head outside to see if the coast was clear, I sat on the windowsill, swung my legs out silently, and let the curtain drop closed behind me.

Without a sound, my gun in one hand and the end of the rope in the other, I moved along the wall, below the windows, until I was just shy of the front corner of the house.

Just a few yards away, around that corner, I heard Earle quietly open the front door. I pulled gently on the rope. Barely audibly, I heard a scraping sound come from the back of the house. I counted to three, and looked quickly around the corner. Earle was gone and Spinney was still at the car, his eyes fixed on me.

With the rope still in hand, I scurried to the door and very carefully looked in. Earle was in the kitchen, crouching by the living room entrance. Again, I pulled on the rope. He tensed and levelled the rifle toward the rear of the building, turning his back to me completely.

Using the doorframe as cover, I pointed my gun at him and spoke softly. "Don't move, Earle — not a muscle."

There was that inevitable slow count of three, that endless moment in which fateful decisions are made between life and death. I wasn't sure of Earle. I didn't even know the man. He'd had a hard life, had his brains twisted around by the very person who should have lent him guidance, and he'd finally given in to the ultimate act of violence. I was fully expecting him to turn that rifle on me to put his misery forever behind him.

But he didn't. He laid it on the ground beside him and placed his hands on top of his head. He was smiling when he turned around. "How the hell . . . ?"

I showed him the rope and pulled it. The table moved a bit in the dark beyond him. "Lie down on the floor — hands behind your neck and ankles crossed."

He did as he was told and I put my handcuffs on him.

"I didn't expect your buddy to come out so fast. I was going to nail both of you inside."

His voice was utterly calm, as if he were sorting out the details of some minor housekeeping mishap. I decided to take advantage of what might be just a temporary state of mind.

"Why'd you kill Rennie?"

He snorted. "You wouldn't be here if you didn't know that."

"Why now?"

"Dumb luck. I saw him pull into Lemon Road when I was coming down Radar. I was feeling bad, thought a drive might clear my head. It sure did. I saw him, followed him, watched him rig a meeting with those fruit-cake bastards, waited 'til they left, and then I cut him open. I've wanted to do that for more years than I can remember. It felt great. You should have seen him go."

I watched him lying on his stomach, his cheek pressed against the cold wood floor, a smile on his face. Now I knew why he hadn't challenged me — the life had already gone out of him. He didn't give a damn anymore.

"The fruitcake bastards — was one of them Edward Sarris?"

He cocked an eye at me, surprised. "Him and some girl. You got all the answers, don't you?"

Didn't I wish. "I'm getting there."

32

Hamilton stopped the car halfway up the hill and watched Sarris's building. Most of it was dark, with only the windows to the far left brightly lit.

"Looks like somebody's still at home," Spinney murmured.

"Son of a bitch never leaves the place," Smith said.

I looked at Smith out of the corner of my eye. For the first time, I sensed a small bounce to his voice. And earlier, while Spinney and I were being debriefed on the Earle Renaud bust, I'd felt somehow that the rigidity with which he'd addressed me from the start had melted a couple of degrees. It was nothing measurable, but it was more than my wishful thinking. For some reason, I'd finally been elevated from being a mere SA investigator and a thorn in Smith's side. It shouldn't have mattered to me one way or the other, but I was pleased nevertheless. It justified the number of times I'd resisted simply writing the man off, as I always sensed Spinney had, perhaps to his own loss.

We continued up the hill, drove around the edge of the building, and parked next to the Cherokee with the "ORDER" license plate. It was only six at night, but already pitch-dark.

Sarris answered our knock with a flashlight in his hand. He led us without uttering a word through the gigantic gloominess of the meeting room to his private inner sanctuary. Hamilton and Smith had never been in that part of the building before, and were obviously surprised by its Greenwich, Connecticut gloss.

Sarris seemed totally distracted, which made me wonder what might have happened during the few hours since Spinney and I had last sat in this room. It might have been that Sarris had had time to mull over Spinney's dire prediction of his fate and that of his organization, but I sensed there was something more, something tangible that had made him realize just how thin the ice was beneath him.

After we were all seated, he fixed me with his large, dark eyes. At some early point in this case, he had focused on me, first as his primary antagonist, and now I thought, almost as a personal nemesis.

"What do you want?"

I looked at the others. Hamilton gave me

a slight nod to go ahead. "We arrested a man named Earle Renaud a few hours ago, for the murder of Rennie Wilson."

"Good for you. Of what interest is that to me?" Sarris crossed his legs nonchalantly, but I felt the gesture belied a subtle tension in his features.

"It turns out Earle had been watching Rennie for quite some time before he stuck him with a knife, long enough to see him meet with you and Julie Wingate."

Sarris remained silent.

"Do you admit to meeting Rennie the day he died?"

"You're the one with the witness, Lieutenant."

"What did you three talk about?"

Sarris propped his elbows on the arms of his chair and made a steeple of his fingers in front of his mouth. I recalled his earlier comment that he'd had a lot of practice appearing in court. He had to walk a fine line with us — to appear accommodating and yet stay clear of self-incrimination. But I sensed from his curtness he was also running on limited reserves, and that the game of cat and mouse was becoming increasingly less rewarding. It was a weakness I hoped to work on.

He finally cleared his throat, opting for a half-truth. "Our meeting was clandestine, not illegal. Mr. Wilson invited us there."

"Why?"

"Oh, he was concerned that Julie Wingate was somehow involved in implicating him in her father's death."

"By planting his lighter under Wingate's body."

Sarris hesitated. "He did mention a lighter."

"Why did you agree to meet with Rennie at all? You were under no obligation to him, were you?"

"Of course not, but Julie was quite upset over her father's death. I thought this meeting might be of some help to her, maybe shed some light on why Bruce Wingate was killed."

"Weren't you a little nervous about being alone in the woods with a suspected murderer?"

"I had no quarrel with Wilson."

"You had no quarrel with a man who'd been blackmailing you for months?"

Sarris sat absolutely still.

"A man to whom you'd been supplying women, including Julie Wingate, because he had information that would shut the Order down overnight? Seems to me that might constitute grounds for a quarrel, even a rather violent one."

"You said yourself you'd captured Wilson's murderer."

"But Rennie Wilson had been framed by the man who killed Bruce Wingate. Wilson wasn't supposed to die; he was supposed to take the fall for the death of a man that had caused you grievous harm. In fact, Bruce Wingate was a challenge to your credibility within the Order." I paused here for a theatrical mix of fact and bluff. "He had killed five of your followers, burned one of your houses to the ground, and was intending on kidnapping his own daughter from under your protection. With Wingate's death and Rennie taking the blame, you took care of two major problems with one fell swoop. Very efficient."

Sarris's eyebrows shot up, in what I was afraid was genuine surprise. "You're saying I killed Wingate?"

"It fits. We have a witness to his murder, and another who will testify that Rennie Wilson was blackmailing you."

Sarris was now visibly perturbed. "You have a witness who says I killed Bruce Wingate?"

"Paul Gorman was also at the bottom of that ravine. Wingate had asked him to come along for backup. He saw the whole thing."

"Well, he didn't see me. I was nowhere near that ravine. Do you think I'd be stupid enough to jeopardize all I've built to kill Bruce Wingate? He wasn't undermining my

464

credibility. The idea's absurd."

"I hardly thought you'd like it. A jury probably will, though, especially when they hear how far you went to keep Rennie quiet, first by paying him off in sexual favors, and then by framing him for murder." My mind was whirling by now, flipping though the facts we'd built up over the past several days, looking for the connections that would widen the cracks in Sarris's composure. Rennie had begun blackmailing Sarris six months ago, more or less. He'd also lost his lighter to Julie Wingate at that time, and she'd been the first woman Sarris had supplied. What had happened six months ago that gave Rennie the ammunition he needed to put the squeeze on Sarris?

And then it came to me, like a bolt from the blue. It fit perfectly, gave a logic to it all. But it needed to be confirmed. Only Sarris could do that, and only if he believed I was already sure of my facts. I sat back in my chair and smiled at him, trying to hide my nervousness. "That must have seemed like a nice piece of irony — framing Rennie for murder — since that's exactly what he was holding over you."

The room was absolutely still. I could hear my own heartbeat thumping away behind my temples, its rapid rate belying my outward calm.

"I don't know what you're talking about," Sarris said in a flat voice, devoid of conviction.

"The child that fell from the bridge, the toddler that supposedly shook off his companion and went running to his death on the streambed below. The child that was actually murdered, and whose murder you conspired to cover up."

"You're bluffing."

"Really? Did you think Rennie would keep that information to himself, a good-ol'-boy redneck like that? Hell, the first thing he did was share some of those women with his best friend in East Burke. Discretion wasn't his long suit — he had you by the balls and it tickled him pink."

Sarris dropped his eyes to the floor. His hands were on his knees, his feet flat on the ground. It was the posture of a far older man, browbeaten and tired, whose resistance had all but drained from his soul. He let out a long sigh. The bluff had worked.

"That child was mentally retarded, did you know that?"

"Yes, I did."

"In previous centuries, its death would have been seen as a blessing, God calling His own back to His breast. And in the animal world, it wouldn't have survived its first day of life. We have surely turned the world on its ear, we civilized men." His voice was bitter.

"Who killed it?" I asked softly.

"His own mother — so hopeful she'd produce something decent and pure, and so shattered when it turned out defective, like herself."

Considering the cast of characters we had, that could only be one person. The realization weighed in my chest like a stone. "Julie Wingate."

He nodded.

I thought of the monstrosity of Sarris forcing Julie to have sex with his own tormentor. The twisted psychosis that would have seen poetic justice in that arrangement could only have belonged to a colossal egomaniac. It was ironic indeed that the same ego had precluded Sarris from simply handing Julie over to the police at the time she killed her child, thereby washing his hands of the entire affair and making himself look like a responsible citizen to boot. The high price of playing God was that when you stumbled, you brought your world down with you.

I did some more mental mathematics, comparing the age of Julie's child to when her parents had said she'd first told them of her "new friends," almost three years ago.

"Julie was pregnant when she joined the Order."

Sarris was still studying the floor. "Yes. I believe Fox overdid it a bit in the recruiting."

"She was living with Fox when he died. I thought you discouraged that kind of attachment."

He shrugged. "He was a close friend, more of a cofounder than a member of the Order. He fell in love with her; I wasn't going to argue. I have to admit, though, I didn't see the attraction."

"Where is Julie now?"

"I let her go," he said simply.

I now understood Sarris's odd mood when we'd first entered his house. Perhaps Spinney's little chat earlier had made an impression. By letting Julie go, Sarris had finally rid himself of his major problem, or so he must have thought until we'd returned to his doorstep.

"Where did she go?" Smith asked, speaking for the first time.

"I don't know. I let her loose like a minnow in the ocean, so that she might just disappear forever."

"How did she leave?" Hamilton asked.

Sarris looked up at him, his brow slightly furrowed. "I gave her the keys to one of those cars outside."

"Would you know which one?"

"A white VW bus." Sarris seemed totally disinterested in us now, and perhaps even in himself. The sense of caution which had made him guarded when we'd first begun to chat had vanished utterly, and he seemed content to answer whatever questions were asked of him. Hamilton and Spinney put handcuffs behind his back and escorted him from the room.

"Well, that's good news," Smith muttered to himself.

"What is?"

"That she took one of those junkers. They've been sitting around for so long, they must be half-rotted inside. I doubt she'll get very far before something breaks."

"Then we can ask her who killed Bruce Wingate."

Smith shot me a surprised look. "You don't think Sarris did it?"

"No, I don't. I think he's as much in the dark as we are."

33

I didn't sleep that night. I didn't even bother undressing. I just lay on the bed with a blanket over me, staring at the ceiling and playing it over in my mind, time and time again. The picture, as such, was almost complete. Like museum restorers cleaning an old and valuable painting, we'd painstakingly rubbed away the obfuscating layers. But what we saw now was confusing — abstract art where we'd been expecting realism. The missing element, we were convinced, had to be Julie, a fractured, self-abused psychotic. At the end of all our rational deliberations, of all our archaeological thoroughness, we were reduced to combing the countryside in search of a pathetically sick girl with a brain full of secrets.

When Spinney called to say they'd found her vehicle, I was in my coat and out the door in under five minutes.

Riding with Spinney through the predawn blackness, watching the icy sheen of the pavement racing beneath our headlights, I wondered what sad conclusion we were rushing to meet. "So where're we headed?"

"Graniteville, near Barre. Our guess is she was sticking to the backroads — Route 5 to 2; Route 2 to 302 via the Perkinsville town highway; something like that, maybe even more roundabout. No way of telling where she was headed in the long run, but she ran out of luck near Graniteville. Busted radiator hose; Smith was right."

"So she's on foot?"

"That's what we're going to find out. Bishop's ahead of us with the others. I figured I ought to call you, considering."

"Thanks."

"Bishop's got a dog with him, and some of Julie's clothes from Sarris's place — maybe they can pick up a scent."

We drove in silence for a while. Graniteville is aptly named, being the center for a handful of huge granite quarries, some of which have been producing for well over a hundred years. I'd heard somewhere that if demand for the stone continued, the whole area could be productive for hundreds of more years. I didn't see how they could miss, considering that much of their stone ended up marking graves.

There was only the slightest hint of predawn grey in the sky when we pulled up next to a cluster of marked and unmarked police cars by the side of a narrow, black-topped country road. As soon as I got out, I saw John Bishop, surrounded by men with flashlights, holding a wad of clothing to the nose of an excited bloodhound. Keeping the clothes in place, Bishop then pulled the dog over to the driver's side of a rusty, battered VW bus.

"Why not just track her?" I asked Spinney as we approached the group.

"Take too long. The engine was still a little warm when we found it. Unless she got another ride, she can't be too far away."

Bishop released the hound to the end of a ten-foot leash. Everybody stood back as the now whining dog darted feverishly back and forth along the ditch bordering the road. As his lithe body flitted in and out of the bobbing flashlight beams, I thought of what it must be like in Julie's position, hearing voices, seeing those stabbing points of light, and being aware that a dog was on her scent. Years earlier, I'd heard of how rabbit hunters in Scotland released ferrets into burrows to encourage the residents to flee into a hail of welcoming buckshot. The trick, apparently, was to avoid hitting the one rabbit that would have the ferret firmly attached to the back of its neck. Despite the obvious differences, I still didn't envy Julie her position.

The dog finally took off into the brush on the other side of the ditch, and with an increased babble of voices, the men crashed in after it.

Spinney jumped the ditch and looked back at me. "Coming?"

"I'll be there."

He waved and vanished into the gloom and the undergrowth. To be honest, I hoped I wasn't there; there were too many undertones to this kind of pursuit to make me want to join in.

Instead, mostly to fight off the early morning chill, I walked up the road a piece, playing my flashlight along the side, not looking for anything in particular. Eventually, I came across a gravel road heading off to the same side the tracking party had taken. The dust showed the impressions of many wide heavy tires — and a single set of boot prints.

Earlier, off Lemon Road, John Bishop had muttered a pet adage, "There are no sharp edges in nature," meaning that it didn't take long for a print's outline to soften on its way back to becoming undisturbed soil. The prints I was looking at were very sharp indeed.

I hesitated a moment, wondering if I should call the others, but they were already tracking Julie. What I had before me were probably the tracks of some quarryman showing up early for work, or maybe a supervisor or watchman. I walked along the road for a quarter mile or so and came to a chain-link gate with a sign proclaiming, CELESTIAL STONE COMPANY — ANDREWS PIT. NO TRESPASSING — VIOLATORS WILL BE PROSECUTED. The sign seemed to confirm my doubts.

I tugged at the lock uniting the chain that held the gate together. It was closed. I pushed at the wire mesh. It swung back a few feet, widening the gap between the two halves of the gate. I looked at the gap appraisingly, contemplating the challenge. Then I saw where the footprints had slipped through ahead of me.

I tried fitting through the gap, with laughable results. I pulled off my coat and sweater and tossed them through ahead of me. If I didn't make it this time, I'd freeze to death — the ultimate diet. I did make it, though, at the cost of several buttons, and quickly put my clothes back on.

The footprints immediately vanished to the side of the road, back to the safety of the brush, so I stuck to the road, going on the hunch that whoever had come this way had paralleled my route.

I knew this still qualified as a wild-goose chase, but my interest was now no longer idle. Kids on a dare usually travel in packs; it helps bolster the courage and affords ready witnesses for later bragging at bull sessions.

This had been very clearly one set of tracks, and that, for obvious reasons, was intriguing. Furthermore, I could still hear my colleagues, though faintly, and they sounded like they, too, were headed in roughly the same direction.

About a half mile later, I came to a clearing, bordered by buildings ahead, and trees on either side. It was a large area, big enough to easily turn an 18-wheeler without going into reverse. Yielding to impulse, I walked over to the edge of the gravel and began looking for the footprints to reappear. I followed the perimeter of the parking area to the most distant spot from the buildings, and there I found them again. I began to feel like a bloodhound myself; it didn't much matter that I probably would end up finding some teenager smoking pot.

There was a large pile of dusty, broken granite blocks that met the bordering trees at a ninety-degree angle. The tracks led me up the pile and over to the other side, and there, glowing slightly in the dawn's struggling half-light, was a sight that damn near made my heart stop.

It was a huge, round pit, the size and depth of a small canyon, about one thousand feet across, and some four hundred feet deep, yawning and utterly silent. The walls were a series of fifty-foot wide, vertical grooves, interspaced with similarly wide buttresses — what mountain climbers call chimneys and ribs. At twenty-foot intervals, roughly a third of these chimneys and ribs were cut with narrow horizontal terraces, on which ladders had been placed as escape routes so the granite workers could use them in emergencies. Some of the terraces interconnected, but most did not. Here and there, usually in the grooves, especially deep terraces had been cut to allow for the placement of large pieces of equipment — generators, winches, elevator boxes for workers to ride up and down, and small wooden foremen shacks. For the most part, however, the terraces were as narrow as ledges, barely five feet wide.

Around the pit's edge were about ten towering pole cranes, all harnessed to each other by an overhead spider's web of steel cables. It gave me the creepy feeling of having an oppressive presence bearing down on me, like a huge, half-seen hand ready to flatten me and flick me into the hole. Instinct told me to quickly extinguish my flashlight and to move as quietly as possible.

I crawled down the other side of the pile and reached a broad strip of flat rock that marked the edge. Moving slowly, a foot at a time, sensing my way partly by the growing daylight and partly by feel, I moved toward the pit. The edge, when I finally got there, was as sharp as a knife — one inch beyond where my shoe rested on flat granite, the cliff dropped to some barely visible milky green water about four hundred feet below. The sight was so destabilizing I had to quickly sit down to regain my balance. My stomach was slightly queasy.

Getting onto my hands and knees, I forced myself to look over the edge. Some twenty feet below me was the first of the narrow ledges, but its ladder was lying flat, instead of connecting it to where I was. It had either fallen with amazing precision, or it had been taken down to prevent pursuit.

I scanned the walls for any activity, but there was nothing. The water-streaked pale gray rock, utterly motionless, seemed to let off a light of its own. This apparent inner glow was in gloomy contrast to the line of dark trees above, and the opaque green water far below. The place was as still as the graveyards it supplied.

Why come here? I thought. I looked to my right, to where the sun was trying to assert some presence. This wasn't an entirely enclosed circular pit — to the east was a narrow opening to the valley below. If someone had been forced to stop here, say by a blown radiator hose, escape by road would be highly risky, especially so near to a vehicle being sought by police. Similarly, cutting across country wouldn't work too well; the woods were thick and, conversely, the area was much more populated than the Northeast Kingdom.

But here was a sort of deranged logic — you could scale down the sides of the pit, dumping ladders as you went, and leave through the opening to the east. Progress would be rapid, direct pursuit would be severely handicapped, and you'd end up miles away by road from where the incriminating vehicle had been left. If the bus was found quickly, the warm engine would actually be an asset, implying you were close, and thus encouraging the police cordon to be so tight that it might even exclude you.

I smiled at the thought. There was one problem, though. Bishop, the dog, and everybody else were hot on Julie's trail, or of someone wearing her clothes. They were way the hell and gone — from what I could hear — on another quadrant of the pit. If they were on the right track, Julie's track, then who the hell was I following? And if she and my guy were associates, why had they taken separate paths?

The first theory — using the pit as an escape route — appealed to me; the second theory had me worried: You don't split up forces if you're running for a narrow exit. But you might if you're setting up an ambush. I looked at the forbidding walls below and opposite me, visualizing what a perfect target a man would be as he slowly climbed down those ladders.

I shook my head. It didn't make sense. You don't ambush the State Police. It would be suicidal; the best you could hope for, even in a perfect spot like this, would be to delay things for a while. I chewed on that for a bit, and finally snapped my fingers silently: That was the whole point — to delay things and attract attention, divert the chase long enough for one of them to get away. A lover's leap.

That's when I heard the stone fall from somewhere below me. It rattled and bounced and ended as a tiny, distant splash.

I began listening so hard I almost stopped breathing. The escape gap was to the east. I was to the southwest. From what I could guess, the others with the bloodhound would appear to the southeast, or right between me and the escape gap.

Swallowing hard, I leaned out as far as I could without losing my balance. I was at the top of one of the buttresses, or "ribs." The ledge below, as narrow as it was, still blocked a full view of the one farther down, which in turn totally hid the rest. I checked to both sides of me, hoping I could get over enough to see the cliff face from another angle. The trees growing out to the edge ruled that out — it would take me too long and I would make too much noise trying to gain a proper viewpoint.

Across the pit I could see tiny pinpoints of light flashing among the trees. The search party would soon become a climbing party — and target practice for whoever was below me. If I shouted or fired my pistol to warn them, I'd lose the advantage of surprise and I might scare off my prey: After all, I was just assuming he was boxed in. It was possible he had an escape figured out other than the obvious one of merely climbing back up his set of ladders.

I backed away from the edge and trotted over to the small buildings, looking for something that might help me reach that first ledge. What I found was a large wooden spool with hundreds of feet of three quarter-inch cable wrapped around it. It was almost taller than I was and probably weighed as much as a truck. I quickly began unlooping cable, thankful I'd packed along a pair of heavy leather gloves.

As quietly as possible, I pulled the cable along behind me, wrapped it around one of the larger granite chunks so the angle would be right, and very quietly paid out about forty feet of cable over the side, making sure the extra twenty didn't slip over the ledge's lip. What I couldn't see was whether the second ladder was standing or had been laid down like the first — the extra cable was insurance.

The search party opposite had broken out into the open. That still gave me time. They had to coordinate before deciding to use their own set of ladders, which I'd already noticed had been helpfully left in place.

I checked the cable again. I'd taken mandatory rappelling during some police training course, so long ago now I couldn't even remember the decade, much less the year. I'd hated it then, even with all the equipment, the safeguards, and the instructors. Now I had none of those. I was going to dangle over four hundred feet of space, the way a boy swings on a rope from an apple tree.

"You are one stupid son of a bitch," I muttered, as I eased over the side and began to let myself down.

I realized I was in trouble one inch after it was too late to do anything about it. Cable, unlike rope, is smooth, and affords no grip for a pair of leather gloves, and as I began to slip faster and faster down the line, I thought that might be the last educational tidbit of my life. I put all my strength into my hands and feet, squeezing as tightly as I could, hoping to at least maintain my speed, if not slow it. It worked, but when I hit the ledge with burning hands, I did so as a solid muscular mass, with no give whatsoever. The shockwave almost blew the top of my head off. I collapsed into a painful puddle, throbbing from my ankles to my neck, totally oblivious to any noise I might have made.

After lying there for a couple of minutes, my focus returned, along with an absolute, stomach-churning fear. I realized suddenly that not only had I almost killed myself going after someone I only thought might be threatening the others, but that now I was stuck on a horizontal sliver of rock five feet wide with a cliff above and a cliff below. Had I been suspended above a fiery pit by sewing thread, I couldn't have been more scared.

I closed my eyes to concentrate. No point going back now. Things couldn't get worse than this. Slowly, I finally got to my hands and knees and peered over to the next landing, hoping I'd find the bastard I was after. Luckily I didn't — I was fully prepared to shoot him on the spot.

Instead I saw a wooden ladder, its outer rails tapering together into the distance until they reached what appeared to be a dime-sized spot on the ledge below. I was sweating like a pig just looking at it. The only source of comfort was that the top rung had been attached to the rock with a metal clip.

I glanced over to the other side. People were clustered around the top ladder there, obviously preparing to descend. I figured if there was somebody setting them up, he'd wait until he had several of them exposed. I gingerly poked my leg over and felt with my toes for the uppermost rung.

The ladder bounced a little under my weight, but it wasn't as bad as I'd feared, especially when I remembered to keep my eyes straight in front of me. I also put enormous faith in that clip, probably more than was due, but by the time I set foot on the second ledge, I was convinced nothing shy of dynamite could move that ladder or any of its peers. I'd conveniently forgotten that the top ladder's attachment had obviously offered no great resistance to my predecessor.

I was still scared shitless, but I now figured I could do it. Across the way, one man had already reached the bottom of the first ladder and another was poised to follow him. I quickly looked over the side.

There was a third ledge, but with a difference. Instead of falling off at each end, as mine had, this one wrapped around to the sides. I was on an "rib" cliff, flanked on either side by two "chimneys."

I crawled on my hands and knees to the far end of my ledge — away from the other searchers — and stuck my head over cautiously. Below me, on the same level as the third ledge, was one of the wide stone platforms I'd noticed earlier, cut to support assorted pieces of machinery. More interesting, however, was the fact that the series of ladders I'd been using switched over to this side and continued on down the chimney from that platform. That meant that anyone descending from the platform would be invisible to those across the way. In other words, there was an escape route, but only from that third level below me. By now, convinced I was right, I scuttled over to the other end and took a peek.

There was a matching rock platform, similarly cluttered, including one of those small huts I'd taken to be foremen offices. Daylight was now truly breaking, the weak sun eating away at the darker shadows, but I still couldn't see any movement. I swore under my breath; I couldn't believe after all this that I'd been wrong. I looked across the pit again. There were three men on various ladders. If I were a sniper, I'd wait for maybe two more at most, pick off as many as I could quickly, split for the other platform, and climb down my way to freedom. By the time they saw me running along the edge of the water below toward the exit gap, it would be all but too late. That thought encouraged me about something else: If this wasn't a suicidal attack, then Julie was still waiting nearby, possibly even at the bottom of the pit, to be joined by her protector.

But it was all still theory — I had the plan and the place, but still no shooter. I lay staring at the little hut, the one place that offered good cover. That had to be it. If it wasn't, however, and I went down there . . . I interrupted the thought. Slowly, and without a sound, I saw the window facing the opposite cliff swing open. I had him.

My earlier fear was flushed away by adrenaline; I trotted back to the ladder and climbed down it quickly to the third level. I knew now I was dealing with a couple of minutes or less. I went over to what I'd mentally coined the escape platform and checked that the ladder going down from it was attached with a clip. It was. I looked around for a tool, something to use as a pry bar. There was a long metal rod lying by one of the machines. I got it under the top rung of the ladder and pulled hard. The wood cracked a little. I repositioned and tried again. This time it split right through, freeing the ladder from the wall. Oblivious to the noise it might make, I shoved the ladder forward, pitching it into the abyss and closing the back door to the shooter. Now, even if I didn't make it, he could only go back up to those above.

There wasn't much sound, however. The ladder was still sailing through the air by the time I made it back to the narrow connecting ledge, and the first gentle clatters weren't heard until I'd almost made it to the other chimney's platform. Still, I was late. Just as I got to the corner, a rifle shot rang out, deafening against all that rock. I saw a tiny figure — the uppermost one — sag against the ladder and then slowly peel away. I didn't watch it drop; I didn't want to waste the time. Instead, I reached around the corner, took aim at the hut with my service .38, and fired two rounds at the shadow behind the window. The glass exploded and the shadow dropped.

"This is the police. Throw out your weapon and show yourself." My eyes shifted to the far wall. I could see minute pale faces looking in our direction. I knew there were binoculars trained on us, so they could see who I was. I also knew they wouldn't risk firing from there, for fear of hitting me. I hoped the other guy wouldn't figure that out, too.

"Come on — give it up."

What he did give up was unexpected. From low on the hut's wall, a chunk of wood suddenly flew off, blown away by the bullet that smacked into the granite near my head — he'd fired right through the wall. The rock exploded like a small grenade, spraying my face and eyes with stone splinters. The pain was excruciating. Blinded, I staggered back, tripped and fell on my side. I reached out for support and felt my arm slip over the cliff edge. For a split second, I thought that was it — my body balanced right at the midpoint, undecided on which direction to roll, until I kicked my leg back and swung myself away from the edge.

I still couldn't see well; I could taste the blood seeping over my upper lip. I rubbed my eyes and blinked like mad, knowing it was now or never for my opponent. About every two seconds, I managed to get a half-glimpse of my surroundings before the blood blocked my vision again. I began backing up as rapidly as I dared, keeping one hand on the wall next to me, hoping to get to the shelter of the other platform before the shooter made his move.

I never made it. In one brief clear-eyed second, I saw his figure duck around the corner, carrying his rifle. I heard its blast just as the back of my head collided with the upright ladder behind me. My head exploded with bright light — a blinding, numbing starburst almost matched by the sudden stab of pain in my left side. I knew I was falling, but not in which direction; nor did I know how to counteract it. My arms and legs didn't respond. I felt almost as if I was falling through water. Only the abrupt contact of my nose to the dusty granite shelf told me I'd fallen on my face.

I lay there, motionless, trying to sort out the numbness, the pain, and the dizziness that engulfed me. I heard the other man's footsteps move around the ladder and disappear to the opposite "escape" platform, out of reach from the State Police. I moved my fingers, trying to feel for my gun. It was gone.

I heard him coming back and lay still. He seemed to hesitate, and then began to climb awkwardly to the second ledge, with something clanking and banging against the side of the ladder. I thought, hell; he's got the pry bar — he's going to leave me stranded. I rolled onto my back and looked up.

My eyes still hurt, and I had to squint, but I could see. He was carrying his rifle, of course, not the pry bar — he no longer gave a damn about me. I got to my hands and knees, and then unsteadily to my feet, pulling myself up with the ladder rungs. I hung there for a few seconds, shaking off the nausea. Even without looking up, I knew he'd reached the next level — the ladder had stopped quivering under his weight.

It angered me that he was getting away, it angered me that I still didn't know who he was, and it angered me to think I'd messed up, that somehow things shouldn't have turned out this way. I swung myself around to the front of the ladder and began to climb.

The pain in my side brought me to an abrupt halt. I looked down at a broad red swatch that was leaking down my pants leg. His bullet must have hit me just above the belt line. I pressed it with my hand — it hurt, but it wasn't unbearable, not like the pain in my head, which still gave everything a slightly pink tinge. I continued climbing, slowly, but steadily, hand over hand, foot over foot.

I could hear more shots above me, and several from across the way. We were no longer so close together, and the others could now feel free to try picking him off. But they didn't have rifles. It didn't mean their bullets couldn't reach this far, but any accuracy was reduced to pure luck. By the time I reached the second ledge, he was almost to the top of the first, where the last ladder lay flat. I just hoped to God he was too preoccupied to look down.

I put my hands on the rungs to start climbing again, but then stopped, my head swimming so badly I had to close my eyes. I could feel my heartbeat through my temples, which felt like they must be ready to burst. With my eyes still closed, I began going up. I was beginning to lose the sensation of the wood under my hands, and the toes of my feet caught under the rungs instead of placing themselves confidently on top. I realized I probably couldn't make it to the top. No matter, I'd get the son of a bitch.

The firing was pretty constant now, more from their side than from his. He, I could tell from the sounds, was struggling to put the last ladder in place. I opened my eyes and concentrated on what I was doing, movement by movement, ignoring that my vision seemed to be closing down from the outside in, and that everything was sounding farther and farther away. I got to the top of ledge number one. He was almost out of the pit.

I grabbed hold of his ladder and shook it. "Stop."

He froze suddenly, clutching the rails, and looked down.

For a split second, everything stopped as we stared at each other. With the humming in my head and the increasing dizziness, I half-wondered if I was hallucinating, going back in time and reviewing the faces of the recent dead. For, above me, his eyes narrowed with malice, was Ed Sylvester's bearded face — Julie's cherished Fox, back from the grave, and here to kill me as he had Bruce Wingate before me. Idiotically, the only thought that crossed my mind was irritation at having been so stupid — we had all relied on Sarris's information in determining the burned man's identity.

I was suddenly aware of the silence around us — again, we were too close together for them to risk shooting. In my dogged pursuit, I'd been too successful: I'd made of myself the perfect target. Sylvester began to fool with his rifle, bringing it around to bear on me.

I ducked under the ladder and put my back flat against the rock. My hands were on the underside of the rungs. I heard the rifle's bolt action snap into place, and the tinkling of a brass cartridge at my feet. All he had to do now was aim and I was dead.

With a sudden, convulsive effort, I put all my remaining strength into pushing against the ladder. It trembled and jumped under my hands as Sylvester began to scramble, trying to reach the top. I felt the ladder begin to give, slowly at first, then with more conviction. I looked up and saw sky appear between the wall and the ladder's top. Sylvester dropped his rifle, which sailed by me on the way down, and grabbed for the cable I'd rigged earlier.

For a moment, we froze there, the ladder

angled away from the wall, Sylvester hanging onto the cable, me pushing for all I was worth. Then, as had happened to me before, the steel line began to slip between his gloved hands. Farther and farther, in gradual slow motion, the ladder tilted into the void. Sylvester began to slip along the cable like a bead along a thread. The ladder twisted away and peeled off to the side; Sylvester continued on his arc out toward the middle of the pit. His gloves were hissing along the cable, smoking with the friction, leaving little plumes that hung in the air. At the end of the forty feet, man and cable separated in sudden, abrupt silence.

I watched him spinning, spread-eagled, until he vanished in a geyser of viscous green water. The scream came from elsewhere far below, thin and high-pitched. My vision reduced to a pinhole, I swung my head to look near the edge of the water near the pit's opening to the east. There was a girl there — half an inch tall from this distance, poised at the escape gap — on her knees with her hands over her face.

I slid down the wall into a sitting position and passed out.

34

The nurse paused, the paper cup still touching my lips. I followed her gaze to my hospital room door. Greta was standing there, a scowl on her face.

"Hey there, Greta," Buster spoke from the corner, where he'd enthroned himself in the room's only armchair, surrounded by magazines.

She ignored him, and the nurse who squeezed past her on the way out. "My God, you look like you been hit by a truck." She shook her head and eyed me with gentle scorn. "I thought you were supposed to be the SA's guy — a paper pusher."

I raised the one eyebrow that wasn't bandaged. "Dumb luck — wrong place at the wrong time."

Greta looked across to Buster finally. "So what did he do to himself?"

"He was shot in the side, damaged his right eye, and suffered a concussion. No permanent damage."

Greta snorted. "They wouldn't know the difference."

I shook my head gingerly. These were two people I'd known for most of my life, playing roles so engrained, it had become almost impossible to see beyond them, until recently. Even now that it was over — the Natural Order disbanding, the Kingdom Restaurant closed, all within the thirty-six hours of my being shot — I sensed a fragility underneath Greta's familiar gruff veneer, the remnants of what I'd witnessed when she'd decked Gorman and had run off to God knows where.

"So what the hell happened? Did Bruce kill those people?"

Based largely on what Spinney had told me that morning on the phone, I related to her what I knew — that Bruce Wingate had returned to Fox's house that night, armed with his .38, to find an unknown man in the house, a newcomer to the Order whom Fox had invited to stay in the house. Fox and Julie, however, were out. Holding the woman and children hostage in the upstairs bedroom, Wingate had sent the man to fetch Julie. When he returned with her, there, on the landing, an argument had broken out. Julie had pulled the 9 mm, shot at her father, missed and hit the newcomer in the throat, the bullet passing through the collar of his down-filled jacket and picking up the feather Hillstrom later found. This was the murder attempt Gorman learned about the night of Wingate's death. Wingate had fled, as had Julie. None of them had paused to think about the smoldering embers spread by the dead man's falling against the stove, and by the time the fire had broken out, the people upstairs were doomed.

"So Bruce lied to me, they both did." Greta looked crestfallen.

"I'm afraid so, to all of us. His only interest was his daughter. That's why he never told anyone that the burned man wasn't Fox. He didn't want anyone to know he'd been in the house later, or that his daughter had killed the man."

Which, of course, had put Fox in the catbird seat. From the supposed grave, he'd orchestrated Wingate's murder and framed Rennie — in his eyes, the two most flagrant degraders of the woman he loved. Had Sarris not then immediately taken charge of Julie, Fox and she could have been long gone. Indeed, it wasn't until this morning that the State Police got Ed Sylvester's dental records from the Bloomington police and found they didn't match the burned body's. That was a surprise to Sarris, also. He too had thought Fox was dead.

"I never believed Rennie did it."

I noticed the set of her chin was almost too defiant. This woman had lost more than she would ever admit.

"I didn't either, Greta. But he sure didn't help his cause any, lying about his whereabouts and running off from the police."

I saw her jaw tighten as she fought for composure. "Silly bastard — always had to do it his own way."

"Are you okay, Greta?" I asked, trying to keep the real concern out of my voice.

"Better than you are."

"You going to be able to hang on to the Inn?"

She looked at me in silence for a moment, pondering whether to deny what was now common knowledge. "We'll see — the other restaurant closing will probably help."

She looked embarrassed to have been so exposed and glanced toward the door.

I let her go with her dignity intact. "Thanks for coming. Good luck."

She smiled, then quickly dug into her ample purse and handed me a small bouquet of flowers. She was gone almost before her mumbled "Get well soon" made it out of her mouth. I looked at the tiny, delicate collection of dried flowers and thought of her secret living room, that equally tasteful, feminine, and soothing enclosure buried inside that rotting heap of a building. Christ, I thought — circles within circles.

"How're you doin'?" Buster asked.

I leaned back against the pillows and shut my one eye, which still ached from the granite splinters. "I don't know. Kind of empty, like after a funeral."

"Rennie?"

I thought about Rennie, another one whose inner soul had been slowly encased in an armature of hard living and bitter experience. But I had mourned him already, even before he'd actually died. "Not him so much — more what he represented."

"The good old days."

"Yeah."

Buster dropped the magazine he'd been holding into his lap. I didn't know precisely how long he'd been here, but it had been most of the day. "The good old days are still there, Joey. You just tried to make more out of 'em than they deserve. They're no cure for what ails you." He then grinned. "Speaking of which, is your friend Gail coming up?"

I smiled at the thought. "Yup. I called her last night, after some of the drugs wore off. She's due in a couple of hours."

"There's your cure, if you ask me."

And how, I thought. The sound of her voice on the phone had done more good for me than anything currently oozing from the drip-bag by the side of my bed. I was looking forward to seeing her, both here and back in Brattleboro, and I was looking forward to strengthening the friendship we'd almost dropped between us.

Part of my resolve, I knew, stemmed from her own enthusiasm. "I think this has been good for us," she'd said last night. "It shook things up a little, the way they should be. We were turning into turtles. I want to make love to you in the backseat of a car, or the floor of my office, as soon as you get better."

I'd laughed at that, threatening my stitches and causing myself a good deal of pain. But she was right. Being in love with another person shouldn't be like standing hand in hand in a minefield, terrified of the slightest movement. Not to do so, however, takes a strong sense of security, and that had only come to me lately, as a result of all this.

I saw Buster was still watching me. "So what happens to Gannet now?" I asked him.

He shrugged. "We go back to work."

It was not a credible line. "You think that'll do any good?"

"Good — bad. Who knows? We're never going to amount to more than what we are. Maybe it'll just bring us back to normal. I'd settle for that."

"You think Greta'll pull it off?"

He laughed and turned the question aside.

"Who else would want the dump?"

But I persisted. "The bank might."

"Oh, Joey. I wouldn't worry about it. We'll take care of things."

By his tone I knew they would, as they always had, for despite the economic forecasts or the demographic predictions, these people were generally pretty good at dealing with what life handed them, and living with the consequences. Be it depression or murder, substance abuse or the visitations of strange outsiders, they managed to hold their stalwart own.

That realization didn't hold much promise, but I thought it was pretty accurate.

Buster seemed to have read my mind, and turned the tables on me. "So, did you get anything out of all this?"

Interesting question. Back in Brattleboro, feeling thwarted and lonely, I'd begun to contemplate my past, which was, as I saw it, my only monument of consequence.

Now, with the endurance of Nadine and Buster and Greta in mind, and with Gail's help, I knew I'd been grossly self-indulgent.

It was time to turn away from what had drawn me back to Gannet.

I nodded to him. "I sure as hell hope so."

THORNDIKE PRESS hopes you have enjoyed this Large Print book. All our Large Print titles are designed for easy reading, and all our books are made to last. Other Thorndike Large Print books are available at your library, through selected bookstores, or directly from the publisher. For more information about current and upcoming titles, please call or mail your name and address to:

THORNDIKE PRESS
PO Box 159
Thorndike, Maine 04986
800/223-6121
207/948-2962